At last
My love has come along...
My lonely days are over
And life is like a song

Oh, yeah, at last
The skies above are blue
My heart was wrapped up in clover
The night I looked at you

I found a dream that I could speak to
A dream that I can call my own
I found a thrill to press my cheek to
A thrill that I have never known

Oh, yeah and you smile, you smile
Oh, and then the spell was cast
And here we are in heaven
For you are mine
At last

Clover's Child

AMANDA PROWSE lives in the West
Country with her husband Simeon and
their two boys Ben and Josh. She was a
management consultant for ten years before
realising that she was born to write.
www.amandaprowse.org

Also by

Amanda Prowse

Poppy Day

What Have I Done?

Something Quite Beautiful

Amanda
Prowse

Clover's Child

HEAD
of ZEUS

First published in the UK in 2013 by Head of Zeus Ltd
This paperback edition published in the UK in 2014
by Head of Zeus Ltd

9 7 5 3 2 4 6 8

A CIP catalogue record for this book is available
from the British Library.

eBook ISBN: 9781781854235
Paperback ISBN: 9781781854266

Printed and bound by CPI Group (UK) Ltd,
Croydon, CR0 4YY.

Head of Zeus Ltd
Clerkenwell House
45-47 Clerkenwell Green
London EC1R 0HT

www.headofzeus.com

For Paul and Stevie
who have at last found a dream
that they can call their own...

27.10.13

Prologue

The old man sat in the rocking chair on the terrace and looked out over the twinkling lights of the distant bay. It was getting late. The night sky and blackened sea merged almost seamlessly. The chirping crickets and hiccupping frogs provided his nightsong. It was still his favourite time of the day. He welcomed the salt-tinged breeze that bathed his face. Tucking the tartan cashmere blanket around his knees, he placed the conch shell on his lap and ran his slim brown fingers over its nodes and cracks. He smiled.

'Well, my darling, it's been quite a day...'

Chapter One

It was cold, the pavement was covered with a sugar-like dusting of frost and the January wind that blew off the water felt like it could cut your cheeks. A large ship painted gun-metal grey was moored against the jetty and its unwieldy hawser stirred and scraped against the wall as the Lightermen's barge made the water swell. The clouds were dark and threatened to burst at any moment. Dot Simpson and Barbara Harrison perched on the flat-topped bollards that stood in rows along the brow of the dock, just as they did in all weathers, in all seasons. When they were little, they had invented elaborate games using the bollards as everything from safe posts during battle to chairs at imaginary tea parties. Now in their late teens, they were more likely to be found sitting there with their faces covered in baby oil, holding up tin-foil reflectors to catch the sun's rays. Tonight, however, they pulled their cardigan sleeves down over their hands and with shoulders hunched forward shouted to each other as their voices navigated the wind.

'I'm bloody freezing!'

'Me too! Dot, look – my fag's stuck to my lip!' Barb opened her mouth wide, to show her mate that her roll-up was indeed hanging free of assistance from her gob. They laughed loudly. This wasn't unusual, they laughed at most things, sometimes because they were funny, but mainly because the two of them were young and free and life was pretty good.

A sailor waved from the deck and the girls waved back before collapsing in giggles. He looked foreign in his dark, woolly cap and double-buttoned pea jacket. He ran up the deck towards them and as nimbly as his heavy boots would allow, clambered up the metal ladder and onto the wharf.

'Shit! He's coming over!'

Barb yanked her fag from her lip and threw it into the wind, where it was carried along a few feet before getting lodged in Dot's hair.

'Jesus! What you trying to do, set me barnet on fire?'

As Dot beat her head with her palms to extinguish any potential flames, her friend sat doubled over on her bollard stool and laughed until she cried. By the time sailor boy reached them, they were slightly more composed. Close up, neither of them fancied him, which was a bitter disappointment to all.

'Hallo!' His voice had the low staccato tones of the Baltics.

Barb waved at him.

'I am new here for some days and would like very much to take you ladies for drink.'

'We don't drink.' Barb looked away from him, tried to sound dismissive.

'What are your names?'

'I'm Connie Francis and this is Grace Kelly.' Dot fixed him with a stare.

'It's nice to see you Connie and Grace, I am Rudolf Nureyev.' Three could play at that game. 'Maybe I take you not for drink, maybe I take you for movies?'

The girls stood and linked arms. Dot cleared her throat. 'That's very kind, Mr Nickabollockoff, but we've got to get home for our tea!'

The two girls ran past him along the dock, laughing and howling, shouting 'GracebloodyKelly?' at each other as they trotted along, homeward bound.

Half an hour later, the Simpsons' front door bell buzzed. Its grating drone was pitiful, like a bee in its dying throes. 'Coming!' shouted Dot, sing-song fashion, casting the word over her shoulder in the direction of the hallway, once again making a mental note that the bell needed fixing. She would ask her dad to have a look at it.

Dot licked the stray blobs of sweet strawberry jam from the pads of her thumbs, smiled and looped her toffee-coloured hair behind her ears. It was probably Barb. Either she'd decided to come round to the Simpson household for her tea after all, or she'd locked herself out of her own house. She felt a swell of happiness.

The front door bell droned again.

'All right! All right!' Dot tossed the checked tea towel onto the work surface and walked past her dad, who was engrossed in his newspaper as usual. She stepped into the hallway, with its narrow strip of patterned carpet, and walked past the glass-fronted unit in which her mum displayed her entire collection of china Whimsies. Looking through the etched glass panels in the door, opaque through design and a lack of regular dusting, she saw her mum staring back at her through the glass in a peering salute. Spying Dot, her mum tapped impatiently at the space on her wrist where a watch would live.

Dot eased open the front door and her mum bustled in from the pavement, filling the narrow hallway with her presence. She used the toe of her right shoe against the heel of her left to ease her foot out of its pump and then reversed the process before stamping her cold feet on the floor and wiggling her stockinged toes. She dumped her shopping bag by the door and shook her arms loose from her mac, making her ample chest jiggle under her chin, then whipped her chiffon scarf from around her neck and rubbed her hands together.

'Blimey, Dot, take your time why don't you. I forgot me key and it's bloody freezing. I've only got a little while to get changed and get back to work!'

'I was just making some toast, do you want some?'

'No, love, I've been surrounded by grub all day, I couldn't face anything. Eat quickly, mind. Don't forget you're coming in with me tonight.'

Dot groaned as she sloped off towards the kitchen. 'Do I have to?'

'I'm not even going to answer that. Do me a favour, Dot, stick the kettle on!' This was code for make me a cup of tea.

Joan watched her daughter tease her roots with her index finger and thumb pinched together. 'You'll never get a brush through that!'

Dot chose to ignore her mum; she wasn't particularly bothered if she never brushed her hair again as long as it was bouffant enough at the back. She yanked the lid from the large, dented, flat-bottomed aluminium kettle, filled it with water and plonked it on top of the gas cooker. As she waited for the whistle, she walked through to the adjoining back room, her hand now pressed flat against her forehead and her arm sticking out at a right angle. 'Mum, do I really have to come to work with you tonight?'

Joan sank down into the chair across from her husband's and delved into her make-up bag. She juggled the magnifying mirror in her left palm and her mascara in her right. She spat onto the cracked cake of black until some of it stuck to the clogged bristles of the brush and proceeded to comb it onto her lashes. She spoke with her lips tucked in, trying to keep her eyes still.

'Yes, you do have to come with me! It's not as though I ask much of you, Dot and not as if anything you might have planned in your hectic schedule can't wait an hour or two!'

'But, God, it's Friday night!'

'I'm sure the Lord above knows what night it is and using his name in vain won't help you, Friday night or not! Now go and wash your face and make that tea.'

Dot trudged through the back room to the kitchen sink.

Her dad looked up from the *Standard*. 'Why's she got her hand stuck to her bonce?'

'She's trying to make her fringe flat.' Joan spat again onto her little brush.

Reg shrugged and shook his head with incomprehension. 'You've only been in five minutes and now you're back off to work. What time'll you finish?'

'I don't know, Reg. When it's done. I've worked bloody hard on this buffet; I hope it all goes all right. Dot better not do anything stupid.'

'Why d'you need her anyway?'

She sighed heavily. 'Oh, don't you start. I've told you, it's a big do for some new family moving into the Merchant's House, military or something, I don't bleeding know! I just know it's overtime and they are paying good wages for someone to waitress, and that someone may as well be Dot! Any more questions?'

'No.'

'Good.'

Joan lifted the brush and started to apply the dark goo to her lower lashes.

'What's for tea?'

'What's that if it's not another question, Reg?'

'Are you asking me a question now?' He smirked.

Joan picked up the multi-coloured crocheted cushion and lobbed it at his newspaper. He ducked and the cushion thumped against the radio speaker.

'Blimey, girl, steady! You just hit Cliff Michelmore in the cakehole!'

'I'm sure he's had worse.' She giggled.

They both laughed as a slow waltz drifted into the room. Reg threw down his paper, struggled to his feet and pinged his braces over his vest, which always made his wife laugh. He hummed along as loudly as he could. 'Come on, Joan, reckon we've got five whole minutes before her fringe is flat and she's made your tea. Let's have a dance.'

He pulled his wife by the arms, she slipped from the green vinyl seat of her chair and he spun her around the back room, trying not to trip on the rug that sat on the tiled floor. Gathering her into a close waltz, he whispered into her hair, which was stiff with lacquer. 'I've just been reading about that *Lady Chatterley* book trial,' he said. 'It's bloody filth that they are trying to pedal, disguised as literature. It's disgusting. I've been following the case quite closely...' He pulled her into him and they swayed around the room in an intimate clinch. She felt the scratch of his stubble against her cheek. His breath came in wheezy bursts, partly from lust and part due to his exertion. 'And I reckon we should definitely get a copy!'

'Oh, behave!' Joan pushed him away, glancing at the cuckoo clock on the wall. 'Gawd, look at the time. Dot!' she yelled in the direction of the kitchen. 'Forget the tea. Come on, we've got to leave right now or we'll miss the bus!'

Dot came in, leading her little sister by the arm, who sported a large orange stain on her white frock. 'She's had an unfortunate incident with a Jubbly. Over to you, Dad!'

'Oh for Gawd's sake, Diane – you're supposed to drink it, not bloody wear it! What are you, a baby? Do we need to put your drinks in a bot bot?'

Dee grinned. 'No! I'm five, I not a baby!'

Reg looked at his wife and eldest daughter as they buttoned up their macs and tied their scarves. 'Is that it then? Are you two off gallivanting and leaving me to it?'

'Looks like it.' His wife smiled as she pecked him on the cheek.

'But this is women's work! And you never did tell me what was for tea.'

'That, my darling, is cos I don't know what will be left over tonight. Might be salad, might be steak! Who knows?'

'Yeah!' Dot added, for no reason other than to join in the fun.

'And you can keep your oar out of it. And by the way, Dot, your fringe n'arf looking curly!'

Dot's parting shot was to poke her tongue out at her dad. 'If the wind changes you'll be stuck like that!' He laughed.

'Oh, well, that explains it; is that what happened to you

then?' She managed to have the last word, this time.

The kitten heels of mother and daughter clicked their way along the Limehouse pavement.

'You working tonight, Joan?'

Their neighbour, Mrs Harrison, leant heavily against her open front door. She took a deep drag on her John Player Special, the smoke from which swirled upwards, further discolouring the yellow fringe that she kept permanently wrapped in two plastic curlers, imprisoned behind a blue hair net. Mrs Harrison ran the grandly named 'Ropemakers Fields Guest House', which for a couple of quid a night provided a bedroom full of clashing florals and mismatched furniture and use of a Goblin Teasmade for weary dock workers who were far from home. Her tall, thin, stooped frame was clad, as usual, in a flowery wrap-around pinny. Her mouth curved into its familiar downward slant and her eyes roamed over Joan and Dot with the usual look of sour disappointment. Dot used to wonder what it would be like if Mrs Harrison ever received some good news – which hadn't happened in all the years she had known her. Would she whoop, shout and yell? She thought not. Dot peeked through the door to the grotty boarding house; it always looked dark and gave off the faintest odour of boiled cabbage. Their neighbour stood with one arm across her flat chest and the other lifting her fag to her thin lips.

'Yes, Mrs Harrison, unfortunately. No rest for the wicked!' Joan hurried past, not wanting to engage any further than she had to.

'That's what they say,' Mrs Harrison replied.

Dot found Mrs Harrison's company boring and depressing, but she was her best mate's aunty, so she had to be careful.

'You seeing our Barb later, Dot? I've got her mum's Avon catalogue here that wants collecting. I'm running low on me night cream.'

Her skin was pitted, furrowed and a little grimy. Dot thought that it would take more than a jar of night cream. 'I might be, I'll tell her when I see her.'

'Thanks, love.' A smile threatened to crease her face but was gone before it was fully formed. Audrey Harrison did not have much to smile about. Her life had been a series of disappointments, starting with the feckless, unfaithful husband that had gone and got himself killed in the war. Although, strangely, once he was dead, his fecklessness and infidelity seemed to have been quite forgotten. As Dot's nan once pointed out, they never seem to bury any crap or useless husbands, only the 'loving and devoted' ones, if the gravestones in the churchyard were anything to go by.

'She's such a nosey old cow,' Joan whispered. The two women laughed as they quickened their pace towards Narrow Street. Just in time to see their bus pulling up to the kerb. Dot screamed and ran ahead, waving her arms and running as fast as she was able in her silly heels on the icy pavement. The conductor waved back and waited until mother and daughter, their faces flushed, had plonked themselves down on the narrow seat that ran along the side of the bottom deck. They laughed as their breath blew clouds into the number 278 that would take them up the road.

Joan Simpson licked her fingers, then wiped them down the front of her starched white pinny, leaving a long smear of mayonnaise across her front. Her mouth mumbled with the inaudible calculations that ensured her pastry always puffed to perfection and her aspic chilled to a fine wobble.

'Tenminutesmoreshoulddoit, thenicanplateitup, getitall out...'

She blew her blunt fringe upwards and wiped the sweat from her forehead with the back of her hand. Her eyes darted between her daughter, who was standing in front of her, fiddling with the collar of her white blouse and pulling and twisting at her black pinafore, and the plate of devilled eggs that she now arranged with deft fingers on the counter top.

'Right, love, listen. The main buffet is all laid out on the trestle in the corner; everyone will help themselves a bit later on. Serviettes, plates and whatnot are already on the table. Just keep an eye out, make sure that no platters run empty, we can refill them in here. Look for anyone that's missing a serviette or cutlery, that kind of thing. You know what's what; it's not as if you haven't done it before. These are just bits to pass around until they eat proper, so let's get them out there and served or they'll be on the turn and I haven't been slaving away all day in this bloody kitchen so that you can ruin my food!'

'I hate doing this, Mum!'

'Really? You haven't mentioned it.'

'It's just so embarrassing. They're always old-timers who smell like lavender and tell me how lucky I am to be a teenager now and not twenty years ago. I know I'm lucky, I don't need reminding by some stinky pensioner every five minutes.'

'Dot, please, just shut up and take the bloody food in!'

'I am! It's just so unfair and anyway, in three years I'll be twenty-one and then I'll be free to do what I bloody want.'

Joan dipped into the metal tray under the counter top and lifted a large serving spoon in her direction. 'Oi! Less of the "bloody", missus. Until you are actually twenty-one, you are not too old for a ladling!'

'A ladling? You just made that up! And you say "bloody" all the time!' Dot concentrated on her outstretched arm, grappling with the wide silver platter that threatened to slide off the folded white linen cloth on which it sat.

'Yes I do, because I can, and when you're as old as me you can swear as much as you like. In the meantime, get that food out!'

Dot drew a deep breath and faced the double swing door that would reveal her in all her shame to the awaiting guests. 'I'm never going to be old,' she offered over her shoulder.

'You're right, Dot. If you carry on defying me and those canapés spoil, you won't make twenty-one – I'll bloody kill ya!'

Mother and daughter laughed until they snorted. Dot shook her head to compose herself. It was bad enough having to go out looking like a prize plum, trussed up like a Christmas pudding, without snorting her way through the crowd as well.

'What are you waiting for now?'

'I'm just composing meself!'

'Composing yourself? Christ alive, Dot! Just get that food out now!'

'All right, all right – I'm going.'

'And come straight back for the vol-au-vents!' Joan bellowed at her daughter's disappearing back.

Dot pushed against the plushly padded velour door with its brass studs, which reminded her of a sideways sofa. She strained to hear the music that was coming from the grand piano in the corner; the sultry tones of Etta James drifted from the gramophone and the musician played along with the record. She glimpsed the bowed head of the black pianist, who with eyes closed and neck bowed was tickling the ivories.

> 'At last
> My love has come along...
> My lonely days are over
> And life is like a song'

She loved the song and she hummed it inside her head as she wandered among the thirty or so guests. This room had always fascinated her: the polished dark-wood floor and the light from the huge chandelier meant everything sparkled. Vast oil paintings hung on the walls, each one of a military man either on horseback or with his weapon of choice held aloft. It intrigued her how such a large group of people could be gathered in one room and yet the loudest sound was the chink of glass against glass, with only the faintest hum of background chatter and the odd tinkle of delicate laughter. In the Victorian terrace where she lived with her mum, dad and little sister it was never quiet. If not loud music from the radio and the bashing of pots and pans in the kitchen, then the whistling of the kettle and the shouts of questions and instructions up and down the stairs:

'CUP OF TEA?'

'ONLY IF YOU'RE MAKING!'

'WHERE ARE MY CLEAN SHIRTS?'

'IN THE AIRING CUPBOARD!'

The fact that someone might be a whole floor away from you was no reason to exclude them from the conversation.

'Would-you-like-a-devilled-egg?' Dot lowered her natural volume and used her posh voice, just as she had been taught.

A bushy-moustached man in naval uniform with flash gold epaulettes practically dived onto the tray. She watched him scoop a handful of delicate white ovals from the platter and cram them into his gob. At least she could tell her mum that someone appreciated her cooking.

'Not for me, dear.' His wife raised her white-gloved hand. A pity; the poor woman looked like she would benefit from the odd devilled egg. She was stick thin and her paisley-print, bat-wing frock hung off her tiny frame. She had drawn her eyebrows way too high on her forehead; like a dolly peg, Dot thought.

Next she infiltrated a group of elderly men and women who collectively smelled of dust and fish paste. 'Would-you-like-a-devilled-egg?' She proffered the tray in the direction of one old bloke.

'Would I what?' he yelled at her.

Dot bit the inside of her cheeks, praying she wouldn't get the giggles and immensely glad that Barb wasn't around; if she had caught her friend's eye, she would have been in hysterics. She gave a small cough and tried again in her low, posher-than-usual voice. 'Would-you-like-a-devilled-egg?'

'Is it something about my leg?' he yelled again.

'Your leg? NO, NO. WOULD YOU CARE FOR A DEVILLED EGG?' This time she over-enunciated every word. It took a monumental effort to stop herself from laughing out loud.

'I'm afraid I don't care for much, lost my brother in the war y'see.'

'I'm sorry to hear that, sir, but can I tempt you?' This time she lifted the tray until it was practically under his schnoz.

'What is that?' he asked, prodding at the softened offering.

'They are canapés, sir.'

'Cans of what?'

Dot felt her shoulders begin to shake. A ripple of laughter was working its way up her throat and down her nose; she felt fit to explode.

'Excuse me a mo, I'll be right back.' She thought it best to make a hasty retreat to the kitchen and compose herself. Turning quickly, she failed to see that another devilled-egg seeker in military uniform was standing not a foot behind her. It was a collision of comical proportions.

The tray of canapés flipped from her arm and stuck to the front of his tunic. Squashed eggs and mayonnaise sat like a cloying, liquid blanket on his jacket. One hollowed-out egg was actually lodged on a brass button. Almost immediately the silver platter hit the floor with an almighty crash. Both parties bent to retrieve the tray and, with perfect timing, bashed their heads together, sending her flying along the newly polished wooden floor and leaving him clutching his forehead with mayonnaise-smeared palms.

Momentarily dazed, Dot was aware of several shouts of 'Oh no!' and the collective gasps of thirty of London's finest watching as she went sprawling. She lay back and looked up at the ceiling, noticing for the first time that it was painted with the most beautiful mural. Fat-bottomed cherubs played harps and lutes in each corner and there was a gold table stacked high with bowls of fruit and flagons of wine. Clouds parted to reveal a heavily bearded God with his arms spread wide and beams of sunlight shining through the gaps. She was captivated. Lowering her eyes from the ceiling, she saw a circle of faces above her. Dolly-peg lady, greedy bastard and the dust-and-fish-paste gang were among them. Someone reached into the circle and held onto both her hands, then she felt herself being pulled swiftly upwards.

Finally upright, her attention was drawn to her right and the smeared khaki and tarnished brass of a uniform that had met with an unfortunate accident involving a platter of eggs. Dot bit her bottom lip. What had she done? Joan would go mad.

She looked up at her rescuer. Her breath caught in her throat and her knees buckled slightly as she swayed. She was staring into the face of a black man and he was holding her hands. She was caught somewhere between fascination and fear; she'd never seen a black person up this close before, let alone held hands with one. But what surprised her more than anything was that it was the most beautiful face she had ever seen. He was the piano player.

'Are you all right?' His voice was like liquid chocolate, deep, smooth and with an accent she couldn't place, like American, but different. His big eyes, framed with thick curly lashes were so dark, she couldn't see where the pupil stopped and the iris started.

'I'm fine. You all right?' she countered, looking at him through lowered lashes and wishing she had put more lipstick on.

'Oh, I'm fine, thank you, but I'm not the one that's been wrestling on the floor with men old enough to know better!'

'D'you think anyone noticed?' She smiled

The pianist cast his eye over the mess and the bemused onlookers. 'No, I don't think anyone noticed a thing.'

Dot exhaled though bloated cheeks and tried to smooth her pinafore.

'Me mother'll kill me.'

'Accidents happen.'

'Yes, but they always seem to happen to me. I better get this cleared up.'

Bending, she gathered up what she could of the gloopy mess, flicking her hand over the floor to rid it of blobs of mayonnaise and egg residue. The doily that had lined the plate sufficed as an improvised floor cloth. Dot stood and held the mess in front of her. She hovered with a confused expression as though she couldn't remember what came next.

The piano player took the platter from her hands and placed it on a small table within reach.

'I think we need to get you some fresh air. Did you bump your head?'

Dot nodded. 'A bit, but I'm supposed to go back for the vol-au-vents.' She pointed in the general direction of the kitchen.

'Voller what? Don't worry; I'm sure nobody is going to starve if you take five minutes.'

She followed as he led her through the muttering crowd and out into the crisp January air. The sky was cloud free and the stars seemed particularly bright and numerous.

'What a beautiful night!' She stared up at the sky.

'Yes it is.' He stared at her, transfixed by the pale skin at the base of her throat.

Dot sat down on the outside steps that led from the back of the grand ballroom to the walled garden below. She fingered a long ladder in the side of her newly acquired black stockings. Damn. She leant against the ornate iron railings that ran the length of the staircase, drank in the damp and breathed heavily. The pianist stood a couple of steps down and watched her with his hands shoved into his trouser pockets. He was of average height, slim, muscular. For the first time, Dot noticed his highly polished brown Oxfords, the khaki twill trousers with their razor-sharp creases, the button-down cream shirt and thin, knitted tie under the ribbed, khaki jersey.

'You look like a soldier on his day off.'

'Maybe I am.'

Dot snorted. She doubted it, unable to picture any soldiers she had ever met moonlighting as a cabaret act. They were always too busy soldiering or boozing.

'You're incredible on the piano, really good. Mind you, I love that song.'

'I love it too.' He smiled, revealing brilliant white teeth, like those of a film idol.

'How long have you played?'

'As long as I can remember – since I was two, I think. I had lessons until I'd mastered it and then pretty much taught myself after that. I should practise more, but you know...' He pictured the ebony grand piano in the entrance hall of his family home, the Jasmine House. He could always find an excuse not to practise.

'So they have pianos where you're from then?'

He looked perplexed. 'They have pianos everywhere, don't they?'

'Dunno, I suppose so. I've never really thought about it, but I can't imagine there being many pianos in Africa. Not plonked in the middle of the jungle. They'd get damp, wouldn't they?'

He ran his fingers around his mouth to stifle a laugh and any sarcasm that might slip out. It wasn't the first time someone had assumed he was African. 'They probably would, yes, but I've been told there *are* one or two pianos in Africa, although that's not where I'm from.'

'No?'

'No.'

'Oh. Fancy that.' Dot was stumped, unable to think of another place on earth that black people might come from. 'I wish I'd learnt an instrument; imagine being able to make music whenever you want to, just because you can.'

'You talk like it's too late; it's never too late, you could learn now!'

'Oh, you're joking! I'd be useless. Look at your lovely long fingers.' She reached out and pulled his hand from his pocket and took it into hers; both were stilled by the surprise and pleasure of physical contact. Dot studied his hand before dropping it sharply. She was fascinated by his palm, which wasn't dark like the rest of his skin but pink, with dark creases criss-crossing it.

'Your hands are all pink underneath!'

He glanced at her with his head drawn back on his shoulders, from beneath furrowed brows, unable to decide if she was thick or sarcastic. 'It would appear so.'

She held up her own palms for scrutiny. 'Can you honestly see me bashing away with this bunch of pork sausages?'

'You have lovely hands and I'm sure you'd make a fine piano player...' He hesitated. 'I don't know your name?'

'Dot.'

'Dot? As in dash, dash, dash, dot, dot—'

'Yep, as in Dot.' She smiled.

'Is it short for anything?'

'Ah, well, there's a tale. Apparently me dad was one over the eight when he went to register my birth in Canning Town. Mum was still lying in and when they asked him my name, he couldn't remember that it was supposed to be Dorothy – after Dorothy Squires, no less! – and so he said "Dorothea", but I've only ever been known as Dot. That's me, I'm just a Dot!'

He studied her face, her wide smile, the peachy skin with the smattering of freckles across her straight nose. Her eyes were wide and sparkling – whether from her bump on the head or something else entirely he couldn't be sure.

'But I think you are more than *just* a Dot. If you hadn't been there to provide the evening's entertainment, I'd still be stuck in there trying not to look bored. You have been the highlight of my evening so far – although the night is young.'

'Ha! Let me tell you, I've met the whole gang up there and I am definitely the highlight of your evening.'

'I think you might be right.' He gave an almost imperceptible wink.

'And when you are calling me Dot, what should I call you?'

'Sol, short for Solomon. My dad wasn't one over the eight when I was registered.'

'Well, lucky old you. And what does Solomon mean?'

'It means "Peace".'

'Is that right?' Dot felt the twist of unease in her gut that she always felt when confronted with someone who was clever; she didn't know anything about anything.

'Apparently so. I am a bringer of peace.'

'Well, that's very comforting coming from a soldier on his day off.'

Sol laughed. 'So what do you do when you're not lying on the floor in a pool of eggs?'

'I don't do this very often. My mum's the cook here and calls me in when they need a waitress; the money's quite good, but to tell the truth I'd rather not. Poncing around looking like this for some unappreciative idiots who just want to fill their faces with anything that's going spare, and my mum never gets a mention or a thank you and she works so hard...' Sol laughed a deep, throaty chuckle.

'And tonight they all seem really old and boring and it's all in aid of another bunch of freeloaders that are moving into the top-floor flat. Well, they call it a flat, but it's actually bigger than most houses and twice as posh, y'know the kind of thing, fancy carpet, fluffy towels and loads of books that they probably never read cos they're all inbred and illiterate.'

'Whoa – harsh!' Sol shook his head from side to side. 'Are they always that bad?'

'Trust me, always. It's where they shove all the waste-of-space top brass that are over here short term. All they seem to do is host fancy dinners or attend fancy dinners and then bugger off back to where they came from. I don't see much work being done – nice job if you can get it!' She knew that she was babbling, but this man's easy smile and open face invited confidences. 'And in answer to your question, when I'm not doing this, I work in Selfridges three days a week in Haberdashery and I bloody love it!'

'Why do you love it?'

'Have you been?'

Sol shook his head.

'The building is beautiful and glamorous; it's been there for fifty-odd years, but it's really modern inside and apart from that, I love material! I would love to make all me own clothes one day and just to see the new bolts of cloth – the cottons, velvet and tweed from all over the world, stacked in every colour you can think of – it's fascinating. And I get to meet really interesting people, fashion designers and buyers who have some great ideas, and girls who are getting married, who spend hours holding swatches of lace up to the light, comparing Chantilly and needle lace. I'd love to design my own pieces one day, dresses and posh gowns.' Dot bit her bottom lip. That had slipped out; she hadn't told another living soul about that. Maybe the bump on her head had loosened her tongue.

'I look forward to buying an original Dorothea one day.'

'Yeah, well, we'll see. I'm only mucking about really. It's just a silly idea. Anyway, I should be getting back.' Dot ran her palm over the drying mayonnaise and wiped her hand on the step. It felt dangerous to share her dream, almost as if putting it out into the real world made it less likely to become a reality. When her future was in her head, it looked perfect and easily achievable, but when it floated among the rooftops of the East End, it got diluted by the smoke and grime. The many buildings, spires and paths between E14 and W1 felt like immoveable barriers that blocked her way.

Dot opened the back door to the kitchen.

'Where in God's name have you been?' Joan's tone was sharp.

'Oh, Mum, I fell over! But no one got hurt. I bumped my head and just had five minutes' fresh air. I'm all right now though.'

'Oh well, as long as *you're* all right, Dot. Blimey, why can you never just do as I ask? There's always some bloody drama with you.' She shoved two platters stacked high with vol-au-vents and cocktail sausages into her daughter's hands. 'Now get these out.'

'Well, thanks for asking, I think I'll survive! Gawd, it's not as if I did it on purpose, Mum.'

'You never do, love!'

Joan watched as Dot stared at the far wall. She was picturing a shop front painted gold and green, with a shiny brass door plate. Two wooden mannequins stood in the window, each swathed in a silk creation, with dainty pointed shoes in coordinating colours on the floor. Models and stars draped in white fur spewed onto the pavement carrying large, glossy bags with the word 'Dorothea' written on the side. What would look best, a gold ribbon or green?

Dot jumped as her mum banged the metal counter top.

'Look lively, Dot!'

'What?'

'Good God, what's the matter with you tonight? You are bloody miles away! Get these out, NOW!'

Dot smiled and picked up the two large platters. When she was a famous fashion designer and Princess Margaret was wearing one of her outfits, she'd remember these moments and consider it to be part of the 'hard life' that had shaped her creativity. *'An original Dorothea…'* now that really would be something.

Through on the other side of the padded door, she watched the small crowd gather round the raised platform on which the grand piano sat. She was rooted to the spot. A sharp-suited man with slicked-back hair and a pencil-thin moustache flung an animated hand around at will, his champagne glass threatening to launch its contents, though it didn't. He stood to the front and, with his other hand anchored in his suit pocket, was clearly giving some kind of speech. His words were interspersed with polite laughter from the great and good standing before him.

Slightly to his right stood a very dapper black man of about fifty, Dot guessed. A healthy clutch of medals sat on his broad chest, hanging from a variety of striped ribbons. Dot heard the name 'Colonel Abraham Arbuthnott' followed by a polite ripple of applause.

His tall, slender wife was sheathed in a grosgrain silk dress of the palest tangerine with ballooned sleeves of sheer voile that were anchored around her narrow wrists by a band of velvet and a single velvet-covered button. She looked stunning, like an Arabian princess. Her arm was linked casually through his and to her right, looking slightly awkward at being so obviously scrutinised, stood the son of the latest freeloading, military-top-brass waste of space to be taking up residence in the Merchant's House – Sol.

'Oh shit!' Dot backed up and using her ample bottom bumped at the padded swing door until she was back in the kitchen.

'All gone already?' Joan grinned, delighted. 'Dot? I said do you need more? What are you playing at?'

'Mum?'

'Yes, love?'

'Can I ask you something?'

'If you have to.'

'If someone called you a freeloading waste of space, would you take that as an insult?'

'How else would I take it?'

'Thought so. In that case, Mum, I think my waitressing days might be over.'

Joan stopped arranging the mini trifles on a tray. 'Oh no, what've you done now?'

'It's not so much what I've done as what I said and who I said it to.'

'Dot, are you having me on, cos this is no time for your shenanigans!'

Dot exhaled and was considering how best to break the news that she had insulted the son of the guest of honour and in reality her mum's boss for the next twelve months, when there was a sharp knocking on the door frame.

The two women stood in silence as the door creaked open. 'Oh shit!' muttered Dot for the second time in as many minutes. It was Sol. He strode over to Joan.

'Good evening.'

'Good… Good evening.' Joan wasn't sure where this was heading; guests never ventured into her kitchen.

'I'm Solomon Arbuthnott – Sol.' He thrust his hand in Joan's direction.

Joan wiped her sweaty palm on her pinny before taking his hand. 'Joan. Hello.' She was unused to this level of formality.

'Joan, I just wanted to say thank you for the amazing spread that you have prepared for us tonight. The food is delicious, particularly the devilled eggs, which caused quite a stir earlier!'

Sol turned and winked at Dot, who found that the power of speech had evaded her.

Joan felt the creep of a blush working its way along her neck and up over her cheeks. It was lovely to have such a compliment. 'Oh, well, just doing my job. It's a pleasure! And if there is anything that you or your family fancy while you are here, just let me know and I'll do my best to accommodate.'

Again Sol stared at Dot and raised his eyebrows. 'There is something actually…'

'Oh, righto, ask away!' Joan nodded, eager as a pup.

'I'd love to see Selfridges. I come from a very small island in the West Indies…' This bit of information he said with added volume and precision, informing any interested parties that it was nowhere near Africa. 'And I'm not sure I can be trusted to navigate the Tube system alone. Do you know anyone that could show me, if it wouldn't be too much trouble?'

Joan fanned her flushed face with the tea towel while simultaneously breaking into a grin. 'Actually yes! Our Dot works there a couple of days a week, don't you, love? I'm sure she could point you in the right direction!'

'She does?'

'Yes! In the Hadashaberry—'

'Haberdashery.' Dot had found her voice.

'Yes, there,' Joan confirmed.

Sol grinned. 'Well, that is a coincidence!'

'Isn't it just…' Dot smirked, feeling a flush of excitement and a wave of anger simultaneously. Was he taking the mick?

* * *

The Arbuthnotts made their way up the wide staircase to their apartment at the top of the Merchant's House. It felt inconceivable that only a few days ago they had been tripping over packing cases and individually pausing on the terrace, drinking in the view of the sparkling Caribbean Sea and the lush junglescape that would be denied them for twelve whole months. They were swapping their island home for the damp cobbles of London because of Arbuthnott senior's role as military advisor to the British government on Caribbean defence.

Vida Arbuthnott had gazed at the misty tips of the Pitons in the distance one last time, knowing she would miss the majestic sight. She was mistress of the grand house and, as an Arbuthnott, was known and respected on St Lucia and all the neighbouring islands. She was renowned for her impeccable taste and for her extravagant parties, whose intricate planning could take months – a hostess of note. Not all the islanders shared her eye for the finer things, however; after one particular soirée, Vida gave all the ladies in attendance a mother-of-pearl soap dish, saying, as she pressed the trinket into the palms of those leaving, 'It's from Paris, Galeries Lafayette...' Most of the guests had never left the island, let alone been to Paris, and rumour had it that in the coming weeks Mrs Arbuthnott was dismayed to see her farewell presents in island gardens, being used for everything from dog bowls to post trays.

As she drank in the view on that last evening at the Jasmine House, Vida had smiled. Her son was sitting on the step, in his running gear, clicking his tongue against his teeth and snapping his fingers at the peahen that obstinately refused to come any closer, despite the lure of the grain in his hand.

'Sol, my dear, how long have been trying to feed that bird by hand?'

Sol replied without turning his head. 'I reckon about four years.'

'And you think tonight, on your last night, she might finally give in to temptation?'

He smiled at his mother. 'Why not?'

'Why not indeed, son. I'm sure she will succumb one day, yes, but maybe not today. Slowly, slowly...'

'That's what I figure, Mumma; slowly, slowly.'

'Well, no one can doubt your optimism. It's a good quality for a soldier.'

'I hope so, or that's four years at Washington's finest military academy wasted!'

'I've told you before, nothing that is an experience is wasted; whether it's a good experience or a bad one, it shapes who you become.'

'What about this experience, Mum? Are you looking forward to sitting in the rain, drinking tea and listening to Queen Elizabeth give her speeches?'

'Well, yes and no. It will be a new experience and it's right that we support Daddy, but all that terrible weather!' Vida shuddered and rubbed her shoulders, which were draped with a pale wrap of the lightest silk. 'I feel cold and miserable just thinking about it. Apparently January is the worst month in which to arrive – cold and rainy.'

'I can't remember the last time I was truly cold and miserable,' Sol reflected as the early evening sun warmed his skin through his singlet.

'Then consider yourself lucky.'

'I do, Mumma.'

Vida ran her hand along the top of her son's shoulders, feeling the taut muscles across his broad back beneath her fingertips. He had vaulted from boy to man without her really noticing: one minute his steps were faltering in the sand, the next he ran along the shoreline with an athlete's determined stride. It seemed to have happened in the blink of an eye.

'Truth be told, Solomon, I don't quite know how I am going to fill my days.'

'I'm sure you'll be busy shopping or planning dinner; you seem to find somewhere to shop wherever we are!'

'You are a cheeky boy, Solomon Arbuthnott.' Vida bent low and squeezed his form against her own. 'But you are my cheeky boy and I love you. Now, I want you to take one last sweep of your room, make sure you have everything you need. The luggage is being collected tomorrow and should arrive in London in about two months, so only put in what you can live without for a few weeks.'

'Mum, I know; we've already been through it. I just hope that my things don't get lost.'

'Lost? Solomon, what a thing to say! It's one of Daddy's ships, of course it's not going to get lost! Don't let him hear you say that.'

'Besides, I think Patience has it all under control, I don't want to interfere.'

'Don't leave it all to Patience; you are the only man I know that still relies on his nanny!'

'What else would she do if not look after me? She loves me.'

'Yes she does and I know you love her. Bless her, she has been crying all day.'

'I hope she has a rest when we're gone, but I doubt it. Anyway, a year will pass so quickly; we'll be back before she notices. And then she can carry on as normal, it will be as if we have never been away.'

* * *

'Think I'll take a couple of the trifles back for Dad and Dee – I've made a few too many – and a slice or two of the cold mutton, save it going to waste.' Joan winked at her daughter; there had to be some perks.

'I'm going to meet Barb, Mum, so you go on home and I'll be back in a bit.'

'Not too late, love, you know what your dad's like.'

'Don't I just!'

Joan placed a couple of bob in her daughter's hand.

'You sure, Mum?'

'Treat yourself, darling.'

Dot looked at the coins in her palm. Money was always tight and she would love to get a replacement pair of stockings or a couple of magazines, but she knew how hard Joan worked and putting meat and spuds on the table was far more important that any distraction for her and Barbara. She popped one of the coins back into her mum's pocket.

Joan smiled. 'You're a good girl, Dot. We'll be all right won't we? As your nan used to say, it's all down to love and luck. And it wasn't all bad, was it? You survived the night, after all that bloody fuss!'

'Yeah, despite falling arse over tit, I live to tell the tale!'

'And our new resident seems very nice – Mr Arbuthnott.'

'I guess…'

'I couldn't make him out, Dot, really. He's a bit formal, shook me hand and everything! You wouldn't think it, would you?'

'Wouldn't think what?'

'That coloured people could be like that!'

'Like what?' Dot felt an inexplicable surge of interest.

'I dunno, I've never really met one before, but I didn't expect him to be posh, like normal—'

'Of course they are like normal. Believe it or not, Mum, they're people just like us!'

'Well, don't let your dad hear you say that, you know how he feels about them!' Joan buttoned up her mac and tied her paisley silk headscarf under her chin. 'Night, darling,' she said, and she left to catch the bus home with her booty in the bottom of her stripey shopping bag.

Dot considered her mum's words. Sol's family might be normal like other wealthy people, but they were nothing like her own. The Simpsons would never live in a huge house with a cook on hand to prepare all their food, and the local bigwigs would never hold a reception for them with as much booze as you could get down your Gregory, and her mum and dad would never have encouraged her to play the piano when she was little so she could blast out those magical notes whenever she felt like it. Dot sauntered out into the cold London night, with the words of the song filling her head.

The skies above are blue
My heart was wrapped up in clovers
The night I looked at you

Chapter Two

Dot's dad, Reg, hadn't always been a chair dweller; he had trained and worked as a sheet-metal worker before being forced to go on the sick with his chest. His wheezing breath was worse at some times than others; if he stayed in his chair and took it easy, it was manageable. His only exertion was a stroll mid-morning to the shop on the corner for his paper and tobacco or an amble into the bookies for a small bet on the gee-gees. The resourceful, industrious Joan had in their time of need increased her hours at the the Merchant's House and just got on with it. Reg was a simple man of simple pleasures who was content with his routine. It would be wrong to say that his decline into ill health had been welcomed, but he didn't lament the loss of his role as breadwinner quite as keenly as others might. As long as his supper was on the table, his wife was in his bed and his kids were happy, he was content.

Twice yearly, when the damp and cold were at their worst, he would take to his bed under a mountain of tartan blankets while Joan ran up and down the stairs with a shallow plastic bowl into which he spat large, bloody gobs of phlegm. She would dab at his fevered grey brow and coo as though tending a sickly child. She loved him.

'Where you off, my girl?' Reg's gravelly voice drifted up from behind his newspaper. His words were always a little muffled; he saw no need to remove the cigarette that was permanently clamped to his bottom lip just because he was speaking. Most of Dot's conversations with her dad, no matter how extended, were conducted from either side of the raised *Standard*. Many was the time she had glanced at the chair by the fire and found herself chatting to Harold Macmillan, Geoff Hurst or D. H. Lawrence about what had happened that day – did Dee need feeding, or who wanted a cuppa?

Dot considered her response. 'I'm going up West; Mum's lumbered me with showing the new bloke up at the Merchant's House where Selfridges is. Could do without it really.'

'Christ, what did she go and do that for? It's not as though we all bleeding work for 'em. I don't know, that mother of yours…' He shook his head.

'S'okay, Dad, I don't really mind.'

'Well you just go careful, love,' he muttered, shaking the invisible creases from the mid section.

Dot clicked the door shut and trotted up the street, picking up the pace. She didn't want to be late, he was practically her mum's boss after all. Mrs Harrison was outside enjoying her umpteenth fag of the day and watching the world go by.

'Off out, Dot?'

Dot held her breath, not knowing how to reply. Of course she was off out, hence she had left the house and was in fact walking briskly in the opposite direction to home. She was formulating a polite yet evasive response when her eyes were drawn to a new notice in Mrs Harrison's parlour window. Three lines that caused the breath to stop in her throat and the colour to drain from her peachy cheeks:

No Blacks.
No Irish.
No Dogs.

Dot looked at the woman she had known her whole life and realised that she did not know her at all and, equally, that Mrs Harrison didn't know her either. Very few people did. There was so much Dot wanted to say – primarily that the only black person she knew lived in splendour with oil paintings, grand pianos and staff and so wouldn't want to stay in her shit-hole guest house anyway, even if he had been welcome. Instead, she nodded and walked on by; it seemed easier.

Dot saw Sol from the bus before it pulled up. Her stomach jumped and her heartbeat quickened at the sight of him, just as it had the first time she saw him. She felt confused. Sol was pacing the corner back and forth, whether cold or nervous, she couldn't tell, maybe it was a little of both. His long gabardine coat with its green diagonal rib pattern emphasised his wiry frame and its large collar was turned up against his beautiful, square chin. She enjoyed watching him unseen for a few moments, free to study his walk, take in his hair with its side part, and notice the way his long fingers curled and gripped each other in an effort to shake off the January morning.

'You look freezing.' She breezed up to him, her breath blowing smoke in the cold morning air; she pinched the front of her leather coat closed at the base of her throat.

'I am! I need to buy a s... scarf.' His teeth almost chattered.

'No you don't, you need to toughen up, that's all, and get used to this London chill. Anyway, it's good for you, it blows the cobwebs out. Least that's what my nan always used to tell me.'

'Well, you can tell your nan I don't think I want my cobwebs blown out if this is what it feels like.'

'I would but she's dead.'

'Oh, I'm sorry...' He looked mortified.

'Don't be – she was a cow most of the time. Didn't really like me much at all.'

Sol looked awkwardly at his feet; he'd never heard the dead referred to with such honesty.

Dot smiled at him, still unused to the slow, rich roll of his Caribbean accent. Some of his 't's were closer to 'd', as was his 'th'. It was a voice that sent a tiny shiver down her spine. She was surprised at how hypnotic she found it, but knew she wanted to hear more.

'Come on.' Dot started to trot along the pavement.

Sol tried to keep up. 'You got quite a wiggle there, girl.'

Dot glanced to her right and smiled again, unaware that she had 'quite a wiggle'. She felt a bubble of happiness swell inside her.

'Where are we going? Selfridges?'

'Maybe, eventually, but I thought we could get a coffee first. It'll warm you up and before I introduce you to people I work with, I want to get to know you a bit.'

'That sounds like you're giving me an interview!'

'You can think of it like that, if you like!'

'What if I don't like?'

'Then you can stay cold and find your own bloody way to Selfridges!'

'Are you always this spirited?'

Dot smiled at him once again. 'Do you want that coffee or not?'

A bell tinkled overhead as she used her shoulder to push the glass door open. The two stepped inside Paolo's, a small, welcoming Italian coffee house whose misted-up windows added to its air of intimacy. A large Burco boiler hissed on the counter, firing steam up to the roof, and there was a deep, acrid smell of burnt coffee beans tinged with the scent of crisped bacon fat. Two older men sat in the corner booth, loading salt-slathered fried eggs onto fried bread and shovelling them into their mouths between drags on roll-ups. Discarded butt-ends smouldered in the heavy glass ashtray, half obscuring its yellow and blue transfer that advertised Pastis.

Dot and Sol slotted into a red vinyl-covered bench in one of the four booths and sat opposite each other with their hands on the wipe-clean Formica top. Sol studied the wall with its signed framed photos of Montgomery Clift, and Elvis in a white tuxedo. He decided not to comment on the fact that the signatures were in identical handwriting and had been written in the same pen. Dot opened her purse and pulled out a sixpence. She considered the mini juke box fixed to the wall at the end of the table and ran through the possible options; her finger hovered.

Sol removed his coat and folded it on the banquette beside him. 'What are our choices? Any Etta?'

Dot smiled at him, glad he'd remembered the song that had been playing when they'd met, unexpectedly thrilled that it wasn't just her who had made the association.

''Fraid not.'

She popped the sixpence into the top slot and jabbed at the rows of letters and numbers until music flowed over them, enveloping them and warming them from the inside out.

'So how are you liking London?'

'Well, they know how to throw a party – I was at a function a couple of days ago and you should have seen the juggler! Eggs flying everywhere…'

'Ha ha. Don't mention it again. I can't relive the shame every time I see you.'

'That sounds like you are planning on seeing me again.'

'I wouldn't bet on it, today might be a disaster. I mean you've already upset me by asking me to give a message to me poor dead nan!'

They smiled at each other, knowing that it was already far from a disaster.

Sol looked at his fingers as he drummed the table top. 'I apologise once again.'

Dot nodded. 'Accepted. Carry on.'

'Well, London seems like a fine place, but to tell you the truth, it isn't a patch on St Lucia. You know what they say, there's no place like home.'

'Is that right?' She had expected a certain amount of flattery about her country, as she was his hostess.

'It's a big adjustment for me. I don't think it would matter if I was in the most beautiful place on the planet – how can you enjoy anything when it's so cold?'

'I guess because we don't know any different, and besides, it's not like it's the Arctic!'

'I can't believe there is anywhere colder than here right now.'

Dot shook her head. 'You're pitiful.'

He ignored her jibe, but smiled. 'And in answer to your question, even though it's too cold to be comfortable, I kind of like what I've seen so far. I like it a lot.'

'Well that's good.' Whether intended or not, Dot took it as a compliment. 'Where is it you're from again?'

'St Lucia, West Indies.'

'St Lucia, West Indies, fancy that.'

'D'you know where it is?'

Dot snorted through her nose. 'I have absolutely no idea! Have you always lived there?'

Sol considered his position on the island: had he always lived there? His family history had been drummed into him over the years, how much should he tell her?

'I was born in the house we live in now and so was my father and his father and so on, as far back as you can think.'

'Oh, that's just like me and my mum – we have both lived in our house since we were born.'

Sol smiled. 'The plot that our house is built on was bought by Mr James Arbuthnott, my ancestor, over one hundred years ago. He made his money in St Lucia and decided to build a home there. He was actually Scottish.'

'Get away! I didn't know there were any coloured people in Scotland.'

'Oh yes, there are lots of coloured people, they are pink.'

'You know what I mean. Anyway, carry on.' Dot placed her elbow on the table and cupped her chin in her hand, rapt by his tale.

'Well, James shipped the finest materials from the far corners of the globe and built the grandest house in St Lucia

– the Jasmine House. I've read some of the letters he wrote, describing what it was like when the white-painted wood caught the sunlight in the early hours, how it gave the whole building a pink hue, and then, as the day progressed, the colour changed to yellow then gold. And he wrote about how, when there's a really magnificent sunset, the whole house glowed the colour of burnt cinnamon. It's still exactly like that. It's magical.'

Dot stared, dumbstruck; it was as if he was reading her a story. She loved it.

'James was born into a rich, successful family, but the amount of wealth he acquired dwarfed even his father's achievements. He was a forward thinker and saw the value in spices, chartering great clippers that transported his sweet-scented cargo all over the world. It took just two years of hauling spices across the high seas before he made enough money to buy his own ships and then he began chartering his boats to others and taking a cut of whatever cargo they transported. Pretty soon he was the wealthiest man in the islands. He had everything a man could wish for. Everything, that is, except happiness.'

Dot leant forward. 'Why wasn't he happy? He had that lovely house!'

'It takes more than bricks, mortar and money to make happiness. And sadly, Sarah, his young wife, pined for her parents, and for the heathery hills of the Scottish Highlands where she had grown up; she dreamed of the snow. And I can understand that – I dream of sunshine!'

'Don't start with that again! Tell me about Sarah.' Dot chewed her thumbnail, as she often did when concentrating.

'Sarah had given birth to two fair-skinned children who also did not thrive in the West Indian heat. Eventually, she couldn't take it any longer and one day she packed her valise and shepherded her small children on to a clipper bound for home. The story goes that on that very same day, just as Sarah and her children were setting sail, Mary-Jane walked barefoot up the path of the Jasmine House in search of work.'

'Ooh, who's Mary-Jane?'

'Mary-Jane was my great-great-grandmother and she *was* from Africa, brought to the Caribbean as a slave to work on the plantations.'

'Oh my God!' Dot placed her hand over her mouth. 'That's terrible.'

'Legend has it that the day Mary-Jane became the mistress of the mighty James Arbuthnott, tropical flowers like hibiscus and lobster claw bloomed in the previously sparse flower beds. The jasmine released its intoxicating scent and birds and wildlife for miles around gathered in the garden paradise, to bask in the love that shone from the two lovers.'

'So she was African and he was Scottish?'

'Yes.'

'Blimey, that must have caused a bit of a stir. I mean it would nowadays, let alone a hundred years ago.'

Sol liked her unfiltered observations, her honesty. 'It did. The household mocked their union, the locals laughed at the skittish young slip of a girl who liked to run barefoot through the gardens and who thought she could be lady of the big house. They warned Mary-Jane that a black and white union would not last, that the master's interest in her would wane and she would be left with nothing, not even her reputation.

But my great-great-grandmother had one response for all those that scorned her: "It cannot be undone; the genie is out of the bottle!" The two lived in a state of bliss for thirty years, until one day Mary-Jane passed away from the flu, brought to the island aboard one of James's very own ships. Apparently he then lay down next to the body of his beloved and died of a broken heart; without Mary-Jane in his world there was very little point in it carrying on beating.'

Dot swallowed the lump in her throat. 'That's so sad, but so lovely at the same time.'

'Their children – Abraham, Saul, Clara and Aloysius – mourned their passing but were happy that their parents would exist in death as they had in life, devotedly side by side. Abraham was my great-grandfather and he and Saul continued to build on their father's success, making the Arbuthnott name one that would always be synonymous with the island of St Lucia.'

'That's like a fairy story.' Dot put her clasped hands in her lap and sat quietly, humbled by his tale.

Sol nodded. 'So, yes, I've always lived there, and my family before me, all in the same house! And what about you?'

Dot perked up and thought about how she might match what she had just heard. She couldn't. 'Oh, very similar to you really! I live in the house that my mum grew up in, and my nan lived there all her life, although we've never had any servants that I know of, unless there's one in the cupboard under the stairs that I don't know about, and it's a darn sight chillier and we've only had an inside loo for the last six years. I think that covers it.'

'You are funny. I've never met anyone like you before.'

'Ditto. Is this your first time in England?'

'No. I came when I was very small, but I don't really remember it. We've only been here for a few days now and my head is still unsure if it's morning or night. I've only been in the new apartment and now here…' Sol waved his arm around in the direction of the door. 'Wherever we are!'

'We are in Stepney. How bad is your sense of direction?'

Sol laughed. 'Pretty bad, apparently, which is surprising because as part of my military training, I've been shown how to find any location in the world by using nothing more than the sun to navigate by as long as what I am trying to find is below the permanent snow line.'

'Is that right?' Dot raised one eyebrow and twisted her lips. It sounded like rubbish.

'Oh yes, it's just one of the many skills that I have acquired. I can also catch and skin a rabbit in less than four minutes and I know how to make a waterproof tent out of a poncho.'

Dot looked him in the eye. 'Well I never. I thank God you are here, Sol, cos the last time I had to catch and skin a rabbit it took me six minutes and my poncho tent was definitely a little bit leaky.'

'You can mock me, Dot, but you never know when these skills will come in useful.'

'Actually, mister, I think I do. Around here your skills are bloody useless!'

Sol was speechless. He had grown up within the privileged walls of the Jasmine House, on an island where his name was known by everyone he encountered. Patience his nanny and Vida his mother had run back and forth to make sure his every wish was indulged. Even at the military academy, his father's name had ensured preferential treatment – and came with its own set of expectations. To this East End girl sitting in front of him, his surname meant nothing at all, which felt both alien and exciting. He laughed loudly, flashing his perfect teeth in Dot's direction.

'Why did you have military training anyway?'

'I'm a soldier.'

'Really? A proper soldier?'

'And you think I insulted *you*? Of course I'm a proper soldier!' He shook his head.

'Oh yeah? What you doing over here then? Don't think there's much soldiering going on here – you're about twenty years too late, mate.'

'It's a covert mission, I'd love to tell you, but then I'd have to kill you.'

'Charming!'

Sol laughed into his coffee. Dot thought she'd better clarify. 'I've never known a soldier before, not a nowadays soldier, only the blokes who fought in the war and are out now. There's a lot of them wandering around, poor souls. Breaks my heart to see the ones that came back loopy, the ones that got landed with the Japs, they was wicked buggers.'

'War makes people wicked.'

'Reckon you're right. It was certainly wicked round our way. Whole families wiped out, fires that burnt for days. Me nan worked in a munitions factory in Clerkenwell and one night during her shift there was a raid; when she came up from the shelter to walk back to Limehouse she couldn't find her way home. Everything was flattened or burning, all the landmarks, buildings, everything that she used to navigate home by, everything she had grown up with had gone. There were people trapped under the rubble and fire crews running from one to the next. She used to tell me about it and I was terrified just listening. The East End was hit pretty bad.'

'I saw pictures, heard about it, it must have been terrible.' Sol nodded sympathetically. 'So I'm your first nowadays soldier...'

'Yes and you're the first black person I've spoken to. I've seen one or two, but not to chat with. I've never known anyone black before.' She lowered her lids; was it okay to say that? She decided not to divulge that she had felt scared of black people before meeting him, having heard only tales of cannibalism and witch-doctoring.

'Your first black person, eh? Well, I definitely have the advantage as I have met quite a few.'

'Do you know other white people?'

Sol laughed. 'Yes of course. Most of my friends from the military academy are white and lots of my parents' friends and my father's colleagues. In St Lucia it's different.'

'So, in St Lucia, is everyone black just like over here everyone is white?'

'Yes.'

Dot smiled. 'I can't imagine that.'

He clapped his hands together and changed the subject. He preferred the ribbing that had gone on earlier to this exploration of race and colour. 'Right, what are our plans for today?'

'Mmm, I'm not sure whether to do a runner and watch you try and find your way home, or take you up West for an adventure.'

'Oh, an adventure sounds good!'

'What would you do at home on a day off?'

'Home, St Lucia?'

'Yep.' She nodded. St Lucia… a name so exotic for a place she couldn't point to on a map, another world that was warm and full of black people.

'Well, whatever was planned, it would start with a good breakfast and then I can guarantee that a large portion of my day would involve the beach – I would either be running on it or swimming in the sea.' Sol closed his eyes and imagined diving, as he often did, head first into the shallow breakers of the turquoise Caribbean Sea at Reduit Beach. He was surprised at the image that leapt into his mind, of him diving into the crystal water with Dot by his side.

'I've never seen the sea.' Dot looked down at her lap, embarrassed.

'Really? Never?'

She shook her head. 'Nope, never.'

'How old are you, Dot?'

'Eighteen.'

'Well in St Lucia you would be about eighteen years too late getting into the water, it's part of us.'

She smirked at him. 'Closest I've got to it is watching the ships come into Limehouse Docks, they sometimes smell like the sea. I often sit on the dock with my mate and look at them, big Russian ships with "Odessa" stamped on the side and piles of timber stacked on them that goes straight into the Montague L. Meyer timber yards. I like watching the barges pulling up to the big ships with lightermen running back and forth like busy little ants. It fascinates me that those massive metal monsters have skimmed over the waves from all over the world and ended up within a mile of my little house. It's amazing that, isn't it?'

Sol nodded, yes it was amazing. He decided not to tell her that his father was not only a military man but also the owner of one of the largest shipping companies in the world.

Dot continued. 'I like to hear the crew of the ships talking in their own language, sometimes I make out it's me that's abroad and not them, I know that sounds daft. I wonder what they make of the stevedores in their woolly hats who natter away in cockney banter; they must think it's all very strange.'

'Where would you go if you could go abroad right now?'

'What, right this minute?'

'Yes, right this minute, anywhere in the world.'

'Would I be back in time for me tea, or should I pack sandwiches?'

'You won't be back in time for tea, but your sandwiches would probably spoil, you can eat out!'

Dot grinned and once again cupped her chin with her hand, her elbow propped on the table, and tried to imagine a world untethered by the boundaries of her immediate neighbourhood, or her family, where she could go anywhere and eat out when she got there.

'Ooh blimey, I dunno. Paris probably; I'd like to look at all the fashion, watch the river and drink wine and sit in a cafe, I'd love that. And America, obviously. I'd love to go to Hollywood and see all the film stars and then I'd get the bus from Hollywood to New York to see the statue of Liberty and the Empire State Building, although not on a day when King

Kong's swinging around on it. I'd eat a hamburger and go to a drive-in movie and sit next to a cowboy! Yep, America – I think I'd love it!'

Sol smiled. For him the novelty of foreign travel had almost worn off, having been hauled all over the world since he was six months old.

Dot continued. 'I may not have seen the sea, but I've heard it, inside a conch shell. My grandad worked in the docks all his life and he gave me one. I held it up to my ear and I could hear the sea swooshing around in there, it was brilliant! I had it for years, but me dad stubbed his toe on it once too often and it got chucked out ages ago. Funny, I haven't thought about it till now.'

'You know, Dot, that shell might have come from the beach where I swim. We eat conch and often the large shells end up as borders around the flower beds in our gardens.'

He glanced up at Dot's wide-eyed expression.

'Don't think I fancy that much,' she said. 'The swimming bit sounds all right, but I'm more of a cod-and-chips girl, with plenty of salt and vinegar. Besides, I don't think we've got plates big enough to hold a bloody massive conch.'

Sol smiled yet again; this girl was unlike any other he had met. He liked the way she looked at the world.

Dot had never taken a taxi up West before; she didn't know anyone that took taxis. She felt a combination of joy, excitement and guilt – if they'd taken the bus or the Tube, they would arrive just as soundly, and the money they'd save could be used for any number of useful things.

'What are you thinking?'

'I was thinking how different the world looks when you see it from a little higher and though the glass of a taxi window.' This was partly true. Dot often travelled underground and if she caught the bus, the windows were more often than not a steamed-up fug of breath and cigarette smoke, meaning you caught the outline of buildings and the flicker of lights but not the detail, the context. She would often wipe the steam from the glass, but the build-up of filth on the outside of the pane still obscured the view.

'That's where I was born!' Dot pointed at the greying facade of the East End Maternity Hospital as they tootled by. 'My mum used to tell me that they'd put up a special plaque saying "Dot Simpson was born here". I believed her for years and I used to tell all me classmates, they must of thought I was a right idiot! Can you imagine? I'm surprised I didn't get a good thump.'

Sol pictured the streets, squares, libraries and schools that were named after his forefathers. It was his turn to feel ill at ease. 'They'll be the ones feeling like idiots when you are known all over for your fashion designs.'

'Oh Gawd, you've got to stop with all that, it makes me feel really embarrassed.'

'I don't see why it should; you've got to chase your dreams.'

'Maybe, maybe not. I sometimes think it's easier to keep things simple and avoid the disappointment.'

'That's not true. Not trying is true defeat and you don't strike me as a defeatist.'

Dot averted her gaze, partly because she didn't want to explain just how hard it was for a girl like her to break out of Ropemakers Fields, and partly because she wasn't sure exactly what defeatist meant, though she knew she didn't like the sound of it much.

She remembered how when she was little, about seven, her dad had tucked her in one night and had told her that they were going to stay in a caravan that summer and that she would be able to paddle in the water, ride on a donkey and eat candyfloss every single day. She had waited and waited, thinking about what it would be like to dig the sand and get in the sea, and she could almost feel the sugary crunch of the pink wisps on her tongue. Then her dad lost his job, went on the sick, and summer came and went and Dot never did get to go in a caravan. She didn't try to explain to Sol that it was sometimes better not to raise your hopes too high.

The taxi pulled up in front of the store. Sol jumped out, shivered, crossed his arms and rubbed the tops of his shoulders with his opposite palms, and reached for his wallet to pay the cabbie. Before Dot got out, the driver scooted the glass screen along and turned to face her, ensuring she could hear him loud and clear. 'I bet you haven't taken him home to meet yer dad, have ya, love?' His mouth was set in an ugly sneer.

'What?' Dot blinked, hoping she had misheard. What did it have to do with him? But there was no time for further discussion. Sol had paid the man, and given him a generous tip, and was holding the door open for her. Her heart lurched. The ignorant pig had managed to take the edge off her lovely day.

'Wow! I can see why you love it, very grand indeed!' Sol shielded his eyes and stepped back on the pavement the better to admire Selfridges' imposing facade. 'Look at the flags on the roof, they're amazing!'

The two laughed as they hesitated at the revolving door, unsure whether they should go in together or separately. Sol stood back and stretched out his arm; Dot swept past him and into the store, careful not to leave a fingerprint on the shiny brass door plate, knowing that they were a bugger to clean. It was a novelty for Dot to be using the main public entrance on Oxford Street and not the staff door around the side.

They lingered over the glass-topped perfume counters and brass and wooden cabinets that held everything from pomade to cologne. Slick-haired, suited gents from the City, wearing bowler hats and carrying black umbrellas, ambled along the walkways, their arms linked with corseted, lipsticked ladies, each preoccupied with the array of goodies and trinkets on display. Sol admired a hand-crafted shaving set of pure badger bristle whose sturdy ivory handles were carved in grooves to resemble colonnades; the whole thing sat in a natty walnut case whose tiny brass hinges were intriguing. He noticed Dot's eyes widen at the price tag and placed it back on the shelf.

'I want to see the Hadashaberry Department!' he declared

Dot chewed her bottom lip. It was one thing to be out and about with a black man, but to parade him in front of her work colleagues was quite another.

Sol saw her flicker of uncertainty. 'Come on! Then I can picture you on the days when you can't come out and play.'

'You'll find that's most days, unless I win the pools!'

'I don't know what you mean by "win the pools" – swimming pools?'

Dot laughed. 'Don't worry about it!' It felt too complicated to try and explain.

Sol and Dot had to stand at the very back of the lift, to make way for a bespectacled lady in a huge fur coat and her large-hatted friend. The stench of several layers of sampled scent sprayed onto their crêpey décolletages hung above them in a toxic cloud. Sol coughed into his bunched-up fist. Dot faced the wall to stem her giggles, but the mirrored confines offered her little shelter.

The ladies bustled out at Lingerie.

'Phwoosh! What was that? I do not want to buy any of what they were advertising. Man! They've burnt the back of my throat.'

The lift boy placed his gloved hands behind his liveried jacket and tried to remain indifferent; he wasn't supposed to join in conversations. Sol caught the lad's smile in the reflection of the shiny brass button panel and said, 'Although I bet that's not the worst thing you've smelt in here, am I right?'

The boy turned around; a cockney, like Dot. 'You're right, sir, sometimes I wish people *would* get in reeking of perfume!' He waved his white gloves in front of his nose.

Dot could have kissed him; the lad's easy acceptance of Sol washed away the memory of the misery-guts cabbie. The lift shuddered to a halt on the fourth floor.

'This is it. We are not staying, mind. Just a quick gawp and then out, okay?'

'Okay!' Sol raised his hands in surrender.

'Ah, Miss Simpson. Not expecting you in today, are we?' It was almost as if the woman had been standing there waiting for her.

If there was one person in the whole store that Dot did not

want to encounter today it was Miss Blight. She peered up at Dot through pig-like eyes framed by elaborate turquoise glasses. As usual, her generous figure was squeezed into a peplum skirt and a tight twin-set, and her fat stockinged feet were shoehorned into high heels. Dot thought it made her look like she had little trotters. She knew it was a mean thought, but it was easy to be mean about Miss Blight because she was horrible to Dot and anyone else junior to her. She worked in Personnel. Dot and Barb agreed that there was no one in the whole of Selfridges who relished administering punishments and sackings more.

'No, not in officially today, Miss Blight, just… shopping!'
'I see.'

Dot watched the woman size up her companion and knew that her visit would be floor-wide gossip within the hour.

'Well, we can pick up about this tomorrow. Have a *lovely* day.'

Dot wanted to challenge her: pick up about *what* exactly? But truth be told, she was as afraid of what the topic might be as she was of Miss Blight. Sol strolled around the counters, thankfully oblivious. He looked at the tiny bone-coloured buttons, sorted according to size in a drawer of many compartments. He twanged elastic, fingered ribbon and flicked through the paper patterns that meant anyone with an average Singer in their parlour and a spool of thread could run up anything from a new oven glove to a wedding dress. He stood marvelling at the bolts of fabric that were stacked in rows according to colour along the far wall.

Dot stood behind him. 'I stare at this every day. It reminds me of a rainbow.'

'I can see why.' Until she had seen a rainbow stretch out to sea as the St Lucian rain competed with the rays of the midday sun, this would be her rainbow. 'Which colour do you like the best?'

'Ooh, I don't know.' Dot ran her palm over the damask. 'I love the dark rose.' Then her fingers massaged the mid-blue drill. 'But this reminds me of a clear summer sky.'

'That's a fine choice, almost the colour of a St Lucian sky. Let's take some with us!'

'What for?' Dot was nervous; a decent amount of the fabric would cost a few days' wages.

'I don't know – you're the designer, you tell me!'

'Oh God, don't start with all that again, 'specially not in here!'

'Oi, Dot!'

Barb marched over to the two of them and folded her arms across her flat chest. She stood with one hip forward, her foot pointing towards Sol in a ballet-like pose.

'Is this him? The piano bloke, the one from the other night?'

'Yes, Barb, it is.' Dot sighed. 'And he's not deaf – are you?'

Sol shook his head. 'No, not yet.'

Barb stared at Sol as she reached up and with one arm still anchored to her chest, teased the ends of her bunches with her fingers and checked her bobbles. Dot had described him perfectly, although she had omitted one small detail.

'I didn't realise he was…'

'So tall?' Dot offered.

'So… exotic,' Barb countered.

The three stood in silence for some seconds. Then Sol coughed.

'Where d'you work then?' Barb was fascinated.

'I'm in the army.'

'What army's that then?'

'The British army.'

'But you ain't British, you don't sound British!'

Dot felt her cheeks flame; her mate was thick sometimes; in fact not just sometimes.

'No, that's true, but I'm from St Lucia and it's part of the British Empire, we share the same queen.'

'Getaway!' Barb unfolded her arms and placed them on her hips.

Sol laughed. 'No, it's true and I fight for your queen and your country. Although I don't plan on doing much fighting over the next year. I'm here as part of the attaché representing the St Lucian defence team.' He decided not to mention that the only other representative of the St Lucian defence team was his boss and his dad, one and the same.

'Oh I see. Blimey, Dot, he's certainly got the gift of the gab!'

'And once again, Barb, he can actually hear you.'

'Barb, can you help us? We would like to take some of this material, if possible; this beautiful shade of blue—'

'What d'you want that for?' Barb screwed up her nose and pulled her confused face.

Sol looked at Dot, who was wide eyed; he read the almost imperceptible shake of her head. She hadn't shared her dream with her friend.

'Because sometimes, Barb, you just need something around you that reminds you of a clear summer sky. Don't you think?'

Barb roared with laughter. 'If you say so! Blimey, Dot, what is he, a bloody poet?'

'Barb, he can *hear* you!'

'All right! No need to shout at me!' she mumbled as she laid the blue cotton on the cutting desk and lined up the edge with the brass ruler. 'Where you going now?'

Dot looked at Sol, a guest in her city. 'I think we might go for a walk in the park.'

'Sounds good!' Sol enthused.

'Do you walk very fast as well as run very fast?'

Sol shook his head, trying to pick up the thread of Barbara's conversation. 'I'm not sure – I can run fast, but I don't know about walking, why do you ask?'

'My dad said that black people have extra bones and muscles in their legs and that's why they make such good runners.'

Barb busied herself with the bolt of fabric while Sol wheezed into a tissue, trying not to offend Dot's friend.

Dot couldn't wait to escape. 'Oh my God, what is she like?'

'She's priceless!'

As they strolled around Hyde Park their conversation flowed without awkward pauses or edits, as though they had shared experience and many years of friendship under their belts. After tea and cake at a Lyons Corner House, their day was nearly done. It was turning into a crisp London dusk: the light was almost pink and the pavement felt hard and cold beneath their feet. Sol was fascinated by the destinations on the fronts of the chunky crimson buses that trundled around the streets, places familiar to him through movies and literature; Trafalgar Square, Greenwich, the Embankment, Highgate – he could jump on any one of those buses and be taken there. It reminded him how small St Lucia was, twenty-seven miles give or take, top to toe.

Dot dipped her chin inside her coat; it was getting chilly. 'Fancy the pictures?'

'Do I fancy what pictures?'

Dot laughed. 'The flicks, the movies!'

'Oh! Sure, what's on?'

'I don't care! I just don't want to go home yet.' She was bold and truthful.

'Well what a coincidence! Neither do I.'

Dot ran ahead. Sol laughed, her words having echoed his thoughts. Pulling his coat into his chest, he followed in her wake.

By the time they'd emerged from the Curzon and had made their way east to Limehouse It was nearly ten o'clock. Rope-makers Fields was dark and for this Dot was grateful; she didn't want there to be any chance of Sol seeing Mrs Harrison's hateful sign, were he to venture that far up the street. A thin mist of rain fogged the air and made the cobbles shine in the lamplight. Curtains were pulled and the only light came from the gaps in nets or mis-pulled drapes, where the dazzle of a light bulb glinted on the damp pavement. Sol ran his hand over the bonnet of the pale blue Austin Seven Mini, the only car on the street; it belonged to the clever boy at Number 29 who was off to university to study something to do with science, according to Mrs Harrison. He peeked inside at the leather seats and tried to picture it bounding along the rugged, sand-filled tracks that led to Soufrière, down on the south-west coast of St Lucia.

Sol walked Dot to the end of her road, as per her request, no further. He tried not to show too much interest in the narrow little houses all squashed together along the pavement. Not to mention the faintly sulphurous odour in the air. It looked poor, it smelled poor and it wasn't what he had expected. Not Caribbean living-on-the-streets poor, but certainly not what he imagined he would find in the capital city of England.

He pictured the Jasmine House sitting high on the hill above Rodney Bay, with its view of the Pitons in the distance. He visualised the eponymous night-flowering jasmine that clung to the wrap-around veranda, filling the evening and early-morning air with its pungent scent. He recalled the way the smell drifted up through the windows, snaking through the freshly painted white shutters and permeating any fabric that hung in the breeze. The French muslin around the frames of the mahogany four-poster beds constantly held the delicate perfume and the mere brush of a finger was enough to release the fragrance into the room. He was beginning to realise the level of luxury and privilege that he had grown up with.

'Thank you for today, for showing me around, for everything.' He kicked his heel against the edge of the pavement.

'No, thank *you*! It's been great! And thank you for my material. I shall give it a lot of thought and try and make something worthy of it, something that will always remind me of today.'

'That's good. It was a day wrapped in clover...'

Dot smiled at the reference to their song. 'Yes it was.'

'Hey, I think I know what I should call you. I think I'll call you Clover. A Dot is something so small and insignificant – that's not a name for someone like you.'

Dot smiled again; she had never felt anything other than small and insignificant. Clover... it sounded lovely.

'Clovers are lucky for some, you know. And it's from our favourite song.'

'I don't think I've ever been lucky for anyone!' Dot beamed, more at the fact that he had said 'our favourite song', as though they were connected. She forgot playing it cool and was now grinning up at him, holding the brown paper bag of sky-blue drill close to her chest.

Sol leant forward conspiratorially. 'I hate this end-of-date moment. In fact I've been dreading it since we first met this morning.'

'Oh, I see; a date was it? And there was me thinking I was helping you out with a bit of sightseeing.'

Sol looked bashful. 'It's difficult for us boys, y'know; we're supposed to take the lead, but I never know whether to lean in for a quick kiss or shake hands. It feels like there are so many ways that I could get it wrong and I don't want to ruin my chances.'

'I'd say your chances are pretty good.' Dot gave him a sideways glance.

'You see, girl, some might interpret that as an invitation to lean in.' Sol placed his hand on her waist and drew her towards him.

'Some might be right,' she whispered.

He moved his hands to the nape of her neck, pushing until his fingers were entwined in her hair, letting the silky strands slip through his fingers. Holding her head fast, he brought his face down to meet hers and hovered over her mouth. She reached upwards on tiptoes and touched her lips against his. The two smiled and touched their noses together.

'I'll see you soon?' He ran his thumb over her jaw. She

could only nod. A gurgle of excitement and pure joy blocked her throat, making speech impossible.

'Clover...' Sol called out from down the street as she fumbled to get the key into the lock.

'What?' She beamed.

'Nothing, I just like saying your name.'

'Daft apeth.' Although in truth she didn't think it was daft at all, she thought it was bloody wonderful!

Dot shut the front door behind her and rested her back against the glass. Her heart raced.

'That you, Dot?' Joan called from the back room. 'Howdja get on, love? I was getting a bit worried. Your dad's gone up already, so keep it down. You're later than I thought you might be. D'yfancy a cuppa? Dee's coloured you in a picture of a bowl of fruit, it's on your bed. Have you eaten? You weren't with him the whole time, were you, love? Did you meet up with Barb?'

Dot breathed deeply, trying to calm her pulse. She touched her fingers to her mouth and pushed at the slight swell of her lower lip. It was as if she could still feel the warmth where his beautiful mouth had touched hers. Her mother could not have guessed that in the preceding five minutes her daughter and the universe in which she existed had been altered. Joan was speaking, but it was a background hum, the details of which Dot could not decipher. Her head was filled with the lilting lyrics *My lonely days are over/And life is like a song* and imprinted behind her eyelids was the image of his face, his liquid brown eyes, his perfect teeth and that sweet, gentle kiss.

Chapter Three

Two days later, Dot let the fire-door slam behind her and stepped onto the busy West End pavement. She had only done a half day, but it was enough, considering how little sleep she was getting. The last couple of nights she had fallen onto her feather mattress physically exhausted. But her mind surfed on a sea of 'maybes' and her body twitched and twisted until the early hours, which made sleep impossible. There was one reason for these distractions – Sol. Sol.

She looped the lime-green chiffon scarf about her neck and tied it into a large bow, enough to lift her drab, mud-coloured mac and American Tan tights.

'I've been thinking about you.'

'What?'

She turned to face the voice, the same voice that had disturbed her sleep and haunted her dreams ever since she first heard it. Her heart thudded and soared, not with shock but excitement. She wanted to throw her arms around his neck with relief. *At last/My love has come along...*

Over the last couple of days, Dot had felt a constant, overwhelming desire to be in his company; any situation or chore that kept them apart was simply a waste of her time. She wished the tone of her reply hadn't been quite so sharp. Of course she had heard and understood him the first time, but she needed to hear the words again. Her imagination was so vivid when it came to Sol, she needed to reassure herself that he was real, needed to seek out any hint that he might feel the same.

'I said, I've been thinking about you. In fact I've been think-ing about you constantly since we met. I can't eat – which as anyone that knows me would tell you, is most unusual – and I can't sleep and it's all your fault.'

'Is that so?' Dot ran her tongue over her teeth, checking for any cerise lipstick that might have adhered there.

'Yep. And to tell you the truth, Lady Clover, it's proving to be a bit of a distraction. I'm finding it hard to concentrate on anything: I can't work, my paperwork is full of errors, I don't hear what is said to me because I am not thinking straight and I don't know what to do. I've considered playing it cool, but I don't know how I'm supposed to do that when you turn me to jelly, which is not cool at all. So I've decided the best option is to come clean, forget cool and be honest.'

'I see. And how long ago is it exactly, since we met and your beauty sleep was disrupted?'

Sol looked at his watch. 'Well I'm not exactly sure, but if I had to guess, I'd say seven days, seventeen hours, twelve minutes and eighteen seconds, no nineteen, no twenty—'

'I get it, Sol, just over a week ago.' She smiled.

'Yes, just over a week. But, seriously, you have not left my head for one second since that moment. Not one.'

Dot felt her gut twist with excitement and happiness. *Imagine! His head filled with her.*

'And what about you?' he pushed, looking at his shoes, his voice quieter now. 'Have you been thinking about me?'

Dot placed her small hands in her pockets and looked down

at the pavement. It was easier not to make eye contact – anything rather than acknowledge the weight of his question. 'Only when I'm awake.'

Her voice was quite small, but Sol heard the lie nonetheless. He grinned. 'It's as I thought, Clover, the genie is out of the bottle!'

'What does *that* mean?'

He leant forward and she had to match his stance to hear his words, which were uttered in barely more than a whisper. 'It means that sometimes the universe conspires and we are merely pawns that have no option but to go with the situation that forces far bigger than us have decreed. And it's not a matter of what we *want*, but whether we have the strength or desire to fight against it.'

Dot sniffed. 'Well, I understood about half of that, I think.'

Dot Simpson had witnessed her mum and dad amiably bumbling along, laughing through the hard times and ploughing on even though sometimes life must have felt like wading through treacle. She'd watched her mum prepare a thousand meals while her dad read a thousand newspaper stories. Their life was like a treadmill of chores and, for her mum, work, with little time or money for fun. Love was the glue that held them together; she would often find them dancing or kissing when they thought no one was looking. But the way Dot felt right now, like a light had been switched on in a dark room, and with her heart aching during the hours they spent apart, she doubted they had ever felt like that. The way she felt about Sol was exciting and confusing in equal measure.

'Sol?'

'Yes?'

'I think it is what I want.'

Sol grinned and squeezed her hand. 'How about that stroll then?'

Dot nodded and linked her arm through his.

* * *

Dot sat at the table in the back room and tried not to comment as Dee swung her little legs in rhythm, kicking Dot's shins from the opposite chair. Dot pushed the boiled ham and pease pudding around her plate, loading up her fork, but not actually lifting any to her mouth.

'You gonna eat that, Dot or just play with it?'

'What?'

'Yer dinner!' snapped Joan. 'You've been shoving it around the plate since you sat down. If you don't want it, give it to your dad or wrap the ham up for tomorrow and I'll make sandwiches.'

'I'm not hungry.'

'No, I gathered that, love. Not sickening for something are you?'

'No, Mum. Just tired, I think.'

'It's all that gallivanting off with God knows who,' Reg grumbled. 'Coming in at all hours. You need a coupla early nights, girl.'

'No, I'm all right, Dad. In fact, I'm enjoying meself for once and ten o'clock isn't exactly all hours.'

'Oh Gawd, here we go – violins, please – what a terrible life you've had! Cooped up here with us wicked parents. Enjoying yourself? I should be so bloody lucky!' Reg forked his daughter's unwanted pease pudding onto his plate.

Joan ignored her husband.

'Ooh, I meant to say, I saw Sol, that black fella today, Dot.'

'Oh?' She tried to sound nonchalant, aware that a scarlet stain of embarrassment had crept along her neck and over her scalp.

'Who's Sol when he's at home?' Reg asked.

'You know, the young darkie bloke that lives in the top flat with his parents; they've come over from God knows where. I told you, Reg, the ones we had the do for a few weeks back.'

Reg nodded and filled his mouth, which was now only an inch or so from the plate in front of him.

'Anyways,' Joan continued, 'he looked proper smart, in a suit, shiny shoes and everything. He was getting into a flash car; don't know where he was off.'

Dot drew a deep breath as she rehearsed the words inside her head. It had to be said sooner or later and it might as well be now. She decided to keep it casual. '*He was off to meet me, actually…*'

'Oooh don't be fooled,' shouted Reg with his mouth full of food, before Dot had the chance to say her piece. 'Whatever he was wearing, they are slippery customers and not to be trusted. Look at poor old Gloria Riley.'

'Who's Gloria Riley?' He had her attention.

'She was a local girl who came to a sticky end.'

'What's a sticky end?' Dee wanted to know.

'Eat your dinner.' Joan pointed at Dee's plate.

Reg leant towards Dot and spoke out of the side of his mouth, not wanting to give Dee any information that might pique her interest. 'It was a couple of years ago now; she took up with a coloured fella that had come to work on the trains. Her family was horrified; her dad chucked her out, naturally. So she goes to this bloke she's seeing with a little bag packed and her savings in her purse, ready to elope like he'd promised and guess what? When it came to it, he had to confess that he had a wife and kids back wherever he'd come from. She was desperate, the poor cow. But that's what they're like, it's different for them. Probably in his village they have umpteen wives and no one blinks a bloody eyelid. Mind you, not sure why you'd want more than one wife, I just about cope with the one I've got! A man could get nagged to death!'

Dot rubbed at her temples to relieve the beginnings of a headache. She swallowed the words she had rehearsed.

Joan tutted at her husband. 'This Sol's nothing like that, he's quite posh and as I say, he was wearing a suit and everything.'

'You can't tell what they're like, love, no matter what they wear. And are you sure it was a suit, Joany? Thought he'd be more likely to be in a loin cloth and have a bloody bone through his nose!' Reg laughed and a small glob of pease pudding slid from his lip and back onto the plate. Dee laughed at her funny dad. He wasn't done. 'And what do they actually *eat*, these people? I bet they've got you rustling up curried goat and Gawd knows what every day! Yuk, you wouldn't catch me eating no foreign muck, the thought of it turns my bloody stomach!'

Dot pushed her plate into the middle of the table. 'Actually, I don't feel that well after all, think I might go and get some fresh air and then I'm meeting Barb. Thanks for tea, Mum. I'll see you later.'

Dot couldn't trust herself not to respond to her dad's ignorant humour. She heard their conversation as she put on her lippy in the hall mirror.

'What'sa matter with her?'

'Hormones, I think, love.' Joan knew this was the one topic guaranteed to shut him up.

'Oh, Christ, a house full of women! It's enough to drive a man round the bleeding bend!'

As Dot and Sol strolled through Hyde Park and alongside the Serpentine the next day her dad's words echoed in her thoughts. She wasn't sure how she would break the news to him now, but she had the idea that once he had met Sol and been bowled over by how brilliant he was, he might come round. She shook her head slightly, laughing at how she must have been confusing her dad with someone else. *He won't come round.*

It was with confidence that Sol now reached for her hand and the two matched each other's pace, in no hurry to arrive anywhere in particular. They stopped only for the occasional peck on the cheek and to share a bag of roasted chestnuts, bought from a vendor who had set up his brazier in a corner of the park.

They stopped at a bench and huddled together under the pretence of warding off the chill. 'I love seeing all these new plants,' Sol said. 'I'm a bit of an amateur horticulturist at home. I find it amazing how you can take a tiny seed and with a little bit of care and attention can watch it grow into something so strong and beautiful. Many of the trees on our land are hundreds of years old; I find that incredible!'

Dot loved his enthusiasm, his interest, but she couldn't help comparing his description with her own back yard at Rope-makers Fields. What would Sol make of the long, thin strip of bare concrete, littered with nothing more interesting than a few metal mop buckets, an ancient wheelbarrow with flat tyres and her dad's bike?

'The grass here is so fine and dense,' Sol continued. 'Our lawn at the Jasmine House is quite the opposite: sparse and spiky. I think the peahens would like roaming about on this all day. And your English flowers seem more fragile, and for that more beautiful. Like poppies... I bet you have some beautiful flowers in your garden, don't you, Clover?'

'Errr, not really much growing in it at the moment,' she replied hurriedly. Dot thought about their back yard at Rope-makers Fields, a long thin strip with patched fencing on either side that denied the area sunlight for most of the day. A large slab of concrete littered with metal mop buckets, an old wheelbarrow with flat tyres and her dad's bike. There was the old outside privy now used as a shed, full to bursting with all sorts of junk that was fit for the scrap heap. A couple of adventurous roses from the Rusalovas' garden peeked over the back fence as though fascinated by the goings on in the Simpsons' house. They withered and died quite quickly. Apart from the clutter, her mum pegging out the washing and her dad having the occasional fag in his vest, there wasn't that much to see.

True, the back two thirds of their yard had once been a lawn, in her nan's time, but that was before the Anderson shelter had taken priority. Now the only thing that bloomed was the bindweed that snaked over its rusting corrugated panels, the beautiful white and pale pink blooms reminding

Dot of tiny gramophone speakers. One small flower bed in the top left corner had been planted with bulbs a few years ago, while her dad had still been able to wield a spade, but you were lucky to get one chrysanthemum a year out of them now. Dot realised with an uneasy stirring in her stomach that she would be embarrassed to show Sol their garden.

'It's cold!' Sol patted his hands together and dipped his chin into his collar.

'When do you think you'll stop saying that?'

'I don't know, maybe when the sun comes out!'

Dot laughed. 'Blimey, you might be saying it for a while then. This is a lovely day, I don't know what you're moaning about.'

Sol leapt up and sprinted off. She watched the grace with which he ran along the path. There was a hint in the March breeze of the warmth to come. Dot couldn't wait to show him London in the summer; they could go for picnics and swim in the lido, it would be wonderful. She thought of her best summer frock hanging in the wardrobe and decided to give it a once-over with a damp sponge to make sure she was ready.

Sol had rounded the bend in the path and stood there catching his breath while he waited for her. She took her time.

'Now aren't you a sight for sore eyes!' Sweeping Dot into his arms, Sol lifted her clean off the pavement. 'I've missed you.'

'Get a grip! You only saw me a few moments ago!'

'Clover, I swear that the second I leave you, I long to have you back again, right by my side. Is it the same for you or am I mad?'

She smiled. 'You *are* mad, but it's the same for me. We must both be mad!'

'How about we go to Paolo's?'

'Where else would we go?' she teased.

'It's our place.'

'Yes it is. If I'd known our first outing was going to have so much significance, I might of picked somewhere a bit flashier!'

'It's perfect. Plus I like to see how long we can hang around before he starts flicking switches very loudly and coughing about a tiring day. So, that's the plan, Paolo's for coffee and maybe some toast, what do you think?'

'I think I'd love to!' *I think I love you…*

The next morning, Dot hung her coat on the peg in the staff room and smiled at the colleagues and customers she passed on her way to her floor. She wondered if they'd seen a change in her over the last month; she certainly felt different. Seeking out the little jobs and fiddly chores in the Haberdashery to try and still her busy mind, she occupied herself with the winding of ribbon and logging of wool, attempting to order the thoughts that competed for space in her head. She imagined the conversation she must have with her dad, pictured him and Sol shaking hands over the threshold of Ropemakers Fields. But try as she might, it was a blur.

'I'm nipping out for a bit of fresh air and a fag, you coming?'

'No, I'm all right, Barb. It's pissing down and I don't want to get me hair wet.'

'Who are you, Jean bloody Shrimpton? What d'you mean you don't want to get your hair wet? Since when have you been bothered about that?'

'I just mean I don't want to spend the afternoon looking like a frizzled drip and with me hair all stuck to me face.'

Barb studied her friend, who was now absorbed in ordering and sorting the packets of dress patterns into a neat row, patting the sides and tops until they were aligned.

'You've been right off today. What's up, you on the rag?'

Dot shook her head. 'No. I'm just a bit tired.'

Barb chewed the inside of her cheek and watched her mate toil. 'Oh my God! It's that bloke, isn't it? You don't want to get your hair messed up cos you're meeting him! I'm right, aren't I?'

Dot sighed as she looked up. 'All right! Yes, I admit I don't want me hair messed up cos I'm meeting him for a coffee. Happy now?'

Barb folded her arms. 'A bit. But I don't know what you're worried for, he's got that horrible crinkly stuff on his head, he's hardly going to worry if yours is a bit flatter than usual. At least you've got normal hair!' Barb snorted her laughter.

Dot felt her heart leap inside her chest as her jaw clenched; she wasn't used to feeling this way when addressing her mate. 'His hair *is* normal for him, and probably his people think our hair is weird, did you ever think of that?'

'No. But it don't matter, does it, cos our hair is how hair's supposed to be and so that's normal and theirs is just… weird.'

'How do you figure out that ours is normal and theirs isn't?'

'Don't be daft, Dot. If theirs was normal hair, everyone'd be walking around with it, wouldn't they?'

'Well of course! And they do where he lives, you dozy cow!'

Barb pulled her mouth into a sideways slant and considered this. 'I hadn't thought of that.'

'You don't say.'

'So why do they have hair like that?'

'Gawd, I don't know! Ask Sol next time you see him. Second thoughts, I am joking, Barb, do not ask Sol that when you see him.'

'My dad says they have that hair to stop their heads being damaged when a coconut falls on it.'

'Well it sounds like your dad talks out of his arse as much as you do, mate. Least we know where you get it from.'

'All right, keep your hair on!' Barb bent over and snorted as she laughed. 'Did you hear what I said? *Keep your hair on!*'

'I heard you. And for the record, I think his hair is beautiful. I think he's beautiful.' Dot ground her teeth.

'Blimey. You do, don't you?'

'Yep.' Dot kept her eyes cast downwards.

'Have I upset you, Dot?'

Dot exhaled. 'I don't know. A bit. Yes.'

'But you and me can talk about anything, can't we?'

Dot nodded at her best friend. 'Course we can. I just find it hard, it seems everyone has something negative to say and I just wish… I just wish someone could be pleased for us.'

'I am pleased for you! Even if other people aren't. I thought Aunty Audrey was going to choke on her tea when I told her! But I'm not other people; I'm your best mate, always.'

Dot nodded. 'I know.'

'But I do think it's going to be tough, because it's different. We don't *know* any coloured people, Dot and it's not just cos he's coloured. It'd be the same if he was normal but from Iceland, people would be interested in what Iceland was like and what it was like living in an igloo and eating nothing but frozen fish.'

Dot looked at her friend and decided there was no point continuing the discussion.

'You go and have your fag and fresh air, mate; I'll tidy up a bit.'

'I don't think anyone will be nipping outside any time soon, thank you, Miss Simpson.' Neither girl had heard Miss Blight approach. 'Can I remind you both that there is a rota for break times and it is not to be deviated from. Is that clear?'

'Yes, Miss Blight.' The girls spoke in unison.

'And have you finished the stocktake on the fabric? I am called upon to submit figures.'

'Yes, Miss Blight.' Again, both girls answered simultaneously, although this time both had their fingers crossed behind their backs. It was their rule: if your fingers were crossed, lying didn't count.

As Miss Blight walked away, Barb held two unlit cigarettes in the extended fingers of each hand and pretended to puff them one after the other. Fake smoking while flicking the V was one of her specialities. Dot collapsed in giggles.

With her hair still passing muster at the end of her shift, Dot pulled her headscarf tighter, jumped off the bus and ran up Ropemakers Fields. And there he was, loitering at the end of Narrow Street, looking handsome and happy. Even the sight of him was enough to fill her stomach with a fizz of joy. It didn't matter that it was raining, nothing did. The two of them laughed at the joy of being reunited.

'Paolo's?' she asked.

'We could, but my parents are at a function so we have the apartment to ourselves. Why don't we go back and I'll make us hot chocolate. We can get out of this rain!'

Dot nodded. 'Sounds lovely. And on the way you can tell me more about your garden. I've been thinking, I'd love a nice garden, y'know. I'd like to grow flowers and all me own veg.'

'Oh, be careful, once you get the gardening bug it can take you over, become an obsession. You worry for the welfare of all these living things that are entirely dependent on you for their survival!'

'Oh Gawd, I don't know if I'm ready for that kind of responsibility.'

Sol looked her up and down. 'I'd say probably not.'

'Behave!' She shoved him playfully. 'I think I'd like to cook what I'd grown. I could do fruit and make jams and crumble; be lovely that, wouldn't it? I've never been much of a cook, it's kind of me mum's thing, but I reckon I'd love cooking for you. I'd experiment and you'd have to eat all my disasters!'

Sol smiled at her. It *would* be lovely.

It felt strange to be in the Merchant's House without her mum – sneaky and a little bit disloyal. This was her mum's place of work and there she was, sliding along the wooden floors without her shoes on, while her boyfriend made them hot chocolate in the kitchen where Joan toiled day after day.

Every footstep, creak of door and rattle of window seemed extra loud, as though betraying her illicit visit to an interested ear. Dot entered the grand ballroom in which they had first met and looked up at the ceiling; strange how she had never really noticed the painting until that eventful night. She walked to the middle of the room and lay on the wooden floor. The more she stared, the lower the image came, as though God and the angels were descending to meet her. She felt warmth flood through her body and took this as a sign, a blessing. She felt at peace, happy beyond measure and optimistic about her future.

Dot jumped up, dusted off her dress and sat at the piano stool on its raised platform. She pressed several keys down at once. The loud thrum resonated in her chest and echoed around the room, bouncing off the majestic military men captured in oil and tinkling the crystal droplets of the vast chandelier.

'There you are!'

'Here I am.'

'Okay, budge up.'

Dot scooted along on the wide, shallow stool to make room. Sol placed two mugs of hot chocolate on the silver coasters on top of the piano.

'I'll play and you sing. We shall recreate the moment I first saw you.' Sol cracked his knuckles and flexed his fingers. 'Ready?'

'No! God, not ready! I can't sing, I'm rubbish, really rubbish. Please don't make me do that.'

'Clover, everybody can sing.'

'Not everybody, not me. I sound like a cat in pain, it's horrible!'

'When is the last time you sang?'

'I sing all the time, but only when no one can hear, in the bath and stuff.'

'Well, just make out you're in the bath then. Come on! No one is listening, you are all alone...'

His long fingers stroked the keys and the magic notes of Etta James's classic tune rose up and danced about Dot's head.

She closed her eyes and listened until the whole song had been played through. Sol continued, starting over, and she began to hum.

After a while, it felt perfectly natural to turn the hum into words, so she started to sing.

'At last
My love has come along...
My lonely days are over
And life is like a song

Oh, yeah, at last
The skies above are blue
My heart was wrapped up in clover
The night I looked at you'

With eyes closed, she massacred the beautiful ballad that had provided the background music to the first night they met.

Sol put his fingers in his ears. 'You're right! Stop! Enough! You really can't sing!'

'Oi!' Dot made to swipe at him. He caught her wrist mid flight, surprising them both into stillness. Dot could hear the blood pulsing in her ears, felt the irregular flutter of her heart in her chest. It was always this way when he touched her. Her breath came in shallow bursts and her senses were magnified. It was as if time slowed.

'I think this is it, Clover,' he whispered, only inches from her face.

'What does that mean?'

'It means that you and I have stumbled upon what most people will spend their whole lives looking for, it means that we will be together. You and me – if that's what you want.'

'Blimey, Sol! You have to slow down! You've only known me for a little while, it's a bit fast, isn't it?'

'I know, it is and I promise you that I am usually so patient; this is totally out of character for me. Just ask my mum, she'll tell you! She's been watching me try and feed a peahen in our garden for what must be years now; every day I call to the hen, offer her a little grain, but she never takes it. I am patient even though she is bad tempered, sneaky and snappy.'

'She sounds like Mrs Harrison.'

'Who's Mrs Harrison?'

Dot shook her head, it didn't matter. Sol sat still and fixed her with his stare, his expression earnest. 'It is a little fast, very fast, that I accept, but here are the facts. I'm nearly twenty-two and, assuming I live until I'm eighty-five, this means we have approximately sixty-three years left on this planet together, no more. The idea of having only sixty-three years with you horrifies me, frightens me. Because it's not enough, not nearly enough.'

He ran his hands over her shoulders.

'How long would be enough?' She hardly dared ask.

'Eternity. I'd settle for eternity.'

Dot bit her bottom lip and felt her heart jump. This was a feeling that she had not known existed.

Sol reached out with trembling fingers and hesitated, trying to calm his breath, which leapt and stuttered in his throat. He stared into her face, trying to fathom the misty-eyed stare. His touch was no more than a fraction away from her milky skin;

they both knew what was about to happen, but being fore-warned didn't make it any less daunting. His fingers breached the space between them. Dot ached to feel him against her.

It was done.

An invisible barrier had been broken, a milestone reached, a curiosity satisfied.

Dot raised her head to receive the kiss that was delivered firmly, squarely on her mouth. It was perfect. Sol lingered afterwards for the right amount of time, allowing her to inhale the scent of him and feel the heat of his body against hers.

Slowly, she moved her face forward again, closing in. He grazed her cheek with his fingertips, igniting a jolt from the point of contact to her core. She kissed the pads of his fingers, before taking his palm and placing it against her chest. Sol stood up from the piano and, still holding her hand, he steered her towards the sweeping staircase that led up to his apartment.

'Supposing your mum and dad are back?'

'They'll be hours yet, but I'll check if you like?'

Dot nodded. Sol opened every door in the spacious flat, while Dot hovered anxiously in the hallway, marvelling at the plush drapes in the tall sash windows and the sumptuous sofas that sat around the enormous marble fireplace. She let her eyes roam over the fancy carpet and the books that probably nobody read, cos they were all *'inbred and illiterate'*... She cringed as she remembered uttering those very words. Had it really been not much more than a month ago?

'The coast is clear!' He beckoned her into the inner corridor.

'Are you sure your mum and dad aren't coming back soon?' She didn't want this to be how she was formally introduced, sneaking in after hours through the back door.

'They are at a formal dinner, long and boring and far away. We've got all the time in the world.'

'All the time in the world sounds good!' She slipped her arms around his neck and kissed him on the lips; it felt wonderful to be able to kiss him with abandon, out of sight and in these very grand surroundings. Sol put his arm around her waist and guided her towards his bedroom door. The two stumbled and kissed as they made their way along the elegant hallway.

'Are you sure this is what you want?' Sol stroked her cheek.

'I'm totally sure, I want my first time to be here and I want it to be you.'

'Me too.' He held her tightly and pushed open the door.

Dot vaguely took in the detail of the room. The large walnut bed with its gold counterpane and bolster pillows. The fancy swags with matching tie-backs and the heavy brocade wall-paper.

She unzipped her dress and let it fall to the floor. Standing before him in her silky slip, she didn't feel exposed in the way that she had expected; instead she felt warm, alive and certain that this was exactly what she wanted.

Sol placed his hands inside her petticoat and tried to find the clasp of her bra. His fingers gripped at the wide elastic and fumbled and twitched against the back of her underwear. He ran his long fingers over the strap, but without success. 'I can't find the hook!'

Dot pulled away from him and looked him in the eye. 'What do you mean, Mr Soldier Boy? I thought you'd been trained. Is my bra hook above the permanent snow line?'

The two young lovers laughed their way towards the bed and landed on the soft mattress in a jumble of arms and legs.

Their pace was measured, the two novices finding their way without awkwardness.

Sol whispered into her hair, 'This is perfect. You are perfect.'

Dot smiled against his skin. For the first time in her life, she felt perfect.

The two dozed for an hour or so. Waking, Dot reached out and took Sol's hand between both of hers. A feeling of pure joy coursed through her veins and left her trembling. She watched his long fingers interlace with her own, his brown skin against her pale palm.

'You know, Clover, every choice has a consequence, a price, and you should always ask yourself if it is a price worth paying.' He spoke while transfixed by their fingers, joined together.

'I don't care what the price is, Sol. I will pay anything to be with you. I didn't know I could be this happy, I didn't know it was possible for *anyone* to be this happy!'

'You are a stubborn little thing, aren't you?'

'I may have been told that before!'

'I've been thinking, about when I leave here...' He waited for her to comment, but she didn't. 'I want you to come to St Lucia. I want to take you home with me. I know it's a long way and I know that it means leaving your family. You don't have to think about it for a while, but these next few months will fly by and I want everything in place when that time comes. I want you to know that I am committed to you, that this isn't some holiday fling.'

'Well I'm glad to hear that!' She laughed and kissed his cheek.

Dot considered the house she shared with her mum and dad and thought about her commute up West three days a week in the rain to sell material and sewing bits and bobs to people that could afford what she could only dream of. In truth it wasn't much of a life.

Sol wasn't finished. 'I want us to live on the island. I can see exactly how it will be. We will live at the Jasmine House and Patience will help you settle in – once she's given you a hard time for having snared the most eligible man in the West Indies and not having a title.' Dot punched him on the arm; he pulled her closer until her head was on his chest. 'You can spend your days designing clothes and then sewing them from the fabric that I will fetch for you from every corner of the earth. The first shop selling "Clover Originals" should be in the islands, with others to follow in America and then Europe. We will get married, and have a very lavish wedding in the garden, when the flowers are just right and then in a couple of years when our children are tucked up at night, sleeping soundly in the nursery with Patience on her bed in their room, I will sit with you in the garden. It's my favourite part of the day, when the sun sinks into the ocean and the day has lost its heat, and we shall bask in the warm breeze that blows across the beach from the Caribbean Sea, watching the lights twinkling from Reduit Beach on the curve of the horizon.'

Dot closed her eyes and lay perfectly still, visualising the scene in its every detail. 'Crickets'll chirp in perfect time,' Sol continued, 'providing our nightsong. There might be the gentle whir of a fan overhead in the great hall or the creak of wood as our rocker lulls us like babies, rocking us back and forth so we have to fight sleep. There is no place like it on earth,

Clover!' She smiled dreamily, not wanting him to stop. 'Your stomach will be full of warm, peppery callaloo, proper one-pot cooking. We will feast on a bowl of bouillon made from pig snout, green lentils, onions, maybe some peas. Oh, it's so tasty and filling that you will eat until you can barely move. I will hold your hand in mine and we'll sit on the deck and smell the jasmine that will fill the air around us. We will sleep with the shutters thrown wide open and the warm wind will flow over us as I hold you tight in my arms, keeping us cool.' He squeezed Dot even closer. 'In the morning we'll drink fresh pineapple juice and feast on mangoes from our trees. We'll run barefoot across the spiky grass and down to the beach where we'll dive into the crystal-clear water and swim all morning, tasting the salt on our tongues and feeling it burn on our skin as we lie under the shade of a palm tree. At lunch-time, we'll eat fresh fish and drink sweet coconut milk straight from the shell. This is how we shall live, getting older and slower with each passing year, but we won't care because we will be happy and we will be together. What do you say, Clover? Will you come with me?'

She reached up and touched his face. It sounded perfect. His description filled her with a warmth that drove the sense of foreboding from her bones. She wouldn't miss the dark mornings, the dirty buses, the rude customers or the cold. She never imagined that there might be a life like that for a girl like her. She swallowed to flush the hard ball of tears that had pooled at the back of her throat. Yes! Yes, she would go with him. Dot wanted to feel the salt water burn on her skin, she wanted to lie in his arms and sleep with the shutters thrown open and the promise of fresh pineapple juice for breakfast.

She rolled over until she was cocooned in the white linen sheet and propped herself up on her elbows. Sol ran his fingers through her hair and over her fine, straight nose.

'Some might think that you were trying to propose to me, Mr Arbuthnott.'

Sol pulled his body free of the blankets and dropped to the floor by the side of the bed. He knelt on one knee and took both her hands inside his. 'Some might be right…'

Dot's eyes filled with tears and her heart beat loudly in her chest. This was it.

'Lady Clover, beautiful woman, I never expected to feel this way. I've played music my whole life without really understanding the words, but then you came along and now suddenly they do make sense to me – *I found a dream that I could speak to/A dream that I can call my own*. In fact everything makes sense to me. Like my whole life has finally come into focus. I love you and I will always love you. There will only be you, always you, for my whole life, and if I can't have you, then I will grow old a very lonely man, tending my garden and thinking about this moment. So, will you marry me?'

'Oh, Sol, yes! I love you. I love you so much!'

He beamed at her teary-eyed face. 'I love you too.' He brought her fingers up to his mouth and kissed the back of her hand. He couldn't wait to make it all happen.

'It'll have to be our secret for a while longer,' Dot murmured, trying not to picture her dad's reaction. 'I need to drip-feed the idea to my mum and dad, let it settle with them. I need their approval and it might take a while.'

'We've got all the time in the world, my beautiful Clover.'

Dot beamed as she eased the front door shut behind her and slid the top and bottom bolts. Even a whole twenty-four hours after her magical evening at the Merchant's House, she couldn't stop smiling. She'd just come from seeing Sol again; they'd been at Paolo's for hours and had then taken a very leisurely walk home.

Her mind felt ordered; for the first time in her life she could see her future and that future was wonderful. She bit her bottom lip to compose her expression; it wouldn't to do be walking around grinning like an idiot. As Sol had said, timing was everything; they would firm up their plans and then tell the whole world! She didn't know what she was most excited about, her marriage to Sol or waking every day with a view of the Caribbean Sea and having her breakfast on the beach. Maybe even a bath in the sea; she wondered if they bothered with bathrooms with so much water around. She pictured herself in the sea with her loofah.

She crept into the hallway and eased her shoes off, picking them up and tiptoeing in her stockings across the floor; she didn't want her heels clicking on the lino to betray the fact that it was well past eleven o'clock. Pushing on the back room door, she was startled to see her dad sat in his chair. It was unusual to find him awake at this hour and even more unusual to find him without his newspaper shield over his face.

'Oh, hello, Dad, I wasn't expecting to see you up! Cuppa tea?' She smiled at him; it was quite nice to have a bit of company as midnight loomed and the dark filled the windows and whistled down the chimney.

He didn't answer. 'Dad? I said, do you fancy a cu—'

'I heard you the first time and no I don't want no cup of tea.'

Dot heard the reedy tone to his voice, noticed for the first time his sinewy arms, flexing in their vest, like a spring coiled and ready to launch. He was angry.

Dot tried to placate him; she knew she was late and that he worried. 'I'm sorry I'm late, Dad. You shouldn't have waited up. I missed the bus and then—'

'Is that what you think this is about, missing the bleeding bus?'

She didn't recognise his aggressive sneer, so unlike him. Her stomach shrank around her intestines; he had never spoken to her like this or looked at her like this. It felt horrible.

'Well, I did! But now I don't.' She gave a small laugh – that was usually enough to lighten her dad's mood.

'Let me ask you something, do you think I'm stupid or blind or both?'

She shook her head. No, no she didn't…

'Cos I'm not and I'm not deaf either and I don't like what I've been hearing.'

Mrs Harrison…

Dot braced herself. She sat down in the chair and carefully placed her shoes on the floor with the heels together before folding her arms across her chest as though this could somehow protect her from the verbal blows that she thought were coming. She was right.

'I always thought you might make something of yourself, Dot, but now I'm not so sure.'

She looked up at him, wanting desperately to tell him that she would make something of herself. She wanted to share her plans, her designs and Sol's idea for shops all over the world. She wouldn't spend the best part of her life sitting in a chair fighting off the cold.

'Your mum and I have always done our best by you, always made sure you never went without.'

Dot decided not to comment that she had frequently 'gone without' and that if anyone had made sure she had anything at all, it was her mum.

'And you repay us by doing this?'

'Doing what?' Dot wondered how much her dad knew.

'You want me to spell it out, Dot?'

'Yes, Dad, I do.' She tilted her chin upwards, projecting a defiance and confidence that she did not feel.

'Wog meat. That's what I'm talking about. My own daughter reduced to wog meat!'

Dot's mouth fell open. Her arms weakened, lost their grip and fell from her chest, dropping limply into her lap. The colour drained from her face as the breath faltered in her throat. Tears pooled instantly and threatened to fall from her eyes, wide with fear.

'I... Dad... I...'

'No. Don't even try and deny it. You've been caught. My own fucking daughter.' He shook his head in dismay. Standing, he gripped the fireplace and stared into the dying coals that glowed and ebbed.

'I wasn't going to try and deny it. I love him.' Her voice

was small, but loud enough.

'Do what?'

This time she spoke a little louder. 'I love him, Dad, I really do!'

'No. You don't! How can you? Urgh, it turns my bloody stomach, it's not natural. It's disgusting!'

'Please don't say that, Dad! I don't care about the colour of his skin, or anything else. I love him and that's just how it is.'

Reg Simpson moved quickly, his arm describing a perfect arc as it flew from the fireplace to the side of her face, catching her mouth with the back of his hand.

Dot held her breath. He had hit her! Her dad had hit her. She saw herself sitting on his lap in her winceyette nightie, a little girl.

'Who you gonna marry, little Dot?'

'I'm going to marry you, Daddy.'

'Well that makes me the luckiest daddy in the whole wide world.'

'Well you bloody should care! "That's just how it is!" What're you talking about? You think the colour of his skin doesn't matter? Let me tell you, it matters a great deal. What d'you think my mates'll make of this? I'll be a bloody laughing stock! How could you? You are a fucking disgrace, if I even think about it I am sick! So don't tell me it doesn't matter – I've never heard the like! What decent bloke is going to want to lay a finger on you after this? Eh? Tell me that?'

Dot struggled to draw breath through her tears, feeling the sting of her dad's slap and the swelling of her bottom lip against her teeth. 'I have a decent bloke and I don't want any other to lay a finger on me.'

'Well that's a good job, cos they won't! You disgust me. Fucking wog meat – my own daughter!' He was shouting now.

The altercation had brought Joan downstairs and she stood in the kitchen now, out of sight, clutching her dressing gown to her neck and with her eyes closed. She wanted to offer comfort to her daughter but knew this needed to be said.

'How could you think that this might turn out all right? You'd have to be stupid or mad – I can't decide which you are, maybe both!

'You've never even met him, never even seen him, so I don't know how you can make a decision and be so bloody horrible when you don't even know the person that you are trying to keep me away from. He's lovely to me, Dad, really lovely and he will make me happy. You always said all you wanted was for me to be happy!'

Reg sank down into his chair and rubbed his face with his shaking hand. 'Does Gloria Riley's story not mean anything to you?'

Dot shook her head. No it didn't, she was nothing like bloody Gloria Riley.

'You think you are so different, but you're not. She was just an ordinary girl like you, from an ordinary family like ours. Let me tell you how her story ended. She was just a bit of fun for her bloke, a distraction. Her mum and dad were finished with her, filled with the shame of it and I can't say I blame them. When the bloke wasn't interested any more, she knew no one else'd want her so she lay on the line between East Ham and Fenchurch Street and was decapitated. I worked with her dad. The funeral was the saddest thing I've ever seen.

88

Her family were relieved that she'd done herself in. It was easier to grieve for her than live with what she had done to herself, done to them. It will ruin you, Dot, it will ruin us, and I'm not about to sit back and let that happen to my family.'

Dot didn't try to stem the tears that ran down her face. 'Please, Dad!'

'There is no "Please, Dad"! I am warning you!'

'Are you saying you'd rather I was dead than seeing Sol? Is that what you are saying?'

Reg looked at his daughter's tear-stained, bruised face. 'What I'm saying is—'

The back room door opened and Dee stood in the doorway in her vest and pants. Dot tried to smile at her little sister so as not to alarm her. Aware of her fat, bloodied lip, she blotted at her tears with the end of her sleeve.

'I heard Dad shouting.' Dee looked close to crying too; her small chest heaved beneath her thin cotton top.

'It's okay, darling. Go back to bed, tin ribs.' Dot tried to use her soothing voice, but speech was difficult.

Reg ignored both his daughters and continued to stare at the mantelpiece.

'What does wog meat mean, Dot?' Dee looked up in sad-eyed confusion.

Dot stood up and ran from the room. It was the final push she needed; she would leave with Sol and go to St Lucia. She would drink fresh pineapple juice and swim in the sea and if ever she felt homesick, she would recall this evening's events and know that she had made the right decision. Her dad didn't understand because he didn't know Sol and it would appear he didn't know her either. She wasn't Gloria Riley, she was different, they were different.

The next morning, Dot hauled her legs over the side of the bed and slipped her nightie over her head before reaching for the black skirt and white blouse she wore for work. She had watched the hands of her alarm clock inside its red leather travel case shuffle around until dawn, trying to fathom how such a revelation of pure joy and happiness could turn into a nightmare within a few hours.

She applied a little lipstick and rubbed a smear of pan-stik across the dark shadows under her eyes and over the slight bruising on the side of her jaw. A slick of black eyeliner and she was all set. She trod the stairs and went straight out of the front door, unable to face any of the family, especially her dad.

'Dot! Dot!' Her mum's calls echoed down the street. Joan tiptoed across the cold pavement in her stockings and drew her quilted housecoat around her body, trying to protect her modesty.

'D'you not want any breakfast, love?'

Dot shook her head, no, she didn't want any breakfast. What she wanted was to hear her dad's apology and to walk to work with a spring in her step because Sol had asked her to marry him! She loved and was loved in return and that should have been cause for joy and celebration.

Her tears gathered and spilled over her pale cheeks, and she dashed them away with the back of her hand.

'Oh, love, come here.' Her mum stepped forward and held her against her chest, kissing her scalp. 'I know it feels like the end of the world, but it ain't. This will all pass, love, mark my words. Your dad's mad and you can't blame him. But he'll calm down in time and we can put it behind us.'

Dot pushed her mum away and stood facing her from the kerb.

'He hit me, Mum.'

Joan nodded. 'I know. He's under a lot of strain at the moment, Dot; it isn't easy for him, with his chest 'n'all. He loves you really. This is for your own good, trust me; no good would come of this, no good at all.'

'I love him.'

'No you don't.'

'But that's just it, Mum, I do! I love him!'

'Don't talk rot! Course you don't. You don't know about love! You might think you do, but it's just a bit of excitement, a bit of a distraction, that's all. You'll know the difference when you really love someone, you wait.'

'I don't wanna wait, Mum. I DO love him and he loves me.' Despite her desperate sadness, Dot couldn't help but smile at this.

'No he doesn't, Dot! He can't! You're too different. It isn't right.'

'Not right? How can loving someone and wanting the best for them not be right? I've told him all my dreams, Mum and he doesn't laugh at me. He thinks I can be someone!'

'Does he now? Well, I've met him, don't forget, he's got the gift of the gab all right, but you can tell him from me that the only way you will be someone is if you stop hanging around with a black man!'

Dot's tears fell freely again. 'I can't believe you are saying that, Mum! I can't. First Dad and now you – I can't believe it. I'm so ashamed.'

'And so you should be, your dad's right, it's a disgrace!'

'No! I'm not ashamed of me or Sol, I'm ashamed of you! You an' him!' Dot pointed back towards the house.

'Don't you get it? You're ruining your future and you're dragging us down with you. We've never had much, but we have always, always been respectable and you are undoing that with one careless fling! There are landlords that would turf tenants out for having anything to do with them – do you know what sort of landlord we have, Dot? Cos I don't know where they stand on it. Are you willing to take that risk on our behalf? Would you see us on the bloody streets, see Dee on the cobbles because you can't keep your pants on? What's your dad supposed to do? Sit back and see if that happens without speaking out?'

'He's never even met him! And yet he feels free to judge him, to judge us. But you, you have, you know he ain't a bad person; you can see that he's smart and clever and he loves me, Mum, he really does!'

'Does he? I tell you what I see, a bloke with the gift of the gab and more money than sense and as if that wasn't warning bell enough, he's black! He's not like us, not like you!'

'I don't want him to be like us, or like me – that's why I love him. He's different and he's amazing and we will have a good life!'

'Oh, grow up, Dot, here's a newsflash for you: life ain't no fairy tale – welcome to the real world!'

The two women were unaware that they were shouting. Mrs Harrison opened her front door, carrying two empty milk bottles that had taken her some minutes to locate, giving her a legitimate reason to open the door,

'Morning, Joan. Dot. Everything all right?'

'Everything's perfect, Mrs Harrison, just bloody perfect.'

Joan trotted in one direction, towards home, and Dot in the other. Mrs Harrison lit a fag and smiled. Some people needed to be brought down a peg or two and that Joan Simpson was too smug by half.

The day could not go by fast enough. By three p.m., when the two young lovers were finally reunited at Paolo's, Dot had worked herself up into a frenzy. She was agitated, angry and sad.

Sol held both her hands inside both his, across the table top in their booth. She had given him the outline of her dad's words, but had decided not to divulge that he had hit her.

'It's not a surprise, but still upsetting none the less.'

'It's a bloody surprise to me!' Dot countered.

'Then you must have had your head in the sand. I see this every day here, every day. Like that taxi driver that drove us up to the West End, remember?'

Dot cringed. She'd thought the cabbie's vile comments had gone unheard. 'How do you put up with it, Sol?'

'I put up with it because I know change takes time. I can't take on the whole world, but I can change my bit of the world, by challenging prejudice and standing up for what is right when I can. Just like my great-great-grandfather did with his beloved Mary-Jane. But it's hard in the face of ignorance.'

Dot felt her cheeks flush, she knew her dad was ignorant.

'Has it put you off me, Sol? I'll understand if it has.'

He laughed and stroked his thumb along her palm. 'How could it put me off you? I love you. It's not conditional, not love in measures. It's just love, one hundred per cent, unshakeable and steadfast. I love you, in all circumstances and whatever may come. In fact, even if you didn't love me back, I would still love you forever.'

'I do love you back, Sol, forever.'

'Well, forgive me for being so blunt, but that's all that matters, isn't it? Not what your dad or some taxi driver thinks.'

'I guess so.' She nodded, wanting desperately to believe him.

'I know so. I'm not after approval or acceptance, I just want you. I want to wake up with you every single day and I really couldn't care what anyone else thinks about that.'

'You make it sound so easy.'

'It *is* so easy. When we are on the other side of the world, sitting on our beach in the sunshine, we won't care how many people in Ropemakers Fields disapprove, we won't think about any of them. It'll be like living in paradise.'

'Or like a fairy tale.' Dot smiled.

'Or like a fairy tale,' he agreed. 'Anyway, good news – my parents are in Paris; fancy another duet?'

The two ran hand in hand through the rain-soaked streets, jumping over puddles and slipping on cobbles like children. They laughed at the sheer joy of being together and Dot knew that she had never been happier. He was right; loving each other was all that mattered.

With her naked form wrapped in a soft blanket, the two sat on the floor in front of the fire.

'I feel like no one can get to us here, we are in a little bubble.'

'That's what it'll feel like when we're in St Lucia.'

'I can't imagine it, Sol – is there enough room for me?'

He smiled at the memory of the Jasmine House and its grand proportions. 'Yes, it's a very large house with plenty of guest bedrooms and a formal and informal lounge, but the best thing is the incredible view. It's like nowhere else you have ever seen.'

'I can guarantee it's like nowhere I've bloody seen, cos I haven't seen anything!'

'You'll love it. It sounds weird but my nanny, Patience, lives with us. She cleans up and cooks and just potters around in the garden.'

'Like a housekeeper or a cook? Like my mum?'

'Not exactly, we have a housekeeper and a cook; she is more there for me.'

'You are spoilt! Well, you've got another thing coming if you think I'll be running around after you n'all!'

'Ha! You'll be like the bad housemaid who poisoned the king when he stayed at Jasmine House.'

'Oh shut up, you are winding me up now!'

'No, I swear it's true, the story has been passed down through the years. Many, many years ago the Arbuthnotts were invited to Carnival, along with the whole household. The lady of the house politely refused as she had a royal delegation staying with her, but that meant she refused on behalf of everyone. A young kitchen maid was so angry and frustrated to be missing the celebrations that she grabbed a handful of nutmeg and shoved it into the cake mix. Too much nutmeg is never a good thing and legend has it that the royal party spent the evening hallucinating. The king was convinced that the floor was the sea and stood on a table, refusing to dive in, before being confined to his bed with violent sickness.'

'Get away!'

'Oh, Dot, it's a lesson not to upset a woman on a mission!'

'You'd better believe it. I'm a woman on a mission, to marry you.'

'That's not a mission, it's your destiny.'

'You make it sound like I didn't choose it, like it chose me.'

'That's exactly right. I didn't choose you, I found you. I feel like I've been waiting for you my whole life without really knowing it.'

'I feel the same. I'm a very lucky girl.'

Sol pulled her close to him and held her fast inside her blanket.

Chapter Five

It was Monday morning and Vida Arbuthnott was already looking immaculate in a cream trouser suit and orange high-heeled boots. Her outfit was a little bit heavy for May, but she had learnt not to take any chances with the fickle British climate. She closed her eyes for a second and leant back on the overstuffed, chintz-covered cushions. She squared the three copies of *Vogue* on the coffee table in front of her until their edges were aligned. Twisting the large diamond solitaire on the third finger of her left hand, she tried to compose herself, rehearse for the conversation that was about to take place. It would be uncomfortable, of that she was sure, but entirely necessary. She stared at the grey, so called summer's day beyond the window and overlaid it with an image of her view from the dining room terrace at home. She missed it. The novelty of stepping through puddles on damp cobbles and breathing in the smog was already wearing a little thin.

The creak of a bedroom door roused her from her musings.

'Good morning, Solomon.'

'Morning, Mumma! Didn't expect to see you up so early, everything okay?'

'Come and sit down, darling.' She patted the chair next to her.

Solomon tied his dressing gown around his waist and sat on the sofa opposite his mother, preferring a bit of distance.

'Are you all right, Mum? You look a bit nervous.'

'Nervous? No, no, but this is a little delicate and so I shan't beat around the bush.' Vida clasped her hands on her knees.

'Oh no, what have I done? Is it the toilet seat thing again?'

'No, Solomon. I want to talk to you about the cook here or more specifically her daughter.'

'Her name is Clover. Yes, what about her?'

'I believe that you may be conducting a little affair with her, Solomon, is that true?'

'Well, it depends what you mean by "little affair"...' He gave a small laugh to hide his nerves.

'What I mean, son, is that rumours have reached my ears and I can't say that I'm particularly happy about what I've heard.'

'Wow, okay, well... I can only guess at what you've heard, but I am seeing her, Mum and I like her, I like her a lot.' Sol sat forward and looked his mother in the eye. 'It's more than a little affair, Mumma, much more.'

Vida ran her tongue over her front teeth before she spoke. 'Listen to me, Solomon, whatever is going on stops now. Right this minute. It's embarrassing for Daddy and me, awkward for the staff and certainly not why we dragged you all the way over here. You can entertain yourself with a cook's daughter at home!'

'Sorry, Mum, I'm a bit confused. Is the problem that she is a distraction to me here or that she is the daughter of staff?'

'Don't try and be clever, you know perfectly well what I mean. You are not a man of the world even if you think that you are. Girls like her will see an opportunity and grab it. She will look at you as the means to a very nice life and you must not allow yourself to get ensnared. By all means have fun, but nothing more. Do I make myself clear?'

'Not really, Mum and actually it's a bit late for all that.'

'What do you mean, a bit late?' Vida's hand flew to her chest.

'I love her and she loves me and that is all there is to it, really.' He clapped his hands together.

Vida was silent for a few seconds before laughing loudly into her palm.

'Oh, darling! My sweet boy.' She composed herself. 'I am glad that you are having adventures, I really am, but it is *not* love. It is not.'

'But it is, Mumma.'

'No, Solomon. It is not and even if it was, I would not allow it, I couldn't.'

'Not *allow* it? This is the 1960s not the 1860s!'

Vida's hand trembled in her lap; this was more dangerous than she had thought. 'I am not prepared to discuss it further. It stops and it stops right now.'

Solomon had never argued with his mother, there had never been the need, but on this point he was resolute. 'No, Mumma, it doesn't, it can't. We want to get married.'

'Married? Don't be so ridiculous!' Her voice was now a shout. 'I do not want to hear such madness again! *Marriage?* Do you honestly think that would be an option for you and someone like her? Grow up, boy!' His mother had slipped into the strong St Lucian accent of her youth, as if she couldn't do angry and well-spoken at the same time.

'I am grown up and that's how I know that I love her and I will marry her.'

'You will not! I can assure you that you will not!'

'Is that right? How exactly will you stop me?'

Solomon sat with his shoulders back and his spine straight. His chin jutted forward – he was a man and this was his choice, his life.

Vida considered this for a moment. 'There are ways, Solomon. Do you think your daddy got to such a position of power by being *nice*?'

'Are you threatening us, Mum?'

'There is no "us"! And I am not threatening you; I am telling you that this madness stops, and it stops NOW! Right NOW!' Vida banged the arm of the sofa.

Sol had never seen her lose control in this way. It alarmed him.

'What in God's name is all the shouting for at this time in the morning?' Neither mother nor son had heard Colonel Arbuthnott enter the sitting room in his leather-soled slippers and silk pyjamas.

Vida took a deep breath and regained her composure. 'Good morning, Abraham, do come and join us. Your son and I are having an absolutely fascinating discussion about why it might or might not be appropriate for him to marry the uneducated daughter of the local cook!' She spat out the last few words.

Arbuthnott Senior scratched at this stubble and rubbed his eyes. It was far too early to be having this debate. 'But *your* mother was a cook…'

Vida rounded on her husband. 'Yes she was! And thank you for stating it so publicly! I know more than anyone what that means in certain circles and if you think that I have worked

100

hard all my life to be accepted and become part of the mighty Arbuthnott dynasty just to have my only son take us right back there with one impetuous, misplaced gold band then you are very much mistaken! This is not what I planned for him and I will not tolerate it! I will not!' Vida stood on shaky heels and swept from the room. 'I shall take my breakfast in the morning room.'

The two men stared at the space that she had vacated. Sol rubbed his eyes and scratched his scalp.

'You okay, son?'

Sol nodded, shrugging his shoulders. 'I guess.'

'She's right though, Sol, a bit of fun is one thing, but you are far too young and inexperienced to be thinking about marriage.' The colonel wandered across to the sofa and sat down, then ran his arm along his son's shoulder.

'But I love her, Dad, I really love her. She is beautiful and incredible.'

He rubbed his son's neck. 'Son, if I married every girl I have ever fallen in love with, I'd have a harem – and if each one was half as much trouble as your mother, I'd be dead.'

A torturous eight or so hours later, Sol was loitering at the end of Narrow Street. It was another hour before Dot appeared. He immediately wrapped his arms around her until he felt the knots leave her shoulders.

'How are things at home?' He almost dreaded asking. In the weeks since her row with her dad, things had become increasingly strained at Ropemakers Fields, she often had to wait and sneak out of the house unseen.

'Still bad. Nothing's changed.'

Sol nodded and reached for her hands. 'Well, if it's any consolation, my parents know too now and my mother has gone a little crazy, but I'm hopeful they will come round.'

'No, it's no consolation at all. I don't understand why everyone is so against us. How can we be happy when what we are doing makes so many people miserable?'

'That's just the point, we aren't doing anything wrong. It's not us with the problem, it's them!'

'You make it sound true, Sol. But the reality is, no matter how loudly you shout at the sky that you don't believe in rain, you are still gonna get pissed on eventually.'

'Yes – but when we get pissed on in St Lucia it's warm and soothing like a hot shower! We will weather the storm, swim in the rain and wait for the sun to reappear.'

'It sounds lovely.'

'It *is* lovely. Look, I don't want us to be miserable – we can sit looking at miserable faces with our parents. We, however, are going to remain positive and confident that all will work out the way we want it to, okay?' He pushed her chin upwards with his thumb.

'All right.'

'That's my girl!'

'I like being your girl.'

'That's good, because I am never going to let you go…'

Back at work later that week, Dot unscrewed the plastic lids on the jars and shook the various-sized buttons into a little brass scoop before refilling the compartments in the drawer. She did this job automatically, preoccupied with life outside the Haberdashery Department.

'All right, Dot?'

'No, Barb, not really.'

'What's the matter? You look like you've lost half a crown and found sixpence.'

'Why did you tell your aunty about me and Sol?'

Barb looked skywards, as though seeking the answer from above, then chewed the ends of her hair. 'I dunno, I was just talking to her and me mum over a cuppa, we always talk about you, you're my best mate! Did I do something wrong? I didn't know it was secret!'

Dot sighed, she couldn't take her anger out on her friend. 'No you didn't. It's not your fault, they'd have found out sooner or later. I guess I was just hoping it would be later.'

'Have they gone mad?'

'A bit.'

'What, cos he's black?'

'No, Barb, cos he wears odd socks! Whaddya think?'

'All right, sarcy cow, don't have a go at me! I really like him.'

'Oh, I know, I'm sorry. God, I seem to be apologising to everyone at the moment. I never thought life could be this complicated. I wanted to fall in love and for everyone to be happy for me; I never thought it could lead to so much grief.'

'You love him?'

It was the only bit that Barb had heard. Dot nodded.

'Oh my God! You do, don't you?'

'Yep, I really, really do.'

'Have you done it?' Barb asked, all ears.

Dot remained silent, running her finger through the buttons.

'You have! I can tell, otherwise you would have said no. Did it hurt?'

Dot shook her head and smiled. 'No, it was lovely, he's lovely.'

'I'm pleased for you, Dot! Best offer I've had is six o' chips with Wally, who used to work with your dad!'

'Ooh, he's a bit quiet, isn't he?'

'He may be quiet but he ain't half a looker and you know what they say about the quiet ones!'

Dot shook her head. No, she didn't.

'Well, anyway, going out with Wally is better than sitting in with me mum all bloody night while she moans about her corns.'

'I guess.' Dot realised how lucky she was to have the love of a man like Sol. Poor Barb. If the best she could do was a date with Wally Day, then she was to be pitied.

'One favour though, mate, if my mum and dad ask, then I've been with you. I tell them I'm meeting you when I go to see Sol, d'you mind?'

'No, course. It makes me feel like I'm part of this fabulous love affair! How exciting!'

'It is, isn't it!'

The two girls giggled into the button trays.

'D'you think you'll get married?'

Dot looked over her shoulder to make sure Miss Blight or anyone else wasn't in earshot. 'I don't *think* we will, I *know* we will.'

Barb gasped. 'Has he asked you?'

Dot nodded. It felt wonderful to be able to share the news that had been bursting to escape.

'Oh my God!'

Barb stepped around the counter and hugged her mate tightly. 'This is mental! I can't believe it. You're getting married! It feels like minutes ago we were playing weddings up on the docks, do you remember? Taking it in turns walking up and down with a net curtain on our head, being the bride, and now you're really doing it!' Barb squealed and clapped her hands together. 'Can I be your bridesmaid?'

'Well who else? Of course you can!'

Barb squealed again. 'Right, we need to start planning this. She grabbed a spool of French lace and held it to her face. 'I'm thinking lace-edged white silk, with back button detail and a large hat, like Britt Ekland.'

'I don't think I want a hat.'

'Not for you, for me, you dozy cow! No, *you* need a head-piece with a bit of crystal and flowers to match your bouquet. Ooh and velvet, you know I love a nice bit of velvet.'

'I was thinking something quite classic, fitted, with long sleeves and a bolero, and I have to admit, I fancy satin.'

'Okay, we'll go with satin, but you need a good girdle, it shows all your lumps.'

'Good point. One thing I am fixed on is how I arrive at the church. I want to arrive in a horse and carriage. I want big horses with flowers up their reins and I want to be sat in the back of a big open carriage, looking like a princess.'

Barb clutched her hands under her chin. 'I can see it, Dot, you'll look beautiful, just like a bloody princess!'

Dot pictured Sol's face turning and watching her walk up the aisle towards him. The truth was, if she was marrying Sol, she wouldn't care what she wore.

Dot walked slowly up Narrow Street and turned into Rope-makers Fields. The sky was bruised with purple clouds. People walked home with collars turned up and hats pulled down. She had loitered at work, offering to stay after hours and sort the stock cupboard. Next she had window-shopped her way along Oxford Street, unable to decide between the green knee-high leather boots that she couldn't afford or the black patent leather ones that she couldn't afford. Eventually she reached her bus stop; she let one bus go, but she knew she had to go home. Delaying the inevitable conflict was only making her stomach more nervous, it was probably better to get it over with. She wasn't sure what to expect, possibly more insults fired in her direction. Her mum would fuss around the table, trying to make out all was well, and her dad would probably sneer at her from behind his paper. Well let him. Sol was right, when they were sitting on a beach in the sunshine, none of this would matter.

'Evening, Dot, miserable night, innit?' Mrs Harrison stood smoking, like the sentinel of Ropemakers Fields, puffing away up into the night sky.

Dot nodded, lacking either the energy or the inclination to engage with her.

The key eased into the lock, Dot slipped off her shoes and put them, heels together in the space under the stairs. She hung her mac on the hook next to her mum's in the hall. It was then that she heard the unmistakeable sound of crying, more spe-cifically her mum crying. She threw her eyes up to the heavens. *Here we go again…* She wondered what the opening shot would be; her money was on shame – '*Oh, the shame!*'

Taking a deep breath, she pushed open the door to the back

room. Her mum was sitting at the table, with Dee to her right. Her sister's little hands fidgeted with the ear of a soft toy. Her dad stood with his back to the fireplace. His lower jaw twisted to the side when he saw her, his nostrils flared slightly.

'Hello, everyone.' She tried to adopt the right tone: warm, not too sarcastic and contrite enough for them to cut her a bit of slack.

'Oh, here she is. You happy now?'

Dot sighed. And so it began. 'I am happy, actually, Dad.' She had decided that defiant and confident was the only way to get through this, even though her stomach still flipped with nerves.

'You are some piece of work! Waltzing in here all high and mighty. What did you do? Have a little word with your boyfriend's mum? It's low, Dot, even by your standards and who do you think will suffer the most? Not me or your mother, it'll be Dee. You can forget Christmas, you can forget tea! How do you propose we keep a roof over our bloody heads?'

'What?' Dot sat down in the chair by the fire, trying to figure out what was going on.

Joan removed the soggy hankie from her eyes, which were red and swollen. Her speech came in breathless stutters. 'I… I… I've lost me… me… job. What am I gonna do?' Her tears fell again.

Dee placed her small hand on her mother's arm. 'S'okay, Mummy, I don't want Christmas anyway and I'm not even a bit hungry.'

This made Joan's tears fall even harder.

'What d'you mean you've lost your job? Why?'

Joan slapped her palm on the table. Her voice was thin

and reedy through her tears. 'Why d'you think, you stupid girl? Fourteen years I've worked there! Fourteen years of my bloody life, scrubbing that massive bloody kitchen, cooking up whatever was asked of me. Putting in the hours. I have never moaned, never put one foot wrong. I've had nothing but compliments on my work this whole time and then you… you whip off your knickers for five minutes of fun and I've lost me bloody job!' Her face, distorted from crying, disappeared behind her cupped palms.

Dee giggled into her palm and whispered to her rabbit, 'Mummy said "whip off your knickers"!'

Dot felt winded, quite literally as though the breath had been knocked out of her. 'It must be a mistake, Mum, I don't understand…'

'Neither do I! I don't bloody understand. I don't understand how I'm gonna pay the rent or put food on the bloody table. I don't understand any of it, Dot.'

Her dad stood with his chest heaving, containing whatever it was that battered his lips, probably because he didn't want to say it in front of Dee. Dot smiled at her little sister, glad that she was there.

Reg marched through the kitchen and they heard the back door slam shut. A fag might calm him down a bit.

'I had no idea, Mum, I swear.'

'That's right, Dot, you have no bloody idea! You think life is some bloody game, where you can flounce around doing whatever you like, but this is the reality, we are now in real trouble. I don't have the rent this month, cos I haven't got a job and I haven't worked till the end of the month so I haven't been paid the full amount. And no rent means no house! And it's all because of you!'

Dot placed her shaking hand over her mouth. She felt sick. What on earth were they going to do?

She couldn't wait to get to Paolo's, where they had agreed to meet that evening, as they often did. Partly she just wanted to get out of the house, but she also wanted to see if Sol could throw some light on the situation.

Sol sat down and took one look at her stricken face. 'What's wrong?' he asked nervously.

Dot stopped twirling the plastic tomato filled with ketchup and gave the man she loved her full attention.

'My mum's lost her job at the Merchant's House.'

'What do you mean?'

'I mean she's been sacked, let go!'

'Why?' Sol shook his head in surprise.

'I was hoping you'd know – well, I was and I wasn't. I don't know what to think.'

'I didn't know anything about it. Is she okay?'

'What do you think? It's her wage that keeps us afloat; I told you about my dad.'

Sol exhaled loudly and went into solution mode. 'Do you need money? I can help.'

'No, I don't need money.' Dot drew her arms around her trunk; she was uncomfortable even discussing it. No matter how bad things got, she would never accept money from him. Pride was pride.

'But when we get married, we'll share everything and it will be irrelevant where it originated.'

Dot stared at her lover. 'To you maybe, and I do appreciate

the offer, but trust me, it feels crap when you've got bugger all to share.'

'Let's go for a walk, walk off the worry!' He smiled brightly.

'No, I don't think I'm up for a walk tonight, Sol. I'll see you tomorrow, love.' She kissed him softly on the cheek before she left.

Dot knew this worry would be a little hard to walk off.

Vida was on the sofa, reading by lamplight; the elegant room was bathed in a golden glow. The logs crackled in the fire - despite being mid-May, Vida felt the chill of the English weather. The record player spun its Motown beat into the room.

Her bare foot tapped in time against the sofa and her silk and lace negligée pooled like liquid over the pale cushion. She chose to ignore her son's entrance, even though his foot-stamping and door-slamming told her he was keen to announce his arrival. She wasn't keen to have her peace shattered.

Sol thundered into the drawing room. 'Mumma, do you know anything about Joan... the cook... about the cook being let go?'

'Good evening, Solomon, how lovely to see you. Have you had a pleasant day?'

'I'm serious, Mum; do you know anything about it? Clover is so upset; her family needs the income, her father can't work. It seems too much of a coincidence that you find out about us and then this happens.' His chest heaved with the exertion of trying to stay calm, polite.

'I have already told you that there is no "us" where that girl is concerned!'

'Please don't start with that again. I just want to know

110

what's happened with the cook.'

Vida turned over her copy of *To Kill a Mockingbird* and placed the flattened Harper Lee on the table. 'Listen to yourself, son – you want to know what happened with the *cook*? Since when have our domestic arrangements been of interest to you? You are a soldier, Solomon and you are an Arbuthnott with a duty to perform. One day you will have to run the companies that Daddy has built up for you. You will have a lot of responsibilities taking up your time and trust me when I say that caring about who is preparing your scrambled eggs for breakfast will not figure.'

'What duty, Mumma? I'm here kicking my heels so that Dad can have me close by, but there is nothing official for me to do here. If it wasn't for Clover, I'd go crazy!'

'So she *is* a distraction!'

'No, not solely. I love her, I really do.'

Vida placed her hands in her hair. 'I need a drink.'

'You don't drink!'

'You are making me want to start!'

Solomon sank down on the sofa, his shoulders sagging, his eyes weary. Mother and son were silent for some minutes. The stylus scratched and hiccupped with a little jump at the end of the record, filling the room with the magnified crackle of static. Both were glad of the hiatus in which they could slow their racing pulses, calm their breathing and order their thoughts.

'I love you, Solomon, you know that, don't you?'

He nodded towards the carpet. Yes, he did know that.

'Daddy and I only want what is best for you and if we thought that settling down with the first girl that has caught your eye, regardless of her background or status, would make you happy, then we would encourage you, welcome her, but this is not the case, darling. The sparkle with which you think she is covered will wear off, quicker than you might imagine, and when that happens, you will be less than satisfied with what you're left with. This would not only be a tragedy for you, but for her also. Trust me when I tell you I am thinking of you both. What right have you to disrupt her life and leave her high and dry when the reality sets in?'

'She does shine to me, Mumma, you are right, and she always will. That is the reality. It's no different than it was for you and dad or James and Mary-Jane, it's love and it's unshakeable, it's fate.'

'For God's sake, do you not *listen* to me any more?'

'Is it because she is white?'

'What?'

'Is that why you don't approve, because she is white?'

'No! Partly. But it's more about her, her life, her very small life! What do you have in common? How would being married to her help your career, your social life?'

'You think I should marry to help my social life?' Sol was incredulous.

'You are making me sound like a monster, but the fact is that these things matter, they are important.'

'They are not important to me!'

'Well, Solomon they should be and it's about time you realised what being an Arbuthnott means.'

'If it means I can't be who I want to be, with the person I love, then I don't want to be an Arbuthnott!'

Vida flinched as though she had been struck. She slipped on

her high-heeled slippers with their marabou trim and padded across the room. Pausing before she entered the hallway, she turned back to her son, slumped against the cushions. He looked like a boy.

'I would have considered giving the woman her job back, but all things being equal, I think it best that she and her daughter are kept as far away from you as possible.'

Sol stared after her, struggling with three new bits of information. His mother was apparently not the sweet-natured woman he had always considered her to be. Secondly, it was his fault. If Dee was hungry in her bed and Clover's family was struggling, it was his fault. And finally, Sol realised, all things were far from equal.

Reg and Joan were still awake when Dot returned from Paolo's. They were sitting at the table in the back room. Dot doubted her mother had moved since tea-time.

'Is Dee okay?' She pictured her little sister's wide eyes of earlier on.

Joan nodded.

'I am really, really sorry, Mum, if anything I've done has led to this.'

'Well, it'd be a bloody funny coincidence if it ain't anything to do with you, wouldn't it?'

Dot ignored her dad; she was too tired for a fight.

'I'm going up Bryant and May tomorrow, see what they've got going.'

Dot sat down opposite her mum. 'Oh no, Mum, surely not! It's terrible up there.'

'D'you think I don't know that? It's stinky, loud and dangerous, Gawd knows what it'll do to me lungs, but you know what? It's better than bloody starving.'

'I wish you didn't have to, Mum.'

'Me too, I wish I still had me nice little job up the road, with all the food that we need and hours that suited, no boss stood over me. I know I used to moan, but I loved it really.' Joan's tears fell again. 'Anyway, there's no guarantee they'll have me up there. I know a coupla girls who've been let go cos they got married, let alone an old codger like me with two kids in tow.' She tried a smile.

'You're not an old codger, Mum.'

'I feel like it, Dot, I really do.'

Dot's heart beat faster as an idea came to her. It was obvious. She would go up Bryant and May tomorrow herself and try and earn the money that her family needed. Yes, she loved Selfridges, but what good was that if she couldn't earn enough to help?

* * *

The next day Sol was anxious. He paced the pavement outside Paolo's, retiring inside only to sip coffee and wait some more.

'Stood you up, has she?' Paolo was unused to seeing Sol without his pretty companion.

'I hope not, Paolo!'

It was a full two hours before she appeared. Sol had drunk so much coffee, his fingers twitched with all the adrenaline.

'Where have you been? I was worried!'

'No need. I had a chore to run, but I'm here now.'

'Yes, you are, and you look beautiful.' He reached across

the table and stroked her face. After any time apart, the sight of her always surprised him; she really was stunning.

'Where have you been?'

'After a job, actually!'

'A job? Designing?'

She shook her head, embarrassed and delighted that he thought someone like her could simply waltz into a job as a designer. 'Not quite! Up at the Bryant and May factory, packing matches. If I'm lucky, I might progress to dipping the boxes in the sand that coats the little strip – but no such dizzy heights for me initially.'

'Why? Why are you trying to work in a factory?'

'Why do you think, Sol? Not because I have a fancy for it; I need to earn money! My mum's been laid off, remember? And it's not as if they have savings – every penny that comes in goes straight out. I can't earn enough in the store, there just aren't the hours available and so this is what I have to do. It's not so we can save up for a television or a holiday, it's so that we can *eat*. You just don't get it, do you?' Dot hung her head; she hated revealing the level of near poverty in which they existed, always one wage packet away from being hungry and homeless.

'I'm sorry. Is it really that bad?'

She nodded. 'Yes, it's really that bad. If Mum doesn't get wages this week, we haven't got the rent. Can you imagine what that's like, Sol? Imagine Dee having no roof over her head, or me dad, who isn't well, not having his bed to go to. I can't let that happen.'

'But you are coming with me to St Lucia?'

'Yes I am and I can't wait, trust me, but that's not for a

year and my family have to live now, right now, today. It's the best thing for everyone.'

'Best for you?' He admired her work ethic, but did not want her toiling away in a factory; he couldn't stand the thought of it.

'It's not all about me. And how can I moan? I'm going to live in a fairy tale with the man I love; a year of packing bloody matches won't kill me.'

'You are amazing, Dot, I think your mum and dad are very lucky to have a daughter like you.'

'I'm not sure that's how they see it right now.'

'They'll come around.' He thought about his own mother and her defiant lack of acceptance.

Dot closed her eyes and sighed; she so badly wanted to believe him. In truth, though, she had been slightly disappointed by her parents' lack of gratitude at her grand gesture. Almost as though she *should* have given up the job she loved in Selfridges and traded it in for forty hours of packing matches in a stinky factory. But she could tell by the relaxing of her mum's shoulders that Joan was relieved. Miss Blight, on the other hand, had seemed not only relieved but entirely delighted, happy even, to receive Dot's resignation. The cow. Dot was tempted to tell her about what her life would be like in a year's time, and that while Miss Blight would still be fat and stuck in Personnel, harvesting joy from the misery of others, she, Dot, would be living on the beach and sipping fresh pineapple juice every day. But she didn't want to tempt fate and besides, knowing how gossip spread like wildfire, whether issued confidentially or not, she couldn't risk Barb informing her mum, who would relay it to Mrs Harrison, who would at the earliest possible opportunity tell Joan and Reg...

* * *

'You look smart, son, off somewhere nice?' Vida stopped filing her nails and cast her eye over her handsome boy, who had clearly made an effort with his appearance.

'Yes, I'm taking Clover dancing. We're going to Ronnie Scott's.'

'Well, how lovely.'

His mother's clipped tone told Sol that actually she thought it anything but. He ignored her.

Dot shut the front door and tucked her scarf inside her coat.

'Well, look at you all spruced up, where you off, Dot? Somewhere nice?'

Dot whizzed past her neighbour. 'Truth is, Mrs H, I don't know where I'm going!'

'Well have fun when you get there!'

'I'll try.' Nosey old cow.

Sol and Dot had jumped off the moving bus before their stop and with his hand on her lower back, he guided her through the streets of Soho.

'Where are we going?' Dot was edgy.

'You'll see.'

'Sol, I really hate surprises, you're making me nervous!'

'Don't be nervous.' He swung around her and crushed her against him. 'You trust me, don't you?'

She nodded up at his beautiful face. Of course she trusted him.

'You look beautiful.' He ran his fingers over her hair, which she had scraped back into a ponytail and fastened with a width of scarlet velvet ribbon.

'You always say that!'

'Maybe because it's true.'

'What did I do to deserve you, Mr Arbuthnott? How did I get this lucky?'

'I don't know. I ask myself the same.'

After one quick kiss, the two almost skipped along until they turned into Gerrard Street.

'Ronnie Scott's?'

'Yup.' Sol beamed.

'Wow, I've never been before!' Dot jumped up and down on the spot with excitement.

The hazy hum of a clarinet drifted up the stairs and out onto the pavement and the tinkling of piano keys started some seconds later.

'Oh, Sol, I don't believe it! Someone's playing Etta!'

She grabbed his hand as the two of them ran down the stairs and into the darkened depths of the jazz club. Dot stopped in her tracks, transfixed by what she saw on the stage. It wasn't someone playing Etta – it *was* Etta!

'Oh my God!' She placed her hand at her throat. 'It's Etta bloody James!'

Sol beamed. 'Dance with me!'

Having dropped their coats at the bar, Sol guided her onto the dance floor. They stood staring at each other for the briefest of moments, unaware of anyone else in the room. And then

Etta started to sing in that rich, velvet voice; she started to sing the words of their song.

> *'At last*
> *My love has come along...*
> *My lonely days are over*
> *And life is like a song'*

Sol placed one hand on Dot's lower back and held her other hand inside his, with her arm crooked against his chest. He pulled her close, until they were as one, swaying gently to the soundtrack to their love affair.

'I love you so much,' he breathed into her hair.

'I love you too.' She spoke to his chest.

> *'Oh, yeah, at last*
> *The skies above are blue*
> *My heart was wrapped up in clover*
> *The night I looked at you'*

'Don't ever let me go, Sol.'

'I'll never let you go, baby.'

He pulled her closer still, holding her tightly against him.

> *'I found a dream that I could speak to*
> *A dream that I can call my own*
> *I found a thrill to press my cheek to*
> *A thrill that I have never known'*

'It will all be okay, won't it?'

'It will all be okay, baby.'

Dot smiled into Sol's crisp white cotton shirt. He pulled the ribbon from her hair and watched her shiny locks fall in a curtain against her shoulder.

> *'Oh, yeah and you smile, you smile*
> *Oh, and then the spell was cast*
> *And here we are in heaven*
> *For you are mine*
> *At last'*

The applause was rapturous. People rose from their seats and whistled and whooped and for the first time Dot and Sol realised just how crowded the place was.

'The two young lovers!' Etta James held out her hand and gestured her appreciation in their direction. Dot blushed and laughed into Sol's shoulder. He gave an impromptu bow.

'That was our first dance!' she gushed

'But not our last.' He kissed her knuckles, her fingers knotted inside his.

He kissed her again at the end of Narrow Street. 'I love you, Clover Arbuthnott.'

'You can't call me that!' She beamed as she said it.

'Why not? You're going to have to get used to it.'

'I shall introduce you to everyone. I'll shout at anyone that will listen, "This is my husband!" Imagine that, me having a husband and not just any old husband – you. The best bloody husband in the world!'

'I love you and I shall see you tomorrow.' He kissed her scalp and watched her wiggle towards Ropemakers Fields.

'I love you too and I'll see you tomorrow!' she half whispered back over her shoulder.

Sol crept into the Merchant's House apartment and loosened his tie. He was relieved that his parents had already retired for the night. He stood in front of the mirror above the fireplace in the hallway and punched the air; he felt invincible! He had danced with his girl in front of Etta James and it had been incredible.

Dot pulled her bedspread up under her chin and kicked her heels against the mattress, squirming with joy and excitement. She didn't care that she was starting work at the match factory tomorrow, she'd forgotten for the moment about Selfridges and giving up the job she loved. She had danced in front of Etta James and she had felt like a film star. She had felt like someone called Lady Clover Arbuthnott.

Sol cleaned his teeth and splashed his face with cold water before changing into his pyjamas. He raked his hair and looked over his reflection in the mirror; he pictured his girl standing behind him. He remembered her in her slip, the way she had looked on their first night together. That's what it would be like when they were married; they would prepare for bed in a shared bathroom with the shutters thrown wide and swap details about their day. He could almost smell the night-flowering jasmine. The very thought sent a judder of expectant joy along his spine.

Dot turned on her side and imagined her lover lying facing

her. She pictured his shoulder gently rising and falling in sleep. She pulled the pillow from under her head and placed it against her chest; wrapping her arms around the ticking-covered feathers, she whispered into its softness, 'Good night, my darling, sweet dreams, my beautiful man,' although how she would sleep with the bubbles of excitement that rose from her stomach and filled her throat was beyond her.

Sol trod the soft wool carpet along the corridor and closed his bedroom door behind him. He glanced at the bureau, the small pewter dishes containing cufflinks and ivory collar stiffeners. Once again he imagined Clover's jewellery and perfume next to his things, a sign of a couple living in harmony, a sign of being married.

He sat on the rather firm mattress and eased the leather slippers from his feet. The silk counterpane had been folded down, as it was every night, to reveal the starched Egyptian cotton sheets. Sol raised his legs and swung into bed, reaching for the lamp switch to click his world into darkness. It was then that the envelope caught his eye. It was perched between the light and his water glass on its silver salver.

The large cream envelope opened with ease, suggesting it had not long been glued shut. He removed the rather bulky contents that had been folded and folded again. It was a thin, old document of some sort, scrawled with violet ink and the occasional flourish of a fountain pen. He placed it to one side and turned his attention to the thick sheet of pale writing paper that was peppered with the unmistakeable green ink that his mother favoured.

Son,

I love you and while it may not always appear so to you, like Daddy, I have your very best interests at heart. Your stubborn refusal to see sense leaves me with no other option than to act before you make the biggest mistake of your life, a mistake that could ruin everything that I have worked for, everything that I have planned for you.

In this envelope are the deeds to a certain house in Ropemakers Fields that I have acquired very recently and not, I can assure you, without considerable trouble.

I am giving you two choices, Solomon. If you go back to St Lucia on the first available flight, these deeds will be locked away and the Simpson family who currently reside there will be able to do so until their deaths, rent free.

If you refuse, I already have new tenants waiting and the Simpsons will be given twenty-four hours to leave the premises.

If you speak to anyone of this, or communicate with that girl in any form, I shall invoke the second option without hesitation.

Mother

Sol placed his hand on his heart, which was thumping irregularly. He swallowed hard, trying to take a full breath. The paper trembled in his hand. He jumped from the bed and ran along the corridor towards his mother's bedroom. But there was lamplight in the drawing room.

Vida sat in the wing-back chair with a cashmere throw over her knees. Sol felt weak beyond measure, too distressed for anger.

He stood in front of her. 'What is this?' He brandished the letter in her direction.

Vida looked unfazed. 'Well, assuming that you have actually read the contents, I would have thought that with your level of education it was all quite self-explanatory.'

'Is this for real?'

'It is absolutely one hundred per cent real.'

'I don't believe you; this has to be some kind of joke. You wouldn't do this, I know you wouldn't.'

Her face was solemn. 'I can assure you that this is no joke.'

Sol sank down onto the floor and sat at the foot of her chair.

'How... how can you do this to me?' He was breathless.

'I am not doing it *to* you; I am doing it *for* you.'

'Mumma... Mum... please, please do not do this to me. Please!'

He swallowed and fought the urge to cry, a feeling that was unfamiliar to this young man who in his short life had had very little to cry about. He folded the paper into his lap and breathed deeply, trying not to weep.

'Listen to me, Mumma, please. I love her! I love her! And you can't change that. I will find a way, I will, because I love her.'

His mother looked over his head towards the fireplace and spoke into the middle distance. 'And that is precisely why I am forced to take this action.'

'Why? Why are you doing this to me, to us?'

'There is no "us", Solomon, how many more times must you make me say that? It is madness.'

'I'll do anything, anything. Please! I can buy the house…' His eyes widened as an idea occurred to him. 'I've got my own money, we don't need you and Dad, Clover knows how to survive! She is starting work at a match factory tomorrow, just to get money, we will be okay.'

'Perfect – a little match girl, good grief.' Vida pinched her nose and closed her eyes. 'And just so that we are clear, you are mistaken, Solomon, your money is my money and I shall see that you don't get a penny.'

Solomon's tears finally broke their banks and coursed down his face. It felt like a never-ending river of sorrow; great gulping sobs shook his shoulders and pulled his vocal chords taut.

'I can't believe that you would do it, Mum. I can't believe that you would put a family on the streets, a little girl on the streets, just so you can have your own way!'

'You would be amazed, Solomon, at what I would and would not do to protect my family, to protect you.'

'I am begging you, do not make me do this, please.'

'You will thank me one day.'

'No… no I won't. Things will never be the same between us. I will never, ever forget this. I will never ever forget.' Sol's pupils shrank as his eyes flashed with anger. His body shook and his throat throbbed with the hidden sobs that fought to escape.

'You are young, so young. I accept that things will not be the same between us for a while, but when you marry the girl that you are supposed to and the Jasmine House is full of tiny children, you will thank me then. You will, you will thank me.'

'The girl that I am *supposed* to marry? Don't you get it? If I can't marry her then I shan't marry anyone, ever.'

'Those are dramatic words for a twenty-two-year-old, but trust me, Solomon, you will marry and you will be happy. This will pass.'

'I must be able to do something. I'll speak to Dad.'

'If you bother your father with this, I will give the order, Solomon and they will be on the streets with their boxes piled around them.'

Sol pictured Dee and Dot with their belongings on the wet cobbles.

'But if you go back to St Lucia, that house is theirs until they die. And judging by the state of the father, that might be just the thing the mother needs. You are giving them a great gift, a roof over their heads, worry-free for as long as they need it. It is more than they could ever have hoped to achieve.'

'Can I... can... can I say goodbye to her, please? I need to see her once more, to explain. I can't just disappear.'

'No. You pack, you get on the plane tomorrow that's heading to New York and you go from New York home and we never speak of this again.'

Sol stood and wiped at his red and swollen eyes. He considered all the options, his thoughts whirring, confused by the cloak of grief.

'You will give them the house?'

'You have my word.'

Sol breathed deeply and wiped his running nose and tears on the sleeve of his pyjama jacket.

'Mum, I just want you to know, my heart is broken. It will never, ever be whole again. I hope that you are happy now.

You have what you want. I'll leave, but she'll have my heart forever, my broken heart.'

Sol walked slowly along the corridor, touching his fingers to the wall where the two of them had so recently bumped and kissed. He wailed like a cat mewling in distress; he couldn't help it. It was as if his soul was weeping.

Vida listened to her son and tucked the blanket around her legs. 'Hearts mend, my son, they mend.'

Chapter Six

Dot poured a cup of tea from the pot and bit her lower lip, concentrating on hiding the smile that threatened to split her face every time she remembered the previous evening. Joan placed a plate in front of her, two poached eggs and a slice of toast.

'You need to eat breakfast, love.' This she delivered with a small smile. 'Are you all set?'

'Think so, don't really know what to expect. I'm a bit nervous, tell you the truth, Mum.'

Joan cupped her hand over her daughter's. 'Course you are, but it'll be all right.'

Dot was grateful for the gesture. It meant understanding, an apology, a peace offering of sorts.

'It'll have to be, Mum, won't it.'

'Yep, it will, Dot. But I promise you, as soon as I've got something that pays half decent, you can go back to Selfridges. I'm not saying I'm happy about the situation, but I do appreciate you trying to fix it.'

Dot smiled at her mum and thought about a beach and pineapple juice; she knew that she would never be going back to Selfridges and until she went to live in her fairy tale, trying to fix things was the least she could do.

She looked at the eggs on her plate and felt a wave of queasiness wash over her. 'Sorry, Mum, don't think I can face breakfast. Reckon I must be more nervous than I thought.'

Solomon had not slept. He had spent the night crouched on his pillows with his arms looped over his hunched-up knees, pondering on how to resolve the wretched situation in which he found himself. Every idea he had, every possible solution led him up a dark alley with no prospect of success and the Simpson family on the streets. In the early hours, he haphazardly packed up his belongings for the trip back to St Lucia, inhaling the vest he had worn the night before, unwashed and bearing the faintest trace of her scent. He knew that what he felt for Clover was deep and pure love, but to see her and her family made destitute as the price for that love was too much for him to contemplate; he loved her far too much for that. Unshaven, eyes swollen and with a pain in his heart and chest that he thought might kill him, he trod the stairs to the awaiting taxi and left London before his beloved had woken. He tried not to notice the swing of the lace curtain on the upper hallway, unable to look his mother in the eye.

It was a beautiful May morning, the cherry trees were in flower and the hawthorns that flourished in many a front garden were drooping under the weight of the pink and white blossom. The sun was bright if not warm and Dot felt a swell of happiness in her tummy, despite the fact that she was off to work in a factory. She had so much to look forward to; it was difficult to contain it all. She had to fight the urge to tell anyone that caught her eye of their plans. If she could, she'd have run down the middle of the street with her arms spread wide, shouting, 'Last night I danced in front of Etta James with my fiancé! And this time next year I will be sitting on a beach in the sunshine!'

Dot caught the bus to Bow and hummed all the way, '*At last/My love has come along...*' She alighted with several other girls, all of them heading for Bryant and May. The previous night filled her thoughts, leaving little room to worry about what her first day in the match factory might hold. She pictured a girl with a red velvet ribbon in her hair, in the elegant arms of the man she loved, being serenaded by Etta James. It seemed unbelievable that the girl was her, plain old Dot Simpson of Ropemakers Fields.

Stepping into Fairfield Road, Dot spied the red-brick building up ahead. This was it. A gust of wind picked up and Dot was hit by a wall of sulphurous odour that drifted from the factory and went right up her nose. Before she had time to react, her gut constricted, sending a wave of vomit from her mouth and out onto the pavement, splashing across her shoes. For the second bout, she managed to find her way to the kerb; holding her hair in a bunch with her right hand, she retched and heaved until her stomach was empty.

'You all right, love?' a woman asked.

Dot, bent over at a right angle, nodded at the ground. 'Yup.'

'You don't look all right.'

Strands of her hair had stuck to her face with sick; Dot pulled them loose. 'I'll be okay in a minute. I'm starting work here today.'

The woman chuckled. 'Oh, love, you want to get yourself up the docs.'

Dot stared at the tarmac and felt as if the ground was rushing up to meet her.

It was a long day. Working in the factory was the exact opposite of life in the Haberdashery Department. She missed the genteel hum of ladies chatting as they browsed, and the sight of her fabric rainbow. Mostly she missed Barb – they rarely went a day without seeing each other.

The noise was deafening, the smell offensive and her role monotonous. She learnt the job quickly and proved capable, if a little slow. On the plus side, when engrossed in the fiddly task that she could complete with ease, fourteen times a minute, her mind was free to wonder to warmer climes than Bow and inside her head, she replayed the previous magical night. She watched it over and over like a movie, saw it from every angle, and each performance ended with Etta's outstretched arm and the phrase 'The two young lovers!'

The best thing about the factory was the group of girls in her section, especially the cousins Milly and Pru, who informed her that this was only a stop gap for them, as both were planning on seeking fame and fortune up West. It was only her first day, but already she was included in the banter, privy to gossip and offered fags, tea and sandwiches by the others. She felt right at home, and while she did miss the refined atmosphere of Selfridges, not having to look at Miss Blight's miserable phizog was a definite plus.

As the bell clanged for knocking-off time, Dot's feet throbbed inside her pumps; the ball of her left foot had stood on a wrinkle in her stockings all day and her scalp itched inside the elasticated hair net. But all things considered, the prospect of going back tomorrow wasn't that bad.

Dot scrubbed her hands and face in the washroom, applied a slick of lippy, patted and teased her hair into place and then walked to the bus stop. She decided to go straight to Paolo's and not waste time diverting to home; if she carried a slightly sulphurous air, then too bad, nothing a lifetime of bobbing about in the warm Caribbean sea wouldn't erase!

She eased into the booth, stretching and flexing her stockinged feet under the table.

'Coffee, love?'

Dot exhaled through bloated cheeks. She didn't feel like coffee, she didn't feel like anything. 'Actually, just a glass of water please, Paolo.'

'Coming right up. Lover boy running late?'

She looked at the door, waiting for the little brass bell to herald his arrival. 'Must be.' She smiled at the prospect of their reunion.

Dot waited for just over an hour, then the fatigue finally caught up with her; she was exhausted. Her head lolled forward onto her chest. Rising wearily, she decided to head home.

'Paolo, I'm too tired. Can you tell Sol I had to go home?'

'Sure, bella. You look exhausted.'

'Yeah, late night last night and a busy day. Can you give him a note?'

Paolo shook his head. 'Do I look like the postman? Go on then, just for you.'

Dot grabbed a pen from the pot on the counter and scribbled on a napkin: *See you tomorrow, soldier boy. Exhausted, but happy! Your Clover xxxxx* She folded it and passed it over the counter.

She sat on her bus and pictured him turning up only to find her gone. Her heart leapt with longing at the thought of him, but she felt dead on her feet. She remembered her sickness earlier, maybe it wasn't the smell that had made her sick, maybe it was a bug; that would certainly explain why she felt so awful. Her bed beckoned and she smiled, still high on the memory of the previous night.

She traipsed up the hallway and into the back room. Joan was palming crumbs from the tablecloth, scooping them into her hand and launching them into the fireplace, where they sizzled and popped.

'Well, that's your first day done. How'd it go?'

'All right, Mum, actually. Nice bunch of girls and that makes all the difference, doesn't it?'

'Yep. Here you are, love.' Joan put a plate of chicken, buttered spuds and greens on the table. She'd been keeping it warm on top of a simmering pan of water for a good forty minutes.

Dot stared at the plate. 'D'you know, Mum, I'm really sorry, but I'm too tired to eat. Think I might have a bit of a bug.'

'Oh, Christ, don't give it to your dad, that's all I need.'

'I won't.' She had no intention of interacting with her dad any more than was absolutely necessary. It didn't matter how much time passed, his words and the fact that he had hit her were there for perfect recall whenever she closed her eyes.

The next day at the factory passed much like the first, albeit her hands and wrists ached from performing the small nimble task with her fingers. After her shift, Dot jumped on the bus and thought she might burst if Sol wasn't waiting for her; it had been too long since he had last held her hand in his. She checked her reflection in her compact mirror: a little pale but otherwise okay. She practically ran to Paolo's, not caring how ungainly she looked as she galloped along the pavement, eager to get inside.

The door bell gave its familiar ring as she pushed it open with her shoulder. No Sol, their booth was empty. Dot took her drink and sank down onto the vinyl upholstery. *Please come soon; I miss you so much.*

Paolo popped up from the cellar. 'Ooh just the girl! I couldn't pass on your note cos he didn't come in yesterday!'

'Oh! That's odd.' Dot was surprised and worried in equal measure. She sipped her Coca-Cola slowly, making it last. With each creak of the door or ring of the bell, she straightened her shoulders and smiled in expectation. But still no Sol. It occurred to her as the counters were wiped down for the night and the Burco boiler was switched off that it was so unlike him to miss two dates in a row, it must be something pretty major to keep him away. As the bus chugged up the road, it clicked – the bug! Of course, she still felt rotten and had even been sick the day before. He must have it worse than her, poor thing. She wished that she could make him tea and snuggle him better in that big old bed at the Merchant's House. What was the saying – absence makes the heart grow fonder? Weren't that the truth. She ached for him.

Sol failed to show at Paolo's for the next two days as well, leaving Dot with a nervous flutter and a disappointed tummy. By Saturday morning, she was beside herself, agitated and snappy. There was nothing else for it; she would have to go to the Merchant's House. She put on her best coat, cleaned her shoes and flattened her fringe. She took care with her make-up, careful not to overdo it; there was a fine line

134

between sophisticated lady who had made an effort and tart.

Dot marched up towards the front door that she had walked in and out of as the cook's daughter since she was four years of age, and as a lover for the last couple of months. She boldly took the stairs, coughed, then reached out confidently for the brass knob, before shoving her hand back in her pocket and running back down the stairs and around the corner.

Her heart thundered in her chest and she fought the urge to be sick again. *Come on, Dot, you can do this, just knock on the bloody door.*

Slowing her breathing, Dot once again trod the steps, this time at a slower pace and with more caution.

She heard the bell tinkling inside as she hovered on the wide stone steps. Dot smoothed her blouse to rid it of any creases but also to soak up the sweat that peppered her palm. She exhaled through bloated cheeks, trying to calm her erratic pulse. After what felt like an age, the door was opened briskly and widely. Dot lowered her eyes until her gaze settled on the face of the diminutive housekeeper. The woman had to be in her seventies, a new addition who didn't know Dot, which made it both easier and harder. She had a bird-like demeanour and bright, fearless eyes that shone from her crêpe-skinned face; her dress was of the palest pink cotton and was starched to within an inch of its life.

'Yes?' Her tone was clipped. Dot wasn't sure if this was because she had been in the middle of doing something or because she'd taken an instant dislike to her face.

'Hello, I'm Dot Simpson, I'm sorry to bother you, but I've come to see Sol. Solomon?' Dot had adopted her posher than usual waitressing voice.

The woman opened the door wide and beckoned Dot inside. 'Wait here,' she said and, without turning her head, strode purposefully towards the back of the house.

Dot stood in the middle of the great hall, which was almost as big as the entire footprint of their little house in Ropemakers Fields. The tiled floor gleamed and the brass door plates shined, fingerprint-free and reeking of Brasso. She glanced at the wide stairs that wound their way up and was tempted to run up them and find her beloved; sick bed or not, she wanted to be with him. She remembered her and Sol climbing the stairs hand in hand, unable to keep their hands off each other, stopping on every other tread for a kiss. She bit her bottom lip and smiled at the secret.

The housekeeper reappeared. 'Follow me.'

Dot was surprised not to be led up the staircase towards the apartment. Instead she was shown into the library at the back of the house, a room she hadn't been in since she'd popped into it by mistake when she was a little girl.

Double doors opened into the imposing room, whose panelled walls were lined with bookshelves that were fit to bursting. Small tables were placed beside leather wing-backed chairs and were littered with beautiful sparkling things: a crystal fruit bowl sat alongside heavy brass curios that looked like ships' instruments.

There was a leather-topped bureau with a stack of papers sitting neatly and squarely in one corner. A large leather-bound blotter and an oversized brass lamp dominated the desk space.

Two tall sash windows afforded a perfect view of the garden and the staircase outside the grand ballroom where she and Sol had loitered on that magical night when they first met.

She recalled the first time she had touched his hands and how she had almost disliked him, wary of his skin colour and defensive in the face of his intelligence. Yet look at her now, they were going to get married!

Dot tried to focus, to calm her nerves. She hadn't known what to expect, had tried in fact not to conjure an image that was too detailed or to imagine the interaction, it would have made her too nervous. The door opened and in walked Vida Arbuthnott. She was tall, muscular but slim, elegant and beautiful, wearing a shirtwaist dress of red cotton, and red patent-leather square-heeled boots that came to her knee. Dot swallowed the bile of inadequacy that rose in her throat. She tried to imagine what it would be like when Joan and Vida met as equals. She'd have to tell her mum to get her hair done and wear her good shoes.

'Come and sit down.' Sol's mother's tone was neither welcoming nor dismissive.

Dot took her place on the little chair in front of the desk. Vida sat on the other side, as if it were an interview.

'You must be Clover?'

'Yes.' Dot smiled and nodded, happy that Sol had given that as her name; it made her sound like someone significant.

'I expect you are here to see my son.'

Dot nodded again. 'Yes, I hope he's feeling better. I've had a rotten bug and expect he's got it too.' Her cheeks reddened at the thought of how the bug might have been transferred: contact, dancing, kissing…

Vida adjusted the large diamond earrings that nestled in each of her lobes and clasped her hands on the desk in front of her.

'A bug? No, no, I believe he's quite well. Thank you.'

'Oh.' A furrow of confusion appeared at the top of Dot's nose. She didn't know what to say. She ran through her next sentence in her head: *'I know this is a little bit awkward, but I think you and I need to get to know each other a bit, Mrs Arbuthnott. I'm really not as bad as you might think I am! I will treat Sol brilliantly because I love him and so I don't want you to worry. After all, we will be related one day.'* She knew it was a lot easier to begin a conversation like that inside her head.

As Dot drew breath, Vida elaborated. 'No, Solomon is not ill, he's gone home.'

'Pardon?'

'My son is not here, he has gone.'

'Gone? What?'

'He has gone home, to St Lucia.'

'Whaddya mean "gone"? How can he have gone to St Lucia?' Dot gave a nervous laugh.

'I mean that he is no longer in London, he is homeward bound. Did he not tell you?'

The smile slipped from Dot's face as she shook her head; it took a while for her brain to register what Mrs Arbuthnott had just said.

'How long's he gone for? When's he coming back?' She stared at the woman who would be her mother-in-law.

Vida gave a small laugh. 'Oh, that Solomon is such a naughty boy! I thought he might have informed you. He is not coming back; not at all. He's gone home for good.'

Dot felt her body weaken and slump down into the leather seat. Her breath came in irregular pants. 'Not coming back?

Whaddya mean? That can't be right... But... he... we were...'
She pictured the two of them dancing in Ronnie Scott's.

'Don't ever let me go, Sol.'

'I'll never let you go, baby.'

Dot didn't realise that she was crying – hot, heavy tears that trickled into her mouth and dripped from her chin. She rubbed her eyes, smearing her eyeliner into a panda-like smudge.

'I think there must have been a mistake! He wouldn't just... He wouldn't... We...'

Vida's voice was calm. 'There is no mistake, Clover. He has returned to St Lucia and he is not coming back. Not ever. He has a life there, a very important life.'

Dot looked at Sol's mother through the fog of tears. 'He said he'd take me with him.' Her voice was small. Her shoulders heaved as she breathed through her sobs. 'He... he said we would get married...'

'Did he now?' Vida shook her head and gave a small tut. 'Can you really imagine him taking *you* back to St Lucia?'

Dot shook her head. No, no she couldn't. Not really. Not if she was being honest, she couldn't. The beach was no place for someone like her, the girl from Ropemakers Fields.

Vida continued. 'He has the gift of the gab, that's for sure, but for him it was just a little fun. He told me so himself, he said you were a distraction.'

'He said that?' Dot's mouth hung open, her eyes closed tight. She thought of Gloria Riley.

'Yes he did.'

'He said that about me?'

'Yes. And I only tell you this, Clover, so that you can put it behind you and move on. I'm sure it's been a fun adventure, but it's over. You *must* put it behind you and move on.'

'He told me he loved me, and I love him. I love him, I really do.' Dot twisted the bottom of her coat in her hands.

'No you don't, dear. It just feels that way right now. Trust me.'

'I can't believe he never even said goodbye…' This Dot said to herself, as though speaking it aloud might help her understand. She felt so confused.

'That tells you all you need to know, doesn't it? If he loved you, would he simply disappear without speaking to you first? If he had wanted you to go with him, he would have made provision for that, but he didn't, did he?'

Dot shook her head. No he didn't. The two sat without speaking for a few seconds, the silence punctuated by Dot's sobs.

'Can I call you a taxi?' Vida was keen to bring the meeting to an end.

Dot shook her head again. 'No… No thank you.' No more taxis for her; she could just about afford the bus fare.

Vida Arbuthnott watched as, for the second time that week, a young person with a broken heart trod wearily down the front steps. She swept her hand over her face, trying to wipe away the guilt that threatened to settle on her. It was for the best.

* * *

Dot lay on her bed and cried for forty-eight hours. It wasn't the small trickle of tears that a stubbed toe or soppy film might provoke – this was different; this time she had absolutely no control. Her tears continued to fall despite the fact that her eyes were sore and swollen shut, her face was peppered with purple blotches and her pillow and the yoke of her nightie were sodden. Every time she closed her eyes she saw the two of them swaying as one, in time to Etta. Every time she opened her eyes, she heard his words, his lies, '… *the lights twinkling from Reduit Beach on the curve of the horizon. Crickets'll chirp in perfect time, providing our nightsong. There might be the gentle whir of a fan overhead in the great hall or the creak of wood as our rocker lulls us like babies…*'

She left the confines of her bedroom only to venture to the loo and this she did on the wobbly legs of a drunk and with the headache of someone who had been on mother's ruin all night. Waves of nausea swept over her, which made eating impossible.

At some point Dee had crept in and placed her small hand on her big sister's cheek. 'Don't cry, Dot, I made you something!'

Dot forced her eyes open and looked at the picture of a rainbow that Dee had painstakingly coloured in with crayons. It reminded her of their day in Selfridges; she thought about the brown paper bag nestled in her chest of drawers and her material that was almost the colour of the St Lucian sky.

'Thanks, tin ribs,' she managed, through a mouth twisted with distress.

It took two weeks for Dot to pluck up the courage to visit Doctor Levitson. He was known throughout Limehouse. He had delivered her and tended to her every ailment since she was a baby, from whooping cough to chicken pox and most things in between. He was the same doctor that had helped

141

deliver Dee, ministered to her nan when she was sick, diagnosed her Dad's dicky chest and lent an ear to her mum when times were darkest. It was going to be an awkward encounter. Dot plodded up the surgery steps and sat in the square waiting room with all the old ladies who sniffed into tissues, rubbed at joints or exhaled deeply for no apparent reason.

Doctor Levitson had always been ancient. He had prominent features, wide-set eyes and large ears from which tufts of grey bristle peeked. The furrows on his forehead were deep and his eyes disappeared into them when he smiled, which he did a lot. Before applying his large hands to his patient's skin, he always warmed them by placing them up his jersey first, and when Dot was little he could make a coin appear from behind her ear, which was quite impressive.

'Mum okay?'

'Yes.' Dot didn't want to discuss her family; it made them seem present in a way that made her uncomfortable.

'Dad resting up?'

Dot nodded.

'Good, good and what can I do for you, little Dot?'

She swallowed. She liked being little Dot, but knew that in approximately twenty seconds she would vault the line from child to woman.

'I've not been too well, Doctor.'

'You do look tired, a little peaky. Your mum said you are up at Bryant and May? How's that working out?'

'S'okay. Nice bunch of girls…'

'Good, good.' He smiled again and was silent, clasping his hands in front of him on the desk. Dot focused on a small hole in the sleeve of his hand-knitted jersey; it had been darned with orange cotton, forming a little nub that drew your eye. Surely Mrs Levitson could have found a better match.

'Thing is, Doctor Levitson...'

He stared at her, waiting.

'The thing is, I think I might be in trouble.'

'I see. What kind of trouble, Dot? The police are chasing you and you need to take refuge in my cupboard under the stairs, or the pregnant kind?'

Dot nodded as her tears spilled. 'The pregnant kind.'

It was the first time she had said the word aloud and it felt terrifying. Two syllables with such a terrible connotation, two syllables with the power to destroy her whole life. She shook inside her coat. *Oh God, Oh God...*

'Okay. Well, first things first, let's do a test and make sure of the facts; otherwise we could be getting in a lather over nothing.'

Dot nodded. Yes, a test would be good.

'And then if you are, Dot, we can take it from there. If you are, is marriage an option, does the father know?'

Dot shook her head and closed her eyes; it was somehow easier to voice the facts without being able to see anything. 'No. He's done a runner. I thought he loved me, we were going to get married.'

'Oh, Dot, if I had a shilling for every time I've heard that.'

She opened her mouth to protest, to explain that she and Sol were different, that they had been in love and she was not like all the other girls who got caught with the promise of a ring and happy ever after, but stopped when she realised she was exactly like that.

'And if you are, you will have to tell your mum and dad, you know that, don't you?'

Dot nodded and could only imagine how that conversation would go.

Four days later, Dot sat in the same chair in front of Dr Levitson and he confirmed what she had suspected for some time. She was having a baby, she was having their baby.

'Promise me, Dot, that you will tell your parents.'

She nodded.

'And sooner rather than later?'

Again the nod. Too stunned to speak and too frightened to move. *What on earth was she going to do?*

Dot decided to wait until she had got her head around the situation before she faced her mum and dad; a couple of days would make little difference. She considered going to see Sol's parents, but decided against it. Her humiliation at the last visit still caused her cheeks to flame. She would just have to figure something out, although quite what, she couldn't begin to imagine.

Joan wasn't sure if there was a magic potion that could cure a broken heart, but she trotted up the path of the doctor's surgery nonetheless. She flicked through a copy of *Woman's Own* until it was her turn. Dr Levitson beamed, seemed pleased to see her.

'Ah, Joan, how are you?'

'Oh you know, Doctor, bearing up.'

'I expected to see you—'

'Yes, I need a tonic or something for our Dot. I'm worried

about her. She's got no energy at all and she can't go on like this, not eating, sleeping all the time.'

'I am delighted that you are being so supportive, Joan. It's not something I see every day and it's a credit to you and Reg.'

'Of course I'm supportive. I'm worried about her, tha'sall. She's me daughter!'

'Yes, she is and, once again, Joan, you are to be commended for your attitude, truly. It's not something I see very often, I'm afraid. The good news is that the heavy fatigue and nausea, loss of appetite and so forth will all fade as she gets further into the pregnancy. It's the first few months that can be the trickiest, I'm sure you remember!'

The next sound was Joan Simpson's body hitting the linoleum floor. She had fainted.

Chapter Seven

Dot was halfway up the stairs with a glass of water when she heard her mum's key in the door. She turned and waited, ready to see if she needed any help with the tea. Her mum clicked the door shut behind her and stood with her back against it. Her skin was ashen, her eyes wide. Dot noticed the tremor of her hand as she removed her scarf. She fixed her daughter with a stare and it was in that single second that Dot knew her secret was out. Joan undid the top buttons of her coat as though desperate for air. As she slipped down and sat on the door mat, she looked broken.

Approaching her slowly, Dot reached out to help her mum stand. 'Mum, I…'

'Don't touch me!' Joan managed beneath gasps. And then, 'What have you done?'

For Dot it was a full ten days of going through the motions. Working, sleeping and waiting. She spent hours sitting on her bed in the wee small hours, listening to her parents' shouts and whispers, which came in alternate waves as they tried to figure out what to do for the best. Finally she was summoned.

Dot trod carefully down the stairs, placing one foot after the other on the worn runner that ran up the middle of each step. She padded along the hallway and eased open the door of the back room. It felt incredible that she had known the

146

room and the people in it – her family – her whole life. This was the room in which she had opened eighteen sets of birthday gifts, blown out the candles on eighteen home-made cakes and rushed in barefoot and breathless to find Father Christmas's offerings on eighteen separate cold December mornings. Yet pushing the door open tonight, she felt no kinship. These people had become strangers and in its way this was more scary and lonely than being upstairs by herself, where she could pretend that there were people in the house that cared about her.

Her dad sat in his vest and concentrated on rolling cigarettes ready to stack neatly inside his old tobacco tin. His braces hung down to his thighs. His flat, broad thumbs had a ring of black grease under the fingernails. He'd probably been fixing his bike. He did not look up from his task, content to let her mum talk on behalf of both of them. Dot noted how his fingers shook as he brought the sticky paper up to his mouth for its lick. Trembling hands that contained the anger and distress that he fought to control; for this she was grateful. He flicked his head occasionally, not to acknowledge her, but to get his long, brilliantined fringe out of his eyes.

'Sit down, Dot.' Her mum's voice was soft. If there was the slightest bit of empathy in her tone, this was cancelled out by the set of her mouth and the narrowing of her eyes, as though having to look at something as unsavoury as her pregnant daughter revolted her. She pointed at the chair opposite Dot's dad. Joan stood slightly behind her husband, with her hand resting lightly on the back of his seat. Dot drew a deep breath and opened her mouth, but then closed it again. It was a further minute before she finally found the courage to speak.

Dot was unsure of the protocol and spoke as she would under normal circumstances, which of course these were anything but.

'Is Dee all right?' It had been ten days since she had seen her sister, who crept mouse-like along the hall and into her bed at night so as not to disturb her 'poorly' big sister.

'You stay away from her, d'you hear me!' Her dad's tone made her flinch. Small flecks of spit flew from his mouth and landed on the rug between them.

Dot swallowed to ease her own dry mouth. 'I'm sorry... I just...' She didn't know what she was apologising for, her confusion made her stutter. She only wanted to know how her little sister was doing.

He pointed a finger towards her face. 'I'll say this to you once: you don't go near her. Do you understand? You don't even talk to her. Is that clear?' His top lip curled.

Dot nodded.

'I don't want her mixed up in all this.' This he addressed to his wife, who nodded in agreement and placed her hand on his shoulder as though that could calm his rage.

Joan coughed, although the lump in her throat would not be so easily shifted. 'Your dad and I have been trying to work out what's to be done for the best. We've been over it night after night and have decided.'

Dot looked at her mum. She wanted to comment that she had a right to be involved in the decision-making process, but knew it would only inflame an already intolerable situation. She kept quiet and waited for the verdict. Her bowels turned to ice and her stomach seemed to shrink around her intestines. She fought the urge to be sick.

'You are not that far gone and so there are options…'

Dot instinctively placed her hand on her stomach. No way, she would never get rid of this baby, never. They'd have to kill her first and if they were going to force her to have an abortion, then she'd rather be dead, so all good.

'But Daddy and I respect our faith too much for that to be considered.'

Dot exhaled. Relief.

'You are going to one of the big houses. A mother and baby home in Battersea. But you can't go there till you're nearly ready to drop, so before that we'll just have to think of a way to keep you hidden, once you start to show. I don't want no one around here knowing anything about it. If you tell anyone, anyone at all, then you can't come back here, Dot. Not ever. We'll be finished, a bloody laughing stock and I will not have my house and my name disgraced. I won't have people talking about me behind my back, knowing my business. But if you stay there until it's born and it's adopted out, you can come home and we'll say no more about it. I'm sure you'll be as relieved as we are to have a solution, Dot. It could all be much worse and if we do like we say, you can move on with your life and put it behind you with the least damage done.'

Dot didn't bother to try and stem the steady flow of tears that trickled down her face. Her cry was the almost silent whimper of the defeated. There was so much she wanted to say. Primarily she would have liked to point out that it wasn't an 'it' but her baby. She also did not want to go to Battersea to live with nuns. But mostly, she did not want her baby, *their* baby, put up for adoption. She could not risk speaking up, incurring their wrath, in case they threw her out there and then. She had nowhere to go and no money. She considered telling Barb, but knew it would be the final straw for her parents if Mrs Harrison and the rest of the street were to find out; it wasn't that Barb was disloyal, but she had never been able to keep a secret. Dot nodded, slowly blinking her swollen, red eyes and fighting the rising desire to scream. After a further minute of silence, she correctly assumed that she was dismissed. She made her way back up the stairs to the comfort of her room, where she began to digest the latest miserable development in the story of her life.

Lying on top of the candlewick bedspread, she stroked her tummy and whispered to her little one. 'I will fight them all the way. I will fight to keep you, baby; don't you worry, darling, they will have to get through me to get to you and I am tougher than I look. Your daddy wasn't interested, but I'll make up for that, you just wait and see. So don't you worry, no one is going to take you away from me.'

Sol's words drifted into her head as they did each hour, various phrases, utterances, promises, all made in deceit, all lies. She knew they were lies, but to recall them hurt just the same. *'The idea of only having sixty-three years with you horrifies me, frightens me. Because it's not enough, not nearly enough. How long would be enough? Eternity. I'd settle for eternity.'*

* * *

Dot carried on working at Bryant and May for another month, then effectively spent the rest of the summer lying on the bed in her little bedroom. At first it felt like a nest, somewhere safe and undisturbed where she could sleep, think, and grow their baby. She revived the games from her childhood, then counted all the flowers within the stripes on the iridescent pink flock wallpaper. She pondered the water mark on the ceiling, from when a tile had blown off the roof and let the rain in, making the stain into as many animals as she could think of and then people and then buildings, although how it could simultaneously be an elephant, Karl Marx and Buckingham Palace, she didn't know.

Joan had a new job at the Queen's Head and things appeared to carry on as normal for the other members of the Simpson family. The noises of the house were familiar: the dull echo of the radio from the back room, as though the presenter and all musicians were speaking and performing through a pillow; the flush of the loo and then the hiss as the cistern refilled itself, the sharp snap of the bolt on the bathroom door. The bang of her mum's big saucepan as it hit the bottom of the sink, usually after the spuds or greens had been drained, as though her wrist had finally tired of carrying the heavy weight. The occasional shriek of laughter from her mum or little sister, probably at something funny her dad had done or said, which might be anything from an impression of Mrs Harrison to putting a tea towel on his head.

After a week, however, these distractions felt like a taunt to Dot's whirring brain. The sounds of normal life seemed strangely magnified, until they deafened her. Every time there was a creak on a floorboard or stair tread, she jumped, waiting to see who or what was approaching. It was usually no one.

One day her mum came up, stood in the doorway and informed her, quite casually, of the grand plan. She had decided to tell the neighbours that Dot had got a job on a farm in Kent, the same one where they as a family had picked hops

151

years before. The farmer's wife was unwell and they had asked if Dot might be available to help out with the kids, cook dinner, that kind of thing. It was certainly a step up from Bryant and May. She overheard her mum and Mrs Harrison chatting one day, heard their neighbour pause from dragging on her fag to comment, 'All them fresh apples, country air and home-cooked food, why wouldn't you? Lucky girl.'

That's me, thought Dot, such a lucky girl.

Once or twice, keeping her head low, she peeked through the tiny gap in the lace curtain and watched the kids playing in the street. It felt like an age away that she had been similarly amused by nothing more than a stick and a scruffy tennis ball. The kids were innovative, resourceful, changing the game to keep everyone interested. One minute you could touch the third lamppost along and be safe, but two turns on, touching it meant instant disqualification – hence the howls of the little girl at Number 26, who could not keep up with the new rules but very definitely did not want to be out. Dot smiled as the little waif called her big brother a 'poo-poo shit head' before stomping off to the kerb with her arms folded high across her chest, sulking at the injustice of it all.

It felt strange that life went on as normal for those around her, while her own world was held in limbo.

When the days were hot, Joan would march in and climb up on the window sill to open the top window. There was nothing suspicious in a mother airing the bedroom of her daughter who was working on a farm in Kent. The metal arm would stick out, pushing the net curtain into a V that would catch any breeze and flutter all day long. This could fascinate Dot for hours, especially the patterns on the wall as the lace filtered the rays and fell back against the glass. On the warmest days, the sound of clicking heels and heavy soles on the cobbles was replaced by the light tap of rubber sandals and the pat and squeak of sneakers. No rain or wind meant that birdsong was louder. People seemed to laugh more, happy to feel the warmth creeping into their bones, driving out their aches.

Sometimes she heard voices she recognised. When it was Barb and her Aunty Audrey, usually chatting about nothing in particular, Dot had to sit on her hands to stop herself from jumping up and banging on the glass; she would have so liked her mate's company.

Dee was kept inside for much of the summer as well, poor little mite; it was almost punishment by proxy. The neighbours had been told that Dot had gone to Kent and when Dot did eventually leave, this would be the story Dee would get told too. Joan and Reg figured that any inconsistency with dates would be attributed to a little girl's confusion. They distracted their youngest daughter with stories, the making of fairy cakes and the colouring in of pictures from her book, which, once completed, were ripped out and stuck on the fireplace with Sellotape. They hoped that she would forget that her big sister was being held hostage in the front bedroom and, for most of the time, she did.

One morning, though, not long after school had started again after the summer holidays, Dot was woken by the creak of a floorboard on her bedroom floor. Her mum usually waited until she was asleep before tip-toeing in, bringing glasses of milk and ham sandwiches that Dot would sip and nibble when and if the fancy took her. Dot opened one eye and was pleased to see Dee's smiling face and not her mother standing there in stony-faced judgement as though the very sight of her daughter was enough to renew the anger, the shame she felt at the situation.

'Hello, Dee! What a lovely surprise. Are you all right, darling?'

Dee nodded. She had been told to stay out of Dot's room and was nervous. She flicked the ear of the stuffed bunny under her arm.

'School all right?'

'Yep, I'm doing tables.'

'You never are! Which ones d'you know?'

'I don't know none yet, but I've got a book.'

Dot smiled. 'That's brilliant! You'll have to learn them all, Dee, and then you can do any sums you want to. You're such a big girl now.' It was true, her little sister had grown in the weeks that Dot had been confined to her bedroom.

'Are you feeling better, Dot? Mum said you've got tonsils.' Dee looked sheepish, she didn't know what 'tonsils' was, but if it meant that her sister was banished to her room and wasn't to be spoken to, she knew it must be bad.

'I tell you what, Dee, seeing you has made me feel a *lot* better, honest.'

'Mum and Dad are having a nap in the front room. They had some beer and now they're asleep.'

'Beer?' It wasn't like her parents to be drinking in the afternoon.

'Yeah, they had a dance and they were having beer because of the rent.'

'Because of the rent?' It made no sense, Dee had probably got the wrong end of the stick, bless her.

Dee nodded. 'They got a letter saying that they don't have to pay no rent. Not just now but not never ever, not until they die!' Wide eyed, Dee delivered the last word with drama.

'That can't be right, darling.' Dot shook her head at her sweet little sister.

'It *is* right Dot! Dad said it was a bleeding good job cos your shenanigans meant that we were nearly bleeding starving anyway! But now they've got no rent and mum's got a coupla shifts up the Queen's Head in the kitchen, he says we'll be all right.'

Dot gave a small laugh, hearing the words 'shenanigans' and 'bleeding starving' coming from the mouth of her little sis, although in truth it was far from funny.

'I've got to go now, Dot, but I hope you feel a bit better. I miss you. I liked it when you had your dinner at the table with us.'

'I liked it too, Dee.'

'I gotta go now. I don't want to get tonsils.'

'Ooh no, you don't. But don't worry, tin ribs, you're a bit too little for tonsils!'

Dee crept forward and kissed her sister on the cheek. It was the sweetest kiss Dot had received in a very long time and made her tears pool instantly.

'Thank you, baby girl,' she whispered through her tears.

Dee poked her head through the door before finally leaving. 'Dot?'

'Yes, darling?'

'Tonsils has n'arf made your belly fat!' With that she clicked the door shut and plodded off down the stairs.

Dot promised herself every day to try and put Sol out of her head, but it was like trying not to breathe. She divided her time between thinking about the time they spent together and imagining what life might be like if he were still here. She spoke to her bump, rubbing at the stretched skin of her stomach and filling in all the little details that she thought her baby might like to hear.

'We used to go to a little cafe that wasn't flash, but your dad said it was perfect. We'd sit for hours and hours talking about nothing much really. I was very happy to watch him and listen to him. He's beautiful, you see, and he told me stories of a place far, far away that sounds like paradise. I thought I'd live there too one day, but it wasn't to be. I expect if he was still here now, we'd be going for picnics and enjoying the sunshine; he hated to be cold.' Dot got off the bed as she remembered something. She opened the wardrobe door and there behind a couple of jumpers and skirts that she could no longer get into was her summer frock, a cotton tea dress with big fat roses all over it. She pulled it from the hanger and remembered the day she had sponged it, making sure it would be lovely for the summer. Her tears spilled at the memory of that day, she could never have envisaged that this was how she would spend her summer.

'I thought I'd wear this for him, but look at me now, baby. What on earth happened?' Dot lay on the bed and placed the dress over her stomach. 'I know it's happened, I know he's gone, but I still can't believe it, if that makes sense. I keep imagining he'll pop up and whisk us away, give me an explanation, because it doesn't make sense, any of it. And I don't want to scare you, but I don't know what to do.' Dot considered her options: she had no intention of giving up her baby, yet every solution she considered led her right back to the facts. With no money, no job, no husband and no home, the prospects were grim.

Dot often dreamed about Sol. Her dreams were always set in the St Lucia of her imagination, where the sun warmed her skin, her hand was always clasped inside his and she felt happy and optimistic about a future with the man she loved. They would drink pineapple juice and lie on soft sand with the ocean lapping at their feet. Sometimes the smell and feel of him was so real that when she opened her eyes a fresh blanket of grief would envelop her, the pain in her heart and chest as raw as just after he'd disappeared. It was like probing a rotten tooth with the end of her tongue.

Try as she might, she couldn't stop loving him. She knew that if only she could erase her feelings for him, life would be a little easier, but it was not to be. It made no difference that the man she loved did not exist, that the man she loved had been a mirage, a fantasy; that in reality he was a liar, a charlatan. She ached for him nonetheless.

Dot also felt an overwhelming sense of disappointment. It wasn't enough that Sol had broken her heart; he had also stamped on her dreams. Escape from Ropemakers Fields to paradise had felt within her reach, but on the day he left, he took that possibility with him. How he must have laughed at her confession of wanting to be a designer, smirked at her seaside that existed inside a conch shell and mocked the fabric rainbow that sat against a panelled wall in a West End store. Well, he was right. A life of success and ambition was laughable for someone like her. His mother's words, delivered so calmly, were there for perfect recall whenever she tried to stop her cogs from turning. *'If he loved you, would he simply disappear without speaking to you first? If he had wanted you to go with him, he would have made provision for that, but he didn't, did he?'* Dot rubbed at her rounded stomach, which pushed against the elasticated waist of her trousers. 'No he bloody didn't.' She smiled bitterly, thinking of his name. 'A bringer of peace, my arse.'

* * *

October finally arrived and with it Dot's last night at Rope-makers Fields. Leaves had started to turn russet and small piles of fallen gold gathered against kerbs and behind bins. The sun was bright and the sky blue; London was at its most beautiful. These were just the kind of days that she would liked to have shared with Sol, probably walking hand in hand along the Serpentine. But the day of her exile to Battersea could not have been further from a walk in the park. It was all arranged, the car was to collect her at five in the morning, when there was least risk of her being spotted by the neighbours as she decamped from bedroom to waiting car.

Dot felt a sense of relief as the morning dawned. Her small suitcase was packed with basic essentials: a couple of nighties, a change of underwear and her hairbrush and toothbrush. Nestled under her things lay a brown paper packet with some mid-blue material in it. Dot had finally decided what she would use it for.

Her dad stayed in his bedroom and Dee was tucked up, sound asleep with her bunny under her chin, so it was left to her mum to wave her off.

'You'll be all right, Dot.' It was the first time her mum had addressed her directly in weeks.

'Will I?' She wasn't so sure.

Joan didn't answer, but instead pushed something into her daughter's hand.

'What's this?' Dot looked at the cotton square.

'It's one of your nan's hankies.'

Dot stared at her mother.

Joan gave her a reluctant, awkward hug. Then, after a quick glance left and right to make sure there were no witnesses, she closed the door.

The taxi wound through the familiar streets of Limehouse, which were silent at this early hour. Dot deliberately kept her gaze inside the car; she didn't want any sharp memories to jab her heart and erode her frail strength. Nonetheless, in her mind's eye she could still picture the east London lanes down which they had walked arm in arm, could still glimpse the ghost of her smiling face as she ran to meet the man she loved, the man she thought she would marry.

Daylight was creeping across London and Dot felt the occasional short-lived flutter of excitement to be out and about. The longest she had ever slept away from home was one night and that was under the roof of her paternal grandma on the night Dee was born. Yet, unsurprisingly, this was the aspect of her forthcoming incarceration at Lavender Hill Lodge that worried her least. Eventually the cab pulled into a driveway in Battersea, passing a square gate house of red brick, whose white-painted window frames and cheerful window boxes full of pretty little red and yellow flowers made it look cute and welcoming. The sight lifted her spirits for approximately ten seconds. Then the car rounded the bend in the drive and stopped in front of Lavender Hill Lodge.

The burly cabbie did not attempt to help her retrieve her

bag from the boot. Instead he watched in the rear-view mirror as she struggled to haul it over the rim without bashing her swollen stomach. He pulled away the second the boot was closed, his small wheel spin on the gravel and shake of his head telling her all she needed to know about where his sympathy lay. It didn't matter. What was one more disapproving click of the tongue and curl of the lip compared to the battle she was about to undertake.

Huge white columns supported the ornate stone portico over the Lodge's double-front doors, which were painted red. Dot placed her foot on the highly polished brass doorstep and peered through the half-glazed doors; the glass was so clean and smear free, she wondered if it was actually there at all. She spied the black and white tiled floor of the hallway, which reminded of her of a giant chess board, a game that she had never learned to play. A wide oak staircase ran up along the right, with decorative acorns carved on the top of the newel post. A wrought-iron chandelier, plain but vast, hung down to just above head height on three large chains. The place looked grand, but not like the Merchant's House, which was more like an art gallery or a stately home; this looked like a church.

There was no obvious bell and Dot was wondering how to knock or draw attention to her arrival at such an early hour when the door was swept open by a tall, bright-eyed nun. Her veil and wimple were pulled so tight, it made her small eyes slant upwards at the corners, and despite her advanced years her skin had the look of alabaster, matt and line free. Her mouth was thin, her lips invisible. Her nose, small enough to be classed as 'button', was too pointed, more like a tiny cone.

'You will be Dot.'

Dot nodded. Yes she will be.

'I am Sister Kyna. Come in.'

The nun stood back. Dot lifted her case and placed it inside the door. She stepped gingerly into the hallway and immediately swallowed to quell the nausea that rose in her throat, a combination of nerves and the overwhelming smell of bleach that filled the air. Sister Kyna was barely able to close the door.

'Come, come – further in, girl. Goodness me, don't tell me you're shy!'

Dot shook her head and released the front flaps of her mac that she habitually held shut to conceal her bump. No, she wasn't shy.

'Of course you're not…' The woman's Irish brogue might have been comforting were it not for the fixed, blank expression on her face. 'Shy girls tend not be sent here in the first place. It's a particular *sort* of girl that comes here and shy is not the word that first springs to mind when describing them.'

This was to be her greeting. Dot swallowed again to try and budge the sob that sat at the base of her throat. *Not here as well*. Naively, she had expected different.

'Oh, come now, it's a little late for tears, don't you think? The good news for you, my girl, is that even for the fallen, our Lord is most merciful and it is never too late to seek redemption for the terrible sin that you have committed. For a sin it is, most grave. You have slipped from his grace and our purpose is to show you the error of your ways and by God's holy hand you will find the path again to righteousness…' Suddenly she clapped her slender hands together and changed tack, as though they had been discussing the weather. 'But enough for now;

goodness, you have only just arrived! Let's get the administrative tasks taken care of and then we can show you to your room and get you settled.' A brief smile caused her lipless mouth to part, revealing small, yellow chips of teeth. Her eyes, however, remained brilliant and fixed.

Dot followed the nun along a corridor and into a small office. The walls were lined with filing cabinets and the room needed a good airing. It smelt of bad breath.

'Sit down.' Sister Kyna pointed to a leather swivel chair.

Dot lowered her bulk into the seat and thought of the last time she had sat in a study on the wrong side of a desk. *'He has gone home, to St Lucia. Did he not tell you?'*

The nun placed her gold half-moon spectacles on the end of her nose. 'I have, as you know, been conversing with your mother, Dot, but there are a couple of formalities to be taken care of today.'

Dot nodded.

'I trust you understand what will happen when the child is born?'

Dot nodded again, not because she *did* understand what would happen when the child was born, but because she couldn't bear to hear the detail, still hopeful that a solution would present itself. A miracle.

'Good, good. Well then, all I need is for you to sign both these sheets of paper; print your name and then sign by the side.' She pointed at two spots at the bottom of the typed documents.

Dot crossed her fingers on her left hand and buried them in her lap; with her right, she signed and printed as instructed. Everyone in the world knew the universal rule: if your fingers were crossed, it didn't count.

'It is some small mercy that, despite the wrong that you have done, God can in his infinite wisdom find a way to make a positive from your transgression. Your child will be welcomed into a Christian household and its spiritual welfare will be paramount. That must be of some small comfort?'

Dot nodded. It was of no comfort at all.

'It is a small miracle every time a flower springs from a worthless pasture.' Sister Kyna delivered this with a smile. Dot twisted her hands in her lap; she didn't need reminding that she was a worthless pasture, she never forgot.

Dot lugged her suitcase from the entrance hall up the wide staircase and along a narrowing corridor. They stopped at one of several identical white-painted doors. Sister Kyna pulled a key out from under her cardigan; it appeared to be attached to a chain on her belt. She unlocked the door and pushed it, revealing a white-walled room with two wrought-iron single beds against opposite walls. Above each bed was an image of Christ on the cross. One bed was neatly made; on the other lay slumped a very pregnant girl who had clearly only recently woken up.

'Are the doors always locked?' Dot was taken aback; having never been locked up anywhere in her whole life, the idea petrified her.

Sister Kyna smiled thinly. 'I think you will find that it was freedom that started this trouble for you in the first place. In you go.'

Dot stepped onto the green linoleum and flinched as the door banged shut behind her.

'Don't listen to her, she is a cow, pure evil!' The girl tried to stand but wobbled back onto the mattress, which Dot would soon discover was actually a straw palliasse. It was covered with a thick grey woollen blanket and starched white bed linen turned over to form a wide, pristine border.

The girl was no more than five foot three tall and yet her stomach was vast, distended beyond recognition, as if she had swallowed a barrel full of beer. She had a wan complexion and her pale hair hung in two thin strips either side of her gaunt face.

'Don't get up!' Dot shouted, partly out of fear for the girl's welfare, but also because God only knew how she would manage to get her righted if she fell.

'Thanks. I'm like one of those blasted shipping tankers that take days to turn around in the ocean! I'm Susan, by the way, Susan Montgomery. But please call me Susie.' Susan gave a small wave from the bed on which she was beached.

'I'm Dot.'

'Is that it? Just Dot?'

'A Dot is something so small and insignificant – that's not a name for someone like you.' She shook her head, this was no time for thinking about Sol.

'Yep, that's it, just Dot.' But to him I was Clover, his Clover...

'Welcome to our luxury suite!'

'I'm sorry, taking up space in your room.'

'No, don't be, it's *our* room now and it'll be nice to have company. I hate being here by myself.'

'I need the loo actually.' Dot cast her eyes around to see if there was a bathroom. 'How d'we get out?'

'Oh, sweetie, we don't. They give us regular loo breaks, but they rarely coincide with when my bladder wants a loo break. For that reason, we have a large bowl under the bed, which

164

we can tip out over there.' Susan pointed at a small china sink on the wall with a hand towel and a small sliver of soap stuck on the side. 'I call my bowl Winston Churchill, as in WC.'

Dot tried not to cry. She could not imagine in a million years going to the loo in front of Susan Montgomery, who liked to be called Susie, no matter how friendly.

'Go ahead, Dot, cry if you like. It's shit, but you'll get used to it.' Susan's tone was quite plummy, it made Dot feel even more out of place.

'I don't want to get used to it!' she sniffed.

'I know, but you do, trust me. Where are you from?'

'London, east. You?'

'Dorset. Miles and miles away.'

Dot sat on the bed and took off her mac.

'Gosh, look at your neat little bump! You look quite gorgeous; you are tiny compared to me.'

Dot beamed. She felt far from gorgeous, but to receive a compliment was lovely nonetheless.

'Mind you, I do have a jolly good excuse for looking like a whale; I've got two in here!'

'Twins? No way! Oh my goodness, I can't imagine…'

'Yes, twins, lucky old me.' Susan patted her swollen bulk and exhaled deeply.

It felt strange to be able to discuss being pregnant, let alone anything else, without fear or embarrassment.

'Oh my God, twins!' Dot shook her head. What was it they said – double the blessing? Or maybe not, in this case.

'It's typical of my luck; I never do anything by halves. I'm the type of girl that doesn't get caught with a joint in the school dorm but a whole bloody dope factory! I'm always the one left holding the baby. Quite literally!' Susan laughed loudly at her own joke.

Dot felt far too desolate to find anything funny. She lay quietly on her side until her stomach cramped with the need to go to the loo; it was agonising. She closed her eyes and drifted into a light slumber.

'That's my girl!'

'I like being your girl.'

'That's good, because I am never going to let you go…'

She practically leapt from the bed when she heard the key in the lock. The bathroom was sparse, functional: the brick-work was painted in white gloss and the floor was covered with a rubberised reddish finish that continued for a couple of inches up the wall. It had the echoey quality of a public loo and smelt like a hospital. Dot noticed there were no mirrors anywhere – not that it mattered, she didn't particularly want to be reminded of what she looked like. When she got back to her room, Susan was occupying the small space between the two beds. She had changed into a pale gold smock whose voluminous fabric hung down from the empire line under her swollen bust.

'You can smirk, missus,' Susie said when she caught Dot looking at her unusual cover-up, 'but yours is in the wardrobe and you need to put it on before breakfast, which is in precisely ten minutes. These are to be worn for all meals and other public duties.'

'Public duties?'

'Don't look so worried, you're not expected to launch ships or open an art gallery, nothing like that; it's just a very grand term for cleaning and other pointless bloody chores that we

166

do en masse while considering *the error of our ways.*' The last few words she delivered with an Irish accent.

Dot smiled. It was impossible not to find Susan entertaining, even at this dark time. She was grateful that she was there. She pulled the smock over her head; it was part overall, part surplus and it looked awful, drab and slightly choirboyesque, which was probably the whole point. Susan laughed at Dot and Dot laughed back. It was the first time she had laughed in months and the duo looked too hideous for it to be anything other than funny.

A different, younger nun – Sister Mary – opened all the doors and the girls from each room filed out to form two orderly queues. Dot gawped and stumbled, trying to comprehend the system. What would Barb or her mum make of this carry-on, she wondered, forgetting for a moment that her mum was not amused by anything Dot did these days, and that it had been necessary to drop Barb, before and during her 'trip to Kent'. The two lines of around ten girls moved like fat drunk ducks, hands clasped in front of them, waddling along the corridor and down a narrow staircase towards the dining room.

Dot was fascinated by the girls, who all looked her age or younger, one or two much younger; all were in the advanced stages of pregnancy. The horrid smocks gave them a certain uniformity, but up close they were all very different. Some girls positively glowed with the radiance of pregnancy, rosy cheeked and chubby; no doubt those from the poorest backgrounds were benefiting from the regular meals that the Lodge provided. Others, herself included, looked exhausted, with black rings below their tear-swollen eyes and sad, drooping shoulders. So many girls with distended stomachs and swollen chests! Is that what she looked like? She assumed so.

A long refectory table sat centrally in the dining hall, with benches along either side. The leaded windows were set in deep sills and the whole room remained in shadow and smelt vaguely of damp and cabbage. Large embroidered banners hung from wooden poles on the far wall. One was of Mary tending to Jesus's wounds on the cross, his horrified disciples looking on. The other was of the bleeding heart, a red pulsing shape with flames leaping from the top and bound by a ring of entwined thorns. They made Dot feel a little light-headed.

On the table were plates of fried eggs, triangles of bread and butter, pots of jam, slices of ham and glasses of orange juice. Dot swallowed the bile of morning sickness that had plagued her entire pregnancy so far. Dr Levitson had assured her it would tail off, but he'd been wrong and she could quite easily have thrown up on the tessellated waxed wooden floor as soon as she smelt the eggs.

Watching the girls swing their legs in an ungainly fashion over the benches could have been quite comical, but the swollen abdomens, altered centres of gravity and ballooning smocks made the process unnecessarily difficult. And then they had to sit in great discomfort without support for their aching backs.

Sister Kyna waited with a calm smile while all the girls took their places. Her eyes lingered longest on those that found the task most challenging, silently chastising them while urging them to hurry. It wasn't enough that they had gone and got themselves up the duff, they were now keeping everyone from their breakfast. Finally she began. 'Almighty God, in whose presence today we hang our heads and bow before your majesty, we ask that you have mercy on the souls of the girls here present. We ask that you forgive the sinful action that the Devil himself has conjured to tempt these poor misguided creatures and we ask that you help them find the path back to righteousness. We thank you, Lord, for the food that we have been blessed with to nourish the poor abandoned souls that they yield. Amen.'

A chorus of 'Amen' rang out around the room. Dot swallowed her tears; this was no time to cry, here in front of all the others. The idea of her baby being a poor abandoned soul filled her with horror. The girls chatted while they ate, not the easy, audible banter of a table at home, but it wasn't silent and for that Dot was grateful. She managed to take a few small bites of bread and butter and sipped at the orange juice.

All the girls seemed to have been allocated tasks and when the meal finished, some gathered plates and glasses, while others headed to the kitchen to assist with the dishes. Dot was handed a long-handled dustpan and brush by an older nun.

'Here, dear, as you haven't been assigned a work group yet, please take this and sweep under the tables and all the chairs. You'd be amazed how many stray crumbs can gather!'

The nun smiled at her and Dot returned the smile hesitantly; what was the catch? This woman seemed genuinely pleasant, not like Sister Kyna at all. Dot nodded and wobbled slightly, any exertion after weeks of lying on her bed left her feeling quite faint.

'I'm Sister Agnes.'

'I'm Dot.'

The sister smiled. 'So I believe. Hello, Dot.'

Dot concentrated on her task. It was just as hard to receive kindness as it was criticism without bursting into tears.

When the morning chores were finished, Dot and Susan lay on their beds and stared at the ceiling.

'Sister Agnes seems quite nice.'

'Compared to Sister Kyna, anyone would seem nice!'

'I guess so.' Dot laughed. It felt slightly disrespectful to be talking about nuns in such a fashion.

Susan propped herself up on her elbow, her stomach spilling onto the palliasse. 'Oh, these beds are so uncomfortable,' she said. 'But once you actually fall asleep on them, they do warm up and then it feels like you're being held in a giant paw!' She laughed at Dot, who was looking nonplussed. 'How long have you got?'

Dot cringed and swallowed. These very private, embarrassing matters had been kept between her and Doctor Levitson and it took monumental effort to discuss them with her roommate, who was still a stranger. It was bizarre that their lives had collided in this way.

'About six weeks.'

'I'm due in four!' Susan was loud, as though she had won the point.

'Are you scared?' Dot ventured.

'Of what?'

'All of it really, giving birth… giving them away.' Dot whispered the last bit; it was the first time that she had said the phrase out loud or even admitted to herself that this might be a possibility. Thoughts of Sol filled her head, as they so often did at the most unwelcome moments.

'When our children are tucked up at night, sleeping

*soundly in the nursery with Patience on her bed in their
room, I will sit with you in the garden. It's my favourite
part of the day, when the sun sinks into the ocean and
the day has lost its heat, and we shall bask in the warm
breeze that blows across the beach from the Caribbean
Sea, watching the lights twinkling from Reduit Beach on
the curve of the horizon.'*

'Yes and no.' Susan anchored her with her response. 'I'm
shit scared of giving birth, who isn't? But giving them away,
no, not fussed really. I'm more than a little bit angry that they
have taken up a bloody year or so of my life! I was supposed
to be going to India with some friends and I had so many plans,
all put on hold because of these little bastards. And not to
mention what they have done to my beautiful flat stomach and
my tits! I used to have amazing tits – I can't see them ever going
back to normal.'

Dot was horrified. Susan read her expression. 'Don't judge
me, Dot, I'm only being honest. I never planned on getting
pregnant and I certainly didn't plan on my whole life being
fucked up by one night of passion. I think it's a bloody big
price to pay for getting stoned, don't you?'

'I…' Dot was literally struck dumb.

'It's not like I'm in a relationship – you know, where you
simply get caught, bring forward the date of the wedding, opt
for a loose-fitting frock, order a trailing lily bouquet that you
hold in front of your stomach all day and night, and, wahey,
seven months later give birth to an eight-pound premature
baby! I'm not one of those women. I'm a party girl that got
unlucky. I can't wait until it's all over, I can't wait to get back
to my old life.'

Dot considered this. To the outside world they were no different; she too was a girl that had got unlucky, a girl who was no good. But there was a difference: Dot knew she would never get her old life back again, not after this.

'Were you never with the dad?'

Susan sighed. 'No. I've a pretty good idea who it is – an old friend, someone I like a lot. He has no idea, which is lucky; I couldn't bear to have things any more complicated than they already are. We smoked a bit, dropped a tab, the rest is a bit hazy. My mother went completely off the scale when she found out, which is how I find myself here under lock and key with the crazy Sisters of Jesus. If I'd had my way, it would have been a quick trip to a certain man in Soho with a bag full of grubby fivers, job done and then home on the bus. I tried every trick in the book, drank copious quantities of gin, sat in scalding baths with mustard in, I even threw myself down two flights of stairs, but these little sods weren't budging, probably stubborn and wilful like me! But no, Mother dearest has some deep-seated conviction in the Lord and a desire to keep her reputation unsullied at the Bridge Club, so the rest is history.'

'You seem to be coping with it well, Susie, if you don't mind me saying.'

'That's because it's not what I want; I am in no way ready for the mundane life of washing nappies and burping a fat baby. It has made me take stock though, made me realise that I need to go out and grab a life, otherwise I'll get swamped by the monotony of the everyday. I feel quite maudlin if I think about it too much.'

'It's funny isn't it; I'd give anything for the mundane life of burping a fat baby, I'd love it.'

Susie shook her head. 'Not for me, I'm afraid. I woke up the other morning and realised that, despite all the things I thought I might become or achieve in my life, unless I try really hard, I am going to be ordinary forever, just like the other 99.9 per cent of the population. I was shocked when I realised that! It was as though I'd always had a sneaking suspicion that I was somehow more special than the 99.9 per cent, but of course I'm not. Which is precisely why I have to create the extraordinary, I have to go and chase the fun!'

'I wish I felt more like that, but truth is I don't want to chase the fun. I think I'd be happy forever with a little house and a child to care for. I'm finding it really tough. I don't want to give my baby away, but I've got no choice.'

'Surely you must have a choice?'

'No I don't, not really.'

'But you must have, even if it means being on your own – women do it all the time!'

'Not women like me. Where I come from unmarried women with babies and no job end up on the streets, simple as that.'

'God, I can think of nothing worse than being saddled with kids for the next twenty-odd years of my life. I've got so much that I want to do, places I want to go. I take it by your face that things are a bit different for you?'

'A bit, but not really. I *was* with the dad, for a couple of months and he was wonderful, well I thought he was. I loved him and I thought he loved me, he said he did…'

Susan smirked. 'Quel surprise, don't they all?'

'S'pose so. I don't really know. He was my first and I believed him when he said we'd get married. I believed everything that he told me. But I guess I'm just a bit thick. The thing is, I wanted so badly to believe him.'

Susan had nothing to say. She watched as Dot's tears trickled down her face and into her ear.

'He's not from England, was just passing through, really. His mum told me that I was a distraction for him and I can see that now, but I got so wrapped up in him, I was so happy, happier than I knew was possible. I really wanted to go and live with him in the sunshine, it sounded lovely. I've never even seen the sea.' Dot's sobbing made further speech impossible.

'Oh, Dot. He sounds like a complete arse. It's far worse to lead you on and give you all the old flannel; it just makes it harder, doesn't it? But the thing is, most of them are like that – well, most that I know. I tell you what, when we get out and this is all over, come to Dorset, I'll show you the sea. I mean it's bloody freezing and you wouldn't want to swim in it, but you can stare at it to your heart's content!'

Dot turned her head and smiled half-heartedly at her roommate, but she knew that she would not want to see Susan again, no matter how kind the invitation.

That night the girls were woken by a loud scream; it was three o'clock in the morning. Both sat up, clutching their chests.

Dot flicked on the bedside lamp. 'What's that noise?' she gasped in fear.

'I reckon it's Jude starting, she's due any day now. Don't worry, Dot; one thing I can say about this lot is that they know what they're doing when it comes to delivering babies – it's the best place you can be. They do it day in, day out and they have done for years; they'll look after her.'

Susan had barely finished her sentence when the next howl began, a bellowing scream that built and built, filling the air and rattling the windows.

Dot shrank down under her blanket and tried to block out the noise. The poor girl, it sounded horrific. Dot shivered at the thought that in a few short weeks it would be her needing the nuns' help in the delivery room.

The next morning the girls came to an arrangement over using their bowls. Susan was happy to complete her morning visit in front of Dot, but the same could not be said in reverse. It took all Dot's courage to ask Susan to turn and face the wall, allowing her privacy of sorts. Susan laughed and called Dot 'provincial'. Dot didn't know what that meant, but was grateful anyway for being able to pee unseen, if not unheard.

As the two columns waddled along the corridor to breakfast, all decked out in their hideous smocks, one of the girls started to whimper and cry, which in turn set a couple of the others off. Eyes darted from under fringes as those that weren't crying tried to smile at those that were. Dot was reassured to see such camaraderie among the group – after all, empathy was in short enough supply on the outside. It was probably just the combination of hormones and the disrupted night's sleep – that girl had sure known how to howl! It was strange to think that she would now be in the separate nursery wing, probably holding her baby. Lucky thing.

As legs were heaved over the benches and into place, Dot caught Susan's eye and was astounded to see tears running down her roommate's cheeks. What on earth could have upset the tough party girl who didn't give a damn about most things, other than the restoration of her amazing bosom, getting to

India and returning to her old life?

Sister Kyna took her position at the head of the table, with the bleeding heart of Christ and his body on the crucifix behind her.

'Jesus Christ, our Father, we ask on this very sad day for you to show your divine mercy and hasten the journey of Judith's dear departed baby who has passed into your care...'

Dot heard very little of the prayer as the girls began to cry and mutter, both to each other and into cupped palms.

'Oh my God, oh no!'

'I don't believe it!'

'Poor Jude.'

'Was it stillborn?'

'What happened?'

No one had an appetite for breakfast; some ate a morsel in silence, most sat in quiet reflection. Within the hour the room had emptied. Each girl had been allocated her chores for the morning and Dot's job was to rake the gravel at the front of the building and collect any litter, leaves and weeds that might spoil its appearance. She was given a wide rake with a wooden handle and a large plastic bucket. Bending down to retrieve small scraps was difficult, but she was glad of the opportunity to be outside, happy to feel the warmth of the morning sun on her skin. She rolled up the sleeves of her smock and set to.

A girl appeared from the back of the building. She was wearing a navy coat and her hair was in a rather elaborate up-do, held in place by dozens of bobby pins; she looked lovely. She was pushing a very high, grand Silver Cross pram with large chrome-spoked wheels that gleamed in the sunlight. She barely acknowledged Dot as she pushed the pram along the gravel; her pace was measured. Dot heard a small sound like a cat mewling – the cry of as newborn baby. The girl stopped and bent into the shade of the hood that was pulled up against the morning's rays. Dot watched as, with trembling hand, the girl stroked and soothed the baby that lay swaddled in its rather fancy carriage.

'It's okay, Gracie, don't cry, darling, Mummy's right here. It will all be okay. There's a good girl, don't cry, Gracie.' The baby seemed to take comfort from her mother's words and after a couple of small hiccups, the crying stopped. The girl stood straight and used the corner of a white cotton handkerchief to blot at tears that now fell from her own eyes. She did this with precision, so as not to smudge her mascara and eyeliner. Dot wanted to ask if she was okay and would have liked to have a peek at the baby, but that would have felt like an intrusion. The girl picked up her pace a little and walked towards the gate house at the bottom of the drive. Dot watched as she knocked on a side door and then pushed the pram inside

Dot worked for half an hour, picking up the odd cigarette butt, pieces of moss and handfuls of dead leaves from the otherwise pristine driveway. Her heart jumped in her chest as a loud shout ripped through the air. 'You fucking bastards! You bastards! She is my baby, you can't have her, she is my baby. I've changed my mind, you can't take her! Please! No! Gracie! No!'

Dot stood still and gripped the rake, her heart hammered inside her rib cage and a wave of nausea swept over her. She rubbed her tummy to quiet the agitated baby that didn't like to feel her distress. Gracie's mum appeared some minutes later, supported by a nun on one side and a doctor in a white coat on the other. Her head lolled on her chest. Her hair had worked its way loose and pins fell along the path as she stumbled forward. Dot noted the black streaks of mascara-laden tears that striped her face. The nun and the doctor were almost pulling her now, and her feet dragged behind her on the gravel, leaving two tracks as the toes of her shoes slid along, like a drunken ballerina. Sister Mary, the neat young nun that had unlocked Dot's door on the first day walked behind the trio, pushing the pram back towards the main building. It was empty.

Dot bent down to gather up the handful of pins, but decided against it. She thought of Hansel and Gretel and their bread-crumb trail – maybe these bobby pins were to help Gracie find her way back to her mum. Dot covered them with handfuls of gravel so they would be there for Gracie to find, if and when she needed to; little metal arrows, showing the way. She raked at the tracks that the girl had created and tried not to think about what had occurred in the pretty gate house with the vibrant window boxes that fooled you into thinking it was a place of joy and beauty.

That night, after lights out, the two girls lay quietly.

'I'm sorry about your friend, about Jude; it must be so tough for her.'

Susan moved, making her straw mattress rustle. 'She wasn't really my friend, but it's shit nonetheless. She's only sixteen. I keep thinking that it was all such a bloody waste, all that heartache, upheaval, distress. To end like that feels doubly cruel somehow. It was all for nothing, wasn't it, if there isn't even a baby at the end of it. I can just imagine the speech that Kyna would have given her about it being *God's will* – that'd be the last thing Jude needed to hear.'

'Susie?'

'Yes?'

'How does it work, giving the babies away? I saw a girl go along today with a pram, to the gate house.' The memory of Gracie's mum, with her hair falling over her face and being dragged along, would never leave her.

'It's quite automatic, fast, apparently. The paperwork that you have already signed gives them permission to put the baby up for adoption and as soon as it's born the system kicks in. It varies as to when you actually hand the baby over, depending on the baby's health, where the new parents are coming from and so forth. Apparently some go a couple of days after they're born, or you could be lumbered for up to three months.'

Dot closed her eyes in the darkness. She would never feel lumbered, she would treasure every second.

'The nuns have a long list of couples, good, church-going people, who are waiting for babies. They pay the Church a handsome fee and they get given a baby. Simple.'

'Do you get to say who you would like your baby to go to?'

'Afraid not, old girl. You do get to see them though, if you want to, through a little grill in the dividing wall, apparently. I don't see the point, personally. I am going to treat it like a transaction: I give the babies away and I get my freedom back – wonderful!'

'I don't want to give mine away and the closer I get to having it, the more panicky I feel about it.'

'The only girls that leave with their babies, Dot, are those whose parents pay for them to leave with their babies. It's the same fee as the adoption money, and some do have a change

179

of heart.'

Dot knew her parents would never pay that. Even if they did have the money, they wouldn't give a single penny. And there was no one else that could help.

'And then there are those that take the ten-pound ticket and go to Australia. They're crying out for people over there.'

'Australia?' Dot didn't know much about Australia, just that it was on the other side of the world and was full of snakes and crocodiles.

'Yep, if you take the ten-pound ticket, they'll load you and your screaming offspring onto a crowded, stinky boat where you will sit for months, going slowly crazy, before arriving in the back of beyond where the likelihood is you will end up married to a heathen who runs a sheep station in the middle of sodding nowhere. *If* you survive the horrendous journey and the blistering heat that will cook you if you sit in it, and the insect bites and life in a swamp, you have the joy of sharing your bed and being grateful for your very existence to a bloke whose only hope of marriage is to buy an English bird who's been knocked up and rejected by someone else!'

'That don't sound like much fun.'

'Good God, Dot, it would be a slow death, a life sentence. I couldn't stand it. If it was New York, I'd be off like a shot, I've always wanted to go there, and I will one day.'

Dot turned to the wall and tried to sleep. Why, Sol, why did you do this to me? Why me?

Chapter Eight

The nuns were singing in the small chapel at the side of Lavender Hill Lodge. It was a beautiful, sweet, melodic cantata that evoked joy and sorrow all at once. The sound carried to where a group of girls toiled in the main entrance hall. Dot dipped her cloth-covered finger inside the pot of floor wax then rubbed it all over the wooden step. She worked on all fours, with her belly smothered by her smock, inches from the floor. As she sashayed left to right, she felt the baby nudge her, probably with an elbow; this baby wanted to sleep and didn't like the movement. It was only when Dot lay in a warm bath – a luxury she enjoyed once a week – that the baby seemed to truly settle, almost as if the warm water soothed the little thing. She swallowed the image of the warm Caribbean Sea, her dreams of swimming in it every day after breakfast.

Susan reached up with a feather duster and removed cobwebs and specks of dust, visible only to the eagle eyes of Sister Kyna, from the wall lights. She carefully removed the fragile glass cloche from a candle bulb as she had been instructed and used the duster to scoot around the fluted edge. Reaching up to replace it, her body convulsed without warning, her hands jerked and the delicate glass shade hit the tiled floor, shattering into a million fragments.

Dot waddled over as fast as she could, crunching the glass underfoot. She placed her hand on Susan's lower back as she bent over, trying to ease the pain.

'Are you okay?' She tried to keep the panic from her voice.

As Susan looked at her friend through her lank fringe, a warm cascade of viscous water ran down her leg and splattered on the black and white floor. 'Flat stomach and pert tits here we come!' she muttered through gritted teeth.

Dot laughed, despite the nervous panic that enveloped the girls. 'Don't try and talk!'

'What's going on here?' It was the unmistakeable cold tone of Sister Kyna. She tutted at the glass fragments, then glanced at Susan.

'I think she's started.' Dot chewed her bottom lip. Talk about state the bleedin' obvious.

'Stand up, girl.' Sister Kyna's voice was firm. Susan struggled to reach standing before another wave of pain doubled her over again. Sister Kyna looped her arm through Susan's and walked as briskly as her encumbered charge would allow towards the nursery wing.

'Clear this mess up!' She cast the words over her shoulder to anyone that would catch them.

Dot lay awake most of the night, thinking about her friend and trying not to be deafened by the silence of their room. Over the last four weeks, she had grown used to Susan's shifts and murmurs throughout the night, the rustle and creak of her palliasse, her frequent, urgent conversations with Winston Churchill and the sips from the sink tap when thirst overtook her. Being alone gave Dot too much thinking time and that wasn't a good thing. She could only liken her situation to living in a nightmare; everything she thought she knew and could rely on had been taken from her, her parents' love and support, the welcoming roof of their little house in Ropemakers Fields, Sol. Especially Sol. It was his absence that she felt most keenly.

By morning Dot was desperate for word of Susan. At the breakfast table she learned that her friend's labour had been relatively quick and that mother and babies, one boy and one girl, were doing just fine.

It was three days later, after breakfast, Dot was back on rake duty, enjoying the fresh air and doing her best to keep the gravel pristine. She wondered how Gracie's mum was doing and was surreptitiously checking that her bobby pin trail was still hidden when she heard a cough behind her,

'Ah, Dot, you'll do. Could you please help me lift this *heavy* bin to the back store?' Sister Agnes spoke a little too loudly and emphasised the word 'heavy', using her eyes to indicate the large metal dustbin in front of them. Dot peered into its empty interior. It didn't look heavy at all, in fact hadn't Sister just carried it all the way around to the front?

'This bin here?'

'Yes, Dot, this one!' She sounded quite indignant.

'But it's e—'

'Yes I know it's "'eavy"! And that word does start with an aitch, you know!'

Dot looked at Sister Agnes's rolling eyes and gritted teeth; she thought the woman had gone stark staring mad!

Propping her rake against the front wall, Dot lifted one handle and the nun took the other. The sister puffed a couple of times, even though they carried a feather weight. They walked with ease across the gravel and up towards the bin store. Plonking the bin down on its concrete plinth, Sister

Agnes looked to the left and right, reminding Dot of the look-out at school who used to patrol the playground while the rest of them smoked behind the girls' toilet block. 'Wait here!' she said, and whizzed off to the side of the building, her wimple flying in the wind.

Dot was left alone and bemused, loitering by the bins. It was a few minutes later that Sister Agnes reappeared, leading Susan by the arm. Dot knew it was Susan, but if it hadn't been for the hair and vaguely familiar face, she might not have recognised her. She looked haunted, and seemed to have collapsed like a deflated balloon, with large dark circles beneath her eyes and no hint of her ready smile or wit.

'Oh, Dot.' Susan crumpled against her friend's body. Dot stretched out her arms and, as far as she was able, hugged the girl's shaking form against her own bulbous belly.

'It's all right, Susie. It'll be okay, lovey.' She patted her back and didn't know what else to say.

Susan drew away sharply and faced Dot, gripping the tops of her arms with bony fingers. She fought to control her tears. 'I had to see you, I had to speak to you and you must listen to me! Forget what I said before. I was wrong. I was so wrong. When I saw them, my babies…' She stopped speaking to try and stem her tears and regulate her breathing. 'They were so beautiful. I loved them immediately, I love them so much. You have to fight, Dot, you have to fight. You were right and I didn't believe you, but… but I love them so much. They've taken my girl already, she's gone!' The last two words she almost screamed, then her knees buckled and Dot held her fast to stop her sinking to the floor. Sister Agnes stood ten feet away, keeping a lookout, breaking several, if not all the rules of Lavender Hill Lodge.

'I called her Sophie and she's gone. I couldn't watch her go, I couldn't. But they are not having my boy, Nicholas. They are not having him. I've taken the ten-pound ticket, we are going to Australia. I don't care about anything but keeping him with me. I don't want to chase the fun, I want ordinary! You were right. I'll live anywhere and marry anyone, I don't care. But I will not let them take my boy and when I can, I'll find her, I swear to God and on my life, I'll get Sophie back. I will! I'll get her back!'

Her sobs made further speech impossible.

Sister Agnes turned towards the girls and flapped her hands agitatedly at Dot, as though shooing away an animal. 'Quick! Go go go!'

Dot walked away as briskly as she could, back around to the front of the building. She retrieved the rake and held it between her palms, tears streaming down her face. Seeing Susan so broken and desperate had been horrible; she hoped with all her heart that she and Nicholas would lead a happy life and that she would one day get Sophie back. Listening to Susan had also got her thinking: maybe the ten-pound ticket was her answer.

Susan's bed remained vacant for the rest of Dot's stay, which gave her the chance to chat to her baby when the lights were out and sleep was slow in arriving.

'Is that the answer, little mate? Shall we go to Australia? I can't imagine what that'd be like, but at least I'd get to keep you. I did love him, y'know, your dad, and I'll love you n'all. Maybe that's what we do, baby, jump on a boat like the ones that I used to see in the docks and we'll go and live in a swamp?

Whaddya reckon? Thing is, I can't really imagine going back to live in Ropemakers Fields. I can't imagine sitting and eating me tea, while my dad reads the paper and Dee kicks my shins under the table. I can't imagine life carrying on for me, as if everything is normal. I don't think things will ever be normal for me again and that makes me really sad, cos I had a lovely little life really, just ordinary, but lovely. Maybe that's the answer; we should go and live in a swamp.'

* * *

November the eleventh, Poppy Day. Dot woke with back ache. This wasn't unusual – the lumps and bumps of the mattress meant a comfortable night was often just down to luck. She stretched and prepared to change out of her nightie, when she realised with horror that she had wet herself. Only she hadn't: her waters had broken and this was it. She looked at the image of Christ on the cross above her bed and sank down onto the mattress. 'Oh shit.'

The room was smaller than she might have imagined and pretty stark. A bright double strip light hung on chains overhead and the rubberised swing doors had no handles. Dot was worried someone might walk in and see her, but as her labour progressed, she cared about very little. A small green canvas cot, like a shallow sling, sat on a table top, awaiting the baby – her baby! She felt a rush of excitement.

She was lying on a trolley bed with her bare feet strapped into stirrups that protruded from each side of the bed at extended angles. The dark cotton gown had been hastily fastened at the

186

back and it slipped down her arms, pooling on her stomach, in a bunched-up mess. To the side of the bed stood a rusting upright trolley holding a large industrial-looking canister of gas and air. A green tube protruded from the top, attached to a face mask; she wouldn't mind a drop of that, whatever it was.

Sister Agnes busied herself among a tray of utensils, clanking and rearranging them. Dot saw the metal glint under the strip light and hoped they wouldn't need any of them.

'How are we doing?' The kindly nun swept Dot's fringe from her face.

'Okay. Sister Agnes... thanks for... letting me help you with... the bin...' She spoke in bursts between her panting breaths.

'You are most welcome, Dot.'

The two women exchanged a meaningful glance.

It was another half an hour before the mask was looped over her head with a length of elastic and she was told to breathe deeply. The mixture left a metallic taste in her mouth and as soon as it hit her blood, the room seemed to soften, voices took on an echoey quality and her limbs felt leaden. The Entonox did little to relieve her discomfort, but she certainly cared less about it. Pointing at the little green sling, she mumbled from behind the plastic, 'That'sfermebaby.'

Sister Agnes held Dot's hand as another contraction built. 'Now, remember what I told you. Breathe, Dot, that's the secret. Good, deep breaths!'

Dot concentrated on the nun's encouraging words and tried to do as she was told, but it was difficult to get a full breath before the next contraction started. It was all going too quickly, too fast for her to have any control over the pain that sliced through her body. There was no time to mentally prepare, brace her muscles or focus. Instead, it was as if the pain was in control, it flooded and weakened her and when it subsided all she felt was blessed relief, thankful for the respite, before the whole ghastly cycle started all over again.

She was aware of a sharp jab in her thigh. She yelped as much with surprise as the sting of the needle. The doctor was standing to her side.

'That's a shot of pethidine. It will relax all your muscles and take the edge off that pain. You will soon start to feel a whole lot better, just you wait.'

Things seemed to slow a little; the calm before the storm.

Bathed in sweat, with her hair stuck to her forehead, Dot tried to control her shaking legs as another wave threatened to overtake her body. She breathed deeply and allowed it to flow over her. She saw Sol's face behind her closed eyes; he was smiling. *That's my girl.* She smiled back. All too soon another stirring in the base of her spine warned of a new volcano building. This one felt different, she instinctively knew that this would be the last push. One, two, three seconds passed and her whole body heaved with relief. She fell back against the thin mattress, feeling like a boned chicken, all soft and supple, the knots and sharp edges removed. She was muted and quiet.

The doctor held up the baby, her baby. A beautiful baby boy, a boy! He had a head of thick, dark curls. Dot cried, he was perfect and he was theirs. She would have given anything in the world at that precise moment to be holding Sol's hand and not that of the kindly Sister.

The baby was wrapped in a white sheet and handed to her.

'Oh! Thank you. Look at him! He's so beautiful.'

Dot peered into the sheet and loosened the fabric; there staring back at her was the face of her son. Her beautiful boy. His large unfocusing eyes blinked slowly as she drew his face up to her own. His skin was downy soft against her lips; his perfect rosebud mouth seemed to form a kiss on her cheek. She placed the tip of her finger inside his tiny grasping hand; his fingernails were minute. Dot nuzzled her face close to his, inhaling his scent – the scent of warmth, love and innocence, with the faintest hint of cinnamon and spice.

Sister Agnes smiled and had to agree, yes, he was truly beautiful.

Dot dozed for a couple of hours as her boy slumbered inside a plastic bassinet in the nursery, where all the babies slept. A couple of other tiny newborns in crocheted bonnets lay in cots, mewling and chewing at scrunched-up fists.

A young nurse wheeled him in and placed him by the side of her bed; the other girl in the room was also brought her baby. Dot lifted him and held him tightly against her chest. He opened his eyes for the briefest second – they were bright blue! His arms and legs were curled up towards his body, his little fists were bunched under his chin; he looked like a beautiful cherub. His lips were full and dark and his skin was darker now than it had been when he was born, more like his dad's.

'Hello, little fella! Hello, you beautiful boy.' Dot beamed at the closed face of her son. She shook her head. How could someone like her have managed to make something as perfect as this.

He started to cry, not with tears – he didn't know about tears yet – but with a little bleat, a small voice of need, and his mum instinctively knew what it was that he needed. Dot unbuttoned her night gown and held his little face against her breast. His greedy mouth latched on and Dot bit down on her lip, it bloody hurt! She smiled though. In spite of the discomfort, she was feeding her little boy! She felt like a grown-up; better than that, she felt like a mum.

'I love you, little Solomon.' It slipped out almost unconsciously, but once she had spoken it out loud, it seemed to make perfect sense: she would call him Solomon. It didn't matter what her mum and dad thought, it didn't matter what anyone thought. Anyway, they were going to Australia and there they could be anything and anyone they wanted to be. It was to be a glorious new beginning; maybe they *would* drink pineapple juice and swim at a beach after all. She smiled and placed her finger inside his tiny hand. He gripped it with his whole fist.

'You are strong, my little man!' She noticed his fingers – long and tapered, piano player's fingers maybe, just like his beautiful daddy. His rosebud mouth continued to suckle, until milk trickled from the side of his mouth and over his curved cheek. His rounded tummy rose and fell as he slept deeply, still gripping his mum's finger.

Later that day, Dot was moved to a little room adjacent to the nursery wing. It felt strange to have her own space, but wonderful to be able to see baby Solomon regularly throughout the day. Her body felt a bit more back to normal; her stomach still carried a post-pregnancy bulge and her bra struggled to contain her swollen chest, but the bone-deep ache from giving birth had almost disappeared.

It was almost simultaneous, when Solomon wanted to feed, she would leak milk, as though she was programmed for his every need. The times when she could hold and feed him were the highlight of her day. Watching him fall asleep against her skin was a joy that she could never have envisaged. To feel the weight of his tiny body against her shoulder was the best feeling in the world. She hated it when the time came to put him in his little bassinet so that he could be wheeled off to the nursery.

When Solomon was not quite three days old, Dot rummaged in her suitcase and removed the brown paper packet that contained her material. *'I shall give it a lot of thought and try and make something worthy of it, something that will always remind me of today.'*

She lay the length of sky-blue drill flat on the table and planned out the shape for a romper suit. Her skilful dressmaker's fingers cut the fabric, using a little vest as a vague template. She pressed the material to her face and inhaled its strange scent; it reminded her of her old life, when she had been a happy shop girl, working in Selfridges and going home to her mum's for her tea. It made her think of the wonderful day she and Sol had spent together when he bought the fabric, and it made her think of her mate Barb, from whom she now felt so remote. Dot folded the seams and used tiny stitches to secure the pieces together. She took extra care, making sure each stitch was equally spaced and precisely the same length; she wanted him to look lovely when they arrived in Australia. Dot smiled at the irony: this was the first 'Clover Original'. She worked diligently until the early hours and on Solomon's fourth day on the planet, his new outfit was ready.

Sister Kyna had sent word to the nursery, asking Dot to visit the office. She walked purposefully along the corridor, almost looking forward to the exchange; Dot was a woman with a plan.

'Please sit, Dot.' Sister Kyna indicated the chair as though there was a choice of where to perch.

'You look well.'

'I feel it, thank you.'

'Good, good.' The nun paused and removed her glasses. 'There are a couple of formalities, Dot, that we need to take care of today. We need to give the child a name.'

Dot smiled at the thought of 'the child'. His name was Solomon, her little Solomon, bringer of peace.

'And the good news is that we have had a development with regard to his adoption. A Canadian couple, based in London – a university professor and his wife, no less – have agreed to take the baby.'

Dot coughed to clear her throat and took a deep breath. 'I do have a name for him, actually, but as far as the adoption is concerned, I'm afraid there's been a change of plan. He's not up for adoption. Can you tell that couple thank you very much, but he's staying with his mum.'

Sister Kyna fiddled with her spectacles and ran her tongue over her thin lips. 'How so, Dot? What has so changed in your circumstance that you are able to keep the boy?'

'It's simple, really. I never wanted to give him up, never, and I hoped I'd find a way around it and I have!' Dot grinned, feeling like she had cheated the system. 'I'm going to take the ten-pound ticket. We are going to Australia!' Dot lifted her chin, determined. Susan was right, women looked after babies on their own all the time, even women like Dot.

Sister Kyna was silent for a few seconds, then she smirked

192

and gave a small giggle that quickly developed into a full-blown laugh. She fought for control and wheezed slightly, then coughed into her bunched-up fist and patted her chest. 'Oh dear, oh dear, Lord give me strength. Is that it? Is that the big plan – to take the ten-pound ticket?'

Dot felt her cheeks flush and her stomach flip with nerves; this wasn't how she had planned the exchange. It had happened very differently in her head.

'Yes, we are going to go to Australia. No one's going to take him away from me.' This time her eyes were on the floor and her chin dipped against her chest.

'I am afraid, Miss Simpson, that it is not quite that straight-forward. Firstly, you willingly signed the papers – legal documents that placed the care and responsibility for the child with the Church. Secondly, it is our absolute belief that the boy will be better placed with a university professor and his lovely wife than in your care—'

'What d'you mean? How can that be right? Who cares what the bloke does for a living, I'm his mum! What can be better for him than being with his mum?' Dot fought to control her pitch and her breathing. She needed to remain calm to get this sorted out.

'He will be given the best education and guidance that money can buy; he will travel and have a rich life. You cannot hope to compete with that—'

'That's just rubbish! I shouldn't have to compete! I'm his mum. It doesn't matter how much money they've got, that's not what makes you happy. I grew up without any money!'

'Yes, and look what has happened to your life. Hardly a glowing example, is it?'

Dot was aware that she was crying. She was angry and upset. She dashed the tears away and continued. 'Anyway, it doesn't matter what you say or what you think, my mind's made up. I don't care what anyone thinks, I'm taking my baby and we are going to Australia. I'm taking that ten-pound ticket!'

Sister Kyna replaced her glasses and paused before delivering the final blow.

'I'm afraid there is no ten-pound ticket.'

'Yes there is! Don't you lie to me! I know there is. Susan's taken it, I know she has!'

'That is true, she did. Maybe I should be more specific; there is no ten-pound ticket for people like you or for babies like yours.'

There was a second of silence while the words permeated Dot's brain. 'What d'you mean, not for babies like mine? He's perfect.' Her mouth twisted from all the crying.

'I think you know to what I am referring. Let's not make things more awkward than they need to be; don't make me spell it out. I will tell you this: you are lucky to find a couple willing to take a child like that, many babies of his sort are not as fortunate. This couple will be taking your child and there is nothing that you can do about it. My advice is to distance yourself from the boy over the next few days, which might make his leaving a little easier to bear.'

Dot's heart hammered, she fought for breath. Feeling light-headed, she gripped the arms of the chair to fight off the faint that threatened.

'You can't have him! I won't let you take him, I won't! No one is taking my boy! Anyway, them forms don't count, I had my fingers crossed the whole time! So it doesn't bloody count!' This Dot screamed.

Sister Kyna ran her hand over her face. 'Oh, dear God, don't be ridiculous! Fingers crossed indeed, I've heard it all now!'

Sister Mary had heard Dot's shouts and now opened the office door.

'Is everything all right, Sister Kyna?' The young nun stared at Dot, who looked like a wild animal about to pounce.

'Everything is fine, thank you, Sister. You may escort Miss Simpson back to her room.'

Sister Mary helped Dot to stand.

'You ain't having him! I swear to God, you ain't taking Solomon from me!' Her face crumpled as her legs folded under her.

Sister Kyna unscrewed the lid of her fountain pen and cocked her head to one side. 'What was the name again?' she enquired, as though she was asking the date, calm and unmoved by Dot's distress.

Tears blocked Dot's nostrils and throat and smeared her lips; her nose dripped. She spoke with the garbled slur of a drunk. 'Slolomon... His name is Sollollomon.'

Sister Kyna wrote 'Simon' in the allocated space. It was close enough.

* * *

Dot unwrapped the yellow knitted blanket in which he was swaddled and removed the miniature terry nappy, held in place by an enormous safety pin with a blue cover on the tip; blue for boys, pink for girls. She laid him in her lap and ran her finger over his tiny feet, gently pinching each of his ten perfect toes and around his little knees, up over his tum and down along his arms. His tiny fingers snatched at the air and she lifted him to her face and kissed his little nose and closed eyes. She snuggled her face against the fold under his chin and kissed all over his face, working her way around to each ear. Whenever she considered the fact that her time with him was coming to an end, she could not breathe, quite literally could not take a breath and so she tried to put it out of her mind.

Dot rocked her baby to sleep and held him close while he dozed, ignoring the nursery rule that baby must be placed back in the bassinet when asleep. She cared little for their rules and gave a look that defied anyone to try and remove him.

'I want us to run away, Solomon. I want to wrap you up and run far away, but I don't even have the bus fare to Southend, what can I do? I can't sleep outside, not with you. And I'm frightened that if they find me, you'll be taken off me and then I don't know where you'll end up. At least this way, my little love, I know you are going to someone that will give you a lovely life.' She kissed his head. 'I want you to know, little man, that you have changed my life in the most amazing way. I might not get to be your mum forever, but being your mum for a couple of weeks is something I will never forget. I had you all to meself for nine whole months and it was such a precious time, darling. There was just you and me and no one to disturb us. You are beautiful, Solomon, and I want you to know that even though he's gone now, your dad, you were made in love, real deep love, even if it was only for a little while. I want you to lock these words away in your head and think about them as you grow up. You are going to be a big, strong boy and you'll have a wonderful life, but try and remember me, Solomon, try and remember these lovely days that we've had together, my love. I know I will, for always.'

Dot fed Solomon and held him against her chest while she rubbed small circles on his back, trying to wind him. She continued to whisper into his ear, desperately hoping that her words would reach his subconscious and be there for recall whenever he needed them.

Sister Mary knocked on her door and poked her head inside the room. Dot knew what the young nun was going to say before she spoke and her tears fell in fat, hot drops down her cheeks. She felt suffocated.

'The Dubois family will be here in two hours to take baby Simon,' Sister Mary began. 'If you could get him ready and wheel him down to the gate house, that would be for the best. Or we could get someone else to take him down for you, if you are not up to it?' It clearly wasn't the first time that she had delivered this speech.

An image of Gracie's mother came into focus; the stoic, dignified manner with which she had performed the last duty for her little girl.

'No, I'll do it.'

The two hours seemed to pass in minutes. Dot bathed her boy, cradling him in one crooked arm as he kicked in the warm water. She gently massaged his skin with the muslin cloth and covered him in talc before putting his nappy and rubber pants in place and slipping him into the white babygro as instructed. She fed him one last time and held his face so close to hers that when he breathed out she breathed in, taking his breath down into her lungs.

The fancy Silver Cross pram stood outside her door. She placed him gently on its tiny mattress, where there was the slightest indent from all the other babies that had been laid down there before him – Gracie, Sophie and hundreds like them. She tucked the small blanket around the edges so that he wouldn't feel any draught. Pulling the hood up, she gazed at his sleeping form, taking mental pictures that she would store away for a lifetime. Dot placed the blue romper suit the colour of St Lucian sky at the base of the pram and set off along the corridor and across the gravel.

She didn't notice the heavily pregnant girl who raked the gravel outside the main entrance, she didn't notice anything, but instead concentrated on putting one foot in front of the other and staring at the gate house that grew larger with each step. Stopping to adjust Solomon's blanket, bringing it up to his chin, she bent low inside the pram. 'Be brave, my little one, be brave. It'll be okay, mate, just you wait and see.' Solomon did not stir.

Dot knocked and the side door was opened. She pushed the pram through and found herself in what resembled a waiting room. A couple of functional, office-type chairs stood against the wall, otherwise the place was bare except for a large oil painting of His Holiness Pope John XXIII. There was a door in the corner and to the left of that a grill with a small sliding cover. Sister Mary reached out to take the handle of the pram. Dot caught her wrist, she wanted five more minutes. But then she realised that she would always want five more minutes and she released her and nodded.

'Make sure they take his little suit,' she whispered hoarsely, every word taking a supreme effort.

Sister Mary swiftly turned the pram, approached the door in the corner and gave a small knock. It was opened immediately.

Even though she had promised herself that she wouldn't, Dot slid the little door on the grill and pushed her face up to it. She saw a man and a woman, older than her, probably in their late twenties; they were smartly dressed and smiling. Professor Dubois had his arms around his wife's shoulders and was gripping her in anticipation; she in turn reached up and placed her palm over the back of his hand. Mrs Dubois wore a cameo brooch at the neck of her blouse, the collar of which peeked from beneath her camel-coloured jersey. Sister Kyna stood behind them with her hands clasped in front of her, looking very pleased with herself. Dot felt a wave of hatred for this woman who called herself a servant of God.

Mrs Dubois placed both her hands under her chin as the pram was pushed into the room and Dot watched as her eyes filled with tears. Dot's own eyes were strangely dry. Sister Mary lifted the baby from the pram and handed him to the woman. Dot swallowed a wave of sickness.

'Oh, Simon! Oh, there you are, look at you!' Mrs Dubois raised his little face to hers and kissed him.

Please don't cover up my kisses, Dot thought. *Remember what I said to you, Solomon, remember that I love you, remember me.* She felt a sharp pain in her stomach as though she had been cut. For the first time in nearly seven months, Dot did not ache for the man who had abandoned her; his face no longer appeared behind her eyelids with every blink. His image had been replaced with that of her baby boy, and there her son's face would stay for the rest of her life.

Mrs Dubois walked towards the grill. Dot shrank backwards,

she didn't want to be seen. The woman spoke into the space, holding Dot's son close to her chest. 'It sounds so inadequate, but thank you, from the bottom of our hearts, thank you! I'd be happy to send you photos or a letter—'

Dot pulled the grill shut and sat on the little chair in the corner. There was no point – as if she'd be able to receive photos! Her mum and dad would go berserk. She felt strangely detached, as though she was floating near the ceiling, looking down on herself and watching proceedings from on high. Even though she could no longer see what was happening next door, she could hear the loudest of the coos and exclamations. When her son began to cry, she stuffed her fingers into her ears and placed her head on her knees. She wanted it to be over.

Some minutes later, Sister Mary appeared with the pram. 'You may take it back to the nursery, Dot.'

Like an automaton, Dot stood on wobbly legs. She laid her hand against the empty mattress that was still slightly warm before straightening up. She pushed the pram outside and onto the gravel. She looked straight ahead and tried not to think about the car that was waiting to whisk her son away to a new life. A better life, a better life than someone like her could ever give him. As the door closed behind her, she heard the unmistakeable, instantly recognisable sound of her son's cry. He was crying again, fresh tears, and there was nothing she could do.

Dot crossed the gravel slowly and made it back to the confines of the nursery wing, where Sister Agnes was waiting.

'Here, Dot, let me take that from you.' The kindly Sister reached over to take the pram handle and in doing so, dislodged the blanket to reveal a small corner of summer's day blue.

Dot pushed her fingers below the cover and pulled out the romper suit with its perfect hand-stitched seams. She sank down onto the floor and covered her face with the small garment. The sound she emitted was part wail, part sob, like an animal drowning in her own tears.

Sister Agnes knelt on the floor by her side and stroked her hair. 'Shhh. It'll all be okay, Dot, it will all be okay.'

'I want my baby! I want him back. Please, please help me. I want him back!'

'Goodness, what is all this noise in aid of?' Sister Kyna stood by the back door, her smile, as usual, fixed in place.

Dot reached behind and, using the wall, levered herself into an upright position. With the romper suit in her hand, she pointed at Sister Kyna. 'This *noise* is because my heart is broken. Broken! I made him this, it was the one thing he could have had from me, the one thing! But you didn't give it to them, you knew—'

'To be quite honest with you, Miss Simpson, do you really think that a couple like Professor Dubois and his wife would want to place their son in a garment like *that*?'

Their son... Their son! Dot was silent for some seconds, gathering her strength, ordering her thoughts. She spoke slowly. 'I don't know what a couple like that would think, cos I ain't no university professor, but I do know this. I may not have any education, but I do have a life, I've had a life! You hide away up here, Sister Kyna, passing judgement on every girl that steps inside the doors, girls that need your help, girls that have no choices, girls like me. And yet you can't pass judgement, cos you don't know anything! You talk about things that you have no idea about, things like love

201

and pregnancy. I feel sorry for you, I do. You'll never know what it's like to lie in the arms of the man you love on a blanket in front of a fire and feel safe and happy. You'll never dance in front of Etta James! You've been so horrible to me, and if it wasn't for Sister Agnes, this place would be hell on bloody earth. I hope you're right about your god being a god of forgiveness, cos when you step up for judgement, you are going to need a lot of forgiveness. You are one wicked cow!'

Sister Kyna was not used to being addressed in this way. Her tongue stuck to the roof of her mouth and she looked ruffled, thrown off balance. When she found her voice, there was only the slightest tremor to betray her. 'Sister Agnes, would you please be so kind as to help Miss Simpson pack her things and escort her to the main gate. She has more than outstayed her welcome.'

An hour later, the unlikely pair of friends stood at the gate of Lavender Hill Lodge. Sister Agnes looked straight ahead and delivered her words into the middle distance. Anyone looking on might have judged from her straight back, clasped hands and remote stance that she was delivering a rebuke, or at the very least a cold farewell.

'I want you to try and remember that this is not the end of your life, Dot.'

'It feels like it.' Dot looked up with swollen eyes.

'Of that I am sure, dear. Of that I am sure. But trust me when I say that you have a lot of years ahead of you and you must fill them in a positive way. Don't turn your back on God through anger; he is there for you if and when you need him. You have brought a beautiful baby boy into this world and the gift you gave to that family makes you forever an angel in their hearts. To give a child such a start is an incredible thing and you are an incredible girl.'

'He was beautiful, wasn't he?'

'Yes, my dear, he really was. And it has been my privilege to be part of your journey. I wish you nothing but the very best of luck, love and happiness, Dot Simpson.'

Dot nodded through her tears and grasped Sister Agnes's hand. 'Thank you. I won't ever forget you.'

'Do you know, Dot, I rather hope that you do.'

Dot sat on the bus that took her to Waterloo station with her suitcase wedged between her feet. It felt strange to be in the outside world. Lavender Hill Lodge had been quiet, almost removed from the real world, and the shouts, beeps and engine growls of everyday life made her jump. She was out of practice being in a crowd, but at least she was anonymous; that suited her just fine.

Boarding the 278, nearly two hours after leaving Battersea, Dot gazed through the bus window as familiar landmarks rushed by. She stared at the Merchant's House, counted the steps up which she had trotted some seven months earlier. *'I thought he might have informed you. He is not coming back. He's gone home for good.'* It was quite a novelty for Dot to be able to recall his mother's words and feel nothing but numb. She now knew there were far bigger things in the world to be lamented.

Standing at the end of Narrow Street, she hesitated, burying her chin in her scarf to ward off the November chill. These were the streets that she had wandered her whole life, she knew them in all seasons and could navigate them with her eyes closed, and yet today she felt like an imposter. The girl that used to play stick in the mud with the kids from the neighbouring streets, the teenager that used to trot along the cobbles in her mum's best shoes, stolen for a night out – she no longer existed. It was as if a veil had been lifted from her eyes and she now saw the harsh reality of her life in every grubby, soot-filled corner that she looked at. Truth was, she had rather liked seeing the world through the flimsy gauze that had diluted the grime, watered down the poverty and smudged the disadvantage until it all seemed quite comfortable. Now that it had gone, she was left with the stark truth of life in Ropemakers Fields.

Picking up her suitcase, she turned into the street that meant home, or at least had used to. Nothing much had changed. The clever boy from Number 29 was still driving his pretty little Mini. The same street lights flickered into life as dusk bit on the day. The same dogs behind the same doors barked at the sound of her footsteps on the pavement and the same voices shouted 'Shudddup, bloody dog!' as they did several times a day.

Mrs Harrison was in situ, as if no time had passed at all. She still displayed the sign that made Dot's stomach shrink. A sign that meant there would be no ten-pound ticket for someone like her, for a baby like hers. She shook her head to rid herself of the image; she couldn't think about him, not now.

'All right, Dot? You're back then.'

Dot nodded.

'How was the farm?'

Dot stared at their neighbour and walked by without speaking, too broken to even pretend.

She reached out with her bunched-up fist and took a deep breath. Was there any other option, anywhere she could go? Anywhere? *Think, Dot, think…* The answer was no, there was not. Closing her eyes, she took a second before she knocked on the door and waited.

The door to the back room opened, flooding the hallway with its light. It was Dee. She peered through the glass and started jumping up and down. 'It's Dot! It's Dot! She's come back from the farm! It's Dot!'

Her mum bustled into the hall and shushed her youngest to one side. 'All right, Dee, calm down, give her a bit of space, she's had a long journey.'

Yes, I have, thought Dot. All the way to hell and back again, miles and miles...

Her mum opened the door and the two stared at each other, strangers now. Joan's face crumpled, it hurt to see the hollow eyes of her wayward daughter – she looked like an old woman. She raised her arms to hug her eldest, but Dot turned away, out of reach, and instead Joan retrieved her suitcase.

'Come on in, love.'

Dee was so excited, firing questions at her sister as she pogoed up and down on the spot. 'Did you get me a present, Dot? Did you drive a tractor? Mum said you might! What were the names of the farmer's kids? I know all me sixes, go on, test me on any six and I know the answer! Six sixes are thirty-six, eight sixes are forty-eight, three sixes are eighteen! See, and I can do them in any order! And I know my fours and fives and half of my sevens! One seven is seven, two sevens are fourteen. Look at my skirt, it's joined to my vest!' Dee stopped jumping and pulled up her roll-neck jumper to reveal a tartan mini-skirt that was indeed joined onto a vest.

Dot smiled at her baby sister. Dee had grown taller and was sporting a large tooth in the front where there had previously been a gap. 'You've got big.'

'I know! I'm the fourth tallest in me class. It goes Alice McFadden, Josephine Ward, Anne Smith and then me! She used her little cupped palm to indicate heights along the wall.

Dot was exhausted trying to keep up with her.

'D'you want something to eat?' Her mum cut in. It was and always would be her first thought. *Can I feed her?* Dot understood this, it had been her first thought too whenever she held her son. Dot shook her head, unable to even consider something as mundane as food.

'Take your coat off then…' Dot half expected her to add '*if you're staying*', as if there were any other option. Her mum reached out and fumbled with the top button of her daughter's coat, as if she was a toddler. Dot brushed away her hand and slid her arms through the sleeves, then hung it on the peg. She felt like a stranger in her family home, a guest who was waiting for an invitation to venture beyond the hallway.

Dee pointed at her sister and laughed with one hand clamped over her mouth. 'Dot's got wet boobies! Wet booooobies!'

Dot looked down and noticed the two pale, wet circles that sat on the front of her shirt. 'It's his feed time.' Two fat tears snaked their way into her mouth.

Joan looked as if she had been struck. She gasped. *A little boy then.* She placed her hand over her mouth; it wasn't just a bump any more, a condition to be hidden, it was a person, her grandson.

Lying on the bed in her little room, Dot stroked the skin of her throat that only hours earlier had felt the weight of her son. She pictured the excited hands of Mrs Dubois, fluttering at her neck in anticipation, waiting to be wrapped around her boy. The same hands which would bathe, feed and change him tonight, would hold his hand when he woke from a bad dream, would clap with delight when he cut his first tooth, said his first word, took his first step. Dot lay with her face in the pillow and let her tears sink into the feathers. She didn't care if she never woke up.

The next morning, with her chest bound tightly with cotton wool pads and strips of muslin, Dot crept down the stairs and into the back room. The last time she had sat within those four walls it had been to hear her fate, the great plan to pack her off to Battersea. What was it they had said? *'Get it adopted out and we'll say no more about it.'* Maybe she should have fought harder. It didn't matter now; she was beaten and broken, with rocks of grief that lined her stomach and sat at the base of her brain, swirling like ugly sediment, filtering each and every swallow and thought. She did not know it was possible to feel this sad and for your heart to carry on beating; she wished it would stop.

Her dad swung into the room and stopped suddenly when he saw her. His look of pity told her how shocked he was at the sight of her. 'Hello, Dot, you're back then,' he mumbled as he delved into his little tin for a pre-rolled fag.

She nodded.

'Are you…?' he began, swallowing hard.

What did he have to feel nervous about? She waited for the rest of the question – *Hurt? Devastated? Destroyed? Angry? Defeated? Heartbroken? I'm all of them, Dad, I'm all of them.*

'Sit down, Dot.' Her mum broke the tension, putting a plate of poached eggs on toast on the table before going back to the kitchen to make tea.

Dot sat at the table and held the cutlery, staring at the plate as though she couldn't quite remember what came next.

Joan plonked the cup and saucer down. 'Not hungry, love?'

Dot stared at her. What did it matter if she was hungry? Her grief blocked her throat as surely as any stopper, making the swallowing of food impossible.

She took small sips of tea. Her mum and dad were in the kitchen; she couldn't make out all of the conversation, but she clearly heard her dad utter the words 'Fucking doolally', and for once in his miserable life he was right.

Dot spent the best part of ten days lying on her bed, unable to converse, eat or look anyone in the eye without dissolving into a shaking mess. Her weight plummeted. She found it hard to get comfortable on the mattress, with the sharp bones of her hips and buttocks jutting against the base. Her breasts, at first engorged and painful, leaked their wasted product onto muslin cloths and an old flannel until eventually the milk stopped, dried up. This was for Dot a whole new level of distress, this was the moment in her mind that she finally stopped being Solomon's mum. She had replayed a fantasy over and over in her head, that the Dubois would turn up at 38 Rope-makers Fields and hand her a carry-cot, in it would be her boy, dressed in his blue romper suit and wailing for a feed. He would cry until she nestled him against her and all would be right with the world as she cradled his dark curls in her palm. Now that she had stopped producing milk, she knew that this could never happen.

One morning, when Dot had finally dragged herself downstairs and was listlessly filling the old kettle at the sink, her dad came in from the garden. The two were still awkward in each other's company. She doubted she would ever be able to erase the words that he had launched at her all those months ago, tiny bombs that had exploded in her head and heart, damaging both beyond repair. She gathered her dressing gown around her body, as though it offered protection, and fixed her eyes on the floor.

'I found this.' He smiled as he stretched out his arm.

Dot looked up towards his raised hand. In it he held the giant conch shell that her grandad had given her when she was little; she thought it had long gone.

'I must have shoved it in the privy years ago, it practically fell on me bonce!' He laughed, trying to elicit a response.

Dot didn't react, though only a few months ago it would have sparked a whole stream of banter between the two of them.

'*Might have knocked some sense into you, Dad!*'

'*Cheeky mare!*'

But that was before. Dot doubted that she would find anything funny again.

Forgetting about the kettle that now whistled on the stove, she took the shell from his hand and, cradling it to her chest, slunk back to the quiet confines of her bedroom.

Folding her dressing gown over her knees, she placed the shell on her lap, running her hand over its contours, stopping at the little nodes and crevices that pitted its surface. Turning it over, she placed her fingers inside the smooth edge. Its pale pink lustre looked manufactured; it was so beautiful, perfect. She pushed her hand inside and tried to imagine what creature might dwell in such a beautiful home, a creature which was apparently considered good eating in some parts of the world, if you had a plate big enough.

Dot shook her hair back over her shoulder, cupped the shell in both hands and tentatively raised it to her ear. Closing her eyes, she listened – and there it was! The rushing of the wind over the ocean, the sound of waves breaking against the rocks and the lapping of the smaller waves against the shore. She could hear the sea! She sat for some minutes, straining to hear more – maybe the people in the sea, or people on the beach, a certain someone on the beach. And then it occurred to her, the most logical thing: if she could hear the sea and possibly the beach, then maybe someone on that beach could hear her. Like a mollusc telephone, connecting her across the miles to the land of pineapple juice and callaloo.

She smiled as she pulled the shell round until it hovered near her mouth. Then she spoke quietly into it.

'Hello… I found my shell, it was in the old privy that me dad stores all his rubbish in. I never thought I'd see it again. I've got something to tell you: I had a baby. I know that's putting it blunt, but what else should I say? That's the fact, I had a baby, a little boy, and he's called Simon. Actually, I called him Solomon, but he's known as Simon now. He's not with me. I had to give him away, to a couple who have money and can do right by him; the man's a university professor, clever. I know Simon will have a good life, I know that's true, but I didn't want to let him go and I get this pain in my heart every time I think about him. He was so beautiful. He looked just like you.'

The conch shell meant finally, Dot had someone to talk to. She did her best to avoid having to interact with anyone else.

She skulked around the tiny terrace like a miscreant, creeping from bed to bathroom to kitchen and then back to bedroom, hoping she wouldn't bump into her parents. The only person that appeared unaffected was little Dee. She would boldly enter her sister's room after school and quote her latest times table at her. Mostly it didn't matter to Dee whether Dot responded or not, she was just glad of the audience. But finally, one evening after she'd faultlessly recounted her 'eights' and still hadn't got any reaction, Dee said, 'You look right poorly, Dot. You don't reckon it's them tonsils back again, do ya?'

And then there was Barb. Dot was home for a full two weeks before word got back to Barb that she had returned from Kent. The evening her friend's bubbly tones drifted up the stairs and under her door, Dot pulled the bedspread over her head and willed her to go away. She wasn't ready; she didn't know if she would ever be. But her mum had other ideas.

'Go right on up, Barb, she's full of cold, but she'll be pleased to see you, I'm sure.'

Dot counted two lies. What did it matter, two more to add to the piles of deceit that multiplied and lodged in every crevice of her mind.

Barb knocked and simultaneously twisted the Bakelite handle until she was stood by her friend's bed. She was a little nervous; it had been a while. 'Hello, mate! Long time no see!'

Dot pulled the cover under her chin and tried out a small smile. The moment the two started chatting, it was as if they hadn't been apart. It was the sign of true friendship, being able to pick up where you left off, no matter how much time had passed.

'Jesus, Dot! You look bloody awful, your mum said you had a cold, but blimey, you look like death! What did they have you doing on that bleeding farm, pulling a plough?'

'Something like that. I can't seem to shake it off.' In those words lay a kernel of truth.

'You gotta get better for Saturday night, we're going out!' Barb clapped her hands together with excitement. 'Wally's mate's in a band and they've got a gig up town, we have to go!'

'I'm not sure. I'll see.'

'No, Dot! Not "I'll see"; the answer is yes! We are going – I've really missed you and we are going, even if I have to drag you there on one of your bloody tractors.'

Dot groaned.

'They're really good, it's Wally's mate Roger who he met on the sheet metal, they're called the Detours and they're fab, so let's get dolled up and make a night of it. We'll pick you up at six. And make sure you wash your bloody hair, you look like an old tramp!' Barb blew her friend a kiss before departing.

Dot hated the idea of having to leave the house, but similarly the idea of spending time with people who would treat her as they always had was quite nice, people that only knew the old Dot. It was something she was going to have to get used to, the fact that a beautiful boy existed in this world because of her and no one would ever know about it. He was her little secret.

Saturday night arrived and it felt strange to wash the grease from her locks and pull on clothes other than pyjamas, a bit like shedding her protective layer. Dot was shocked at how much weight she had lost. The side zip on her dog-tooth-check pencil skirt pulled up with ease; she remembered buying it at the market when her biggest worry had been how to best show off her curves. She looked at her profile in the bathroom mirror, ran her hand over her flat stomach. Could it really have contained a little person, or did she dream him? She wondered sometimes.

Reg was at the bottom of the stairs. 'You look lovely, you really do.' He smiled as he wound a woollen scarf around his neck.

She tried to respond, breathed in to speak, but the banal words of thanks or other minutiae refused to pop into her mouth. She could only envisage shouting at him, *They took my baby, I have nothing and you made me do it!* It was better for both that she simply gave a little nod.

Roger and his band picked Dot up in a white van. As soon as she climbed in, she wished that she had stayed at home. The air was thick with cigarette smoke and their banter only irritated her. It felt juvenile and so very insignificant to be laughing at rubbish when she was grieving. Roger smiled at her in the rear-view mirror; rather than excite her, it made her feel sick. She could only picture Sol and the way he had looked at her and the way it had made her feel. And then she pictured the bright blue eyes of her baby boy. She looked away. How could she begin to explain that she wasn't like other girls. Not only was she uninterested, she was broken.

The band hauled their equipment round the back of the nightclub while the others found an empty booth inside. Dot tried to smile and join in, but it was exhausting.

Wally sidled up to her as she loitered alone. 'Not dancing?'

Dot shook her head. No, no dancing for her.

'Wha'ssamatta? Everyone likes a dance. Come on, I'll take you for a spin.' He tried to grab her hand, which she quickly buried in her lap.

She ignored him. Stupid, idiot Wally. She willed him to go away.

'Not talking to me? Come on, Dot, cheer up, it may never happen! Barb told me you was a laugh, but all I can see is a miserable-faced cow that won't join in!'

Dot felt her tears welling. Again she shook her head. How many more times was she to find herself backed into a corner? Why couldn't people just let her be, hadn't she suffered enough? She wanted to shout at Wally, *Actually it has happened. I gave my baby away eighteen days ago.* Eighteen days, that was all. She wanted to grab the microphone and shout it to the crowd! Maybe then Wally and everyone else might leave her alone.

Dot gathered up her bag and her cardigan. 'Tell Barb I'll see her soon. I've got to go.'

'Don't go! I'm only pulling your leg!'

She stood outside the club and could hear the compere announcing the bloke who had eyed her up in the back of his van. 'With his band the Detours, it's Roger Daltrey!' The band started to play their loud music and Dot pulled her collar up; she didn't think the Detours would get very far with a racket like that.

Dot sat on the bus and wondered if she would ever go back to how she was before. It was as if getting pregnant meant that she had left the queue of life and everyone had moved up a space, so that her place had disappeared. And no matter how hard she tried or how polite she was, no one was going to budge up and let her back in.

Back home and in the refuge of her bed, Dot placed the shell on her pillow.

'I've had a rubbish night. I was thinking on the bus on the way home how messed up everything is. You don't know about our boy, I don't know where you are or where he is and our boy will know nothing about us – how strange is that? We are three people that'll be connected forever, but I'm the only one that knows it. Not that there is an "us", I realise that. Never was an 'us', and that makes me so sad. Goodnight, darling.'

* * *

Dot left the main gates of Bryant and May with the papers sorted. They would write to her when there was an opening, which would probably be in the New Year, after the Christmas break – a different shift from her previous one, a different job. Night work. She figured that might suit her. She could creep out when most people were creeping in, keeping her interaction with the rest of the human race to a minimum.

Since returning home from Lavender Hill Lodge, she had got into the habit of not speaking and it was harder to break than she might have imagined. As far as her parents were concerned, being mute effectively meant being deaf as well, and they spoke freely in front of her, as though she couldn't hear them.

Joan busied herself at the head of the table while Reg sat waiting and Dee played with her metal spinning top on the tablecloth, fascinated as the circles and specks turned to lines as it whirred and fell over, as if exhausted by the exertion.

216

'It'll do her good to get back to work. Won't it, love?' Joan addressed this to her daughter as though she were a bit simple, then cut the buttery crust of the apple pie with the dishing-up spoon and dolloped large helpings into the four bowls.

Reg spun his spoon between finger and thumb, waiting impatiently for the custard to tumble and his afters to be served. 'Let's hope she's got a bit more to say for herself there than she has here, or they won't put up with her!'

'Leave it, Reg…'

'Christ, can't a man express his opinion at his own dinner table under his own roof? Is this how we have to live now? Treading on bleeding eggshells when she's in earshot? Dinner times used to be fun, d'you remember that? Laughing and chatting. I can't live like this, I really can't!'

'For God's sake, Reg!'

'Don't shout at me, Joan, this ain't my fault, the fact that you lost your job an' we've been put through the mill. It's cos she wouldn't listen, we told her it would end in disaster, but she didn't bloody listen! It ain't my fault!'

Joan threw the apple pie spoon down on the table and a large gob of custard splattered against the cotton cloth. She placed her hand against her forehead and rubbed at her temples.

'What? I'm only saying the truth. It ain't my bloody fault she's come back a bit soft in the bleeding head, is it?'

Dee started to cry. She didn't like hearing her mum and dad shouting at each other like this, it made her tummy feel scared. Dot scraped the chair away from the table and shut the door behind her; she didn't fancy apple pie after all. She climbed the stairs, taking care not to tread on the steps that creaked; she wanted to be silent, she wanted to be invisible, she wanted to disappear.

As Dot lay down on her bed, names of girls she knew from school and from work flashed through her mind, girls who had slept with loads of blokes and not been caught out. An image of Susan Montgomery popped into her head: *'Tits and India, here I come!'* It was so unfair. Those girls still attended communion, dressed demurely and got away with it, living however they chose and with their reputations intact. She, on the other hand, even though she'd only slept with the one man, a man she had loved, the man she was going to marry, was forced to carry a label and was open to ridicule because she had got unlucky. It was so bloody unfair. For the first time in a long time, Dot prayed, though not to a benevolent God – she'd stopped trusting in him a while ago; this was more like popping a note into a glass bottle and casting on the ocean to see if she got a reply.

She closed her eyes. 'Please, give me a way out of here. I'll go mad if I have to stay under this roof. I will, I'll go bloody mad.'

A couple of days later, Dot ventured out. She jumped on her old bus and rode the familiar route to the West End, then wandered along the streets with her hands deep in her pockets, watching shoeless assistants in shop windows prepare their Christmas displays. They positioned fat-bellied Santas and sacks of foil-wrapped gifts, placed fake icicles on invisible wires and sprinkled the whole space with silver and blue glitter. She had never felt less like celebrating Christmas in her whole life. She wished she could go to sleep and wake up in January – or May might be better.

She found herself outside Selfridges and pushed through the revolving door that had made her and Sol giggle back at the beginning of the year. The counters were decorated with silver tinsel and tiny bells, miniature Christmas trees with minute glass baubles. The whole store looked beautiful and smelt of baked apples. Dot meandered among the counters, spritzing Chanel on her scarf, admiring Dents leather gloves in the palest blue and fondling French lace handkerchiefs that were far too good to use.

She took the escalator and without thinking about it found herself in the nursery department. She studied the sturdy prams and matching carry-cots filled with hand-knitted blankets and soft toys. Changing mats with matching nappy buckets were set among stacks of terry-towelling nappies. Nursing bras for mothers with natty little flaps that folded down for feeding, rocking chairs with strategically placed cushions 'for comfortable nursing' – they had it all. Dot stood next to a display of matinée coats, hats and matching booties, all with delicate white ribbon trim, tied in tiny bows. She was surrounded by pregnant women whose anxious husbands hovered, and women with well-wrapped newborns in strollers, seeking dummies, feeding bottles and sterilising units.

'Can I help you at all, madam?' The young girl smiled.

Dot did a double-take to check she was talking to her. 'Oh, just looking thanks.'

'Well, if you need any assistance, I shall be over by the counter.'

Dot smiled; she had been similarly trained on how to approach not encroach, assist but not push. The girl had got it spot on.

'My little boy's at home...' She didn't know why she said it, it just popped out.

'Aaah, lovely. How old?'

'He's nearly six weeks now.' Six weeks that had passed so quickly.

'Well, you look very well on it! Is he a good sleeper?'

'Is he a good sleeper?' Dot repeated the question as her tears fell. She stared at the young girl, who looked aghast, highly embarrassed by the display. She had been told to expect 'high emotion' from some young or expectant mothers, but this was off the scale.

Dot sobbed. 'I don't know, I really don't know. He's called Simon now.'

'Can I call someone for you?' The girl held Dot's arm, she was sweet, sincere.

Dot thought about the one person who might have been able to make things better, the one person who had caused the whole sorry mess to start with and she cried even harder.

'No, no, but thank you.'

With her head bent, she took the escalator and ventured out into the cold.

Christmas Eve had always been her favourite night of the year. Ever since she was little, she had felt the magic in the air. Lying in her bed, with her eyes screwed shut and her feet tucked up inside her nightie, she was always convinced she could hear the jingle of the bells on Santa's sleigh and the pitter-patter of hooves on the roof as the reindeers parked up. She never failed to leave a raw carrot for Rudolph and a glass of milk and two biscuits for Father Christmas. In recent years she had laughed as her dad insisted that Santa preferred a glass of stout to a glass of milk. She and Dee weren't so sure. This year, she sat in her room dreading Christmas Day, the first of many that she would mark without her son.

She ran her fingers over the inside of her shell. 'I wonder how you do Christmas in the sun? Do you still have pictures of snow everywhere and icicles like we do? Do you have the same fat Father Christmas? I can't imagine it; I don't think it'd feel Christmassy if it was warm. I should've asked you, there's lots of things that I wished I'd asked you. I don't know much about your family, what it was like for you growing up in St Lucia. And there are things I never told you; did you know I'm allergic to strong cheese? It makes my throat go itchy! Our little boy'll be getting on, eh? I expect he'll be spoilt rotten tomorrow, his first Christmas. It's been bloody freezing here. You wouldn't be able to stand it – I remember you didn't cope too well in March, let alone now we've got a bit of snow. But it's the wind that gets you, goes right through you, blows your cobwebs out, and I know you weren't too fond of that. I'll think about you tomorrow, but then I think about you every day so that's no shocker. I wonder if you'll think about me?'

Dot was woken by her little sister's squeals. 'He's been! He's been!'

Plodding down the stairs, she took the seat next to the hearth and wrapped her dressing gown around her legs. The fire roared but only seemed to heat the space directly in front of it, as if the wind whipped the warmth up the chimney and blew it at the birds perched in a long line along the roof. Dot rubbed her thighs with her palms; she felt cold.

Dee tore the wrapping from her *Bunty Annual*, revealing a suspiciously toasty-looking Bunty on the front who was ice skating yet wearing nothing more than a mini Santa dress to cover her modesty.

'Yeeeees!' Dee jumped up and down in her nightie, delighted with her pressie. Next came a Barbie in an air hostess outfit. The little girl was beside herself with joy.

Dot reluctantly, awkwardly, received her gift of tights and a jar of bath salts. She felt like a guest that had turned up at the last minute and whom the family felt obliged to ask to stay for dinner, even though they didn't have enough veg.

That night, as snow fell on the cobbles of Ropemakers Fields, Dot held her shell in her arms and rocked it almost as if it was a baby. 'I've been thinking about whether it would have been better never to have met you, better never to have known that another kind of life existed. Then I wouldn't know what I was missing, but that would be all right, cos I wouldn't know! But then I think about not having Simon and even though my heart is ripped in two, proper ripped in two, I wouldn't have missed those weeks when I fed him and held him and he slept on me. I wouldn't have missed that for the whole world. Night night, Happy Christmas.'

A few days after Christmas, Dot once again donned her coat and slipped out of the front door unnoticed, in need of some air and a change of scenery. She hadn't really planned where she would wander but soon found herself outside Paolo's. It had been months since she last set foot inside. *See you tomorrow, soldier boy. Exhausted, but happy! Your Clover xxxxx*

She pushed the door with her shoulder, uncertain as to whether reopening this wound was a good idea or not. The place was warm as usual, but strangely darker, grubbier and smaller than it had been on previous visits, as if in the cold light of day and without Sol's love to polish her world, it had lost its fairy-tale sheen.

'Here she is! Merry Christmas!'

'Merry Christmas.'

'Blimey, girl, I thought you'd fallen in the docks! Long time no see.'

Dot smiled. 'Can I get a coffee please, Paolo.'

'Certainly, love. Coming right up. Your usual seat?'

She nodded and slid into the booth. She stared at the table top and pictured their hands joined together across its shiny surface. She daren't look up, couldn't bear to see the empty space that used to be filled by him. Instead, she made out she was waiting for him, killing time like she used to, wondering if her eye liner was straight, her hair all right, her breath nice...

'There we go, gorgeous.'

Paolo placed the dinky cup and saucer in front of her and she stirred the thick, frothy contents. It smelt lovely. He loitered before returning to the sanctuary of his counter. Wiping his hands on his apron, he slid into the seat opposite: Sol's chair.

'Your fella coming in?'

Dot shook her head. 'Nah, we split up.' It surprised her how easily she could utter the words that stung her mouth like poison.

'I did wonder, as we haven't seen you both for a while. But I have to say, I'm shocked, I really am.'

'Really?'

'Yeah! I see all sorts in here – charmers who think they can woo a dozy tart with a bacon sandwich and a few words of chat, players who come in with a different bird every week. And then there was you two. I thought you made a smashing couple.'

'I thought so too, but he did a runner!' She chewed her bottom lip, trying to make light of her heartache.

'What? Never! Gawd, he didn't seem the type. Well, all I can say, he must've had a bloody good reason, cos he was as smitten as ever I've seen.'

Dot stared at him, her eyes wide. She swallowed the bubble of happiness and excitement that rose in her throat. 'Did you think so?'

It was the first time that anyone had confirmed what she thought she knew. Paolo, a witness with no axe to grind or any background knowledge, was able to tell her what she had longed to hear, confirmation that it hadn't all been in her mind.

'Yeah, absolutely. I don't mind telling you that I used to watch you together. That was the real deal if ever I've seen it, the way you looked at each other, the way you were together. It was something else. I thought that you two would have gone all the way.'

Dot beamed. Maybe, just maybe what Paolo was saying was true. Sol *had* loved her after all, and maybe he did have a bloody good reason for disappearing in the way he did and if that was the case, she wasn't mad after all.

'It felt like love.' She smiled

'Well, mate, it certainly looked like it.'

'Thanks, Paolo, that means a lot to me. You'll never know how much.'

'You're welcome. D'you know, I don't even know your name.'

'It's Clover.'

224

The euphoria of Paolo's words didn't last long; in fact it had worn off by the time she got home. It had only confused her more. If Sol had loved her as he said he did, why did he bugger off? Dot dozed, curled up like a little ball, lying on the mattress and wishing she could sink into it.

The rapping on her door roused her. 'Yep?'

Barb pushed the door open and popped her head around the frame. 'You decent?'

'Come in.'

'I was worried about you leaving on your own the other night, thought we'd agreed we'd all travel home together. You didn't even stay for the music. They were brilliant. Wally said you just upped and left like you'd had enough.'

Dot remembered his sarcastic tone, his jibe. 'Yeah, something like that. Sorry, Barb, I just wasn't in the mood.' As she spoke, her fingers plucked at the tiny loops of the candlewick bed-spread.

'D'you fancy a walk? Thought we could go and sit on the docks, it's been a while.'

Dot looked at her friend; it had been a while, a while since they had spent any time together, a while since they were close. She felt a pang of guilt.

'Why not? That'd be lovely.'

Barb visibly brightened; she had clearly missed her mate.

The two strolled along as the sun sank behind the buildings and the chimneys puffed away, shooting plumes of fine black fog up into the night sky. Dot pictured her neighbours in those houses, gathered around the hearths, with gravy-filled turkey and ham pies made up of Christmas leftovers and mugs of tea. In a few days' time it would be another year. Dot looked forward to putting 1961 behind her, but, equally, the thought that 1962 would be a year in which she wouldn't see her son, that this time next year she would be thinking, *I have not seen him this year*, was too awful to contemplate.

The water shimmered, reflecting the street lights and red and green flashes from the lamps on the boat decks. The girls took up their familiar seats on the dockside bollards.

'It's been a while since we came down here. We used to do it all the time, didn't we; just sit and natter.'

'Yep, it was all we did, Barb!'

'But funny how it was enough. I've had some of my best times sitting here in all weathers mucking about with you.'

'Same.' It was true, before Sol, that was normal life and she had been happy.

'D'you remember that Russian bloke, that day when I chucked a fag in your hair?'

'Yes!' The two rocked and giggled. That had been a funny day, one that would stay with them.

When the laughter subsided, Barb coughed, gathered her courage. 'I've been worried about you, mate.'

'Oh, you don't have to worry about me. I'm all right.'

'I know you say that, but I have and I am. You ain't yourself, Dot, and you haven't been for a while.' Barb fell silent. Having given her friend the cue to open up, she waited for the explanation. None was forthcoming.

She tried again. 'I've missed you.'

Dot knew Barb was sincere. 'I've missed you too,' she replied, although in truth she had been so preoccupied over recent months that her friend had rarely entered her head.

'I've been wondering, did that farmer do something to you?'

'What?' Dot momentarily forgot the lie that had been cast. The question caught her off guard.

'That farmer at the hop-picking place, did he do something to you or someone else there? Were his kids mean cos you were looking after them and not their mum?'

Dot sighed and gazed at the water. *If only...*

'No, no. Nothing like that. I'm fine, honest!'

'But you ain't fine, despite what you say. I know you ain't. You haven't been fine since you were seeing that black bloke...'

'Sol.' Dot would only tolerate him being referred to by name.

'Yeah, him. I'm trying to figure it all out, Dot. You and me was real close and then you started seeing him an' it was like I didn't exist, an' I'm not moaning, I understand what it's like when you just wanna be with someone, I do! But then you bugger off to work for the farmer bloke and I had to find out from me Aunty Audrey, you never even said, you just went and we were supposed to be best friends. And then you come back and it's as if someone has put a Dot lookalike in your house, someone that looks like you and sounds a bit like you when you do eventually talk, but it's like... it's like someone turned your spark off, put out your flame, you look empty.'

Dot was grateful for the encroaching darkness and the fact that she could cry into the night without being seen. That was exactly how she felt, as if someone had put out her flame – empty. She placed her hand on her flat stomach – empty. Her nipples tensed inside her cotton bra, desperate to feel the seeking mouth of her newborn, her son, her Simon.

'I'm sorry, Barb—'

'No, I don't want an apology,' Barb fired back. 'That's not what I mean. I just wanna know if I can do anything to make it better. I want the old Dot back.'

Dot laughed; the old Dot didn't exist any more. The old Dot had drifted along with her head full of inconsequential rubbish, preoccupied with how to make people laugh and the state of her fringe, working hard to get enough money to have fun, an easy life. The state in which she now existed allowed no space for frivolity; her experience had left her so changed, so broken.

'I am sorry, Barb. I've neglected you, I know, but the thing is, I fell for Sol completely and I thought he was the one.'

'I thought so too, never seen you so smitten and he couldn't take his eyes off you! I was planning the bloody wedding!'

Dot smiled, still unable to control the rising tide of happiness at having a second person in a week give her this sweet information. She had loved him so much, missed him so acutely that even this felt like a connection of sorts, a link across the miles and confirmation that even if their relationship had been only temporary, it had been real.

'And then he left without saying so much as goodbye; no explanation, nothing. It broke my heart, mate, literally broke my heart and I don't think it will ever feel better, I really don't.'

Barb crouched beside where her friend sat and placed her hands on her mate's knees, like a mum trying to console a fallen toddler. 'Look at me, Dot. It will get better, I promise you it will. We've all been there, love, and it does get better, it gets easier and the next amazing bloke that comes along will rub out the old bloke that you used to think about all the time, he'll take his place. It'll all be okay.'

Dot knew this was Barb's truth and she appreciated her friend's concern, but she also knew that what she had felt for Sol was a once in a lifetime love that no 'new person' could ever come along and erase. And even if this wasn't the case, the longing she felt for their child put her loss in a whole other league. Dot hoped that Barb would never know that sort of heartache.

'Thanks, Barb, you're probably right.'

'I am right. I ain't as stupid as I look!'

'And what's been happening with you, what's your news?'

Barb stood and plunged her hands into her pockets, facing the water with her scarf wound around her neck to ward off the chill.

'Not much change, really, except I've been seeing quite a bit of Wally – he's all right. We haven't… y'know… but I reckon we will and then who knows?'

'Be careful.'

Barb turned her head and smiled. 'I will, thanks for that, Mum!'

'I just don't want you to do anything silly, I don't want you to mess up your life.' *Like I've messed up mine.*

'I won't! Anyway, I could do worse than end up with Wallace Day. He's never going to set the world on fire, but he's reliable, earning, and it's just easy, cos he knows me mum and dad and your mum and dad and it just feels… easy.'

Dot pictured the tall, thin Wally Day who had worked with her dad on the sheet metal. She saw his gangly arms and legs, his almond-shaped eyes, small chin and large teeth. She couldn't imagine kissing a mouth that wasn't perfect like Sol's. She didn't want Barb to settle for 'easy', throwing her lot in with a strange fish like Wally, who rarely blinked, laughed or expressed an

229

opinion that wasn't a repetition of what the person before had said. She wanted Barb to know what it felt like to come alive when another human being said your name, touched your skin and promised you sunshine.

But Barb wasn't finished. 'Anyway, what's the alternative? I ain't getting any younger.'

'You're only eighteen; you can do anything you want.'

'Can I?'

'Course you can. What would you do right now, if you could do anything, anything at all?'

Barb considered this; her answer was already battering the inside of her lips, clearly not the first time she had thought what she would do if only she could.

'I'd like to be a hairdresser on a cruise ship.'

'Really?'

'Yep.' Barb nodded. 'I'd like to sit in a massive ship as it hurtled through the waves. It would have chandeliers and sparkling wine glasses – like the *Titanic*, but without the sinking. I'd do the hair of all the ladies before they went to posh dos in long frocks and they'd all be stinking rich and give me massive tips that I would spend when the ship docked wherever it was going!'

'Knowing your luck, Barb, it'd dock right here in Limehouse Basin and you'd end up in the local chippie with a fist full of tips!'

'That'd be all right, I'd treat everyone that came through the door to six a chips and a pickled onion!'

'Generous to a fault!'

'That's me. And what about you, Dot, what would you do if you could do anything for a job, anything at all?'

Dot looked out over the water. 'Well, it sounds daft, but I'd like to design and make clothes, not just any clothes, but posh frocks, beautiful gowns that ladies wear as they descend grand staircases before getting whisked around a shiny wood dance floor...'

'Mate, I think you'd be brilliant at that. You've always had a good eye an' I used to listen to the suggestions you made to girls who were getting dresses made, it was always perfect.'

'I'd call it Clover Originals.'

'Why "Clover"?'

'Because clovers are lucky!' Dot's response was instant.

'Well, I'd like to wear a Clover Original.'

'Would you?'

'Course, if I had enough money – you sound a bit pricey!'

'Well, it ain't going to happen, mate, but thanks for your custom anyway!'

'D'you know, it's been lovely tonight, just like old times.'

Dot smiled. Yes it had, almost – if you didn't count knowing that she would go home now and cry herself to sleep.

Barbara stood up and dusted her palms against her hips. 'Come on, I'm off to meet Wally up the Barley Mow. You come too.'

'No, I don't want to be no gooseberry!' *And I want to go home to be on my own and sit with my shell.*

'Don't be daft! It's only Wally. Please, Dot, c'mon.' Barb took her friend's hands and pulled her into a standing position.

'All right then, just one drink.'

Barb was delighted. 'That's my girl!'

'I like being your girl.'

'That's good, because I am never going to let you go...'

231

The three had been sitting around the sticky-topped table at the Barley Mow for a couple of hours. The girls watched as Wally flipped Ind Coope beer mats, adding one at a time until he had mastered seven, for which Barb gave him a small clap. Dot was sipping her third gin and orange of the evening. She was definitely out of practice – it had been a long while since she'd had a drink, but she enjoyed the fuzzy euphoria it brought. It was so pleasant to escape from the exhausting reality of everyday life, so she carried on. She slumped against Barb and as she struggled to angle the rim of her glass correctly, half of it slopped down the front of her shirt.

'Oooh, Dot's got wet boobies, again!' She roared with laughter.

'I think I'd better get her home!' Barb chewed the inside of her cheek; this was not how she had envisaged their night out ending.

'S'all right, Barb, you go get your bus and get on home. I'll probably have to carry her anyway.'

Barb looked at her wristwatch. 'Shit!' Her dad would have been expecting her home ages ago.

'Are you sure, Wall?'

'Yeah, go on, I know where Reg lives, it's almost on me way anyway.'

Barb stooped and gave him a big kiss that smacked against his cheek. 'D'you know, you're smashing, you are!'

'Dot!' Barb shook her friend's shoulder. 'Wally's going to see you home. Will you be all right?'

'I'm a disgrace, shameful!'

'Yes you are!' Barb laughed, thinking Dot was talking about her inebriated state.

It took Wally twenty minutes to persuade Dot to leave the pub and not to spend the night with her head on the table. He placed one arm around her waist, hooked the other under her shoulder and the two of them wobbled along the cobbles like a couple of dancers whose fandango had left them in a horrible tangle.

Dot stumbled, pitching forward and crushing Wally's winkle pickers at least twice. 'I think I'm gonna be sick...'

Wally steered his charge up the alley at the end of Narrow Street and pointed her in the opposite direction. Dot bent over, breathed deeply and waited. No sick, yet.

'Sorry, Wally... Imnotusuallylike this...'

'No, I know. Don't worry. I've heard you've been having a bit of a rough time. Although why anyone'd chuck over a girl like you, I don't know.'

'I don't know either.' Dot hung her head forward and wobbled on her heels. Wally reached up and caught her arm. She started to cry, doing nothing to stem the flow of tears.

'I had to let him go! I didn't want to, he was crying, I could hear him crying through the wall and I couldn't do anything about it...'

Wally pulled her into his chest and patted the back of her head. 'Don't worry about him now, Dot, he was probably just feeling guilty, the bastard! Don't you feel sorry for him, he's a grown man – crying, for God's sake, whasamatter with him? It was his doing in the first place!'

Dot looked up at Wallace Day, her face streaked with tears and mascara. 'I'm sorry.'

Wally didn't hesitate, it was the moment he had been hoping for. Leaning forward, he bent his head and pushed his lips against hers. Dot was shocked and jerked backwards, smacking her head against the alley wall. His hand reached up to pull her head away from the wall, to try and make it better. Dot pulled back, banging her head again.

'Gawd, Dot, mind your head!'

'I don't want to kiss you! Of course I don't!'

Dot retched as her drunken stomach finally decided to release its poison. She turned around and vomited against the wall, splattering her shoes and tights as her tears fell down her face.

Wally Day placed his hand on her back. 'It's all right, Dot, you've just had a bit too much to drink. It'll be all right.'

'Fuck off, Wally! Leave me alone!' She shoved him with both hands.

Wally placed his hands in his pockets. 'I was only trying to help you.'

'No you weren't. You tried to kiss me, you idiot.'

Dot shook with equal measures of fear and anger. She was sober enough to know that he was supposed to be her best friend's bloke. 'How could you do that to me… to Barb?'

'It's got nothing to do with Barb!'

'She's your girlfriend!'

'No she ain't! She's just some dozy bint that turns up all the time, she ain't my type.'

Wally stepped forward to take her arm and guide her home. Dot ducked under his arm; she didn't want his help. Walking as quickly as her quaking legs would allow, she tottered up Narrow Street.

Mrs Harrison took a drag on her fag and for once was speechless.

Dot wobbled past as though her neighbour wasn't leaning on the door frame staring at her.

She paused before putting her key in the lock; she had never gone home drunk before. She wondered if they would be able to tell. Dot spat on a tissue, removed the smudged mascara from under her eyes and tired to fix her hair. She took a deep breath and opened the door. A more rational Dot might have gone straight up the stairs and into her bed, but this was no rational Dot, this was a Dot with a good measure of gin and orange juice sloshing around in her blood.

Joan sat at the table in the back room with the standard lamp pulled close to her chair; she was sewing a name label into Dee's gym knickers. Her dad was as usual face deep in the paper.

Dot swayed, but would have sworn she was standing still.

Her dad looked up from behind the *Standard*. 'Look at the bloody state of you. Is that what we've got to look forward to now, you coming home in God knows what state, stinking like an old brass? Or am I not allowed to comment on this neither?'

'Wh'as it to you if I do? It's got nothing to do with you what I do with my life!'

'Blimey! At least you've found your voice! And you're right, Dot, it's got nothing to do with me that you've buggered up your life, but if you think you can bring this behaviour over my doorstep, you've got another thing coming. How much more do we have to put up with, eh? We used to be a happy family!'

'Did we? I don't remember. I'll never be happy here again, Dad, never. I won't forget the names you called me and I won't ever forget that you hit me. You hit me! When I needed help the most, you weren't there for me!'

'What did you bloody expect? You nearly destroyed this family and you still can't see it. Mum lost her job, we nearly lost our home. Do you know what that means? I mean really what that means? If you are in any doubt, my girl, go up the arches by the station. You'll see families just like ours, with little Dees and old men with dicky chests just like me, they'll be lying there covered in filth on a pallet, waiting for the cold to do its worst. They are homeless and helpless and we were one step away from that cos of you! And the worst thing is, you still don't see it. It's a disgrace!'

Dot wobbled and put her hand on the wall to stop herself from falling. 'Oh yes, I know I'm a disgrace! I had a spiteful nun telling me how much of a disgrace I was in that bloody place you sent me to. She was wicked and some of the things they made us do were horrific. They took Gracie and Sophie and Simon; I reckon Jude was lucky in some ways. D'you know that they make you take your baby to the people who are going to adopt it and then you have to wheel the empty pram back, like a walk of shame, while your tears fall and your heart feels like it has been ripped from your chest and your tits leak and you can hear him crying and you know he wants you, cos you're his mum, but you know that you can never ever go to him and stop that crying, not just on that day but never ever for the rest of his life!'

Reg scrunched the paper up and threw it on the floor. Joan looked on, pale and stricken.

'And what's the alternative, you cocky madam? Bringing the little bastard back here to live among us? How well would that go down, Dot?

'Don't call my son that! Do not! And in answer to your

question, Dad, I don't know how well that would'a gone down, because I was never given the choice! I wish you didn't give a shit what anyone thinks, cos then I might have my boy!'

'That's the problem! You didn't give enough of a shit what anyone thinks or you wouldn't have done it in the first place!'

'Christ! You make it sound like I committed a crime!'

Joan finally piped up. 'Maybe you did, in God's eyes.'

Dot turned to her mum, who had been unnaturally quiet at the table. 'In God's eyes? Oh please, Mum, how can you say that? You don't even go to bloody church! You just pick and choose the bits that suit you.'

Joan folded her arms across her chest. 'You can say what you like, but that doesn't change the fact that you let us down, Dot, in the worst possible way.'

Dot let out a small laugh. 'I let *you* down? Jesus Christ, I expected shit from him...' She pointed at her dad. 'But you! How could you do that to me Mum? You've had babies and you knew what I was about to go through and yet you never said a bloody word, packing me off, nearly due without one single word of advice. And d'you know what, Mum? One word of kindness, just one, would have made the biggest difference to me, far better than giving me a sodding hankie! But no, I got the cold, silent treatment as part of my punishment, part of making me suffer. And all because I fell in love with the wrong man – and I did fall in love, it wasn't just sex! I loved him! I really loved him.' Dot's tears started to fall. 'And I would have gone to the other side of the world just to be with him. I was going to leave, leave you, this shit hole of a house and this bloody country where people judge and condemn me, when all I am guilty of is falling in love.'

237

'D'you think you're the only one?' Her mum spat the words. 'The only girl ever to have had her heart broken over a little crush?'

'A little crush? I was going to marry him! I had a fucking baby, your grandchild! A little boy that someone else gets to wash, feed, bathe and sing to sleep every night just because his dad had the wrong colour skin! It's a fucking joke, you think you can sit in a church, say a few prayers and make it all all right? How? How can you justify what you did to me, to us? How can you justify your horrible, horrible views? What kind of church is that?'

'It's not just me, it's the whole world, it's how it is.'

'Just because it's how it is does not mean it is how it should be!'

Reg was not done with his part in the discussion. 'Very profound, Dot, but this is the real world!'

'Do you think I don't know that Dad? Do you think after what I've been through, I have some sweet little fantasy about life? I've got a son in this world that doesn't even know I exist. How is that fair? Why should he be denied his proper mum and dad just because you had a problem with his dad's skin? Think about it, Dad, both of you; play it back in your head and think about that for a minute. How fucked up is that?'

'He left you, Dot.' Joan spoke quietly yet forcefully; it was time it was said. 'He left you without so much as a by your leave. That is not what people that love you do. I know that you are angry and you can try and lay the blame on my shoulders if it makes it easier for you, but I ain't the one that buggered off at the first sniff of a problem. Whether you like it or not,

238

the fact is you gave him what he wanted and he left you. And now you are paying for that.'

'He wanted to marry me.' Dot slid down the wall, her legs crumpled like paper beneath her body. The shouting had cleared her head, she felt nearly sober.

'Did he? Did he really? Think about it, Dot, did he really?'

There was a pause while the three mentally reloaded. All were exhausted, wanting the confrontation to end, but they knew that this was possibly the only chance to get it all out and put it to bed.

'No matter what Sol did to me, Mum, *you* let me down, you and Dad, but especially you. I don't even mean telling me what to expect about giving birth or anything like that, which would have been kind, but you knew what it was like to fall in love with a baby, you knew what was going to happen to me and yet you didn't give me one word of hope, nothing to prepare me for having my heart ripped out, nothing. And I will never ever forgive you for that.'

Joan leant over and tried to hold her daughter. 'I've suffered too,' she said. 'D'you think I wanted to see my family torn apart like this? D'you think this is how I pictured you having your first baby?'

'Mum, if there's a scale of suffering, I'm at the top, trust me.'

'Get away from her, Joan.' Reg was clenching his fists now. 'Listen to yourself, Dot.' She looked up at her dad. 'You are one selfish cow. Since when did it become all about you? When did you become the most significant person in this family, Dot?'

Dot slid back up the wall and stood tall; she smoothed her coat against her body and pushed her hair behind her ears.

'From now on I want you to call me Clover, not Dot. A dot is something small and insignificant and I am not insignificant, because I am someone's mother and that makes me something amazing.'

As she turned and left the room, then padded up the stairs to her bed, her parents exchanged a long look of incomprehension. This was it, she had finally gone proper doobleedin' lally.

* * *

Two weeks had passed since the showdown. And while it had been painful for both parties to give and receive such honest opinions, it had helped to clear the air. The atmosphere was no longer heavy with unspoken insinuation, sentences were no longer stuttered from dishonest mouths as everyone edited and whispered their words. Dot had stopped skulking in the hallway, embarrassed and awkward. She was not back to her chatty self, she never would be, and her demeanour was that of someone who lived with a heavy burden, but she certainly felt better having voiced her grievances and exorcised some of the horrors of Lavender Hill Lodge. In some small way the family could now move forward, albeit a different family to the one that used to live at 38 Ropemakers Fields. Everyone understood now just how fragile the ties of family life were, how they could be severed forever. Dot had learnt that the certainties of her youth – knowing that her mum and dad would always be there for her, no matter what – were unfounded. She now knew that they would only be there for her if she did and said what they expected, within their accepted boundaries. She envied Dee her ignorance, her assumption that her mummy and daddy would fix everything.

Dot was woken by the clinking of cutlery and the banging of drawers. Popping on her slippers, she sloped down the stairs and headed for the kitchen.

'Pass me the best tablecloth, Dot.'

Joan spoke as though her daughter had been present all morning and had not only just appeared, with mussed hair and still in her pyjamas. Dot yanked open the drawer in the sideboard and pulled out the white linen cloth with the pressed-out lace pattern along its border. The cloth they used for Christmas lunch, birthday teas, Easter Sunday, wakes and other special occasions. After which it would be boil-washed, ironed, starched and returned to the drawer for its next appearance – and that was today, apparently: January 14th 1962; not a date of note, as far as Dot could remember.

She handed her mum the cloth. 'Why are you using the best cloth and why are you laying the table so early?' It was only eleven a.m.

'Cos your dad has a guest coming for Sunday lunch and I want the place to look nice. You give yourself a good strip-wash and come down looking nice. An' I don't want no misery-guts face or silent treatment, just a nice normal Sunday lunch, all right?'

Dot shrugged. A nice *normal* Sunday lunch – that'd be her mum skivvying away with a plucked chicken, a peeler and a sack of spuds before shoving everything in hot fat to roast for an hour. They would then eat in silence around the table, interspersed only by her mum's occasional tuts as her dad splashed gravy on the table and by Dee moaning about how much she hated sprouts. Her dad would then take his afters to his chair by the fire, shovel the pudding/pie/trifle into his mouth and then fall asleep for an hour while she and her mum washed, dried and put away. Why they would want anyone to come and witness the merry tradition, God only knew.

Dot did as she was told, pulling a comb through her hair and slipping into a grey polo-necked jersey and black skirt. She put a slick of eyeliner on each eye and, hey presto!, she was ready to eat Sunday lunch under the watchful eye of one of her dad's cronies. She hoped it wasn't slobber gob Steve, the balding bore with a florid complexion and nasal laugh.

She picked up the shell and placed it on her lap.

'I've been thinking this morning, what it would've been like if you'd come here for lunch. I was thinking that if only they'd spent a bit of time with you, they wouldn't have been able to help falling for you, just like I did, cos you were so clever and funny and polite. I remember you telling me all about your garden and the plants you used to grow and about your peahens that you try and feed. I'm sure that if they'd just given you a chance, you would have won them over, and then what, eh? Maybe we would have just gone and got hitched and sailed off into the sunset. He'll be just over two months now. I bet he's big. I'm not sure what they do at two months, do they smile yet? I don't know how I can find out. It'll be our anniversary next week, did you know that? One whole year since I met you. I'll talk to you then of course. Gotta go now though, love, me dad's invited one of his mates to lunch. I'm dreading it really.'

Dot was halfway down the stairs when the door bell rang out its whiny, grating serenade. She could make out a male form standing on the other side of the etched glass: tall, thin and with dark hair. Opening the front door, she stepped forward, then stopped still.

'What d'you want, Wally? If you've come to apologise about the other week, then it's too bloody late. You knew I was pissed and you was right out of order, not only to me, but to Barb 'n'all!'

Dot folded her arms high across her chest. Her face flushed and her body shook as she recalled his hand on her back, his mouth looming larger as it came in for a kiss.

Wally stared at her with his unblinking eyes and held her gaze. 'Actually, Dot—'

But before he had a chance to finish his sentence, Dot's dad came up behind her and opened the front door wide. 'There you are, Wally! Come in, son!'

Son? Surely to God it wasn't Wally that was the special guest!

Dot sat as far away from him as the size of room and chair configuration would allow. She barely spoke and when she did, had to bite her lip to stop from mentioning what he had done to her after offering to walk her home. The pig. She watched as he chatted to Dee, making her laugh with a napkin fashioned into a puppet that gobbled up her fingers and spat them back out again. She watched how he overloaded food onto his fork, using it like a shovel; how he chewed with his back teeth and how his front ones hovered irritatingly over his bottom lip. Her dad had made an effort and was wearing his pressed shirt with the sleeves rolled up and his hair brilliantined into place. It made her angry to think that her parents thought they had to dress up for someone like him or that Wally might be considered the distraction that was needed. It made her cringe to think that they thought he was a potential match for her, an equal. Is that what they thought she was worth, bloody Wallace Day?

Wally and Reg sat in the chairs by the fire and laughed at memories of their days on the sheet metal, the foremen who knew bugger all about the job in hand and the factory owner who had been born not only with a silver spoon in his gob, but apparently one stuck up his arse as well.

Dot washed the plates in silence, unable to talk to her mother, who at least twice jabbed her in the ribs and reminded her to 'Be nice!' Dot swallowed the bile in her throat, remembering just how *nice* Wally wanted her to be.

Wally stepped into the kitchen with two empty bowls. 'Cor, Mrs Simpson, you know how to make a mean custard, that was lovely!' He smacked his lips together.

'Well, I should hope so, Wally. I've made enough of it in me time!' Joan giggled, coquettish, glad of the compliment.

Dot was stood a couple of feet from him and could smell cheap scent. She immediately compared it to the way Sol smelled – expensive soap, hair oil and a natural smell like cookies and spice. She had found it intoxicating, surreptitiously sniffing at his scalp and temples when he dozed in her arms.

Her parents waved Wally off after what felt like hours.

'Well, that was nice.' Joan stripped the table of her best cloth and headed towards the sink. It would get a good soak overnight before hitting the twin-tub in the morning. 'He's a nice boy, Reg.'

'Yes he is. I told you.'

'Liked my custard, he did, and ate a good dinner.'

Dot looked from one to the other. How? How could it be that Sol, who treated her like a queen, like Lady Clover, would not have been welcome at their grotty dinner table and yet Wallace, who would take advantage of her in a dark alley and had the manners of a goat was considered a *nice boy*? It was beyond her.

Dot couldn't wait to get out of the house once Wally had finally disappeared and was relieved to find Barb waiting for her at the end of Narrow Street, as agreed. They headed off for a wander and to find somewhere for a cuppa. Dot felt awkward not mentioning Wally's visit, but it was hard to know how to phrase it: '*You know, the bloke you love, who I detest and who my parents want to fix me up with.*' It was a non-starter. The two girls linked arms and matched each other's pace.

'How's it going up Bryant and May?'

Dot shrugged. 'Not so good, actually, mate. I've got a start date, but I think I might need to get my nerves in better order before I try going back.'

It was a huge admission that things were far from okay with her. Barb recognised the branch.

'You'll get there, Dot. Blimey, I used to think you was the strongest girl in the world. You'd never take crap from a bloke and you'll get back to that, once you get over that poet soldier arsehole.'

'Don't call him that.' Dot laughed a little.

'I can't believe you're defending him! He was a proper shit to you.'

245

'I know, but it wasn't entirely his fault.' Dot considered what he *didn't* know. 'Thing is, it's up to us to make lives for ourselves. We should take chances and grab at opportunities, not wait for them to be offered to us.'

'I s'pose so.'

'I know so. Don't just settle, Barb. Please don't ever settle for anything less than what you really want, anything other than what will make you really, truly happy.'

Barb stood still and looked at her friend. 'But supposing no chances or opportunities come along? Then I'll be on the shelf and you'll see me smoking on the pavement in all weathers with a face as miserable as sour milk, begrudging anyone smiling the air they breathe – I'll turn into Aunty Audrey!'

'That ain't gonna happen to you. You should train as a hairdresser and try and get on that cruise ship. I want you to have an adventure; I might get stuck here, so you need to have an adventure for us both!'

'Christ, don't talk like that, you sound like your life is over!'

It is. I hate waking up, I'm broken. My life is over. 'It's not that, it's just that I love you too much for you not to have a bloody brilliant life!'

The two girls hugged.

'I n'arf lucky to have a mate like you, Dot. I don't know what I'd do without you.'

'Well, you'll never have to find out. We're gonna grow old together and we'll sit with a nice cuppa in our bed jackets and talk about when we was young.'

'But we'll have an adventure before that, right?'

Dot painted on a smile. 'Oh, you betcha!'

* * *

It was a Saturday night and Joan was gathering up the gravy-smeared plates and the salt and pepper pots from the table.

'That was lovely, Mrs S,' Wally patted his stomach, which despite being flat was able to put away vast quantities of Joan's fare. She called it a good healthy appetite. Dot thought him greedy.

'Glad you enjoyed it, love. I like to see a man eat well. But for Gawd's sake, Wallace, please don't call me Mrs S – it makes me sound ancient. Call me Joan.'

'All right, I will. Thanks, Joan.'

Reg winked at the boy who had clearly won his wife over.

'Fancy a pint, son?'

'Rude not to.'

Reg punched Wally on the arm; they were cut from the same cloth. Similar in so many ways, and the admiration was mutual. 'Be with you in a minute. I'll just pay a visit before we go.'

Wally strolled out into the street and rocked on the pavement in his winkle pickers. He zipped up his leather jacket, extracted his comb from his back pocket and smoothed his hair back.

'Wally?'

He looked up and saw Barb, who was leaving her aunty's.

'All right, Barb?'

'Yeah, I'm… I'm fine. What you doing here? Looking for me?' She smiled, happy at the thought that he had sought her out, nervous because she had her work clothes on and didn't like him to see her so dowdy looking. She was supposed to get straight home, had promised her mum, but sod it; she'd go to the pub with Wally. Going out when it wasn't planned felt like much more of an adventure. She put her hands on her hips and stood in front of him.

'Looking for you? No.' He looked beyond her down the street. His tone was dismissive.

'Oh.' She didn't know what to say. Tongue-tied and awkward, she took a step backwards and hovered on the cobbles, caught between confusion and embarrassment. Her arms slipped down to her sides.

'I thought you'd come to find me when I saw you, thought me mum might have told you I was here.'

'Your mum? No. Joan's just cooked me tea and now Reg and I are off up the Barley Mow for a pint.'

'You and Reg?'

'Yeah. Dot's staying in, she's knackered.'

'Is she?' Barb felt an overwhelming desire to cry. Her best friend and her boyfriend had just had their tea together and now he was going out with her dad – it didn't make any sense... Unless... unless...

Barb rubbed her cheek, considering how to ask the question that shot into her mind, nervous about how to ask it and also wondering if she should; she didn't want to make a fool of herself.

'Is there something going on here, Wally, something that I should know about?' Her lip trembled.

'Depends, Barb, on whether what is going on with me and Dot is anything to do with you. And quite frankly, I don't see that it is.'

Barb hesitated. She was confused, upset. '*Going on with*

you and Dot? I don't understand, Wally. Why are you talking to me like that? What are you saying?'

'Oh dear, I can see she hasn't told you...'

'Told me what?' Barb's voice wobbled under the strain of not crying.

'Well, put it this way, Barb: you and me is mates, but with Dot... things are a bit more than that.' He winked. 'If you get my drift.'

She placed her hand to her chest. 'What? Are you are bloody kidding me?' She shook her head, it made no sense. 'But I thought... I thought you and me was together, Wally.' Her tears trickled down her face. Her humiliation was complete.

'You and me are friends, Barb, you know that. With Dot it's different. No hard feelings, eh?'

'No hard feelings? She is my best friend! Was. She was my best friend.'

'Look, I gotta go, don't want to keep the in-laws waiting!'

'*In-laws*? What the fuck's going on here?'

But Wally had already stepped back inside 38 Ropemakers Fields, the house that Barb had merrily trotted in and out of her entire childhood. She was determined never to set foot over the threshold again.

Unaware of the exchange below her window, Dot lay on her bed waiting for the door to close and Wallace Day, the bloody creep, to leave. She stroked her shell and spoke into it softly as it lay on her pillow.

'One whole year ago today! A whole year! In some ways it's gone so fast it feels like weeks and in other ways it feels like a whole lifetime ago. I remember every second of that night, I remember getting ready to go out, I didn't want to go, but me mum nagged me to go and help. We laughed as we ran for the bus. I remember the first thing I saw was the top of your head, bent over the piano. I didn't see your face first off, but I heard the music, our Etta, and I was humming the tune inside my head while I took the food around. *At last/My love has come along…* And then we went outside, didn't we, after I'd made a right fool of meself. You held my hands and pulled me up off the floor and it felt like you had rescued me. You asked me what my name was…' Dot was crying now. These days it was as normal for her as breathing, to be battling against huge, gulping sobs; quite normal. 'And I told you – Dot. But you was having none of that, you said I needed a bigger name, a better name. I felt like a bloody film star! I did. That night, Sol, when I got home and went to bed, I couldn't sleep, I could only think about you, about your face. It's still like that one whole year later. I can't sleep and I can only think about your face. Why, Sol, why did you leave me? I miss you so much, I really miss you.'

Dot cried until there were no more tears, just the sleepy, dry, heaving breaths that punctuated her night and shook her from slumber in the early hours.

The next morning, Dot woke with a clearer head. She decided that it was time to try harder. She could never go back to how she was before, she knew that, and despite all her prayers and wishes, her life was not going to stop – her darn heart just kept on beating. The idea of spending the rest of her days under a cloak of misery was too awful to contemplate. Bracing herself against the sink in the bathroom, she tried out a smile in the small square mirror at which her dad shaved and her mum applied her night cream.

Dot headed to Paolo's, as agreed with Barb a few days before. She couldn't wait to get inside and have a good natter, secretly hoping that Paolo might again make reference to her and Sol; that would brighten her day. She had also decided to tell Barb of the significance of the little coffee shop, let her share in some of the magic.

Barb was standing outside with a fag clamped between her two raised fingers and one leg bent, her foot flat against the wall.

Dot waved as she approached. 'Hello, mate. Blimey, it's taters, inn'it?'

Her friend stared at her.

'What?' Dot waited for the punch line, the quip. What was Barb looking at? 'Y'all right, Barb?' There was an uncomfortable second or two of silence. 'Barb? Say something!'

'You are a bitch, Dot, a fucking bitch and I want you to know that I ain't stupid.'

Dot was speechless.

'I'll never forgive you, never, not in this lifetime. You know everything about me and you have been laughing at me all this time. Well, let's see who's laughing in a few years' time. I'm going to make something of my life; I will be a bloody hairdresser and I will go on a cruise ship and you will still be stuck in this shit hole. I won't give you a second thought, either of you. It's a low trick, Dot, and I never had you down as someone like that!'

'What are you talking about?' Dot was still undecided if this was a joke.

'You know what I'm talking about. I stood by you through your little love affair, I let you make out you was with me all them nights when you was with your bloke.'

'And I was grateful! I am!'

'Yeah, so grateful you upped and pissed off to bloody Kent without so much as a by your leave. I had to find out from Aunty Audrey, like I didn't count, wasn't even important enough for you to tell.'

'That's not how it was, Barb, even though that's how it seems. I needed you then and I need you now, more than you know.' Dot wanted to tell her more, but she couldn't risk the truth being made public.

'Yeah, looks like it! You've got a bloody funny way of showing it.'

'What d'you mean? When you need me, I'm there for you and it's the same for you with me. It's always been like that and it means the world—'

'Is that right? I can't believe I sat there the other night, with you telling me to go for it, get trained, have an adventure. What was it you said? *Cos you loved me too much for me not to have a bloody brilliant life!* More like you couldn't wait to get me out of the way. I can't believe I fell for that shit. You and Wally must have been pissing yourself behind me back. I'm so angry, I've never been so angry! You lost your lover boy a long time ago, Dot, and congratulations, you just lost your friend.'

Dot laughed out loud. 'Me and Wally? Are you mental?'

'Yes, I must be not to have seen it before. Are you going to try and deny it?'

'Barb, I don't know what to say to you. You can't think that me and Wally—'

'Are you telling me he hasn't been to yours for Sunday lunch or for tea last night or out with your dad and God knows what else behind my back?'

Dot was stunned. 'Well, no, I'm not going to deny it. Yes he did and I was going to tell you but—'

'There is no fucking but! He told me what's been going on and I am finished with you. Just fuck off, Dot, fuck off and leave me alone. You are welcome to each other!'

Her friend broke into a run and disappeared up the road.

'But, Barb, please, it's not true! I love Sol and there's no room for anyone else, let alone someone like Wally. Barb, please, you're all I've got… you're all I've got…' Dot doubted that her whisper had reached her friend's ears.

Chapter Ten

Dee spun round and round in a circle until she felt so dizzy that she had to lie with her eyes closed on their mum and dad's bed. It had been pushed to one side, giving them the maximum space to get ready in. After a few seconds the room stopped spinning and she assumed the same position with her arms spread wide and started twirling again.

'Look, Dot! I'm a bally dancer! 'Cept Miss King said I can't do bally cos I'm a fairy elephant. I don't care anyway cos I'm going to be a air hostess. Look, Dot, look at me petticoat, it's like a bally petticoat, all sticky out. I'm going to jump off the stairs and see if my frock makes me float down. How high up shall I jump from – shall I go halfway? Dot, how high shall I jump from? Dot?'

Dot sat at the dressing table under the window in her parents' room and stared at the reflection of her sister in the triptych of mirrors. The plastic daisy headdress had slipped from the crown of Dee's head and now sat half under her chin and half around her face. Dot felt exhausted watching her as she twirled and jumped, all the while emitting her incessant babble of chatter and questions. She was like a hyperactive meringue.

'Be careful, tin ribs.'

'I'm always careful, and I'm strong, Dot. Punch me in the arm as hard as you can and I won't even cry!' Dee slipped her arms from her white hand-knitted cardigan and pushed a scrawny bicep towards her sister. 'Go on, punch me as hard as you can and I won't cry, I promise. Go on!'

'Dee, I am not going to punch you.'

'Shall I punch you first and then you punch me back?'

'Dee, I'm not going to punch you, ever. And please don't jump down the stairs, you won't float, you'll only break your bloody leg.'

'If I break my bloody leg, can I still be your bridesmaid?'

Dot hated the word 'bridesmaid'. It reminded her that she was a bride. If Dee broke her leg it would only delay proceedings. She was quite sure that even if she broke *her* leg – or her neck, come to think of it – her parents would find a way to cart her up the aisle and get her off their hands.

It had all happened so fast and she'd had precious little chance to stop it. 'Wally is a good bloke and he wants you,' her mum had said after another of those interminable Sunday lunches. 'It's time you started to look at the glass as half full. We ain't gonna let you sit around here with a face like a smacked arse all day, doing bugger all and looking miserable. We've got to act while there's a chance, Dot, or you will be an old maid. It's not as if you work...'

Dot had bitten her bottom lip at that. The shame – even more shame ladled onto the pile of shame that filled her gut. She had been unable to hold down the job at Bryant and May, unable to walk past the gates where she had thrown up on that first morning without feeling so distressed and panic-stricken that her legs wouldn't carry her forward. She had been pregnant with their baby and had wasted precious hours thinking she had a bug, that *he* had a bug. Why had she not legged it round to the Merchant's House and shaken Sol awake? It might have made a difference.

Her parents were right. Wally wanted her and she had no other options. And Barb had been right: take the easy route.

Dr Levitson had said it was her nerves. Dot knew it was no such thing, but she sipped thrice daily at the tonic meant to calm her nonetheless. It wasn't nerves; it was heartbreak. Her broken heart looked for every opportunity to remind her of what she'd nearly had. The bus that wound its way to the factory in Bow was the very same bus she'd sat on the morning after the most magical night of her life, when she had danced in front of Etta James. Thoughts of the West End sparked memories of her fabric rainbow, then of the hand-stitched romper suit and the moment Mrs Dubois had pushed her ever so pretty Christian face up against the grill while she held Dot's son. These terrible, painful thoughts were only ever a postal district, a street, a mention away.

'But does it matter that I don't love him?' she'd asked her mum.

To Dot it seemed obvious: just like in the song, love and marriage went together. To her parents, however, love had nothing to do with it.

Joan's face had puckered and her nose wrinkled as though Dot's sentiments had a stench about them. 'Love? Listen to yourself, Dot. What makes you think love is so important? Cos I'm here to tell you it isn't. Love is what happens in the films, love is a little spark of fancying that dies, Dot; it dies. What matters is security, having a roof over your head and food in your belly. That, my girl, is real life, not chocolates and flowers and a quick fumble that gets your heart racing.

256

Your dad and I are the exception, he knew what he was getting with me and I did with him. For you it's different and what you and that fella had was different, it was a fling.'

'We had so much more than that!' She wanted to tell her mum how sometimes when she looked at his face it was as if she'd discovered happiness for the first time; of the way her hand fitted so snugly inside his, it was the closest she had ever felt to coming home. But she had neither the confidence nor the audience for such a speech.

Joan wasn't done. 'Did you? Did you really, Dot? Where has this "love" got you? I'll tell you, shall I?'

Dot had known she would.

'It's got you in a whole heap of trouble, shredded your nerves and put me and your dad through the mangle. And all for what? A bucketful of memories and regrets. It has nearly ruined your life and smashed my family. No, my girl, we have tried doing things your way and that hasn't worked out. This time, you'll listen to us and we are telling you that you will marry Wally.'

Dot nodded. It was easier. Marry Wally, grow old and die. She couldn't see anything else.

Her dad lowered the paper to add his tuppence worth. 'And just so we are clear, you are packing up and leaving my house in three weeks' time and that is either to marry Wally or to go on the street, as you put it. Thems is your choice!'

'Nice to see you being as supportive as ever, Dad.'

'Don't you dare cheek me! I've told you your choices and that's the bleeding end of it. I can't believe we are even having this conversation. You should consider yourself very lucky that a decent bloke like Wally wants you and that we didn't chuck you out months ago. It's not only what you've done, it's the fact that you weren't sorry or embarrassed, not even a bit. Trust me, I thought about chucking you out, it was only because of your mother that you stayed.'

Oh I trust you.

'And you are also very lucky that we've taken an interest. Lucky that someone, anyone, wants to take you on. In my day you'd have been on the scrap heap after your bloody antics.' He gave an exaggerated shudder of revulsion.

'I don't feel very lucky.'

'And whose fault is that?' Joan chipped in with her arms folded high across her bust and her lips set in a thin line.

Mine. It's all my fault. I thought love was important.

'Can I have lippy on like you, Dot?'

'What?' Dee's question brought her back to the present.

'Can you do my lips like yours?' Dee pushed her mouth forward into a grotesque pout.

'Sure.'

Dot dabbed the lip brush on her sister's mouth, then placed a bit of loo roll between her lips. 'Press them together.'

Dee closed her mouth on the paper, leaving the smallest, palest cupid's bow.

Dot stroked her little sister's face. 'You look lovely.'

'You don't, you look fed up. And you're s'posed to be radiant and gay today.'

Dot couldn't help but giggle. 'Is that right? Where did you hear that?'

Dee shrugged and twitched her head. 'Will you do sexing when you're married?'

258

'What?' Dot hoped she'd misheard.

'My friend Marcia says you can do sexing when you get married. Her sister got married and has done sexing three times and she's got three babies. Mum and Dad have got us two so they have done it twice. So are you and Wally gonna do sexing?'

Dot shook her head and thankfully was spared from responding as Joan bustled in, already wearing her turquoise shantung coat with matching mini-dress underneath.

'You nearly ready?' Her tone was coaxing, trying to put a happy spin on the day. Her anxiety manifested itself in impatience: grabbing the hairbrush from the dressing table, she pulled Dee over to the bed and, wedging her youngest child between her knees, she started to brush at her curls, trying to rearrange her headdress.

Dot spoke to her mother's reflection. 'I don't know if I am ready, Mum. I can't think straight.'

Joan pointed the hairbrush at her oldest daughter. 'I'll tell you now, Dot, don't you dare start, don't you dare! Cos I've had it up to here!' Joan indicated her exact level of exasperation by placing the hairbrush against her chin. 'I've worked day and night on that spread and I'm not about to see it all go to waste because of more of your bloody shenanigans. You have to try, Dot, you do. This is your chance.'

Dot stood up in her under-slip and stockings, her face a little more made up than usual, but not much. 'My chance for what exactly?'

Joan paused from her brushing and swallowed. She looked near to tears. 'Please let's not go over this again. Just try, that's all I'm asking.'

'You're quite right, Mum. Far better I spend me life in abject misery than you let your ham sandwiches and cheese and pineapple on sticks spoil.'

'D'you know what, Dot, I'll be bloody glad when I wake up t'morra and you are not under my bloody roof!' Joan yanked at Dee's defiant curls and pinned plastic daisies where the fancy took her.

'You're hurting me!' Dee squealed. 'Ow!'

'Me too, Mum. It's the one thing that makes this whole pile of shit in which I find myself bearable – the fact that I can get out from under your bloody roof!'

Joan leapt up and stood inches away from her daughter. 'I don't know what's happened to you, I really don't!'

Dot stared at her mother. 'Don't you? Do you really not know what's happened to me? Cos I do wonder sometimes. You act as if nothing has, but it has, Mum, something so big that I will never ever get over it.'

'And by the love of Christ don't we know it, wallowing in it day after day, dragging us all down with you! Bad things happen, it's called life!' Joan shook her head and reached inside her bra for her hankie. 'I can't go through it again, not today. You are driving me nuts!' Joan stalked out and left the two girls alone.

'You mustn't say "shit", Dot. Swearing makes your face ugly, Miss King told me that.'

Dot smiled. 'She's right.'

'Can I do my eyes with your make-up?'

Dot stood up. 'Course,' she mumbled, and walked into the hallway and down to her room.

As she sat on her own bed for the last time as a single woman,

Dot placed the shell on her lap and felt it jab at her skin through the thin silk of her slip.

'I can barely say the words: today is my wedding day. Not the wedding I dreamed of, to the man that I love, and not through choice, but it still feels like a betrayal. I want you to know that in my heart I'm yours and you are mine. This wedding will feel like a sham, a fake, because every waking morning and last thing at night I will think of you, just like I always do. It will always be you, Sol, always. I'm up the creek without a paddle, mate, and I can't find a way out – I must be living above the permanent snow line, whaddya reckon? This feels like my only route out and so I'm taking it. But I want you to know that if you ever come back for me, I will run into your arms faster than you can say pineapple juice. I just want you to know that.'

Dot placed the shell inside her suitcase, on top of her clothes, setting it alongside her copy of *Anne of Green Gables*. She stuffed in her pillow and then snapped the locks shut. Her room had gone from being her childhood refuge to a prison; she wouldn't miss the four drab walls. She was surprised that her ocean of tears hadn't seeped through the floorboards and weakened the joists so as to make the bed and all the furniture go crashing through the floor onto the buffet below. That would certainly spoil her mother's spread.

Dot, her mum and dad and Dee gathered in the hallway. There were no gasps from the father of the bride or tears from the mother; instead, her dad enquired, 'Has someone locked the back door?' and that was it, off they trotted.

They walked to St Anne's on Newell Street, a grand looking building whose ornate architecture only emphasised the mediocrity of their nuptials. Iron bars and mesh sat over the windows, installed by a fed-up vicar who was trying to deter the vandals that regularly targeted the poor box. They walked quickly, as though late for the cinema or the chippy that was about to close. There was nothing in their expressions or demeanour that suggested they were a wedding party – except for the fact that Dot was dressed like a bride. She had let her mum pick the dress, so little had she cared. It was a simple A-line of duchess satin with an empire bust and a row of daisies sewn around the neckline. It came to just above the ankle; she teamed it with matching character shoes that fastened with a metal hook and a little hoop. Her elbow-length gloves were the same colour as the dress, just a shade off white.

Her parents had decided that as this was a church outside their faith but inside Wally's, it didn't really count and so it wasn't breaking any rules. In any other circumstances, Dot would probably have found such skewed logic amusing, but there was very little that was funny about her predicament. She had, like many girls, carried an image of her wedding day in her head since she was small. The details had always been sketchy, but the general picture had always included her in a white lace creation, with a bunch of lily of the valley in her hand, her mum crying into a cotton hankie and a dashing groom, beaming as he reached for her hand with a twinkle in his eye. This image had come into sharper focus when Sol had proposed; then she'd seen herself in a classic fitted dress with long sleeves and a bolero in matching satin. She'd wanted to arrive at the church like a princess, sitting in a big, open carriage drawn by horses with flowers up their reins. He would turn and watch her walking up the aisle; then he would beam as they stood side by side and uttered the words that would bind them even tighter.

Joan strode towards the church, pulling Dee by the arm. Her dad hesitantly held out his crooked elbow. Dot placed her hand inside and rested it on his arm. He patted her fingers with his other hand. It had been a long time since they had touched. He didn't look at her, but spoke to the middle distance. 'I love you, Dot. Always have and I've only ever wanted what's best for you.'

He continued to stare ahead. She was silent. It was too late for his words to act as a salve, the damage was done. Dot had thought stronger emotions might have accompanied her big day. But no, it was just the same anaesthesia that had gripped her since she had returned from Lavender Hill Lodge. It was, in fact, horrible to be led to her fate by the one man that she used to trust.

Dot took a deep breath and looked skyward; one last silent wish for a different solution. As she lowered her eyes, they fell upon a shadowy figure standing to the left of the cedar tree at the side of the church. Her heart lurched in her chest. The figure side-stepped behind the wide trunk, moving quickly, not wanting to be seen – but not quickly enough to hide the familiar hairdo and favourite jacket of her friend Barb.

I'm sorry, I'm so, so sorry.

Reg and his daughter marched a little too quickly down the aisle. The pews were empty on the bride's side, bar her mum, Dee and Mrs Harrison, who was perched on one of the back pews, not exactly invited, but no one was going to turf her out. Dot noticed that she had removed her curlers for the occasion, the nosy cow.

Wally stood in front of the altar in his black drainpipe trouser suit; she hadn't noticed how tall he was before. Dot felt sick. Wally turned to face her as Reg delivered his daughter; she felt like a parcel, wrapped in off-white satin. He smiled, not with love or longing, not the way that Sol had smiled at her so many times; this was more of a nervous smirk, like when an awkward teenager is given a compliment. He took her hand and placed it on his crooked arm.

'You look really lovely.'

She was sure he meant it, but rather than encourage or reciprocate, she closed her eyes for a second as if to say, 'Leave it out.'

As they exchanged vows, Dot stared at his mouth, studied his profile, noticed he had long eyelashes; she'd never looked at him for this length of time, this close up. She watched his mouth as it turned towards the vicar, moved up and down, uttered the words that completed the transaction and sealed her fate. It didn't feel real, any of it; it felt like a horrible dream.

'I now pronounce you man and wife!'

Dot closed her eyes and fought the urge to scream. Strangely, she wasn't filled with panic, but something closer to numbness, as if a slow burn of indifference had been lit in her veins that would smoulder away for the foreseeable future, filling every gap inside her until the fight finally left her.

Wally and Dot, the new Mr and Mrs Day, led Wally's parents, sisters, aunts and uncles, cousins, neighbours and mates from the sheet metal in a laughing, smoking procession along the street to 38 Ropemakers Fields. They poured into the house, filling every corner with their back-slapping, fag-toting banter. They were a family of strangers who dived into her mum's buffet, stuffing sandwiches and sausage rolls into their gobs, digging into trifles and popping cubed cheese into greedy mouths. She felt sick, again. It was as if she was invisible, and when one of the Crimplene-clad fatties hugged her to their cigarette-scented bosom and welcomed her to the family, it shocked her as though it must be a case of mistaken identity.

Her dad put the record player on and some of the aunts shimmied a little where they stood, with paper plates held aloft to a Motown track. Dot looked at Wally as he drank pale ale from the bottle and sat on the arm of her dad's chair. One of the aunts caught her staring, 'Oh bless her, that's a look of love alright, you love him don't you girl?' Dot was unable to reply, she knew the answer was no, not tomorrow or the day after that or the day after that…

Joan smiled at her from the other side of the room. Unusually, Dot stared back. What was her mum saying, with her covert smiles and wave? *I'm proud of you; it's done, look forward, not back.*

Someone put a slow waltz on and Dot felt the tears pooling in her eyes; she missed her lover, oh God! She couldn't cry here, not in front of all these strangers. Wally, engaged in conversation with some of his mates, kept glancing nervously in her direction; she wished he wouldn't, didn't want to feel responsible for his misplaced concern. She ventured outside and looked around her at the back fence, she wondered if the Rusalovas saw any of the goings-on in their back garden or wondered about the family that lived a few shelter panels away and yet they had never really spoken to. She would have liked to have seen the garden that yielded the occasional rose, a thing of beauty that accidentally bloomed in this barren shit hole of a back yard, remembering how she'd been too embarrassed to tell Sol the truth about their excuse for a garden.

'Here she is!'

One of the guests was clearly delighted that she had been located.

'We want to get a photo, Dot.'

Her stomach flipped. *Oh, please, not a photo!*

Wally sauntered over and removed the fag from his lip, tossing it into the flower bed that on occasion produced a chrysanthemum. He put his arm around his wife's waist and pulled her towards him. Dot drew breath sharply and was about to push him away when two things registered: firstly, everyone was watching, she was trapped; and secondly, he was entitled, she was his wife. *His wife.*

Dot tried to find a smile, but it was difficult. Just as the photographer was about to click the button, capturing them forever, Dee popped up beside them. It was the first time Dot had properly looked at her little sister since they'd left the house. Only now did she notice the inch-high blocks of bright-blue eye shadow that Dee had caked under her eyebrows and all over her eyelids, and the circles of black eyeliner she'd drawn around the blue. Dot beamed at her lovely little sister, who looked part clown, part panda. She smiled and at that precise moment the shutter clicked, capturing forever the grinning Wally and his laughing bride. She looked beautiful and happy and for that split second she was.

The crates of beer were soon drained and the men loosened or removed their ties, rolled up their sleeves and with braces hung down onto suit trousers, threw their arms around the next fellow's shoulders and started the singing. Her dad was in the thick of it, pissed and happy.

A couple of the aunties who were sozzled on sherry slept open-mouthed in the back room, their heads lolling against the lace antimacassars on the settee. Mrs Harrison hovered, sniffing around the depleted buffet and having a good look at the decor while she had the chance. Joan ran back and forth from kitchen to table, capturing her guests' compliments as if they were butterflies, ready to pin and dissect them at a later date. She replenished empty plates with slices of pork pie and tipped crisps and Twiglets into Tupperware bowls.

Dot sloped off to her room – her old room, as it was now – stepping over her niece by marriage, who was snogging her latest spotty beau on the stairs. She changed into her grey pleated mini-skirt and polo neck, placed her wedding dress on a hanger and hung it on the wardrobe door, running her fingers over the silky skirt. *What a waste of bloody money.*

There was a rap on the door and it opened straight away. She expected to see the flushed face of her mum, but it wasn't Joan.

'Hiding up here, are you?' Wally put his hands in his pockets and straightened his shoulders, trying for masterful, but achieving awkward.

Dot drew breath to tell him to get out, when again a wave of realisation hit her that she couldn't – she was his. She plopped down on the single bed as the strength left her legs. She felt uncomfortable and nervous, she'd never had a bloke in her bedroom before and she didn't like it.

'Reckon we'll push off in a minute, if that's okay.' There was a quiver to his voice.

She nodded into her lap.

These were the first words they had properly exchanged as man and wife. They were strangers.

Dot carried her suitcase into the hallway and spied Dee sat on her bed, kicking her legs and chatting to her stuffed bunny. 'Don't cry, bunny, you silly sod, course you're gonna see her again! She's only going to Walthambloodystow.'

Dot knocked on the door frame. 'Y'all right, tin ribs?'

'Yep.' Dee looked up, her face smudged with blue eye shadow and the remnants of strawberry jam around her mouth.

'Now, I've told Mum that you should come and stay with me. How you fixed next week?'

Dee visibly brightened. 'All right, I think!'

'Great, that's settled then. We'll get fish and chips and you can help me get settled.'

'F'ya like.' Dee beamed.

'I do like. Keep learning them tables, Dee, you're gonna need them if you want to be an air hostess.'

'D'you think I'll be a good air hostess?'

Dot dropped to her knees in front of her little sister. 'I think, Diane Simpson, that you can be anything you want to be and that you can go anywhere you want to and whatever you choose, you'll be bloody brilliant at it!' She kissed her firmly on the cheek and stepped out of the room.

The guests at 38 Ropemakers Fields crammed into the hallway and spilled out onto the pavement. Holding fags and bottles in the same hand, the strangers waved and hooted as Dot placed her suitcase in the boot of Wally's cousin's car. Her dad was waving with his eyes half closed, so pissed he could barely keep them open.

Joan stepped forward. 'Bye then, Dot.' She leant over and kissed her daughter on the cheek. 'Well, that's it then, me first-born off me hands!' She tried out the joke.

Dot bent her mouth towards her mother's ear. 'Consider yourself lucky, Mum, that you had me under your roof for nineteen years. I only had my firstborn for fourteen days.'

Joan pushed her hand against her mouth as her eyes clouded with tears. She threw her arms around her daughter's neck, holding her tight. Her body shook as her tears fell. 'I did it for you, love, and I did it for your future. You wouldn't have had a life! And I loved you too much to watch that happen.'

'He was so beautiful, Mum.'

'Did he... did he look like you?' she stuttered through her tears.

'No.' Dot shook her head. 'He looked just like his dad.'

'What's his name?'

'Simon. His name's Simon.'

'Simon.' Joan repeated.

Dot stared at her mum before climbing into the back seat of the Austin Cambridge, her boots squeaking against the grey vinyl upholstery. Wally hung out of the open window, his fag resting on his lip, waving and enjoying the salacious nudges and winks from his mates. Dot pretended to search for something in her handbag; she couldn't bear to look at the posturing pack of strangers, to watch her childhood home getting smaller and smaller or see the stricken expression of her mum in the rear-view mirror.

The drive from Limehouse to Walthamstow was not a long one, half an hour at most, but for Dot it might as well have been another continent. Her mum and dad's house had been a refuge of sorts and the cul de sacs of this East End corner were all she knew, having lived there her whole life. She could walk the streets with confidence, knowing every lane and house en route. Every time she ventured from the house she would raise her palm at several neighbours, people she'd grown up alongside, whose children she'd been to school with or who knew her mum. The corner shops, pubs and bakeries were guaranteed to hold a familiar face: Limehouse was her family. It felt inconceivable to her and more than a little bit frightening that this had come to an end. Tomorrow she would wake in a different neighbourhood, where she didn't know the bus routes, or where to pick up a loaf, or who lived to either side of her.

It was late afternoon by the time Wally's cousin dropped them off, beeping the horn in a rhythmic tune as he left. The two had ignored her as they drove, talking about West Ham – the Irons' chances in the league, was Fenton still up to the job, and the various skills of Geoff Hurst and Martin Peters. She had felt excluded, awkward. How had she come to be in a strange car with these two people, heading God knows where on her wedding day? *Her wedding day…* It was still surreal.

She had kept her eyes fixed on the passing shops and lock-up garages as the two discussed her.

'Blimey, Wall, she's quiet. You know what they say about the quiet ones…'

Dot felt her cheeks flush, but made out she hadn't heard.

The cousin wasn't done. 'Maybe once she starts she won't stop, rabbit rabbit, nag nag…' He lifted his left hand from the steering wheel and snapped his fingers against his thumb like a crocodile; this was supposed to represent Dot's gob apparently. 'And you'll look back on this moment and wish that she'd shut her cakehole!'

Wally laughed. 'I don't know, I think I'd like to hear her chatting. Her mum and dad chat all the time, don't they, Dot?'

She shrugged.

'You got the keys, mate?'

Wally fished in his inside pocket and pulled out a key ring with a miniature pint of beer on it, complete with plastic foaming head. Attached to this was a shiny silver Yale key.

Dot had taken little interest in the planning for her nuptials and even less in the council place that Wally had acquired for them to live in. It hadn't seemed in the slightest bit important, until now. Dot had believed up until the moment that she stood at the altar that something would occur to stop the wedding and therefore prevent her moving to a place she had never been to before. It had to; surely no force on earth would want to see her hitched to a stranger that she disliked.

Please, please let me have a garden. Dot hoped that she would have a bit of outside space; it didn't have to be acres, but a small patch, a square, anywhere that she could grow veg and cultivate a bit of grass, somewhere to escape to, breathe, be alone.

'I'd love a nice garden, y'know. I'd like to grow flowers and all me own veg.'

'Oh, be careful, once you get the gardening bug it can take you over!'

'I think I'd like to cook what I'd grown. I could do fruit and make jams and crumble; be lovely that, wouldn't it? I've never been much of a cook, it's kind of me mum's thing, but

271

I reckon I'd love cooking for you. I'd experiment and you'd have to eat all my disasters!'

Wally bent to pick up the suitcase. Dot beat him to it and gripped the handle; she wanted to show him that she didn't want or need his assistance. She followed her husband across the tarmac car park in which they had been deposited. Wally shoved his hands in his pockets and looked a little sheepish. Almost as if he didn't know how to act, as if he hadn't thought much past this point either. He had been quite cocky all day – the big man, the groom – but right now, without the audience and with his quiet bride trailing in his wake, he didn't know what to do or say. It was excruciating.

Dot looked around at the pale concrete buildings that surrounded her. Each block of flats was five stories high and was joined to its neighbouring block by sky-high walkways. The buildings formed a square of sorts. Each was identical, each balcony or walkway faced the other, the only difference being that one block had front doors painted red, another green, another blue. Dot and Wally's block had yellow doors.

Dot walked timidly behind Wally, trying not to look over the third-floor balcony to the patch of tarmac below, in which she could see large communal bins and a couple of vans. There would be no garden here for her. She thought about Rope-makers Fields with its squashed-together terraces and cobbled streets with wide pavements and tall sycamore trees planted every twenty feet. Tonight it felt like a different world. Here, everything was square and cold to the touch: concrete, moulded and formed into slabs. The windows had no familiar sashes

272

or stained glass, but instead were large single panes that looked functional, but not homely.

Dot could not imagine living in one of these boxes, so close to other families in other boxes, some above, some below and some on each side. She couldn't imagine opening a front door and not finding herself on the street but instead on a walkway high up in the air, like a bloody pigeon. She couldn't envisage opening a back door and not stepping into the back garden to check on the progress of the determined chrysanthemums. She was breathing the cool night air but felt inexplicably claustrophobic. Placing two fingers inside her polo neck, she pulled the woolly fabric away from her skin, as though she was struggling to take a breath.

'Here we go.' Wally stopped at a yellow door that looked exactly like all the others and put the key with its little swinging beer glass in the lock.

Dot wondered what that expression meant. Here we go, home at last; or here we go, the first step into a concrete prison that will trap us until we wake one day and realise we are already old – a slow death.

Wally glanced at her face, but could make out little in the failing light. He disappeared inside and flicked the bare bulb into life in the square hallway. Dot hovered on the walkway, wondering how far she could get if she ran – not very far, she figured, not without a penny and only a change of undies and very little else in her crappy little suitcase. She considered the tradition of carrying the bride over the threshold and was grateful that her new husband had not attempted it.

She stepped inside, holding her case with both hands against her chest. She could see the small galley kitchen straight ahead and spied a frying pan full of bacon fat sat on a two-ring burner on the worktop. Wally had obviously managed to master the art of bacon cooking in the week that he'd had the keys, but not washing up. He came from a side room.

'This is the front room.' He stood aside to let her pass.

It was a square room, with an electric fire and nothing else; no curtains, no furniture and not so much as a lampshade.

'All it needs is a woman's touch, but you can get it done up, eh? Get all the bits and bobs you want to make it home.' He tried out a small smile before striding out. Dot followed him. He stood in the hallway and pointed to three identical doors. 'Bedroom, box room...' The third door at the back of the hall was open. 'And our bedroom.'

Dot swallowed the bile that rose in her throat; the way he'd said 'our bedroom' made it quite clear that they would be sleeping in it together. Of course they would, they were a married couple. That room was not empty; its windows also had no curtains, but there was a mattress on the floor with a candlewick bedspread on it, almost identical to the one she had slept under for most of her life. This fact did not give her any comfort; in fact, it just made her feel more homesick, more isolated and more desperate. It was as if she was lost – where was she? And how could she be homesick for a home that no longer existed except as a fantasy.

Dot was speechless: how could she spend even one night in this environment with this man? She looked at the bare concrete floor, which was peppered with splats of the white paint that had been used on the ceiling. They reminded her of tears.

'Why did you marry me, Wally?'

It was the first time she had spoken to him in hours and the question caught him off guard.

He too looked at the floor, as though that was where the answer lay for them both.

'You're lovely... Who wouldn't want to marry you?'

She looked at him and, despite the compliment, felt nothing but a wave of pity – not only had he trapped her, but he'd unwittingly trapped himself too.

'Don't you think people should really know each other before they get married? Or be in love?'

'I think it'll all come in time, Dot. It'll all come in time if we let it, if we work at it.'

There was nothing else for Dot to do but nod. Any words that might have found their way out of her mouth would have severed this quiet optimism and she could not be that cruel.

For Dot and Wally Day it would be a very long time before such sentiments would be discussed again.

Dot brushed her teeth in the cold bathroom, grappling with the unfamiliar taps on the pale green sink before slipping into her nightdress. The rayon skirt clung to her legs; she tried to pull it away from her body and felt the tiny pins and heard the crackle of static against her skin. She patted her hair into place and put some talcum powder on her armpits before trying to slide into the room unseen. But Wally was sitting up on the mattress, leaning against the wall, smoking a cigarette. The bedroom light was off, but an orange light from the street lamps flooded the room with their glow.

Dot was fascinated and sickened in equal measure by his naked white torso. He was very slim: wiry, with tight bunches of muscle to either side of his belly button. His skin was near translucent, revealing clusters of spider-like meandering purple veins. She doubted that his body had ever seen sunlight. It was inevitable that Dot would compare his body to that of the only other man she had seen naked. Sol's brown skin had shone. His strong arms and broad, muscular chest on which she used to love lying her head had felt like home. The two men could not have been more different, and that at least was some small mercy, for had Wally been a poor imitation of Sol, it might have been confusing. Tonight there was no confusion: if Sol was warm, Wally was cold; if Sol meant strength, Wally weakness; and if Sol was love, Wally was indifference.

Dot tiptoed around the mattress to the vacant side and crouched down, pulling back the corner of the bedspread with a trembling hand. She climbed in and lay as stiff as a board on her left side, facing the wall, shivering with cold and fear. She screwed her eyes tightly shut and prayed, prayed that he would let her sleep. She wasn't comfortable but was far too nervous to pull her nightie further down her legs or change position so her knees were not resting on each other. Her feet were cold and her muscles tense, but still she didn't move, didn't want to risk any part of her body inadvertently touching any part of his.

An hour passed, maybe more. Dot listened through the pretence of sleep as Wally drew rhythmically on his cigarettes and flicked ash into a glass ashtray that he'd placed on his thigh. He coughed a few times, a phlegm-filled rattle that reminded her of her dad first thing in the morning. She sniffed surreptitiously at the pillow from her childhood bed, knowing that it would soon lose its perfume of apple shampoo, hairspray and Coty L'Aimant.

Finally Wally placed the ashtray on the floor with a thud and slunk down on the mattress. He pulled the blanket up, which loosened it from Dot's grip under her chin. She ground her teeth and tried to stop her limbs from shaking. Pushing her eyelids even closer together, she held her breath, which meant she then exhaled more loudly and obviously than she had intended, betraying the fact that she was awake. There were a couple of seconds of stillness when she thought she might have got away with it before she felt his thin hand grip her right shoulder.

Dot felt herself jump; her arm jerked. He didn't attempt to move her, thankfully. Instead he gently squeezed her shoulder and touched the hair that hung down her back.

'Night then.' He withdrew his hand and turned over.

They lay like actors, both feigning sleep, both praying for and dreading the relief that daylight would bring. It would mean they could leave this room, but what would they do tomorrow? With no wedding for distraction, it meant a whole twenty-four hours in each other's company, with nothing to say and nothing to do.

Dot heard the change in his breathing and knew that he slept. That was when she started to cry. Hot, silent tears leaked down over her nose and cheekbones and into the pillow. She cried both with sadness at her newly married state and with relief. She had expected a violation – how could she not? They were man and wife. It wasn't just the thought of having to lie with a stranger, it wasn't even the revulsion she felt at her husband's physique. It was much more than that. Wallace would be entering a space, both physically and mentally, that had been the sole reserve of her love, her Sol. It would be an invasion that threatened to erase the perfect memory of their union and dilute the act of creating Simon.

Dot lay awake long after Wally slumbered, appreciating the solitude. She blinked into the ether and tried to answer the big question: how long could she live like this, with this man, in this horrible, cold flat before she started to lose her mind?

Chapter Eleven

Three months had passed since their wedding. Three months that for Dot Day might as well have been years. She lived in a state of silent agitation when Wally was around and in a state of silent agitation when he wasn't around, waiting for him to come home – not that it would ever feel like home. Joan and Reg had visited once; it had been awkward and embarrassing. Wally and her Dad had bantered as they always did, recounting the hilarity of the wedding reception and arranging to meet soon in the pub. Their jollity merely highlighted all that wasn't being said. Joan tried not to make too much of the sparse surroundings of her daughter's marital home, although her raised eyebrows and sharp intake of breath spoke volumes. She tried not to comment on the lack of food on offer or the dark circles that sat beneath her daughter's clouded eyes like two bruises. The four sat in the front room, with Dot and Wally on cushions on the floor. After one hour Joan commented that they did not want to miss the bus and everyone had nodded, no one publicly acknowledging the fact that there was a bus every forty minutes. No one insisted on another cup of tea or delayed their exit with one final story. Another hour would have been unbearable. They promised to bring Dee next time; she was doing well at school, they said, and this was the only time Dot smiled, when she pictured the bundle of energy that was her clever little sister.

She woke bright and early and did as she had every morning since her arrival in Walthamstow: squeezed out a healthy dollop of Ajax, scrubbed the worktops in the kitchen, cleaned the two-ring hob and mopped and dried the kitchen floor. Then she wiped around the stainless steel sink until it shone, ran the carpet sweeper over the lino and the concrete floors, flicked a duster over the fireplace and rubbed over the two vinyl chairs – donated by Wally's mealy-mouthed, whinging mother – with a damp cloth. This took approximately twenty minutes and that was her list of chores complete for the day.

Wally had been signed off the sheet metal for a while with his back and had got into the habit of sleeping in until mid-morning. He would appear at around eleven a.m., having sloped from the bedroom to the bathroom to the chairs in the sitting room, where he would yawn and stretch with a look of happiness on his face, reminding Dot of a retarded cat. When he did appear, unwashed but dressed, flat-haired and with the indent of a pillow crease on his grey cheek, she would slip into the bedroom and fling open the window on its tilt, trying to rid the room of the smell of him. It was the musky tang of male sweat and smoker's breath; no matter that she knew what to expect, Dot had to fight her gag reflex or would have thrown up all over their mattress. She longed to wake in a room that smelt like her childhood bedroom, sweet and untainted by adult scents, or indeed in a room that smelt of Sol, expensive cologne and sensual oils. She would stare out over the roof tops, taking great gulps of air before throwing the sheet and bedspread over the mattress and plumping the two pillows just so.

Wally, enjoying his first fag of the day, would mutter 'Are you hungry?' as she passed the door. To this she would give a little nod and reach for the frying pan in the kitchen. He was nervous around her and did not have the courage to ask outright if there was any breakfast. Dot fed Wally twice a day. Every day. Eating breakfast so late meant that this meal was a kind of lunch/breakfast hybrid, consisting of fried bacon between two slices of white bread and tomato ketchup, washed down with a mug of strong tea. At around five p.m. Wally would be hungry again and she would present him with either more bacon, again served between two slices of white bread and tomato ketchup, or a fried egg between two slices of white bread and tomato ketchup. Every Wednesday and Friday night she would fetch fish and chips from the chippy in the new precinct on the ground floor and they would eat it out of the wrapper with their fingers. Every time Dot lifted the scalding batter-wrapped cod to her mouth, she thought of Sol and a large conch on a large plate.

Dot placed the white china on the arm of the chair and waited for Wally to stop scratching his chin so that he could eat his breakfast.

'Ooh, bacon – lovely!'

She knew he was lying, but couldn't figure out why – or why the lie was delivered in the veil of a compliment; did he think she cared? 'I could do you some toast?'

'Toast? Nah, bacon'll do, but I reckon if you carry on like this, I'll turn into a bleeding pig!' He laughed, hoping that it might be infectious. It wasn't.

Dot stared at the man who never used cologne, who didn't sing or dance, who scratched himself with abandon and never cleaned his teeth. She didn't say a word.

Wally took a large bite, filling his mouth with half the sandwich. 'I thought you might like cooking, what with your mum being a cook and everything.' A small blob of wet bread landed on the chair; she resisted the temptation to clean it up right away.

Dot shrugged in response and wandered into the kitchen to scrub the frying pan. She replied to Wally in her mind, as she often did. *Truth is, Wally, I do love cooking, I just don't want to cook for you. If I was married to Sol, I would strive every day to make something wonderful that we would eat together and laugh about before falling into bed. Truth is, Wally, if he was the man I shared this flat with, I'd live in this horrible place, with its shitty kitchen and its cold floor, and I would be living wrapped up in clovers. In fact, as long as I was with him, anywhere and anything – a tent in a blizzard or homeless in a jungle – would make me happy. And the exact opposite is true of you, of us; if you put us in a mansion and gave me jewels, I would feel the same as I do now. I would wake with a desolate heart and want to run away, because you aren't him and you never will be.*

'I'm going out.'

Dot nodded in his direction. He was probably off to meet one of his creepy mates up the pub. Not that she cared; it was a relief to be alone. As soon as the front door clicked into the frame, Dot wiped her hands on her skirt and went into the bedroom. Pulling her suitcase from the corner of the room, she flipped up the locks and removed her shell from beneath her underwear. She carried it with both hands into the sitting room, sat in the chair only recently vacated by her husband and placed it on her knees. She breathed deeply and spoke slowly. She wanted every word to reach him.

'Me again. Things pretty much the same here. I know I should try harder, but it's difficult. Wally ain't bad, but he's not you. He's not fat or wicked, but truth is it could be Billy Fury that I'm shacked up and I'd feel exactly the same. I want your skin, your face, your voice and anything else is not good enough. I can't help wondering what it'd be like living with you, here. We'd be all right, wouldn't we? We'd be more than all right. I was thinking earlier that we'd be fine anywhere. I'd make you apple crumble just like I promised and we'd find nice places to walk with Simon. It'd be brilliant. See, I don't need no formal and informal lounge – whatever that is when it's at home. I just need you, that's all, just you. Being with you was like being home.'

Dot considered her next phrase. She drew breath and smiled, wanting to talk about Simon some more.

'What the bleeding hell are you doing?'

His voice took her by surprise; she jumped. Dot looked up and into the face of her husband. She hadn't heard him come back in, had been too engrossed to hear the key in the lock or the rattle of the front door. She was mortified, embarrassed to have been discovered. Not because of what Wally might think, but in case their exchange could be heard on a beach far, far away.

'N… nothing. I'm not doing nothing!' She placed her hands protectively around her shell, hugging it close to her lap.

'Who the fuck are you talking to?' It was a rare flare of aggression. Wally flexed his fists by his side.

'I wasn't talking to no one.'

'I can see that, cos you're sat here all on your tod, but you

283

were talking to someone as if they were here, telling him you'd make bleeding apple crumble...'

Dot stared at the floor and felt the creep of a blush over her neck and face; he must have heard it all. *Oh God...*

Wally bent down. Crouching on the floor in front of her, his voice was once again quite soft. 'And what I really want to know, Dot, is who you'd make apple crumble for, while I choke meal after meal on bacon, always grateful that you are making me something, no matter how boring or tasteless it is?'

Dot ignored the question.

Wally continued. 'Nah, you don't have to answer, love. I bet I can guess. I bet I know who all this is in aid of. It were that bloke you were seeing before, weren't it? That darkie bloke who had first pickings. Barb told me you had a fancy for a bit of foreign.' Wally breathed deeply and stood, placing his hands on his hips, figuring out how to continue. 'I reckon you've got some bloody nerve. You marry me, live here, never show me the slightest bit of kindness or interest and as soon as me back's turned, you sit chatting to some bloody bloke on the other side of the bleeding world who didn't give a shit about you and yet you talk to him like he's royalty, and me, muggins here, I'm just the annoying bastard that's put a roof over your head! I'm the idiot that puts up with your bollocks and what do I get in return? I get nothing, fuck all!'

Dot let her tears fall. What did it matter, it was the truth.

'Still got nothing to say?' Wally stood and stared out of the window at the concrete nothingness that was their view. 'I knew you was damaged goods, as they say, but I had no idea that you were mental. You are, y'know; you are bloody loop the loop. Jesus, I reckon even that Barb would have more about her. I mean she weren't no looker but, Christ, it'd be better than this!'

Dot remained silent. Maybe he was right, who knows? Maybe he and Barb would have been happy. How had it all gone so bloody wrong?

He turned towards her. She watched his expression, saw him deciding what to do next. Where could they go from here?

He reached forward and grabbed at the shell. She raised her elbows, making it hard for him to get a grip, clutching it to her chest. 'No! Get off! Leave it alone, Wally, it's mine!'

The two tussled over it like toddlers.

'We is married, love, what's mine is yours and all that… Let go!'

'No!' she shrieked, louder than he would have thought possible. 'Don't you touch it, Wally, it's all I've got left of him! It's all I've got left!'

These words gave Wally the impetus he needed. With one hand he hooked the shell from her grip and with the other he pushed her head back against the chair.

'Is that right, all you've got left of him? You've taken the piss out of me for the last time. Apple crumble? I'm your fuck-ing husband!'

Wally stood, slightly encumbered by the bulky shell in his hand.

Dot jumped up after him. 'Please, Wally! Please give it back to me… please. My grandad gave it to me.'

Wally hesitated for the briefest second before opening the front door. Dot ran behind him but was too slow. He stood on the walkway and hurled her precious shell out into the daylight. Dot watched with her hands outstretched, as though she could somehow prevent the inevitable. The shell seemed to fall in slow motion, allowing her to follow its course out into the middle of the empty space below, turning and falling before it hit the concrete floor, shattering into a million pieces. For the rest of her days, Dot would be able to picture that moment with clarity; closing her eyes, it would always be there for perfect recall. She watched the shards splinter and bounce with a violent pitter-patter.

Wally stormed off, angry and embarrassed by what he'd done. Dot stood transfixed by the fragments of shell that littered the greyness below, the sun glinting off the tiny slivers of pink. She slid down the wall and sat in a ball at the base of the walkway. She felt calm and strangely disconnected. She knew that she would never talk to Sol again. And finally she had the answer to the big question: three months and five days. It had taken three months and five days for her to start to lose her mind.

As night began to fall, she crept back inside the flat and crawled on all fours across the hallway and onto the greasy mattress. She heard the laughter of kids outside, knowing that never again would she laugh with joy. Never again would she kiss the lips of the man she loved or place her hand upon a male chest with longing. Her heart had split, would never heal; her broken spirit meant she would exist as a husk, all feeling and vitality stripped away forever. She would grow old and lonely inside this marriage with a heart that yearned for the man she could never have. Her body would cherish the memory of the times their skin had touched and that magic spark that had ignited within her.

She closed her eyes and pictured the two of them sitting in Ronnie Scott's sipping champagne with fingers entwined, staring into each other's eyes; they had been unaware that these were the last few hours they would have together. What would she have said had she known? What could she have done? It probably would have made little difference. The universe had conspired and Dot and Sol were reduced to mere pawns that had no option but to go with the situation that forces bigger than them had decreed. She lay her head on her childhood pillow and fell into a deep, exhausted sleep.

The front door slammed against the wall in the early hours, waking her with a jolt. Wally bumped along the hallway, muttering to himself before walking into the door frame of the bedroom and tripping over his shoes. He entered in a cloud of alcoholic fumes; the pungent odour stung her nose – beer and whisky, if she had to guess. He removed his trousers and fell onto the mattress in his shirt and socks. Dot lay still, staring into the manmade orange glow. She became aware of a movement on Wally's side of the bed; his shoulders shook and his body heaved as he cried into his pillow. Unable to speak words of comfort, she placed her hand on his back and patted him, the way one might a child that was distressed but whom you didn't know.

Wally's words were muffled against the feather-filled ticking, but Dot heard them loud and clear.

'Enough. I've had enough.'

Dot's heart leapt. He was right: this was no way to live. The last part of her functioning heart had been thrown over the balcony along with her shell. She didn't know where they could go from here, but she felt sorry for them both.

It was a bright, frosty morning, the kind on which, not so long ago, she would have stomped the streets of Limehouse, wandered down to the docks and into the cafe for a cuppa, chewed the fat with Barb. Dot dashed the tears from her cheeks and placed her hands on the worktop. She bit her top lip with her bottom teeth; she wanted to make this sadness stop, but she didn't know how. In one palm was the bunched-up striped tea towel with which she had been drying up last night's chip plates. Her fingers formed little pyramids that supported her weight along rigid arms. Her hair hung forward, enabling her to hide behind the toffee-coloured curtain. It was three days since her shell had been destroyed and yet still the memory of it tumbling through the air was enough to make her tears spill. It was ridiculous, really; he had never touched it or even seen it and yet it was an object that she felt linked her powerfully and magically to the man she loved. It was also the last link to her childhood, and her grandad, although she had to admit this fact had been thrown onto the heap of misery for good measure – its connection to Sol was the reason she cried.

'Come on, Dot, get a grip.' She'd been doing this more and more recently, speaking in a quiet yet commanding tone, trying to self-soothe, take control.

Her husband crept into the kitchen, his black-socked feet making his entrance almost silent. She turned to see what it was he wanted: a cup of tea? Sandwich? She noticed the dark bruises of consecutive sleepless nights that sat above his cheek-bones; his pinched face and sallow skin. But there was something else: he looked as if he had been crying again, though she didn't know him well enough to mention it.

'What we gonna do, Wally? We can't go on like this, can we?'

It felt strange to cleave the silence that sat between them like a block of ice and even stranger to break it with a topic of such gravity when their usual exchanges were about cups of tea and passing the tomato sauce.

Wally looked her in the eye. This itself was progress; he had been avoiding eye contact with her since they had exchanged vows. He leant against the wall and studied her from top to toe. Running his hands through his hair, he kept his fingers on his scalp as he closed his eyes and breathed deeply. Finally, he rubbed his palm over his face and chin before swallowing noisily.

'Come and sit down,' he said quietly.

Dot followed him into the lounge, throwing the tea towel on the worktop and wiping her hands down her skirt as she walked across the small square of lino that covered the floor.

The gas fire gave off a gentle hiss as the two sat on the squeaky vinyl chairs. Dot placed the thin crocheted cushion over her lap and put her clasped hands on it, a barrier of sorts; Wally leant forward. With his shirt sleeves rolled high against his biceps, he placed his elbows on his knees; his upturned face was only feet from hers.

'I'm sorry about your shell. I shouldn't have broken it.'

'S'okay.' Although of course it wasn't.

'You've met me mum and dad...' He spoke slowly, in a considered fashion; he was calm.

Dot nodded, unsure where this was going.

'They're bloody useless. Always have been. I remember when the letters came home from school about the eleven-plus, my teacher thought I could do well. I put it on the mantelpiece and told my dad that there was an open day at the Grammar; I asked him if he'd take me. He looked up and said to me "Wha'for?" As though the very idea of me going to a place like that was so ridiculous there was no point. He's very political, my dad, and has always banged on about the responsibility of the working man. He told me that if I went to the Grammar, I'd get ideas above me station. I wanted to ask what my station was exactly, but it wouldn't have got me anywhere. My life was pretty much mapped out, I guess. They're not only useless with me; they're rubbish for each other. Never supported each other, never made the other one happy. And then I went to your house one day with your dad, when he was on the metal. I couldn't believe it, Dot. I stepped through the door into that warm hallway and before I'd hung me coat up, your mum was rushing around making cups of tea and getting the fruitcake out the tin. I felt like a bloody king. They were laughing at something on the radio, I can't remember what now—'

'Probably something stupid,' Dot cut in, thinking of all the little private jokes and shared joys that used to fill the back room while the fire roared. It had been a happy place, a refuge, before…

He continued as though she hadn't spoken. 'I remember thinking, I want to live like this. I want someone at home that's pleased to see me and gets the fruitcake out when a visitor comes though the door and who laughs with me and dances to any old rubbish on the radio.'

Dot suppressed the image of dancing in Sol's arms – the pictures of him holding her were like little daggers that hurt every time they jabbed at her heart and mind.

'Then I met you and you were so beautiful and so sparky. I never thought you'd look twice at me, like me…'

I didn't. I don't.

'But your dad said you were a bit shy, really, and that you'd had a rough time and that you just wanted someone to look after you.'

I did want someone to look after me, but it wasn't you.

'And I thought, I can do that, I can look after her and I s'pose I thought that we'd end up with a house like your mum and dad's, a happy house, with the radio on.'

'Wally, I—'

'No. Let me finish. I ain't good at talking and I need to say this, Dot, while I can. I thought you'd be grateful to me some-how and I know how that sounds, but I thought it. I thought you'd be glad to be getting married after that other bloke did a runner and that we'd grow together, if you like, get to know each other a bit and then who knows… But that's not how it's working out and I never knew I'd be this lonely being married and I know you're lonely too.'

Dot nodded. *Yes, I'm lonely, so lonely.*

'I'm awkward and embarrassed. I don't know where to stand or sit, what to say or how to say it and this flat feels small and I feel big in it. That's why I go out all the bleeding time, just to give us both some space. I sit in the park sometimes and I sit on me tod and I breathe out and my shoulders unknot and I don't feel so sick or uptight like I do when I'm here, cos I know you don't want me here, but the trouble is I live here!

It's my home!' Wally realised that he had raised his voice. He waited a second and then continued, quiet again and under control. 'I know this situation ain't really your fault, but the thing is, it ain't really my fault either. And you're right, this is no way to live, it's no life. And so we need to talk about things. We need to sort things out.'

'We do, Wally, I know.' Her stomach flipped at what might come next.

'There's lots you don't know about me, Dot. In fact, you don't know anything about me. I've been saving and saving; that's why I ain't bought stuff for the flat, because I always wanted to own me own house and I've got enough for a deposit. I don't know if that will make you happy, but it would make us more secure. I wanted to go looking at places together and make a plan for our future, but I can see that there isn't any point. The fact is, you're my wife, Dot; we are married and that means that we will be together for a very long time, probably for the rest of our lives, but I don't want to spend the rest of my life with someone that doesn't wanna be with me. I can't.'

They were both silent for some minutes, allowing the enormity of his words to sink in.

'What do you think, Dot, is that fair enough?'

She nodded. It was more than fair enough.

'So, I've come up with a plan of my own. The way I see it, we either make a go of this marriage and live like a normal husband and wife or we call it a day. And the only way we can make that decision is if you sort out what's going on in your head.'

Dot's pulse raced; was he asking for a divorce? The thought of being a divorced woman who had been an unmarried

292

mother… What would she do? Where would she go? But could she continue living tethered to a man she didn't love, a man that repulsed her because he wasn't Sol? No, she couldn't. He was right, it wasn't really his fault and that wasn't fair.

'So instead of putting a deposit down, I've gone and spent the money.'

Dot stared at him; why was he telling her this? What did it matter, it was his money. He had probably frittered it down the pub, up the bookies, so what? Owning a house wouldn't have changed a thing, of that she was sure.

Wally lifted his bottom from the chair, making his bony thighs rise up against the slack of his black cotton trousers as his hand snaked into the back pocket. He pulled out a white envelope that wasn't sealed. Holding it by the edge, he bounced it against his upturned palm as if considering whether to give it to her not.

Oh my God, divorce papers… *Where will I go?*

'I want you to go away, Dot, for a week or a month, what-ever it takes. I want you to sort out what it is you need to sort out and when you've sorted it you have to make a decision. You either stay where you are and make a life there or come back here and make a life with me. Not just a make-do life, but a proper life, like a proper married couple, with the radio on and proper dinner and intimacy.' The last word hung in the air, the glue that would bind them or the reason they would part.

He held out the envelope. Dot reached out and grasped it with the tips of her fingers; he gripped on to it for a fraction of a second before releasing it into her care. She turned it over and lifted the loose flap. Her fingers delved inside and touched the stiffened card. As she drew it out with caution, her eyes scanned the words, the text, the figures, the facts… Wally had indeed been saving and had used his house deposit money to buy her a ticket, a return ticket. A ticket to St Lucia.

Dot stared at the piece of card that at three inches by ten inches was so much bigger than the sum of its parts. She bowed her head to her chest and inhaled deeply until her breath had returned to its normal rhythm.

She considered reaching out to touch his knee or give him a hug, but decided against it.

'Thank you! Thank you, Wally.' She smiled at her husband, then jumped up and kissed him hard on the mouth. He pulled her towards him and kissed her back; it left them both breathless.

Wally almost leapt from his seat, grabbed his coat from the back of the door and was gone. There was a flicker of disappointment in his eyes. She realised that deep down, despite his brave rhetoric, he had probably hoped that she would refuse it and stay in Walthamstow.

Dot studied the ticket and documents in her hands. BOAC-Cunard would whisk her off to New York, then Barbados, with several short stops at islands en route and finally a little island hopper would take her to the beaches where her lover swam. It was as if a dark cloud had been lifted from her mind. Her spirits soared and her heart pounded. She placed the pieces of paper against her chest. 'I'm coming, Sol! I'm coming!' She jumped up and twirled around the room like a ballroom dancer who had lost her partner.

Chapter Twelve

Her little case had been packed without too much deliberation. It wasn't as if she had a winter and summer wardrobe. She put her summer frock in, a couple of fine-knit cardies, her vests, pants, socks, a nightie and one pair of cropped trousers. In London, any variation in the weather simply meant wearing more or fewer layers: the actual clothes remained pretty much consistent. It was therefore without heed to the heat of the Caribbean that she folded her dress and underclothes and laid them on top of each other. If it was too hot, she would simply leave off her stockings. Her one concession had been the purchase of a bathing suit. It was navy with large white spots on it and a pretty bow that sat just beneath her bust. As she fingered its thin straps and high-cut legs, her breath blew out like cold smoke in the chill of the autumn morning; she couldn't imagine wearing it.

The first plane was big and noisy – not that she cared; she had far too much to occupy her mind. It was amazing and unbelievable to think she was actually making the journey. The only people she had seen getting on and off planes, acting as though they were boarding a bus, were film stars and pop groups that had been snapped on the steps and plastered on the front of the *Standard*; to be among their number was surreal. The excitement was tinged with awkwardness and embarrassment at travelling alone – she didn't know the routine, where to go, what to do and wished that she had someone to share the little things with. A wave of guilt swept over her as she realised how much Dee would have loved it; then, when her thoughts finally turned to her husband, who had sacrificed his dream to make this possible, that sent another wave of guilt shooting through her veins.

On the plane, she was too shy to ask for help with stowing away her luggage, and having to unbuckle her seat belt and make her way to the tiny loo were also daunting prospects. But the staff were so attentive that they more or less talked her through every step, including her transfers. The model-like air hostesses had beautiful faces, orange lipstick and immaculate suits and they waltzed up and down the aisle balancing glasses full of ice and fizzing gin and tonics. Dot stuck to water and lemonade, it felt safer.

It wasn't until she was on the plane that she considered, really considered what she would do when she arrived. Such had been her joy at the prospect of seeing Sol that she hadn't thought about what she should say if she tracked him down or even whether it was a good idea at all. Her heart leapt and her stomach churned at the prospect of being near him again. She figured she would know what to say when the time was right.

When the plane reached its full cruising height and those around her started to relax, she finally dared to look down from the window at the clouds below. She was above the clouds! Imagine that. It was a beautiful sight and one that she would never forget. She was in the sky! With clouds above, and clouds below. It suddenly occurred to her that she had always thought that this was where heaven might lurk. Dot screwed her eyes into slits to focus better, trying to look into the gaps between the vapour, but looking for what, she did not know.

When she was small she used to lie on her back in the garden and stare up into the clouds looking for those same gaps, trying to peek at heaven. She fully expected to see fat-bottomed angels draped in bed sheets directing thunderbolts and volleying Cupid's arrows. She could now see this wasn't true. Come to think of it, she knew that space was beyond the sky, so where exactly was this heaven that she had searched for so fervently? Maybe it didn't exist and if it didn't exist, where had her nan gone? Where was Jude's baby now? Was that it? A few years or seconds on the planet, then, poof!, you just disappeared forever? Surely not, otherwise what was the point? Dot realised that she knew very little, including why she was schlepping halfway around the world in this metal tube. What did she hope to accomplish? If she was being honest, she hoped to run into his arms and never leave. That was what she hoped to accomplish. Poor Wally would eventually find someone else and when he was old and grey with a clutch of grandchildren running around his knees, he would thank her for setting him free. Barb's tear-stained face ducking behind a tree flashed behind her eyes.

As she descended the aircraft steps in St Lucia, surveying the concrete strip, Dot felt elated at having finally arrived. She had expected to feel exhausted – it had been a long, draining journey – but instead she was alert, already registering in her mind each new feeling and sensation. Tiny homes with tin roofs sat only a few feet away on the other side of the runway. The London airport had had a rather grand red-brick terminus with comfy seats and a cafe, but here in St Lucia there was a long, low bungalow and a stall selling refreshments under a hand-painted sign. A gust of hot air filled her lungs: new smells, new sights and a new temperature. Her stomach tightened in anticipation; she was getting closer to him, they were once again in the same country. Reunion was only a fingertip away.

She was transported from the airport in a little green open-topped Land Rover with bare metal doors and a steering wheel that grew from the floor like a tiny sapling. It bounded up and down the steep, dusty tracks, through dense jungle where the fronds of giant palms tickled her arms as they drove past. The flowers were such vibrant colours – fiery reds and electric blues. Nothing like the little gold chrysanthemum that occasionally popped its head up from the grey dirt mound at Ropemakers Fields. She hadn't known that flowers like this existed. Bananas hung from trees in big, fat bunches and the heavy-looking rounded green fruit on the other trees were mangoes, apparently.

An hour later, the car broke out onto the coastal road and there it was in front of her, framed by lush forest and jungle-covered mountains – the sea! Dot pulled herself up against the door frame and stood, despite the protestations from her driver. She didn't care; she wanted to see it all, unable to take her eyes from the pale blue ocean that went on forever and the clusters of giant palm trees that fringed the beach. Yachts peppered the horizon, and the sun smothered everything with a hazy glint of heat. It was beyond beautiful, it was just as he had described; it was paradise.

Dot's rose-print summer dress clung to her sweaty skin, and her hair, which she'd gathered up into a neat chignon, now hung limply in strands around her face, the rest of it blowing backwards in the breeze. She could never have imagined the temperature; it was so strange to be breathing in hot air, like when you accidentally opened your gob under the dryer at the hairdresser and got a lungful.

The car wound its way through the streets of Castries en route to Reduit Beach. Small crowds of children pressed forward as they passed, some snickering into their palms, others reaching with outstretched arms. Dot stared at them; she had only ever seen the occasional black person and felt a slight frisson of anxiety to find herself the only white person among the crowd. The kids were fascinated in return; for most, it was the first time they had seen anyone white and they wanted to touch her hair and stare at her face.

She thought of Barb, remembering their conversation, it seemed like a lifetime ago, *'Don't be daft, Dot. If theirs was normal hair, everyone'd be walking around with it, wouldn't they?'* *'Well of course! And they do where he lives, you dozy cow!'*

It was late afternoon when she arrived at her little beach hut at Reduit Beach. She grinned at the sight: it was pretty and perfect. It reminded her of a gingerbread house in a fairy-tale book. It was wooden and painted sugar pink with bright blue curtains in the little windows. A wide wooden step led to the front door – perfect for taking in the mesmerising view. The key, as promised by the travel agent, was taped under the mat. Her little home comprised two rooms. In the bedroom stood an old brass bed that sagged in the middle; it was covered with a pristine white counterpane on which four fat feather pillows were stacked high. She considered the bed she shared with Wally, the greasy mattress in the curtainless room, but then checked herself. How many fancy beds would her ticket have bought? Quite a few probably. She was still in awe of his act of kindness and surprised by the eloquence with which he had summed up their dire situation, almost giving her permission to abandon him, possibly forever.

The sitting room had a wicker sofa with plump sprig-leaf-patterned cushions on it and a cream and green tartan rug thrown over the back; she couldn't imagine needing that. There was a multi-coloured rag rug on the floor and a small stove and a sink in one corner with a square of mirror above it. Local prints of beaches and palm trees hung randomly in clusters. Most were at jaunty angles, having shifted on their hooks. She fought the need to straighten them. Her bathroom was at the back of the hut with a shower pipe jutting from the wall; the water was warmed by the sun while it sat in a small tank on the roof. It ran straight onto the sandy floor, where there was a latrine hole – her loo. She was shielded from view by walls of rush matting that formed a cubicle of sorts. It was perfect.

Dot placed her little suitcase on the floor and kicked off her shoes. She pulled out the remainder of the pins from her hair and, shaking it loose, stepped out of the front door and onto the hot sand. She dug her toes in and savoured the way the small mounds of salt-like grains piled up to fill the arches beneath her feet, cushioning her every step. She tentatively walked forward. After only a few minutes, she felt the sting of the sun against her skin, her hair lank against the damp sweat on her neck. She remembered Sol shivering and rubbing his palms together for warmth as he waited on an East End street corner with the frost beneath his heavy shoes. *No wonder he'd looked so bloody cold.*

Tiny translucent crabs shot down minute holes as her footsteps approached the shoreline. White bubbling waves fizzed on the sand before disappearing to leave a jagged, darkened line.

She ignored the stares of fellow beach goers, dark-skinned locals whose muscles rippled and dripped with sea water. Their comfort in this intense heat would have made her feel foolish had she considered how much of an outsider she was. Instead, she looked straight ahead and took small steps until the Caribbean Sea washed over her feet and lapped at her ankles; it was warm and welcoming. Dot grinned. She was really here; she was really in the sea! Bunching up the skirt of her dress with one hand, she held it just below her knickers and strode forward until the water pushed past her knees; tiny fish darted around this new object in their territory. Tomorrow she would put on her new bathing costume and she would sit in the sea. She couldn't wait.

Dot showered, washing away the sweat and fatigue of the day and night she had spent travelling, then pulled on her cropped trousers and a sleeveless top, and strolled along the beachfront to the cafe from which music pulsed. It took all of her courage to go in alone, but then she told herself it was no different from Paolo's cafe, just a bit warmer. Choosing a table outside, Dot slid onto a bench and watched the sun sink down into the ocean. As it did so, flaming torches and strings of light sprung to life along the shore and beach road. She had no idea that places like this existed; it was like a different planet.

'What can I get you?' The woman spoke with the same gentle roll as Sol. She was petite, like an elf, with close-cropped hair, high cheekbones, large, hooped gold earrings and brass bangles around the tops of her arms. She was wearing a tiny, triangular halter-neck top, without the need for a bra, and a floor-length patchwork cheesecloth skirt. She looked amazing.

'Oh, can I have a Coca-Cola?'

'Sure. And to eat?'

Dot thought of eating conch and her stomach flipped. In fact, the thought of eating anything made her wince, but it had been a long time since she'd had food and she knew that when the fatigue kicked in, she would need something in her stomach. 'What is there?' She bit down on her bottom lip. Wednesday night in the flat was chippy night – was it Wednesday night? She couldn't be sure.

'We got a callaloo special?'

'Sounds lovely.'

And it was, just as Sol had described it, warm and peppery. *'Oh, it's so tasty and filling that you will eat until you can barely move.'*

'How long you staying?' the woman asked as she cleared Dot's empty bowl.

'Truthfully, I dunno, maybe a week, maybe forever!'

'Forever, eh? I better make another batch then. I'm Cilla by the way.'

'I'm Clover.'

'Clover, that's a pretty name. Well, I'll see you around, Clover.'

'Yes, I hope so.'

'Honey, I know so! How many girls like you d'you think are strolling around a small place like this?'

'I guess not many…'

'You'd be right, not any! Where ya from?'

'London.'

'Hey, my uncle is over there, working on the Tube. His name is Grayson Amable, he lives in Ealing – do you know him?'

Dot laughed out loud. 'Course I don't! Ealing's miles away from where I live and there are millions of people!'

Cilla looked more than a little offended.

Dot did her best to make amends. 'But if I do see him, I'll send him your love.'

Cilla sniffed, smiled and nodded, satisfied, before leaving.

Despite the excited bubbles that grew and burst in her stomach, sleep was fast in arriving. Dot was lulled to sleep by the gentle sound of the small waves lapping the shoreline, the rustle of trees and the chirps and trills of insects and frogs around her. It was like magic. *I'm here Sol, I'm right here.*

Without a clock or watch, she had no idea what the time was, but judging from the sounds of laughter and chatter on the beach, it had to be waking-up time. Dot stretched on the large brass bed and leapt to her feet, then peered through the little curtain, just to make sure it wasn't an elaborate dream. No, it was real! The sea lay in front of her on this beautiful beach, just as she had left it the night before.

A quick splash in the shower and Dot squeezed her shapely form into her new bathing suit. She was glad there was no tall mirror to dent her confidence; had there been the opportunity to study her lumps and bumps, she would have chickened out of wearing it in public. Slipping her frock over the top, she donned her sunglasses and made her way down the beach to the cafe, feeling quite at home for a girl who had previously travelled only a handful of miles in any direction from the neighbourhood of her birth. In truth, she felt like a different person; she felt like Clover.

Cilla was dancing on the deck to the strains of a slow beat with her arms raised above her head. Dot wondered what it must feel like to be that happy, that abandoned.

'Don't you love Laurel Aitken? Morning, Clover, sleep good?'

'Yes! Thank you. Phew, it's hot!' Dot fanned her face with her hand.

'You'll get used to it, especially if you're staying forever. What you having for breakfast?'

'Have you got any fresh pineapple juice?'

'Coming right up.'

Dot sat back in her chair and let her eyes wander along the shore. Families dumped their towels and bags in sandy heaps on the beach and ploughed into the sea. Everyone seemed so confident and familiar with their surroundings – there was no tentative toe dipping required. She watched as old and young, big and small dived headlong into the small breakers, disappearing only to emerge feet away like interested seals popping their heads above the water.

Cilla placed a large glass of pulpy juice in front of her.

Dot held it between her palms. 'Can I take it down to the beach?'

Cilla nodded and shrugged, indifferent.

Dot ambled over to the group of palm trees that threw their spiky shade out across the sand and sat with her back against a ridged trunk. She pushed her sunglasses up onto her head, all very Natalie Wood, and took a sip. It was sweet and cold and utterly delicious. 'So that's what this feels like.' She smiled.

A little boy aged about two waddled across the sand and into view, pursued by a slightly older brother who looked none too pleased to be on child-minding duty. Dot watched as the toddler's fat little feet pounded the sand, revealing a glimpse of pale sole each time he lifted his foot. With arms pistoning up and down either side of his round tummy, he ran as fast as he was able until a small rock that lay hidden from view tripped him. He fell down and wailed, with a mouth full of tears and a curly head full of sand. She didn't realise she too was crying until she felt the hot tears drip onto her arms as they lay across her drawn-up knees.

'Simon... My Simon...'

Dot returned to the cafe and ordered a coffee. Sitting with her back to the sea, scanning the little beach cafe that already felt familiar, she decided to make a plan. She couldn't hide away down here for her entire stay, so once she was acclimatised she would seek out her lover.

'You look miles away.' Cilla placed the coffee on the table and sat down opposite her.

'I'm just thinking, I need to go and see someone, a friend of mine. I've come all this way just to see them, but now I'm here I'm not sure how to find them.' Dot was unsure of how much to tell.

'Well, if they live around here, chances are I know them. It's a small place and I've lived here my whole life! What's their name?'

Dot swallowed, her confidence was evaporating. She had little choice but to talk to Cilla, she was her link to this new world.

'His name is Solomon, Sol, Sol Arbuthnott.'

Cilla smiled, which turned into a laugh that shook her whole body. She giggled, with tears glinting in her eyes and one hand at her throat. 'Oh, Clover, you have friends in high places! The Arbuthnotts are big shots around here, girl! Trying to find someone that *doesn't* know them would be harder!'

Dot looked at her lap. She had known that Sol's family were wealthy, but not that everyone would know them. This made her quest both easier and harder. She felt swamped by the enormity of the situation.

Cilla continued, 'And today is your lucky day.'

'Oh, why's that?' Dot laughed.

'He is right over there…' She pointed with her arm outstretched and index finger directed over Dot's right shoulder.

Dot felt rooted to the spot. She wanted to turn around, but her shaking legs wouldn't budge. Her hands gripped her coffee cup and her tongue stuck to the roof of her mouth, making speech difficult.

'Is… is he really?'

'Yes, and if I'm not mistaken, he's coming this way.'

Dot gasped and placed her trembling hand over her mouth. 'Oh my God.'

Cilla watched the colour drain from Dot's cheeks and saw the fear flicker across her eyes.

'Think I'll leave you to it. Holler if you need anything.'

Dot's heart raced. She could hear the blood pulsing in her ears and was sure she would have fainted had she been standing. It was surreal. She sat for what felt like an age, waiting to hear his footsteps approach and climb onto the wooden deck of the cafe. The old man nursing a bottle of rum in the corner disappeared into the background, the music overhead faded until there was just her and the empty chair opposite, waiting.

She remembered grabbing a pen from the pot on the counter at Paolo's and scribbling on a napkin, *See you tomorrow, soldier boy. Exhausted, but happy! Your Clover xxxxx*. She had folded it with a tired but happy heart, confident that he would be given it within the hour. She hadn't known he was already heading home, back to paradise. She hadn't known she was carrying their baby. She hadn't known a lot of things.

She heard the creak of the timber as he climbed onto the step and the scrape of a chair and then silence; he hadn't sat down. She felt the heat of his stare against her back. He had seen her. She closed her eyes and waited. His bare feet shuffled across the floor, four paces until he was stood by her side; she heard his sharp intake of breath. He moved slowly until he was in front of her.

'Open your eyes.' It was a whisper.

Dot slowly raised her lids and it was as if it had been seconds and not more than a year since she had seen his face. He shone, this beautiful man. He stared at her in disbelief. His skin was darker than before, there were new lines etched around his eyes and he had lost weight; some of the muscle had slipped from his bones.

He continued to whisper. 'I dreamed about you last night. I wished you to me, just like I've wished you to me every night since I last saw you. Am I going mad? Are you really here? How—'

'It's a long story...'

'Oh, your voice! Your voice! I've missed it. I've missed you... every second.'

Sol pulled the chair away from the table and almost fell into it as the strength left his legs. He was wearing a shirt with the collar up and the buttons undone and tennis shorts. He gripped her hands and held them inside his own, crushing them to his face; it was almost painful.

Dot looked up into the face of the man she loved, the man she would always love. 'You broke my heart.' She cried, unable to stop the flow of tears.

Sol nodded and let his own tears fall. 'I broke my own.'

'You said you'd never let me go, but you did.'

'Oh, Clover, my Clover, I never let you go in my head or my heart, never.'

I had a baby, I needed you. He was perfect, he was ours.

He shook his head. 'We can't talk here, where can we go?' He was thinking aloud, not really asking her.

'I'm staying along the beach…'

Sol stood and reached for her hand and just like that she placed it inside his palm, where it fitted snugly; it felt like coming home. The two walked along the beach as though they had never been apart, able to breathe and think for the first time since they had been parted, without everything being filtered through the grief of separation.

Cilla watched them from the kitchen window. 'Oh dear, oh dear, there's gonna be big trouble up at the Jasmine House.'

Dot pushed open the door of her little hut and Sol followed. They had walked in silence; there was so much to be said that it was difficult for either of them to know where or how to start.

The moment the door closed, Sol stepped forward and pulled her to him, holding her tight against his chest with her head under the crook of his chin. He kissed her scalp and breathed in her scent. She reached up and placed her fingers against the skin at the base of his throat, feeling the pulse of his heart.

'I can't believe you're here, I keep thinking I might wake up and you'll be gone. I've imagined holding you so many times.' He smiled as he spoke.

The two made their way over to the sofa and sat at either end, facing each other. She gripped his legs and he her arms, entwined on the cosy space, unable and unwilling to be separated.

Sol continued. 'And if this is all I ever have, these few minutes of seeing you, touching you, hearing you, then I will die happy. I've prayed for so long for one more touch, one more kiss.'

Dot reached up and ran her fingers over his face, confirming he was real. She bent forward and kissed his mouth, a sweet kiss that sent a ripple of joy through her entire body. Sol lifted her until she lay flat against him, her dress open, allowing her skin to touch his along their legs, faces and chest where her swimming costume dipped away. He ran his hands over her form, kissing her hungrily and with a need that he had forgotten he possessed.

'I love you.' His words were a magic salve that confirmed what she thought she had known. She hadn't imagined it: he loved her. He loved her!

'I love you too, always.' She looked into his face, just inches from her own. Then she placed her head on his chest and spoke into the air. Safe in his arms, words now flowed with ease.

'I came to find you, y'know; I thought you must be poorly. I saw your mum, and she told me you had gone.'

'You did? I didn't know that.'

'She didn't tell you?'

Sol shook his head.

'She told me that if you had loved me, you wouldn't have gone without saying goodbye, and that made sense to me – you wouldn't, would you?'

'I had no choice.' His voice was small.

'Everyone has a choice, Sol.'

Dot remembered a conversation she'd had with Susan at Lavender Hill Lodge. *I wish I felt more like that, but truth is I don't want to chase the fun. I think I'd be happy forever with a little house and a child to care for. I'm finding it really tough. I don't want to give my baby away, but I've got no choice.*

'Surely you must have a choice?'

'No I don't, not really.'

'Not always, my darling. Sometimes you are presented with information or an ultimatum so compelling that you can't choose what you want.' Sol recalled his mother's dogged determination to ruin Dot's family; he was still convinced she would have done it. But Dot clearly did not know about the bargain he had struck, didn't know about the rent in Ropemakers Fields, and he didn't want to divulge any confidences; it was up to her parents to tell her, not him. And if he was being honest, it now felt as if he had given up a little too easily and that thought was harder to stomach than any other. 'I promise you that any decision I made, I did it because I believed it was for the best and never, not for one second because I wanted to leave you.'

'Was it because of your mum? Did she make you go?' The idea occurred to Dot as she remembered the cool way Vida had delivered the facts in the study at the Merchant's House.

'Yes.' It was all he could say. 'I have barely spoken to her since; she and my father have moved to another house on the island.'

Dot sat up. 'So you're living in that big house all on your own?'

Sol drew himself up on the sofa and Dot caught sight of it, glinting in the sun. She didn't know how she hadn't noticed it before. On the third finger of his left hand, a shiny gold band.

He shook his head. 'No, I live there with my wife.'

Dot flinched. It was as if she had been punched. She held her breath and tried to allow the information to seep into her brain. *A wife, 'my wife'. He was married. He had married someone that wasn't her.*

'You got married?' Her voice was a squeak. Hot tears flowed again.

He nodded. 'I sort of had to.'

Dot looked up suddenly, as if remembering for the first time. 'I did too.'

'You married someone?' It was Sol's turn for the kick in the stomach.

She nodded. 'I don't love him, I can't. I can only love you.'

Sol pulled her against him and held her close. He stroked her toffee-coloured hair. 'I don't love her either. I can't.'

'Me dad more or less kicked me out and I couldn't think of another option. It felt like my only chance and so I took it. I haven't been able to think straight at all since you went.'

Sol's story was similar. He thought about the weeks spent drunk and isolated, unable to function sober as the memory of her hurt too much. 'Oh, my love.'

'We live in a shitty flat and I can't bear to be in the same room as him and when I do look at him, I realise all over again that he is not you and I can't stand it.'

Sol pictured the long table piled high with food at the Jasmine House, where he and his wife ate with the finest silver, in silence. How he longed for the easy chatter over a sticky table top in a cafe in damp, dark London. He pictured the bed and its fine Egyptian cotton, how he hovered on the far side until his wife fell asleep, leaving him free to relive every moment of lying with his Clover, replaying every word, every flick of the hair, every giggle until they were indelibly etched on his mind.

'Does he know you are here?'

Dot nodded against his chest. 'Yes, he bought me a ticket and said I had to sort meself out. He said that the way we were carrying on wasn't fair on him or me, and he was right.'

'I'm very grateful to him – which sounds ridiculous, because I would also like to punch him in the face for marrying you. And yet I have no right.'

'No you don't, Sol, not really, and he ain't a bad man, he's just not you and never will be, which in my eyes is a crime. I feel sorry for him, really, poor sod. Oh God, Sol, it's such a mess.'

'It is a mess. I only know one thing and that is I love you, my Clover. I worried that it was all in my head, the way I felt, the way you made me feel; I worried that I might have imagined it or I thought that you might hate me after running out on you. I couldn't bear the idea of it, but the second I saw you again today, I knew, I knew that it was real, that we are real and that nothing will ever come close to this feeling, nothing ever. You are the love of my life now and for always.'

'Don't ever let me go Sol.'

'I won't ever let you go, baby.'

Dot didn't know if this was true or even possible, but her heart swelled with joy upon hearing those words again, just the same.

By the time he left, the day had once again sunk into the ocean, and the night animals were coming out to strike up their tune. Dot felt a mixture of elation and exhaustion. She lay in the middle of her big brass bed and ran her palm over her form, where his hands had touched.

'Sweet dreams, my darling boy.' She slipped into slumber with a smile on her face, feeling as she had before, before he had broken her heart, before Simon had ripped it out.

The next morning she was woken by a rapping on the door. Grabbing a sheet and swirling it over her underwear, she ambled into the sitting room, where she caught sight of herself in the square mirror above the sink. She was smiling, her cheeks held the apple-pink blush from the first kiss of sunshine and her hair was messy; she had never thought she looked so pretty. She beamed as she answered the door.

'Cilla! Come in! What time is it?'

'Early. I brought you some breakfast.' Cilla dumped a basket of hot rolls onto the little table with a glass of pineapple juice and a mug of hot coffee.

'Oh, bless, that's so kind of you.'

'I was also a bit worried – you didn't resurface yesterday…'

Dot noted the twitch of Cilla's eyebrow, the smirk around her lips and felt her cheeks flush. Nothing – well, nearly nothing – had happened yesterday between her and Sol, but she could see how it might look to the outside world.

'We had a lot to catch up on; it's been a while.'

'I'll say! My God, you could have lit up St Lucia with the electricity coming from you two. Y'know he's married, right?'

'Yes. I am too.' She didn't know why she divulged this, as if it made any difference.

'Look, Clover, I don't know you very well. In fact I don't know you at all, but what I do know I like. You seem like a sweet girl and I'm telling you to be careful. You don't want to mess with the Arbuthnotts and their like, they are powerful people.'

'I think I'm quite safe with Sol!' Dot laughed at the idea of her beautiful man being feared.

'Oh him, yes! But his wife's people are not so nice. They own most of Martinique and let's just say they didn't get it by playing nice. Okay?'

Dot nodded, but felt far from okay.

Sol found her dressed and ready for the day. No sooner had she opened the door than he swept her up and carried her to the bed. He threw her down on the white counterpane. Ignoring her squeals and yelps, he kissed her hard, running his hands through the hair she had spent twenty minutes styling and smudging the lipstick off her face and onto his own.

'I missed you! God, I feel like a child. I slept so well last night. I woke up laughing! Actually laughing, because I knew you were close by. I love feeling like this and I love you. I can't stop telling you: I love you, I love you!'

Dot kissed him back. 'I love you too!'

The two kissed and held each other tight, resisting the over-whelming urge to strip off and find comfort as they had in his grand bed in the Merchant's House. It was as if the rules had changed and both were aware of what was at stake.

Finally, jumping up, Sol gripped her wrists and pulled her from the bed. 'Come on, we are going on an adventure!'

Dot just had time to grab her sunglasses and the glass of pineapple juice before they jumped into Sol's scarlet open-topped sports car.

'Ooh, this is flash! And there was me thinking you fancied that little Mini in Ropemakers Fields. What's this then? I like the colour.'

'It's an AC Shelby Cobra, the only one in the Caribbean!'

'Fancy! Think I'll stick to the bus.'

'God, I've missed you.' Sol kept glancing to his right as though to confirm that she was sitting in his car. He placed his hand on her thigh as if to anchor her and stop her disappearing at any moment.

Dot sipped her pineapple juice and tried not to spill it as they rounded corners and bumped over dips in the road. The roads got narrower and narrower, until Dot began to worry what might happen if they met another car coming from the opposite direction. The thick canopy of leaves made a roof over the track that dripped with the recent rainfall. The two chattered and laughed, each queuing up the next item on the agenda – so much needed to be said. The car stopped abruptly at the edge of a small forest.

'Here we are.'

He smiled at Dot, his beautiful open smile that gave her a glimpse of the man behind it, a good man who would have made a wonderful father to their son.

He strode with confidence through the forest. Dot followed

in his wake, tripping as her urban feet, more familiar with the grey slabs of English pavements, struggled with the alien terrain. She trod gingerly over tangled roots and fallen branches.

It was worth it. One more step forward and she found herself in paradise.

The bay was horseshoe shaped, on a gentle incline that allowed the crystal-clear blue water to lap its shore. The fine sand was undisturbed. The trees of the wood behind them cast gentle shadows and shady pockets over the beach. Mother Nature had dotted palm trees where the jungle met the sand. It was perfect.

'Oh, Sol! This is like something out of a film, but even better! I've never seen anything like it. It's beautiful.'

He lowered his frame onto the sand and Dot sat next to him, bunching up her frock to tan her calves. She was self-conscious about stripping off to her swimming costume, preferring to keep herself a bit covered. There was no need for a towel or a blanket; this was the way to do beach life. She ran her fingers through the sand and let the gentle wind lift her hair and her spirits.

Sol lay back on his elbows. 'You have no idea how many times I have dreamed of showing you this place. I often come here on my own and, as mad as it sounds, I talk to you. I chat about my day and I wonder what you are up to and I like to remember things we did together, walking along the Serpentine...'

'It doesn't sound mad at all. In fact I've been talking into a bloody shell, one of them big conch shells that you told me were on the beach. I thought you might be able to hear me, so I used to tell you all about my day and about our s—' Dot's tongue tripped over the words, but this was not the time.

'About our days together, our Sundays, strolling and drinking coffee.'

Sol stood up and peeled off his shirt and unzipped his shorts to reveal his swimming trunks underneath. 'Come on.' He pulled her up from the sand and helped her ease her arms from her dress, letting it fall in a heap.

'You look beautiful.' He ran his hands over her shoulders.

'So do you.' His beauty had not faded and to be this close to his almost naked form was enough to make her forget that they were both married and weren't still the free and hopeful couple that had loved with abandon in another time zone under a rainy sky.

Grabbing her hand, he galloped down to the shore; she had no choice but to keep pace with him. The two ran into the sea. Instantly her head went under the water; it felt incredible, invigorating and healing. The two splashed and ducked beneath the waves, squealing like toddlers before coming together to hold and be held in the warm current. Sol kissed the salt water that sparkled on her eyelids, and peppered her face with small kisses. He lifted her in the water and twirled her around, causing the water to ripple and froth around them.

'I want to take you back to the beach hut and I want us to spend the night together. I need you, Clover, my wonderful girl.'

Dot nodded and, closing her eyes, placed her head on his shoulder. 'Yes. That would be wonderful. We can sit in the quiet and talk. There is something I want to tell you, something I have to tell you.' She tried to think of how she might begin. *'His name is Simon…'*

They lay in the sun and laughed at the memories of traipsing around the West End like lovesick puppies, caring little for anyone or anything. Neither mentioned the last few days they had spent together; it was still too painful to recollect what came next.

'How is Barb getting along? You haven't mentioned her.'

'We kind of fell out and I don't see her any more.' Dot swallowed the lump in her throat; she missed her mate.

'Well, you need to put that right at some point. Friends are precious.'

Dot nodded, knowing that it was very unlikely she would ever see Barb again and if she did, God only knew how they would find a way back to friendship.

'Where do you live now?' He couldn't bear to picture a marital home.

'Walthamstow, in a modern block of flats. They're ugly and I don't have a garden.' She didn't want him to envisage the place she shared with another man and avoided giving him too much detail.

'You don't have a garden?' This for him was unthinkable. He shook his head. 'I don't like to think of you living somewhere ugly.'

'It makes no difference to me. If I can't live with you, then it's all irrelevant.'

'I'd live in the ugliest ditch in the world if I could curl up with you every night.' He meant it.

'Me too.' She reached over and kissed his mouth. Trying not to think of the torturous nights she spent feigning sleep and avoiding contact with Wally, poor Wally.

'Your mum and dad doing okay? Dee?'

She nodded, unwilling to allow them entry into this little slice of paradise. This was Clover's world.

'Are you still proper soldiering?' She laughed.

'You are so cheeky!' Sol dived on top of her, kissing her face and rolling her in the sand, squashing her beneath his frame.

When the sun had dried them, they jumped back into the car, which was cool from sitting in the shade.

Sol revved the engine and reached over for one final kiss before they drove off. 'I need to make a stop-off on the way, is that okay?'

'If you like. Where d'you need to stop off?'

'I want to pick something up from home, but don't worry, I can park at the back and nip in and out in minutes.'

'Is your wife there?'

He nodded at the floor, unable to hide his guilt and nerves and yet so powerfully driven by the love he felt for his Clover that it overshadowed both of these negatives.

'Oh God, Sol, it feels horrible to be sneaking around like this.'

'I know, but it doesn't feel like sneaking around, it feels right. I love you and if I hadn't been forced to leave you, I wouldn't have to sneak around, married to someone that I don't fucking like, because I would be married to you and I would never have to sneak anywhere, ever in my whole life. I would be happy!' He smacked his palm on the steering wheel. It was the first and only time she would hear him swear, see him lose his cool. 'I'm sorry. I shouldn't have said that word in front of you. I'm just angry at what I have had to miss and having you with me again has made me realise how very miserable I've been. So, forgive me for swearing, but I want no forgiveness for grabbing at the life I should be living, the life

I could have had if other people had not interfered and ruined things for us. You asked if I am still a soldier – yes, I am, but in truth I've been at home, struggling. I almost lost my reason because of my grief at losing you, and I'm not better yet.'

Dot stroked the side of his face. 'It's okay, it will all be okay. I love you and that's enough, isn't it?'

He kissed her on the mouth. 'I hope so, I really do.'

Sol stopped the car in a leafy lane, high up and surrounded by jungle. The grey roof of the house could be seen poking above the trees. It was huge. No wonder his mum had thought she wasn't good enough; maybe she was right. Dot would have loved to have gone inside and had a look at where her beloved lived. She wanted to see the veranda that she had imagined on so many nights, picturing the two of them rocking in their swing seat, just as he had described it. She wanted to climb the staircase down which Sarah Arbuthnott had fled and up which Mary-Jane had skipped. Instead, she sat alone in the front seat of the car, all but hidden from view by the abundance of surrounding trees, waiting like a thief on the look-out, which in a sense she was. She began to fidget, taking the pins out of her hair and retwisting her bun.

'Hurry up, Sol!' she whispered as her sense of foreboding grew. She heard a noise approaching from behind her on the track; it was distinctive and yet took her a few seconds to recognise the sound of horses' hooves. Two huge horses plod-ded up the lane. She could see them in the rear-view mirror and prayed that they would turn off before they reached the car; how she would explain her presence she didn't know. She angled the mirror so she could see better.

One of the women she recognised instantly. 'Oh shit!'

Vida wore a full riding habit despite the heat and laughed loudly with her mouth open as she patted the flank of her horse. *'Can I call you a taxi?'* Dot's heart raced. The girl on the horse next to her looked young. Dot felt her bowels turn to ice. The dark-skinned beauty with the flawless complexion and beautiful face was undoubtedly Sol's wife. She held the title of Mrs Arbuthnott, something Dot knew she would never be called. But that was not what caused her heart to race. The young wife of the man she loved was also very pregnant.

No! No… Oh my God. This changed everything.

The two women broke into a gentle trot and turned off right, towards the stable block. Dot placed her head in her hands and wanted to run away, but she was trapped, as she so often was, in a situation over which she had very little control. She was thinking about her baby, big brother to the child the girl was carrying. Life was cruel. For want of a different mother-in-law with a different set of tolerances, she would be the one living in this big house, on this paradise island and her little boy would be swimming with his dad instead of living in another country with two people that weren't his real parents.

Sol made her jump as he raised the boot and placed a box inside it. He clambered into the driver's seat before noting her expression.

'What's the matter? Don't look worried – I wasn't seen and I've left a note. We have the whole night together.' He held her hand and kissed her fingers.

'What's your wife called?'

'It's not important.'

321

'It's important to me.'

Sol sighed. 'Her name is Angelica.'

'Is she pretty?'

'Where is this heading, Clover?'

'Please just answer me.' *I'm testing you.*

Sol paused, considering how to respond. 'Yes, she is very pretty and everyone tells me how lucky I am. But it makes no difference to me; I am in love with you and so she could be the prettiest girl on the planet, what does it matter? All I know is that she is not for me; you are.'

Dot nodded. 'Is she pregnant?'

Sol pinched the bridge of his nose with his thumb and fore-finger, then nodded. 'Yes, she is.'

'Is she happy?' Her mouth quivered, although no tears fell.

'I don't see how she can be. I think she is distracted by being pregnant, but I don't see how she can be happy when her husband is a stranger to her and spends most of his time thinking about someone else. It's a farce. Her parents are keen to be a bigger part of St Lucian life and I am the means to that. It's an arrangement.'

'Don't you want to be a dad?' This she whispered. Biting her tongue to stop from saying, *'This will be your second child – you have a son, a beautiful son! They took him away from me.'*

'Please don't make me say it.'

'Make you say what?'

Sol turned until he was facing her and cupped her hand in his palms. 'I don't want to have a baby with anyone other than the woman I love and that woman is you. Every time I look at her pregnant state, I picture you and I dislike her a little bit more each time for tying me into this sham of a marriage. So help me God, that is the truth and it makes me a monster.'

'Take me home, Sol.'

The car wound its way down towards the beach as the day slipped into night and the huge golden sun sank behind the sea. Dot stepped over the threshold of her little hut and lit the candles that were placed on every available flat surface. The room glowed with the flickering lights as her shadow loomed large against the wall. Sol lifted the cardboard box from the boot of his car. He came into the shimmering cabin and smiled at his love. It had been an unforgettable day.

He sat next to her on the sofa and held her hand. 'You didn't say a word on the way back.'

'No, I know, just thinking.'

'What were you thinking?'

'That when happiness is taken at the expense of someone else's and the consequence is misery for them, it's not right. It's too high a price.'

'But shouldn't people think of themselves sometimes? Don't we deserve happiness?'

'I don't know. I know that I love you; I love you more than I ever thought possible and I know I always will. But can I hurt Angelica, can I hurt her little baby? I don't think so.' She shook her head and once again pictured Barb's distraught face, followed immediately by Gracie's mum being dragged along the shingle driveway.

'Stay with me. Please stay with me. We can work something out.'

'Can we? Like what? Me hiding from view in the passenger seat for the rest of me life?'

'No, of course not. I can buy us a house! We could have a house like this; we could sit on the veranda each night and—'

'No. Stop.' She placed her fingers over his mouth. 'I can't let you tell me anything that won't happen, anything that isn't true, no matter how much we want it to be, cos it hurts too much when it's taken away from me.'

'But it can be true; we could find a way.'

'You'd be sneaking from her to me and back again – that's not honest. She would hate her life and eventually I'd hate my life. I don't want to share you with someone that has had your child; I love you too much for that, I couldn't stand it. You'd start lying to your child and eventually, Sol, you'd hate yourself and your life too.'

'I hate my life now!' This he shouted. 'I just want you. I only want you. Please, Clover. Is it that you don't want to leave London? That's okay. I don't care any more about anything. I could start over, I could come back with you!'

She gripped his hand. 'And leave your child? No. I can't have that on my conscience.' *Not again, not two babies robbed of their daddy because of me.* 'I've decided, Sol, this is what I wanted to tell you, I'm going home.' *I'm giving this little baby a daddy.* 'I shall go back and carry on best I can, but I shall always love you and now I can be happy, cos I know that you will always love me and in some ways that's enough. It killed me when I thought I'd been wrong about you, about us, but I wasn't, was I?'

Sol stood and she followed. 'No, my darling, you weren't. I love you.'

Dot heard her mother's words inside her head, unwelcome and yet wise. *'Love? Listen to yourself, Dot. What makes you*

think love is so important? Cos I'm here to tell you it isn't.
Love is what happens in the films, love is a little spark of
fancying that dies, Dot; it dies.'

Sol stood and reached for her hand. 'Let's go outside. It's
my favourite part of the day, when the sun sinks into the
ocean and the day has lost its heat; we'll bask in the warm
breeze that is blowing across the beach. We can do like I
always said; watch the lights twinkling from Reduit Beach
on the curve of the horizon. I want to hold your hand in mine
and sit on the deck and smell the jasmine that fills the air
around us. I want to spend one night with you, with the
shutters thrown wide open and the warm wind flowing over
us as I hold you tight in my arms, keeping us cool. And then
just as I've dreamed, in the morning we'll drink fresh pineapple
juice and feast on mangoes. But only after we have run across
the beach and dived into the crystal-clear water and swum,
tasting the salt water on our tongues and feeling it burn on
our skin as we lie in the sunshine under the shade of a palm
tree. Please, please, Clover, don't send me away. Let us have
one night just as we have always wanted, one night that will
sustain me for the rest of my life. One night that I shall think
about when I am old. What do you say, Clover, will you give
me one night?'

She reached up and touched his face, wet with tears. 'Yes.
One night.'

'But first…' Sol walked over to his cardboard box on the
little table and reached inside. 'This has been lying around for
years.' He pulled out a gramophone, winding the handle with
his right hand. 'The last time I danced with you, I didn't know
I was saying goodbye. This time I do.'

He pushed the little sofa to one side and rolled up the rug. 'Come and dance with me, my Clover. Let's pretend we've got forever...'

The static crackle of the record filled the little room. Sol pulled her close and with one hand on her lower back and the other holding her outstretched hand, they waited, both knowing what was coming next. And then Etta started to sing in that rich, velvet voice. She started to sing the words of their song.

> *'At last*
> *My love has come along...*
> *My lonely days are over*
> *And life is like a song'*

Sol drew her closer still and with her arm crooked against his chest held her hand inside his. She felt her form melt against him, until they were like one, swaying gently to the soundtrack to their love affair.

'I love you so much, and I always will.' He breathed into her hair, his words stuttering through his tears.

'I love you too.' She spoke to his chest.

> *'Oh, yeah, at last*
> *The skies above are blue*
> *My heart was wrapped up in clover*
> *The night I looked at you'*

'Don't ever let me go, Sol.' Her voice cracked, her vocal cords straining against her distress.

'I'll never let you go, baby.'

He pulled her closer still, holding her tightly against him.

'I found a dream that I could speak to
A dream that I can call my own
I found a thrill to press my cheek to
A thrill that I have never known'

'It will all be okay, won't it?'

'It will all be okay, baby.'

Dot smiled into his chest. Sol ran his fingers through her hair and watched her shiny locks fall in a curtain against her shoulder. 'You are so beautiful.'

'Oh, yeah and you smile, you smile
Oh, and then the spell was cast
And here we are in heaven
For you are mine
At last'

Chapter Thirteen

Dot ran her fingers through her hair and knocked on the front door. She exhaled and dug deep to find a smile. Wally twisted the Yale lock and stood staring at his wife.

'Hello, Wall, pop the kettle on, I'm dying for a cuppa.'

Wally stood rooted to the spot. He swept his eyes over her tanned face and tousled hair; she looked lovely.

'You're back then.'

'It would appear so.'

'And are things…'

'Are things what, Wally?'

'Are things sorted?' This he addressed to his socks, nervous of her answer.

'Yes, things are sorted.'

His mouth twitched into the beginnings of a smile. 'So you're staying?'

'Yes, love, I'm staying. Now, are you going to let me in for that cuppa or do I have to chuck something else off the balcony before I get me own way?'

Wally reached out and lifted her suitcase from the walkway. Dot followed him into the hall and surveyed the flat in which she would spend the rest of her days.

'Well, someone's been busy!'

Dot noted the fringed lampshades that had been placed over all the bare bulbs. A large mirror now hung over the fireplace and a nest of tables was separated into three and placed either side of the chairs with a lacy doily on each. Floral curtains hung in the lounge and in the bedroom, where the greasy mattress had disappeared and been replaced with a large divan.

'I thought if you came back, I wanted it to look nice for you.'

'Well, I did and you have.'

Her husband beamed.

'Thank you, Wally.'

'S'all right. Your mum helped me. I'll put the kettle on.' He pushed past her into the kitchen.

He filled the kettle at the sink with his back to the hallway. Dot couldn't see his smile or the way his mouth moved in silent thanks.

A few minutes later, the two were sitting in the vinyl chairs, holding mugs of their restorative brew.

'I got you a present actually.'

'Oh yeah?' Wally wasn't used to receiving gifts.

Dot pulled out a Bush radio from her suitcase. 'I thought it'd be nice to have a bit of background music, we could even have a sing-along!'

'Gawd, have you ever heard me sing?'

'No, but I reckon if you're half as bad as me, we'll get all the dogs in Walthamstow howling!'

When the tea was finished, Dot washed up the cups and felt her fatigue wash over her. She smiled. This was a world away from flights around the globe, sitting on a deck with the sun on her skin or swimming in the warm ocean and sipping fresh pineapple juice. That was a life that belonged to Clover.

But she wasn't Clover, she was Dot, Dot Simpson from Rope-makers Fields; and this was her life, a life that she would live the best she could.

'You turning in?' Wally's voice was shaky, issued from behind her. She turned to face her husband. 'Yep, nearly done.'

He nodded.

'Oh, and Wall?'

'Yep?'

'Tonight is our first. We are starting over, remember?'

He nodded. 'I remember.'

She reached out and squeezed his arm. 'Thank you, Wally. I don't only mean for what you've done in the flat, I mean thank you for everything. It was an amazing thing you did and you did it just for me. I shan't ever forget it.'

'Dot?'

'Yes, love?'

'Don't ever mention it again.'

Wally went into the bathroom to clean his teeth. They were starting over. He whistled out the last tune he had heard on the radio, Etta James's 'At Last'.

* * *

Dot lay on the hospital trolley, staring at the dazzling strip light overhead. The radio on the nurses' station sent the gentle tones of the Four Seasons wafting down the ward. '*Sherry Baby/She... e... rry, Can you come out tonight...*' Dot laughed. Yes, please, Sherry, do come out tonight. She couldn't go through another day and night of this. Her contractions were evenly spaced, her labour had slowed and the pain was manageable. One of the nurses had given her a rubber band to play with to distract her mind, but had the woman entered the cubicle while the last contraction was building, Dot would happily have shoved the bloody thing where the sun don't shine. She sincerely hoped they had something stronger available if she needed it. Her paper-thin nightie was none too warm and she was glad of the pale blue wool blanket that she could pull up under her chin. Her toes were snug inside some rather fetching white socks.

'Can we call someone for you, Dot?' The young nurse who had earlier removed the flaming red nail polish from Dot's toes and fingers popped her head around the curtain, into the cubicle.

'Yeah, please. My husband. I gave the other nurse the details already. It's Wallace Day. He's probably already on his way.'

'Righto, let me go and check on that for you.' She smiled sweetly with crinkled eyes and the faintest hint of pity. Whether because Dot was in the middle of her labour without any company or support or because of what she was about to endure, Dot couldn't be sure. The nurse needn't have worried, Dot knew the drill. She kept checking herself, having to stop from blurting out that it wasn't in fact her first child and there was no need to explain what was going to happen next, she had lived through it once before.

If anything, she felt bored. It had already been a couple of hours and after the initial excitement and euphoria, it was now tedious, waiting for the action. Even though she'd had nine months to get used to the idea, she still didn't quite believe that she would be walking out of here with a baby. A baby. She tried to visualise herself with a swaddled bundle; she couldn't. It was as if the disappointment of going home once again without a child would be too great to handle, so she wasn't allowing herself to believe it until it happened.

'Oh, here we go again, eh, Dot?' She cringed, having spoken aloud, remembering that there was only a floral-print curtain between her and the rather posh woman who sat with her attentive, brow-mopping husband in the cubicle next door. She hoped they hadn't heard.

'Here she is.' Her mum's voice cut through her thoughts and brought her to the present as she whipped back the floral curtain.

Joan rushed forward and palmed the fringe away from her daughter's forehead. 'You all right, my girl?'

Dot nodded and fought the desire to cry – probably a combination of hormones and relief that someone was finally there.

'How you doing?'

'M'okay.' She nodded.

'S'all all right, darling, your mum's here now.' Joan hitched the elastic waist of her trousers and pulled the plastic chair up to the side of the bed. Taking up position, she clasped her daughter's hand between her own; she cooed and clucked as though Dot was the baby.

'Have you told Dee?' Dot murmured, sounding far more baby-like and vulnerable than she had before her mum arrived.

'Course I have. She was desperate to come in, but I've told her she has to wait her turn. She's driving me crazy. You know how excited she gets.'

Wally stood at the foot of the bed, feeling quite redundant. Dot could see his relief at the fact that there was only one chair in the cubicle and Joan had commandeered it. It made her smile to see his nervous air – what did he think he was going to have to do?

Dot wasn't sure how she was going to cope giving birth again. It was certainly different so far. Being treated with respect as a married woman expecting her first child made her proud and delighted in a way that had been impossible the last time. The way her mother soothed and fussed over her made her gut twist. It felt like only moments ago that she had been eased into stirrups and forced to undergo the trial of childbirth alone, before then being obliged to give her son away to a very high bidder.

How was it that things had changed so much for her in such a short space of time? How was it possible that with the addition of a small gold band she was able to walk with a straight back and a defiant smile while she carried her husband's baby, her main concern being how to afford the clothes that best flattered her pregnant frame. How was it possible that this baby was 'a little bundle' whereas her last had been an 'it', a thing to get adopted out. How was it that one simple certificate meant there was no talk of shame, no stain of illegitimacy that would blight every course of action. It was a world where marriage counted and if you weren't married, you didn't count. Dot was glad of the change in her circumstances, not wishing to endure anything like her experience at Lavender Hill Lodge again. Yet she found it torturous that for the want of a piece of paper and a tiny sliver of bent gold, she could have walked down the street with her bump on display and not been confined to the miserable bedroom of her childhood; she could have asked questions and read books about pregnancy and birth, instead of having to guess, worrying about which of her symptoms were 'normal'. She would not have been forced to hand over her baby boy, an act that would define her whole life. This one act was the reason she now sat in a state of near denial, waiting for the arrival of a baby for whom she felt very little. A baby conceived with her husband, who was still a stranger in so many ways.

Dot spoke to Wally for the first time. 'You coming in or out, Wall?'

He hovered by the curtain, on the edge. 'D'you need anything?'

She shook her head. 'No, love, just looking forward to getting home.'

'Does it hurt?' He looked genuinely concerned; it was his fault after all.

'Not much.' She winced as another contraction built.

Wally smiled and nodded. This was no place for men. 'I'll go and phone your dad, give him an update, and then I'll pop back.'

Dot laughed, knowing he would be gone for some time, finding any excuse to loiter outside until it was all over.

Dot cast her eyes around the maternity suite. She may have been well into the advanced stages of her labour, but she was lucid enough to take in all the detail. It didn't matter that nearly two years had passed since she'd given birth to Simon; the passage of time had done nothing to dilute her distress. When she saw the instruments for childbirth and nodded at the masked nurses and midwives bustling to and fro with syringes and lotions and potions to ease their patients' discomfort, she was back in the delivery room at Lavender Hill

Lodge, where the only comfort she'd received was from a kindly nun. She felt the pain in her heart as keenly as she had when she walked across the fine gravel with a Silver Cross pram that was empty of her baby, her Simon.

Dot expected to feel guilty. How could she look at the baby she was able to keep and not reflect on the one that she had given away. Guilt, however, was not her overriding emotion as the linen-wrapped bundle was placed in her arms. It was love. Dot felt a huge rush of love that she had forgotten was possible. Her little girl was perfect and beautiful. She mewled and gurgled from under her blanket. Dot peered in and beamed.

Sitting on the edge of their bed in their little flat, with her dressing gown wrapped around her trunk, Dot stared into the little white cot. Sherry stilled and turned her head in the direction of her mum.

'Hello, little one. Hello, mate.'

The baby opened her eyes and blinked. Her mouth opened and closed and her little legs kicked against the base of the cot. Dot felt her heart constrict and her stomach knot. The baby's fine covering of hair looked quite ginger in the light. Her nose was flat and her eyes, slowly blinking, were already inquisitive, taking it all in. Dot loosened the little blanket and lowered her head towards the baby girl.

'Well, well, look at you, funny little thing. I'm your mum, yes I am, forever and ever. No one is going to take you away from me. You are stuck with me! God only knows what we did to get something as gorgeous as you!'

Dot reached into the cot and scooped her baby girl into her arms. Cradling her small head in the crook of her neck, she inhaled deeply. It reminded her of holding Simon. Her eyes misted over and the breath caught in her throat as she held Sherry's downy head under her chin. 'Oh, it feels lovely to hold you, little one. I'll do my best for you, I promise. I will love you and tell you everything I know – which isn't much. I'll try and help you follow your dreams because dreams are very important, my girl. Mine were taken away from me, but I'll try and make it different for you. In fact, I am going to tell you a secret...' Dot lowered her voice to a whisper. 'I still think of my dreams every single day and night. I think about a little boy who was a scrap of a thing just like you, only with the beautiful honey-glow skin of his daddy. And I think about watching that little boy swim in the warm crystal sea before I wrap him in a big, fluffy towel and give him fresh pineapple juice to drink while we sit on the sand leaning on that big palm tree.'

Dot did nothing to stem the tears that trickled down her face. 'I told you I was a daft old thing. Ignore me, my darling girl; I'm just a silly old cow with her head stuck in the clouds. But it's hard not to miss him. Even after all this time, when I think there is no gap in my armour, something knocks me sideways and the ache for his dad is as strong as it was on the day he left me. I loved him, you see; more than I ever knew was possible, and I still love him now just the same, just like it was yesterday. He shone to me, like a bright light in a very ordinary world; made me feel special. One day I might tell you about the night I danced in front of Etta James, *the* Etta James; it was the best night of my life. It was our first dance, but not our last.'

'Who are you talking to?'

She hadn't heard Wally creep along the hallway, but his intrusions didn't alarm her any more. 'Who do you think? Your daughter!' She turned towards her husband. 'Do you want to come and say hello?'

Wally shuffled from foot to foot and hesitated. 'I will later.' His nerves were palpable.

'She's tougher than she looks, love, and isn't she beautiful?'

He stared at the baby. 'I guess so, but when they're babies they all look the same, don't they?'

Not all of them, thought Dot as she placed the three-day-old Sherry back in her little cot. *Not all of them*.

'What's that you got there?' Dot noticed for the first time the piece of paper in her husband's hand. 'Is it her birth certificate?'

Wally nodded sheepishly. Dot approached and noticed that he smelt mildly of beer. He and Reg had clearly stopped for a couple of halves to wet the baby's head on their way to Canning Town.

'Well let's have a look!' She grabbed at the certificate that Wally held by his side. This was how Sherry had actually been registered as Cheryl. Dot marched into the lounge, staring with her hands on her hips at her father who was sprawled on the chair in front of the fire, napping with his hands folded over his chest, 'Oh, Dad, not again!'

* * *

Dot put her baby girl down for a nap and plonked herself down into the chair. She was exhausted. Wally was at work and she thought she might grab forty winks as Cheryl slept. No sooner

337

had she sat down than the front door bell rang. Dot rubbed her face and eyes, then walked down the hall to open the front door. Her breath caught in her throat and her eyes widened; there was the briefest moment of hesitation before she spoke.

'Barb! Oh my God, it's lovely to see you!'

The two stepped forward until they were standing with their arms wrapped around each other.

'Come in! Oh, please come in!' Dot wished she wasn't so scruffy; her mate looked immaculate.

'Your mum gave me your address, said you've just had a little one?'

'Yes, come and see her.'

Dot and her old friend crept into the small bedroom and peered into the cot in which the little girl slept. She lay on her back with her arms over her head, her fat little cheeks sucked in and out as if she was feeding and her tummy gently rose and fell as she breathed deeply.

'Oh, mate, she's beautiful.'

Dot beamed, not at the compliment, but because Barb had called her 'mate'.

'I ain't half missed you.' Dot felt her eyes misting over.

'I've missed you too.' For the second time in as many minutes, the two women hugged. Then they wandered into the kitchen to make a cuppa.

'Wally not here?'

Dot blushed.

'It's all right, Dot, we have to mention him at some point!'

'He's at work.'

Barb nodded. 'We've got to talk about it, Dot or it will always sit between us like a massive boulder.'

Dot placed her hands on the work surface and addressed the wall. 'I know, but I feel so embarrassed. I felt bad enough when you were angry with me, but now you are being nice, it's worse somehow!'

'I could always clock you one if that'd make you feel better?'

Dot turned to face her friend. 'No you're all right.' The two laughed.

'I never wanted to hurt you, mate, never. Truth was, I was pushed into it a bit, and I know that sounds like a crap excuse, but it's the truth. I was a mess after Sol, a bit doolally if you like, and I wasn't really right again until I got pregnant, with Cheryl.' Dot felt her cheeks colour again. This was for two reasons: the verbal confirmation that she and Wally had slept together – as if their child weren't proof enough; and also her need to clarify in her own mind which pregnancy she was talking about.

Barb removed her fur coat and smoothed her fitted frock. 'I can see that now. I think I wanted him to like me, just cos he was so good looking…'

Dot jerked her head up – was Barb talking about her husband? *So good looking?* She realised that she never really looked at Wally for who he was; her eyes were veiled with an image of Sol that filtered everything.

Barb continued, 'And I got the wrong end of the stick a bit. Wally and me was only ever mates and I misread him being nice to me, thought it was something more. I was desperate for someone to want me, anyone, really, and he was around. I s'pose I wanted what you had, a proper fella.'

'Oh, Barb. I'm so sad we didn't have this conversation sooner. I honestly thought I'd never see you again.'

'Well, a lot of water's passed under the bridge since then.'

'Hasn't it just! You look fabulous, really well.' Dot was conscious of her own scruffy trousers and jumper mottled with baby milk.

'I'm off, Dot. I'm doing what you said and I'm joining a big cruise ship, not as a hairdresser, but as a hostess and I've come to ask you a favour.'

'Blimey, I don't see you for years and you come for a bloody favour?' She laughed.

'I need an amazing evening dress, something really knockout, and I would like you to make it for me.'

Dot put the teaspoon down and gave her friend her full attention. 'What? Are you winding me up?'

'Nope. You said I should follow my dream and I am. I shall travel in luxury all over the Caribbean – can you imagine that, Dot? A girl like you or me heading off to the Caribloodybbean?'

Dot shook her head. 'No I can't.' She crossed her fingers; everyone knew that if your fingers were crossed, it didn't count.

'I remember you said your dream was to design frocks and so I want to make one of your dreams come true. I want to wear a Clover Original when I arrive for my first big dinner.'

Dot placed her hand over her mouth. 'Oh, Barb, supposing I'm not very good?' She pictured a little blue romper suit that hadn't been deemed good enough.

'It will be perfect.'

The following week, Dot sat staring out of the bus window. It had been too long since she had jumped on a bus and gone up West. The shop windows sparkled in their pre-Christmas finery;

pounding the busy pavements gave her an energy she hadn't felt in a long time. She window-shopped in Lady Jane, noting that skirts were getting shorter and shorter and eyelashes longer and fatter. It was easy to lose touch now that she was a fully occupied mum. Making her way to Selfridges, Dot entered through the front swing door and headed for the nursery department, where she selected a pair of pink crocheted booties with a little pearly button on the side, perfect for her little girl. Next she jumped in the lift and went straight up to Haberdashery.

She didn't recognise anyone in the department and, thankfully, no Miss Blight, the old cow.

'Can I help you, madam?'

A young girl with an East End accent approached with a smile. She couldn't have been more than sixteen.

'Yes please. I want some sheer fabric to make a dress.' Dot pulled out a pattern from her bag and showed the girl the design.

'Ooh, that's lovely!'

Dot beamed. Yes it was, if only she could do the picture justice.

'What colour were you thinking of? We have a whole range across the back wall.' The girl indicated with her outstretched arm.

Dot turned her head and there it was – her fabric rainbow. She wandered over to the bolts of material and ran her hand over the sheer silks and mossy tweeds. The smell transported her to another place, another time. Her fingers came to a standstill.

'I think this one. It is the colour of St Lucian sky, Caribbean blue.'

'Have you been there?' the young girl asked as she pulled the fabric across the wide cutting table, her pinking shears in her hand.

'Yes I have.'

The girl looked at Dot with wide eyes. 'I've never been anywhere, don't think I ever will.'

'Where are you from?' Dot asked.

'Forest Gate.'

Dot nodded. 'And if you could go anywhere, where would you go?'

'America. I'd love to go to America.'

Dot noted her name badge. 'Well, Roberta, let me assure you that a lot stranger things have happened than a girl from Forest Gate finding her way to America.'

'I hope you're right!' Roberta beamed. 'Although knowing my luck, I'd find me way there, but not me way home again!'

'Ah, that's the thing. If you are meant to find your way home, you will, I guarantee it. It's all down to love and luck!'

A month later, Dot stepped off the bus in Narrow Street and thanked the conductor who'd helped lift the pram down the big step. She pushed Cheryl up and round the corner into Ropemakers Fields and spied Mrs Harrison leaning on the door frame with a fag clamped to her gob.

'Cold, innit, Dot? Reckon the weather's on the turn.' They were so familiar, she spoke as if she had seen her only an hour before and not more than a year ago.

'Yeah, you want to get inside, you'll catch your death out here, Mrs H.'

'Let's have a look at her then.' She stepped onto the pavement and removed her fag before peering into the hood of the pram. 'Oh, she's soundo.' Mrs Harrison sighed. 'Bless her, she's beautiful, Dot, really is.'

Dot was aghast to see tears falling down Mrs Harrison's leathery cheeks, sending her eyes instantly bloodshot.

'You all right, Mrs Harrison?'

The old lady nodded and sniffed. 'Takes me back, that's all.'

Dot tried to work out why she was so distressed. Mrs H was childless – the careless, feckless Mr Harrison having died before they'd managed to reproduce. 'Oh what, to when Barb was born? You must have been a very proud aunty. I'm meeting her at me mum's, as it happens.'

'No, not to when Barb was born… To when *I* went to work on a farm in Kent, Dot. I was fifteen, but I remember it like it was yesterday.'

'Oh, Mrs H…'

'I whispered to him, my little boy. I told him where I lived and I told him to come and find me. I promised I'd never move house and I haven't, even though I haven't got a single happy memory here and I've had to run it as a boarding house to keep it on. I promised him I'd stand outside in case he couldn't find me and that I'd wait until my dying day. I'm still waiting.'

Dot looked at the woman she had known her whole life and realised that she did not know her at all.

Joan ran out onto the pavement in her slippers. 'Here they are! Reg, they're here!' Taking the pram by the handle, she manoeuvred it into the hallway, then whipped her granddaughter out from beneath the covers and took her into the back room, where a nice fire roared.

'What did she want, the nosey cow?' Joan enquired as Dot shrugged her arms from her mac.

'Oh, the usual, Mum, just passing the time of day.'

'I've made Wally a nice stew with a bit of fruit cake for his afters.'

'He'll be happy.' Dot smiled. 'He'll be here soon as he's finished work.'

Twenty minutes later the door bell rang and in rushed Barb. 'Blimey, it's taters out there! Right, where is it?'

'Gawd, give me a chance! You've only just walked in the bloody door. It's upstairs.'

The two girls thundered up the stairs as they had a million times before and flung open the door of Dot's old room. And there it was, hanging on the back of the door.

Barb stared at the creation in the most vibrant blue she had seen. 'Can I try it on?' she whispered.

Dot nodded.

Barb slipped the silky material over her head and felt it fall down over her body. The single strap ran over one shoulder to attach to the gathered bodice at the front. The fabric seemed to drape itself around her form, its elegant folds accentuating her tiny waist. It was part Grecian, part haute couture. It was perfect.

'I love it, Dot, I really love it. How do I look?'

'Like a bloody film star, mate.'

'Like Grace Kelly?'

'Yep, like GracebloodyKelly.'

'Fancy a walk up the docks, Dot?'

'Yeah, I'll get me coat.'

Barb changed out of the frock and the two thundered back down the stairs.

'Jesus Christ, you sound like you're coming through the bloody ceiling!' Reg shouted from behind the newspaper.

'Sorry, Dad.'

'Sorry, Mr S.'

Joan, sitting opposite her husband, held the sleeping Cheryl in her arms. 'And where might you two be off to?'

'We're just off for a walk, Mum. Won't be long.'

'That's a good idea, you two go and catch up. I need to get Wally's dumplings in, but your dad can look after the baby.' With that she rose and plonked the sleeping infant in her husband's awkward arms.

'Oi! I can't look after a bleeding baby! It's woman's work!' Reg hollered as he shifted his elbow to make sure Cheryl's little head was properly supported.

'I shouldn't worry, Reg, Dee'll be in from school in a bit and you won't get a bloody look in. I'd make the most of it if I were you.'

Dot and Barb slipped from the room. Dot peeked through the tiny gap and spied her dad kissing his granddaughter's scalp.

'You is a right little bobby dazzler, nearly as lovely as your mum, but not quite, but then I'm biased, aren't I? She stole my heart on the day she arrived and she ain't given it back yet.'

'Everything all right, Dot?' Barb asked as her friend sniffed back her tears.

'Yep, everything's fine.'

The two linked arms and made their way to the docks, where they perched on the flat-topped bollards. The wind started to bite as it skimmed the choppy water. They pulled their cardigan sleeves down over their hands and with shoulders hunched forward shouted to each other as their voices navigated the wind.

'I'm bloody freezing!'

'Me too! Dot, look – my fag's stuck to my lip!' Barb opened her mouth wide, to show her mate that her roll-up was indeed hanging free of assistance from her gob. They laughed loudly. This wasn't unusual, they laughed at most things, sometimes because they were funny, but mainly because they knew that life was pretty good.

Dot felt a pang as she remembered the last time she had laughed like that, a time before she had loved, a time before she had suffered loss. Her mum was right about one thing: life was a bucketful of memories and regrets, it weren't no fairy tale. She considered the life that stretched ahead of her, a different life from the one she had once planned, but a good life nonetheless. She would take comfort in the small things and be thankful for her calm heart and clear mind. Dot was a survivor. She knew she could get through just about anything, with a little love and luck.

Epilogue: Forty-five Years Later

Simon slowly trod the brick path that led through the wrought-iron gates and up to the majestic front of the Jasmine House. He took in the wide, white-wood terrace with its clusters of rattan furniture and vintage fans operated by pulleys suspended from the awnings. The large sash windows allowed a glimpse into this mansion from a bygone era; the polished wooden floors, brass ceiling fans and wooden louvered doors reminded him of the pictures he had seen of the plantation houses in history books. The ancient palms swayed overhead, providing cool shade from the heat of the midday sun. Conch shells peppered the flower-bed borders and the beds themselves were so beautiful that they drew your eye, planted with a luscious display of variegated shrubs and bursts of flowers in fiery shades, arranged with colour-coordinated precision.

The sweeping lawn was of the deepest green, with none of the bare patches that blighted most grass on St Lucia. Simon recognised the patient hand of a dedicated gardener. Jasmine plants climbed over trellises and arches, filling the place with their heady scent. The delicate white flowers hung in drooping bouquets, clustered around entrances and walkways, giving the whole garden an air of matrimonial elegance. Where the blooms littered the path, Simon squashed them underfoot, releasing their perfume with his every step. He looked down at the path and there under his sandal he spied a brown metal hair pin, the sort that would hold a bun in place. It was rusted, old. Its V-shape looked like a little arrow, pointing towards the front door, guiding him home. He stooped and picked up the fiddly little thing and for some reason decided to pop it into his pocket, a memento.

He coughed as he approached the front door and noted the slight tremor in his right hand. He was nervous. He reached out and curled his fingers around the brass bell pull, hesitating slightly before releasing it. The action was so much more than the simple ring of a bell: it was a summoning across decades, an echo back to the past and the levering open of a chest of memories that might have been sealed a very long time ago. He hadn't planned what he would say, but prayed that God would loosen his tongue and give him the words when the time was right.

He heard the bell tinkling inside as he hovered on the step. He smoothed his shirt to rid it of any creases, but also to soak up the sweat that peppered his palm. He exhaled through bloated cheeks, trying to calm his erratic pulse. After what felt like an age, the door was opened briskly and widely. Simon lowered his eyes until his gaze settled on the face of the diminutive housekeeper. The woman had to be in her nineties, with a bird-like demeanour and bright, fearless eyes that shone from her crêpe-skinned face; her dress was of the palest pink cotton and was starched to within an inch of its life.

'Yes?' Her tone was brisk. Simon wasn't sure if this was because she had been in the middle of doing something or because she'd taken an instant dislike to his face.

'Hello, I'm Simon Dubois, Reverend Simon Dubois. I've

just opened the mission up at Dennery and wanted to come and introduce myself.'

She seemed unmoved by either his speech or his status. Simon smiled at her and opted for a different tack. 'I am sorry to disturb you, but I was hoping for a word with Major Arbuthnott, if it's at all possible.'

She opened the door wide and beckoned the reverend inside. 'Wait here,' she said and, without turning her head, strode purposefully towards the back of the house.

The great hall in which Simon found himself was vast, almost as big as the entire footprint of the mission in which he now resided. The dark mahogany floor was polished to a high sheen; the same wood formed the treads of the wide stairs that wound their way up, forming a wide gallery that ran to the left and right at the top of the staircase. The history of Simon's ancestors was all around him, if only he'd known where to look. Each stair had a rounded dip in its centre, eroded by the daily tread of feet across a hundred and fifty years. The anxious fleeing feet of Sarah Arbuthnott, desperate to return to her native Scotland; the light bare feet of the beloved Mary-Jane, eagerly skipping from the bedroom to the kitchen; the dancing steps of Patience, up and down countless times a day at the behest of the charge to whom she was devoted; and the weary booted steps of Simon's father, each touch leaving the imprint of a heavy heart, laden with what if's and echoing into the silent rafters of an empty house. Vida Arbuthnott had many years to reflect on her words: '*When you marry the girl that you are supposed to and the Jasmine House is full of tiny children, you will thank me then.*' She passed away without being thanked or becoming a grandma. Sadly, Solomon's ex-wife had miscarried their child and they divorced very quickly after. Angelica had returned to Martinique, where she remarried, this time to a man that loved her, and went on to become mother to twin boys, and then a grandma.

A giant fan whirred half-heartedly from beneath the domed ceiling, chopping at the heat of the day and sending it downwards to bathe the beautiful objects that had been placed on half-moon tables – vast, ornate china lamps with woven conical shades, silver-framed photos of broad-chested military men, and sparkling crystal decanters with silver name-plates looped over their fat necks.

The housekeeper reappeared. 'Follow me.'

Simon did not have to alter the stride of his six-foot-three frame to accommodate the old woman; she was nimble. Double doors led into a huge study that was dominated by a desk that sat centrally, surrounded by shelves that bulged with leather-bound books and journals. Here, more small tables, placed beside leather wing-backed chairs, were littered with beautiful sparkling things: a crystal fruit bowl sat alongside heavy brass curios that looked like ships' instruments.

The leather-topped bureau was ordered, despite its clutter. A stack of papers sat neatly and squarely in a wire basket. A large leather-bound blotter had a Mont Blanc pen set and a chunky glass-and-brass inkwell lined up along its top edge. An oversized brass lamp shone from the corner and various pots held a selection of pencils that Simon noted were all perfectly sharpened. Simon stared at a glass shadow box on the wall, approximately eight inches wide and double that in length. It contained nothing more than a length of velvet ribbon, once red, but now faded with age and sunlight into the colour of a dark rose.

The room was open to the garden; tall shutters were pushed back to the sides, making the space at one with the outside. Some of the more daring ferns were growing inwards with their pointed tips dipping into the cool shadows. The deck continued around the back of the house and on the top step, with his back to the room, sat Major Solomon Arbuthnott. His arm was extended and with his palm cupped he beckoned towards the peahen that strutted majestically in front of him.

Simon hadn't known what to expect, had tried, in fact, not to conjure an image that was too detailed, or to imagine the interaction; that would surely be a path to disappointment. Solomon Arbuthnott was smaller than he might have expected – muscled but slim, and with none of the bulk or height that gave Simon his presence.

'Come and sit down.' The major spoke over his shoulder in a tone that was neither welcoming nor dismissive.

Simon took his place on the top step of the deck and pulled his knees up under his arms; his large feet, comfortable in deck shoes, hung over the edge. He studied his father's profile, old but still in good shape, with the line-free face of a man half his age. His hair was white and close cropped, his shoulders still had good definition, but were let down by the slight bow of a spine that had spent too long bent over a desk into the wee small hours. His cream linen trousers were bunched up around his thighs, revealing cotton-socked feet inside tan-coloured Oxfords.

'You feed her like this?' Simon was curious.

'I hope to, one day, yes. But maybe not today. Slowly, slowly...'

The major turned to face the new reverend sitting on the step next to him. 'So, reverend, eh?'

Simon nodded.

'I read about your project up at Dennery; it's a noble thing. How many kids you have up there now?'

'About twenty, sir, but that can change on a weekly basis.'

Solomon nodded. 'I'm sure. You after funding?'

Simon gave his deep, throaty chuckle. 'Always! But that's not why I'm here today.'

Solomon smiled. 'Well, good for you. Is it a happy place?'

'Yes, it really is. We don't have much, but it's happy!'

'It takes more than bricks, mortar and money to make happiness,' Solomon stated.

'I agree. And community support is vital, which is why I thought I would come and introduce myself—'

'And then the next visit you ask for funding?' Solomon interrupted.

'Something like that, yes.'

The two laughed in the same throaty chuckle.

'I didn't want to impose on you and your family, I just thought—'

'Oh, there is no family to impose on.' Solomon interrupted again. 'Just me, Patience and Mrs Harrison here.' He pointed at the peahen.

'Mrs Harrison?'

Solomon smiled. 'Oh yes, it's the law at the Jasmine House, all peahens have to be called Mrs Harrison.' He pulled a white cotton handkerchief from his pocket and dabbed at his eyes.

Simon drew breath. This was the moment to come clean, to tell the major the true nature of his visit. To introduce himself and express his desire to, in some small way, get to know the man that had fathered him.

'Do you like gardens?' The major's question rather threw the moment.

Simon considered his response. 'Yes, of course. But I have never lived anywhere long enough to plant anything and watch it grow and now we are planting food for practical and economic reasons and so there's little time or room left for the luxury of flowers.'

'It's been my greatest joy, this little patch of heaven here, my oasis.'

Simon nodded. He looked at the old man and realised that there was no value in bringing the past to his door, no reason other than personal curiosity to shatter the peace of this man's existence, to upset the delicate balance of the life that he shared with Patience and the latest Mrs Harrison.

He stood and dusted at the seat of his pants. 'I should be getting back. I really just wanted to say hello and I've disturbed you enough already. Sir, it was a pleasure to meet you.'

The major stood and outstretched his hand. Simon shook it gently. He looked at their wrists so close together, wrists that carried the same blood.

'Please call me Sol – it's short for Solomon, it means bringer of peace.'

Simon smiled. 'Is that right?'

Neither of the men knew that for the want of a more composed mouth, less clogged by the tears of heartbreak and frustration, and a less spiteful nun, they would both be called Solomon.

Sol looked at the face of the reverend and continued to

353

hold his hand; it was a second that would change the course of both their lives.

He placed his other hand over the hand of the one he already held, cupping the large palm of the reverend inside both of his. His words were considered, slowly delivered, as his tears pooled.

'Oh my goodness, you have her eyes, my son.'

Amanda
Prowse

Turn over for book club notes, an exclusive
sneak preview, and to discover more
about Amanda Prowse.

Clover's Child

Notes for your book club

This story is set in the 1960s in London. How does the author evoke the place and time in her writing?

Lyrics of the Etta James song 'At Last' can be found throughout *Clover's Child*. What role does music play in the novel? Why do you think this song is so significant?

The prologue of the novel is set long after Dot and Sol's romance. What effect does this have on the way you see Dot and Solomon when you first meet them?

Dot's family have firm views about race and class. Do Dot's opinions differ to those of her parents? If so, why do you think that might be?

Solomon's mother also has firm opinions on race and class. How does Vida's own background affect her feelings about Dot?

Solomon's mother forces him to make a terrible decision. Did he do the right thing? Do you think Dot would have done the same thing if she were in his position?

Dot never tells Solomon that she is carrying his child. If she had been able to tell him, would it have changed his decision?

Why is Joan so angry with Dot when she learns she is pregnant?

Wally knows that Dot is in love with Solomon. Why does he marry her? And why does he encourage her to visit Sol after they are married?

Do you think Dot made the right decision to go back to her life with Wally? Do you think she is content with the way her life has turned out?

At the end of the novel, Solomon guesses that Simon is his son. Why do you think Simon chooses not to tell his father who he is initially?

Amanda Prowse

A Little Love

'A modern-day love story' *Daily Mail*

One

Pru donned her dressing gown over her pyjamas, stretched the thick socks over her feet and tiptoed through the hall, closing the flat door quietly so as not to disturb her cousin Milly, who slept soundly in her bedroom further down the hall. She slipped down to the basement. This she did on occasion when the bakery was closed, usually in the dead of night when sleep proved elusive and always with the snap of excitement at her heels as she did so, covertly.

Her alarm would not pip-pip for another three hours, yet instead of resting her head on her plump, feather pillow there she was, wandering along corridors and punching alarm codes into locked doors, looking over her shoulder and tip-toeing like a thief.

Using only minimal lighting, eschewing the wealth of machinery around her and the complicated recipes that she and Milly had honed over the years, she set about doing what she always did on these night time jaunts, running up a batch of fairy cakes using a wooden spoon and a ceramic bowl, just as she had been taught.

Pru fastened the apron around her waist before laying her ingredients and tools in a row on the counter top. She felt the familiar jolt of happiness, knowing that she was about to begin and had everything she needed to execute her plan. It felt exactly the same now as it had all those years ago, casting her eye over the white flour, the bowl of sugar and the greasy lump of margarine splayed on the saucer where it sat next to the shining, clean bowl, awaiting her attention.

She smiled as she tipped the margarine and sugar together and began creaming them into a thick paste. She savoured the gritty crunch on the back of the spoon as it smashed the crystals against the crackle-glazed side of the china bowl, pushing and churning until the mixture billowed with tiny bubbles of air and her fingers ached. Next came the spoonfuls of plain flour, a drop of essence, baking powder, the egg and gradually more flour. Pru couldn't fully describe the lift to her spirit or the bounce to her step as she watched the dry ingredients transform into a pale golden batter that passed the dropping test. There was no great science to knowing when the mixture was ready, instead she used this tried and tested method, lifting the spoon and watching to see how the cake mix fell, too quickly meant it was too thin, calling for more flour and more mixing. Whereas a blob that refused to shift from the back of the spoon, required more liquid and a light mix. The perfect consistency, meant the batter dropped slowly into the bowl with jaw clenching expectancy.

The anticipation as they baked filled her stomach with butterflies. While they cooled, she made a strong cup of coffee to go with, before decorating them true to her Nan's instruction, sparsely, and with hundreds and thousands that sat on a tiny misshapen pond of white icing, both of which had been a luxury. She would then pop the soft, vanilla scented sponges into her mouth and allow the sugar to spread its warm satisfying sweetness across her tongue and the icing to stick to the roof of her mouth. She gobbled them greedily and quickly, all of them.

'I know you are shaking your head and tutting at me, but don't judge me, Alfie! I could have far worse habits.' This she uttered into the ether with her eyes raised skyward and a smile about her mouth as she licked a stray blob of icing and a couple of sprinkles from her lip.

As proprietor of the world renowned Plum Patisserie, Pru had access to any number of delicate, iced fancies and sweet, sugar-dusted morsels each and every day, and yet none of them came close to the sensation of eating a warm fairy cake, gobbled illicitly in the wee small hours, made to her Nan's exacting recipe and method. The parcel of moist cake not only made her mouth water, but if she closed her eyes, she was back in their grotty kitchen in Bow, a little girl again, working diligently at their wobbly enamel-topped table. It was a time before she knew of the world beyond their front door, before drive and aspiration had yoked her to the winding upward path on which she climbed. Her nan, stood at the shallow, china sink, wearing a pink wrap-around overall which had worn thin at the seams and her brothers, with pinched cheeks and a ring of grime against the back of their necks, hovering around the large, china mixing bowl, with dirty fingers scooping at fine lines of cake mixture that they deposited into their eager mouths. The smell of the fluffy, little ingots baking would almost drive them to tears. Clustering around the stove, unusually silent, waiting.

Her Nan would then turn them out of the bun tin onto a wire rack on the sideboard. The scented steam that they gave off hypnotised them. And it would feel like an eternity before she would allow them to take one each. When they finally got one of those little cakes in their mitts, wide-eyed and with a mouthful of sweet crumbs, it was a moment of bliss in an otherwise bliss-free life and it was wonderful. For Pru, nothing represented success as much as her ability to eat a whole batch made in the kitchen of Plum Patisserie. She never told anyone about her trips down to the big kitchen, it was another little secret for her to keep.

Pru laughed to herself as she perched on the edge of her bed and applied the Crème de la Mer moisturiser to her face and throat. It was six a.m. but she had the speed of movement and alertness of someone who had been up for many hours, fancy. She touched her fingers to her temples where at the age of sixty-six, her once lustrous locks had now thinned, it was a habit she had acquired along with pushing up her eyebrows with her finger as if she could for a second or two, re-create the wide eyes of her youth, before gravity had done its job and they had taken on their hooded appearance.

'I was lovely once wasn't I? Not that I really thought so at the time, despite what Trudy said. I never had her confidence, blimey, who did? She was something else wasn't she? So, so long ago. I don't know why I'm thinking about that, Alfie, our little flat in Kenway Road, my life in Earls Court. We had some fun, tough times, but happy times. A lifetime ago. You're the only one I tell everything,

362

but I know you're a secret keeper, aren't you my love?'

This she addressed to one of several silver framed photographs on her bedside table. This particular snap was of a man astride a moped, he was looking over his shoulder, with a roll up hanging from his bottom lip, it was black and white and even though had been taken decades later, could have come straight out of the sixties, he had an air of James Dean about him or maybe that was how just she preferred to think of him, an anti-hero rather than a hopeless, addicted drop-out.

He smiled back at her with eyes that crinkled into laughter, peeping from behind black-framed Raybans that with his head tilted down towards the camera, had slipped down to the end of his nose. Pru loved this photo. There weren't that many flying around of her family, owning a camera was never a priority, but his smile and the setting on what looked like a bright, sunny day, meant that she knew he had this one good day or more specifically, this one good moment on this one good day. She hoped that when things got bad for him, the memory of this might have sustained him. As usual, he didn't reply.

Pru meandered around the flat in her soft grey, jersey pyjamas and dressing gown, with a cup of hot, black coffee balanced on her palm; she hummed and walked room to room, finding it calming to walk around and see that everything was just as she had left it the night before, harvesting reassurance from the order in which she lived and gaining confidence from knowing she was the owner of so many lovely things. The pictures were straight, cushions plumped and object d'art positioned just so. Although she had to admit that barring a messy burglary or natural disaster the likelihood of it not being were extremely slim.

She sat on the chair at the little walnut desk in the corner of her bedroom and let the bank statement flutter in her palm. She no longer paid heed to the black figures and their commas, lined up in neat rows, it was more of an inquisitive glance to see that payments had gone through and a reminder of where she was in the month. Gone were the days of shuffling balances and debts around to keep suppliers happy, juggling dates and orders to ensure enough money sat in the accounts for wages. The business had reached a point a couple of decades ago where the takings had significantly outweighed their costs and once the scales had tipped in their favour, they had never looked back. She unscrewed the lid of her Montblanc fountain pen and placed a tiny cross by the payment that was referenced CM – one thousand pounds had gone through on the fourteenth, just as it did every month and had done for the last ten years. If she did the maths, it caused a ball to knot in her stomach and a tide of panic to rise in her throat, so it was better that she didn't. Pru folded the paper sheets and clipped them into the leather file that she stowed back in the drawer.

After showering and blow-drying her auburn hair into its blunt bob, Pru sat down at her dressing table where she applied the merest hint of taupe lip stain and one wand-slick of mascara. She rubbed her fingers over her temples. She had never thought she would become this older lady. Any imaginings she had in her youth, placed her in her mid twenties, old enough to know best and still young enough enjoy herself. And yet there she was, hardly recognising the face in the mirror and it had happened in a heartbeat. She sighed and pulled her lower teeth over her top lip in the mirror, making her neck and chin taut, the way it used to look. A liberal spritz of Chanel number five and she was set for the day. She accessorized her navy trousers with a white silk blouse and two rows of pearls that hung in differing lengths against her small, high chest. She slipped her feet into navy penny loafers; her foot wear of choice on days like these.

Pru held her breath and pulled the blind. She watched a white transit van pull up on to the curb with its hazard lights flashing, delivering to Guy all that they might need for a day of baking and trading. On the opposite side of the street, two young men in dinner jackets, with ties loose about their necks and a wobble to their saunter, walked arm in arm. No doubt homeward bound at this early hour. She smiled; there it was, Curzon Street, just as she had left it.

She worried that one day she might pull the blind and see the traffic of the Kenway Road a few miles across town in Earls' Court, as if she had dreamt her success, her home in Mayfair, her Italian marble flooring, espresso machine and walk-in closet and was still there, living that life. Back then, although her surroundings had been drab, she had herself been full of life: a young girl with a defiant stare and a gut full of determination.

The day that she and Milly had arrived at the six-storey terrace in Kenway Road, they had thought they were invincible, immune to the regret and recrimination that came with old age. It was the last of a long line of places that she and Milly had painstakingly ringed in the small ads, and from the moment they arrived, they knew it was the place for them. A statuesque, elegant woman opened the door wearing a silk kimono and smoking a thin cigar in an ivory cigarette holder. She introduced herself as Trudy; she lived in a flat on the top floor. Pru walked to one of two deep-set sash windows on the landing that gave her the most incredible view across the London skyline, all the way out to Fulham and beyond. She let her eyes skim the horizon and red brick chimney pots. This would be the start of their journey, here among the west London rooftops, living with this elegant worldly woman. Pru followed Trudy down a narrow hallway, noting the way she swept along on her high heels, which made her look refined and sophisticated, sexy. She was going to practise that walk and when she had enough money, buy herself a pair of high heeled, red patent leather shoes, just like Trudy's.

'Who's David Parkes?' Milly asked. She had stopped at a framed certificate that hung on the wall and pointed to it.

'David was my brother.' Trudy sighed, 'He died a couple of years ago.'

'I'm sorry.' Pru offered as she rolled her eyes at Milly who was always jumping in feet first.

Pru and Milly told Trudy how they wanted to open their own bakery with a shop and a café, where they would make the most delicious cakes and bread that London has ever tasted. Trudy didn't laugh or mock the way others had when she shared this, instead she nodded and blew large O's of cigar smoke, before pressing her full, carmine painted lips together.

'I think people without dreams are only living half a life and that's a life I wouldn't want to live.'

Pru had been impressed, Trudy sounded like a poet.

'But it's no good dreaming unless you are prepared to work really hard. You have to dream it and set yourself a path to make it happen. A dream won't put food on the table or money in your purse.' Pru subconsciously patted the purse in her pocket, which contained their first weeks rent, bus fair and a lucky coin with a hole drilled in it. It was the sum total of their combined wealth. Pru nodded, wondering what they would need to do to clear their path – the one that led straight to the shiny, glass window of Plum's Patisserie.

'What's your dream then?' Milly asked over Pru's shoulder.

Trudy gave the younger girl her full attention, and drew on her cigar, 'To have a little love in my life,' she offered as she turned her back and walked forward, 'I think that's everyone's dream, really.' Dear, dear Trudy.

Pru closed her bedroom door and popped her head into the kitchen where she spied Milly, clad in a tiger onesie.

'What are you wearing?' Pru shook her head.

'It's new and quite possibly the cosiest thing I have ever owned. I might never take it off.'

'That'll be nice in the front of house.'

Milly dipped a large croissant into her coffee before lowering the soggy mess into her mouth.

'Gross.' Pru commented.

'It's what they do in France!' Milly spoke with her mouthful.

'Maybe, but you're not French, Mills.'

'What? You are kidding me! Mon Dieu! I had no idea. I thought I'd imagined growing up in Bow and I was actually from a fashionable little suburb of Paris!' She winked at her cousin.

Pru grinned as she left the flat and trotted down the stairs, taking a deep breath she opened the door of the café. She and Milly took it in turns to do the early check on the bakery and it was her turn this week. In truth, after two decades in these premises, and with the celebrated, Guy Baudin at the helm of a trusted team, it was more a cursory nod to all that she was around, a reminder of who was boss and the chance to monitor quality rather than get her hands stuck in.

The cleaners in their blue nylon tabards and with their hair scraped up into untidy knots were hard at it, buffing the brass fixtures with yellow dusters and mopping the pale, waxed wooden floor. The sun had started its creep through the large window that displayed the Plum Patisserie logo, working its way up like the revelation of a dancers fan until the whole room was awash with light. Tiny white bud-roses had been placed in slender, finger-sized vases on every table. The glass display unit, which they had re-created to mimic those found in the Parisian coffee houses of the eighteen hundreds, gleamed. The tiered, glass cake stands and fancy china plates with hand-painted flowers and swirls, delicately kissing their fluted edges, sat shining, awaiting the scones packed with jam and cream, soft iced buns, frosted sponges and flaky pastry masterpieces, stuffed with marzipan and dotted with an almond, which those with a sweet tooth would devour with a cup of hand blended French roast coffee.

She particularly loved this time of the morning, before the customers arrived, before the problems arose, before tiredness crept over her aging joints.

'Good morning all!' Pru offered with a singsong note, many of these girls spoke little English, but could glean enough from her tone to reciprocate with a nod and a smile.

'This looks lovely, thank you.'

The girls smiled and nodded in return.

Making her way down the twist of staircase, she placed her foot on the last step, the wood creaked unexpectedly beneath her weight and she gasped, placing one hand at her breast and the other against the wall, trying to steady her heart rate. She exhaled and leant on the wall, using her index finger and thumb to wipe away the tiny dots of perspiration that had gathered on her top lip. She placed her flattened palm against her chest, trying to calm her flustered pulse.

'Come on you silly moo.'

It still had the power to do that to her, the flash of a memory, an image, a sound. It could transport her back to a time she would rather forget.

She waited a second and dug deep to find a smile before taking one final step and pushing on the wide double fire door with its brass edged porthole glass window. Immediately, she was engulfed by the smell of fresh bread, baking in the oven. She never tired of the warm scent; it cocooned her in a blanket of well-being and was evocative of full tummies, log fires, cosy rooms and all that was homely.

'Good morning, Guy.'

'Is it? I'm not so sure!' He slammed his clipboard with its checklist on the stainless steel counter top.

This was entirely expected; Guy lived his life with his fingers, tense against his flustered, plucked brow and a sigh hovering in his throat. Whippet thin and groomed to within an inch of his perma-tan, Guy lived off caffeine and on his nerves.

'What's up?' Pru refrained from adding, now. Guy was undoubtedly a worrier, a panicker and a drama queen, but all that was forgiven when she considered his insistence on the inflexible standards both in and out of the kitchen. His attention to detail and design ideas kept them at the forefront of global cake design. He was the jewel in her crown, an analogy that he particularly loved.

'I specifically ordered extra lemons for our dessert du jour, lemon posset with almond crusted shortbread, and they have sent me my standard order. These people drive me crazy! Are they trying to ruin my day? How can I deliver what I promise with this?' He poked at a large net of sorry-looking yellow fruit and turned down his mouth as though he had been presented with road kill rather than inadequate waxed citrus.

'I expect they haven't set out to ruin your day intentionally, they probably just forgot or got muddled, you know how it is when an order deviates from the norm, it often gets confused somewhere along the line. We could always send someone up to the supermarket to grab you some more lemons?'

Guy placed his hands on his hips, 'well, I suppose we will have to.'

Pru as ever, noted the slight flicker of disappointment that crossed his face when a solution was easily and quickly found.

'Also, Guy, can we get someone to fix the bottom stair that comes down from the café. It's got a creak.' She gave a small cough.

'Oh, Pru! You and your creaks! I could have a man here every day, fixing one creak or another. This building is over two hundred years old, it's going to creak!' He raised his hands up to the sky with flattened palms.

'And as I've said before, I don't mind if a man or a woman for that matter, has to come every day or indeed, every hour of every day and I don't care it what it costs. I can't have the stairs making that noise. Any of them, at any time, I can't. Okay?'

'Okay.' He shrugged, before muttering something inaudible in his native French.

'How's the window display coming along?' Pru knew she could easily distract him and if she were being honest was keen to change the subject. In between the double-fronted café and the front door that lead to their apartments, sat a tall bow window, emblazoned with the Plum Patisserie logo, the window was all that was left of the Victorian pharmacy that had been knocked through and subsumed into their current corner premises. The space behind it was a little over five foot in depth and

371

with no particular purpose other than decoration; it was the ideal space in which Guy could showcase the latest Plum creations. The little gallery had become one of the most photographed spots in Mayfair. This pleased Pru no end, whether for a magazine or as one of a tourists haul of snaps, the fact that her logo and cakes of such breath-taking magnitude were being ogled, meant great advertising.

He clapped his hands under his chin, instantly diverted from his lemon crisis, and lack of empathy when it came to stair repair, 'Oh, Pru, oh my! It is beyond exquisite, its divine. No, its beyond divine, it's epic, it's… words fail me.' Guy placed his middle three fingers over his pursed lips and blinked away tears that threatened.

'That good huh?'

He slowly nodded, unable to fully articulate. 'Mais oui and more!' He was quite breathless.

Pru smiled, she was used to this, each of his creations was always similarly lauded and the funny thing was, it was always entirely justified.

'I can't wait to see it. Any luck with the new trainee?'

'Don't. Even. Go. There!' He held up a palm in front of her face. 'Every single person they have sent has been completely useless. I have the same conversation with the agency after every sorry interview. I tell them repeatedly, I don't need bakers! Bakers are ten a penny, no offence intended, Pru,'

'None taken.' She was a baker and proud.

'But I don't need a baker, I need an artiste! Someone who has the eye, the touch and the imagination, someone who can turn sugar paste into pure fantasy, someone who can make the dreams of others into reality! Is it too much to ask?' For the second time in as many minutes he looked close to tears.

Pru stared at him in silence, fishing for a suitable response and wondering if this was the job description he had given the agency, before giving up and abandoning the topic altogether. 'I'm nipping out this morning. Bobby has a dress fitting in Spitalfields, but Milly is around if you need anything.'

'Oh, a dress fitting? How exciting! I saw the lovely couple yesterday afternoon, strolling hand in hand like love's young dream. Oh my goodness, so beautiful together! Can you imagine what les enfants will look like? They are a couple that heaven blessed for sure.'

'I know, Bobby's a lucky girl. She certainly doesn't take after me; she takes after her mum, Astrid. She was the most beautiful girl I'd ever seen.'

It wasn't a topic she normally discussed. Bobby's mum had disappeared when she was three months old, leaving her in the care of her drug-addled boyfriend to pursue a life in India. Ironically, it probably saved her life. Astrid too was fond of the recreational drugs that formed the backdrop to Alfie's life, but left before he progressed to heroin and the habit that would eventually kill him. She told Alfie she needed space and enlightenment, which he thought was a bloody shame, as what their little girl needed was a mummy who wasn't over six thousand miles away needing space and enlightenment.

'Oh Pru, she most certainly does take after you. You are

beautiful inside and out. I can see you now,' he raised he hand as if shielding his eyes, 'you could model for denture cream or stair lifts!'

Pru threw a napkin at him and turned on her heel, smiling as she did so.

No Greater Love

Amanda Prowse's NO GREATER LOVE sequence is a series of contemporary stories with love at their core. They feature characters whose histories interweave through the generations: ordinary men and women who do extraordinary things for love. They are stories to keep you from switching off the bedside lamp at night, stories to remember long after the final page is turned...

Amanda Prowse

Amanda Prowse was a management consultant for ten years before deciding to pursue her ambition to write. Her husband, Simeon, is a soldier, and they live in the West Country with their two teenage sons.

You can contact Amanda via twitter, @mrsamandaprowse or via her website, www.amandaprowse.org

Amanda Prowse

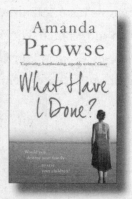

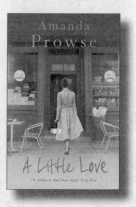

Stories to remember, long after
the final page is turned...

Find out more at www.headofzeus.com